This book was purchased with
funds from the
Bauriedel Family Grant

W9-ATZ-382

EUR

HUMBOLDT COUNTY LIBRARY

What readers are saying about Conor and the Crossworlds

"Hello from The only radio station in the world owned and operated by kids, WKID 96.7 FM, located in Clearwater, Florida. For years we were looking for an exciting book to read live on air to our listeners. All the books that we thought would be interesting to read on air turned out to be very confusing to our listening audience, but three years ago we received our first book from Kevin Gerard titled Conor and the Crossworlds. After receiving the book we thought it was just going to be another boring book, BUT NO! JUST THE OPPOSITE! This book was awesome!! Not only did we love it and were able to relate to Conor because he was our age, but our listeners really loved to hear us reading the story on air every night. They begged us not to stop reading it due to the great suspense of the story. Every night when we would stop reading for the night the phone would start ringing with listeners very upset and wanting to know what happens next, of course our response was "you will have to tune in tomorrow night." If we ever had a night that we were unable to broadcast we would receive hundreds of e-mails and phone calls. We just wanted to say thanks again for writing such a great, exciting story and we look forward for the next book." *– Adam and Eric – WKID 96.7, Clearwater, Florida*

"The Conor and the Crossworlds series is one of the best series I have ever read. It is full of action and friendship and a bunch of stuff it is awesome!!!" *– Alicia – Desert Hot Springs, California*

"Conor and the Crossworlds is the perfect blend of fantasy and adventure. Action around every corner.....Conor is my favorite character for his courage and bravery! People can relate to him." *– Andrew – Portland, Oregon*

"I'm from the high school in Burlington, Vermont that you visited. I didn't really get a chance to properly thank you, so I'd like to do that now. Not only is your series, Conor and the Crossworlds, one of the most imaginative, brilliant and overall best fantasy reads ever, you've also inspired me to write more than I can ever express. Keep speaking at schools; you're very motivating, and I'm so grateful for your stories and kind words. Thank you!" *– Matt – Burlington, Vermont*

"I think that Conor and The Crossworlds is a genius series! They made me want to read again; they are definitely my all time favorite books. I think Conor's stories will be a huge success. I can't wait for the next one!"
— *Max – Desert Hot Springs, California*

"Thank you again for the gift you gave to my son. He has never been so excited about reading and wanting to read. That is the best gift of all."
— *Penny – La Mesa, California*

"In the book series of Conor and the Crossworlds, I loved the stories at the very beginning when I started reading them. I personally admire Conor because of his bravery and courage to put other people before himself, and I loved the fact that there are creatures that have powers that no person can ever imagine. When I started this series I was hooked from the first page and couldn't wait for the next book to come out. Now after three, I can't stop thinking about the next book to come out and try to imagine what could happen in the next book..."
— *Jacob – Norco, California*

It's amazing! I can't wait to read the next books and search around for pictures; I draw pictures of my characters all the time, you know. But not nearly as good as this and thanks by the way, but my writing could sure use a lot of work. Someday I want to be able to write clever things, I want to make people totally understand the feelings of the characters in my story. I love your books, they just draw me in, I can't put them down and I'm hanging on every word. Someday I hope I can write like that. You're a real inspiration, you know that? You actually take time out of your day to read stuff like this and talk to the people who love your books. I wish other authors would do that. It makes me happy.
— *Flickerstripe – Desert Hot Springs, California*

"I am so very impressed. I remember the darkness from the third book more than anything, although the second book had such cool fight scenes and new characters. For some reason this story is pure pleasure for me, I think because it was quite visual and exciting, but also very tender. The ending was absolutely amazing, it evoked all the feelings you would expect from an extremely well-written fantasy."
— *Karen – Tierrasanta, California*

"Hi, it's Ryan.

Big fan!!!!!!!!

Love the books, but, I'm thinking you should make a movie.

I want to see what colors the places are, I want to see how big they are.

I can see the pictures; I just see them in black and white.

And I'm almost done with the second book.

I met you at the Clairemont branch Library 50th Celebration.

That's where we bought the first book.

Who won the key thing, or is it still going on?

Please reply..."

— *Ryan — San Diego, California*

"The Conor and The Crossworlds books are great! Full of drama and adventure, it has everything a book worm needs to be satisfied with the book she/he devours! It's a suspenseful adventure, waiting to pull you into the journey and complete it."

— *Shannon — Oceanside, California*

"I have been reading the series since Kevin came by my school. It was and will be full of emotion, exciting characters, and meaning. All the books have great plots, and I can barely wait for the next couple of books. Conor is a perfect mixture Harry Potter, Bobby Pendragon, and Percy Jackson."

— *Wesley — Indio, California*

Conor and the Crossworlds, Book One, is our new #1 of our top ten books checked out in the library. YEAH! Congratulations!

Linda — Vista Middle Magnet School, California

"Now that the Harry Potter series is over, it's time to find a great new book series, and Kevin Gerard has the answer. His new book series, Conor and the Crossworlds, is possibly the next great teen book series."

— *Titan Toll Chronicle — Glendale, California*

"I like your books. They're very suspenseful. I think your books will be worth more in the future. What I think I'd like to see in your next book would be more characters. I like the design on the front cover of Book Three.

— *IMS student — Riverside County, California*

I am in the sixth grade. I like all of the characters you put in the Conor and the Crossworlds books. I even liked the words you put in the books and the action in the story and how you describe it.

– IMS student – Riverside County, California

The characters that you put in the book are amazing. I can actually imagine in a dream a giant cat taking me for a ride in the sky. You have made some really amazing books."

– IMS student – Riverside County, California

"I just love the Conor and the Crossworlds books! When I pick them up I can't put them down! I feel like I'm in another world!"

– Jocelyn – Manchester, New Hampshire

"I love the Conor and the Crossworlds books because they have a really good plot. I like how in an instant Conor's life goes from ordinary to getting to experience being in an alternate world beyond imagination. When Conor starts gaining abilities from serving as a warrior for the Crossworlds creators, it makes me wish I could escape to an alternate world of my own and meet majestic cougars like Purugama. The third book "Surviving an Altered World" is my favorite because of the quest for the five keys. The plot for the third book was awesome and the scavenger hunt that the author did for the five keys that went across the United States was a lot of fun! That's why I love the Conor and Crossworlds books. Not only that but I've always liked writing, thanks to this series I am inspired to write so much more!"

– Jade – Lumberton, Mississippi

"Kevin Gerard's Conor and the Crossworlds series is an essential "must have" for any library or fantasy fan. Conor's story stands out in the ever-growing fantasy genre as a fun, safe adventure for all ages. Mr. Gerard's work does not stay on our shelf very long and patrons are eagerly awaiting the next installment."   *– Michael – Hattiesburg, Mississippi*

"Reading Conor and The Crossworlds is like watching a movie in your head, and not spending time on the T.V. so my parents don't get mad."

– Shannon – Oceanside, California

"When you came to my middle school you said you would give me a copy of your book free if I got mine published. I am proud to say that my book is 452 pages long and is on its way to 3 different publishers! I hope you are ready to hand over that book!"

– Lucy – Desert Hot Springs, California

"Crossworlds
Conor and the Crossworlds
Replenished my soul with every page
Only something with
Significant power
Sinks within my gaze.
What it must be like to live
On champions glade
Right beside the champions
Like Eha, Therion, Ajur, and Maya
Don't forget Surmitang and best of all Purugama
I will seek refuge in the Crossworlds."

– Wesley – Indio, California

"I love these books because they are very adventurous. Every sentence traps me inside the book as if I am in it. I never want to stop reading these books. I just love them so much."

– Joseph, La Jolla, California

"I would like to say that all three of your books were very well written and interesting, although the first one was our favorite. Even though Conor is the main character Purugama is our favorite character. One of our many favorite parts in all of the three books is when Purugama is fighting Drazian in the beginning of the first book. The first couple of pages in the first book got us hooked and they were all exciting and they made us want to read the whole series. Can't wait to read the next book."

– Ben & Tyler – Manchester, New Hampshire

Conor
and
The
Crossworlds

Book Five:
The Author of All Worlds

KEVIN GERARD

Crying Cougar Press™
San Diego, California

Published by Crying Cougar Press™
San Diego, California

Edited by Katie Chatfield
Cover art by Justin Gerbracht
Cover design by Molly Nicholson
Interior illustrations by Jennifer Fong
Typesetting by Julie Melton, The Right Type
Cover photograph of Kevin Gerard taken by Share

APPRECIATION:

The creation of these novels would not have been possible without the effort of many individuals and organizations. I'd like to acknowledge them at this time.

If it weren't for all of the wonderful, hard-working, and underpaid school and public librarians everywhere, Conor and the Crossworlds might not enjoy its present popularity. The dedication you show to your students and patrons is remarkable.

I had a stroke of good luck when I found Katie Chatfield. She has edited each of the books in this series, with wonderful results I might add. I've always said that it's the task of an author to let the story fall from his or her mind onto the paper or keyboard. It's the editor that cleans everything up and makes the story great. I trust Katie's judgment implicitly – she once told me to rewrite the entire ending of <u>Surviving an Altered World</u> – I had a brief moment of "Harrumph" and then did exactly as she ordered. Of course the book's strength increased ten-fold. If you need editing services, I highly recommend her – kt_gaeng@yahoo.com

The Art Institute of San Diego has provided me with a group of talented illustrators. I'm sure if you Google any of these names you will find a wealth of information on the internet about these fine artists.

Justin Gerbracht has drawn all of the covers for the Conor and the Crossworlds novels. He drew the first cover at the tender age of nineteen. Although the picture of mighty Purugama carrying ten-year-old Conor on his shoulders is still the favorite for many readers, my favorite cover shows Seefra in one of his many altered forms walking calmly through a tempest toward Conor and Janine. Justin is a lead illustrator for Buzz Monkey Software in Eugene, Oregon.

Jennifer Fong came on board during the creation of <u>Surviving an Altered World.</u> She is a very talented artist and a pleasure to work with. I can be quite picky at times and she shows great patience with me. My favorite illustration of hers is the depiction of Surmitang and Therion peering over the crater at the tiny pit bull who moments before had Maya in his sights.

Wilfredo Gago Jr. contributed drawings for <u>Peril in the Corridors.</u> When I looked at his first illustration I knew I had found a unique talent. His work confirms my opinion that the second book in the series is by far the best. The one-on-one battles Conor gets into with the destroyers are magnificently illustrated. I believe Wilfredo is also employed by a video game design company, this one located in Los Angeles.

If I hadn't been invited to Readers' Week in Nevada in 2009, I might never have learned about Julie Melton and her company, The Right Type. When everything is prepared, the edits, the illustrations, and the cover, Julie takes all of it and readies the files for the printer. I wouldn't trust anyone else with this essential function. For information and quotes about book design e-mail her at julie@therighttype.com.

Authorhouse produced the first version of Book One: Breaking the Barrier. Due to promises I'd made and some unforeseen circumstances, I needed the book fast. They produced it and made it available for purchase in less than a month. They also gave away quite a few copies to school librarians around the country. Say what you want, but there are some definite benefits to enlisting Authorhouse to serve as your initial guide on a publishing journey.

Cold Tree Press initially produced Book Two: Peril in the Corridors. Peter Honsberger and Amanda Butler were a delight to work with. Cold Tree was very professional, definitely my best experience with a subsidy publisher. The quality of the book they produced easily matched those put forth by any major publisher in New York. Unfortunately, the souring economy made things too difficult and Peter had to close up shop. I wish him well in all future endeavors.

Mill City Press produced the first printing of Book Three: Surviving an Altered World. Their model was quite different than Authorhouse or Cold Tree, and although communication was at times difficult, they did produce a quality book. They also try to keep as much money as possible in the author's pocket, which I was certainly happy about.

After speaking with a diverse group of individuals over the years, including a Los Angeles writer named Christopher Meeks and writer/editor/promoter guru Carolyn Howard-Johnson, I shifted gears and decided to throw in with a publishing company in San Diego. Crying Cougar Press not only produced Book Four: Charge of the Champions and Book Five: The Author of All Worlds, they also re-issued the first three books under their imprint. The arrangement is beneficial for all parties concerned and it gives the Conor and the Crossworlds series a bump in credibility.

Thank you all for your valuable input and encouragement.

FOR WALTER WILLIAM RUMSEY,
WHEREVER YOU ARE, MY FRIEND

BATTLE RANKS
COUNCIL OF SEVEN

CREATOR
ABILITIES:
Corridor Construction

Power Allocation

Animation of Life

MAGIC – *Untouchable*

IQ – *Advanced*

BATTLE SKILLS – *Exceptional*

CHAMPION
ABILITIES:
Corridor Travel

Power Transference

Structural Manipulation

MAGIC – *Extraordinary*

IQ – *Superior*

BATTLE SKILLS – *Excellent*

SEEKER
ABILITIES:
Corridor Travel
Unlimited Vision
Superb Trackers
MAGIC – *Limited*
IQ – *Good*
BATTLE SKILLS – *Formidable*

GUARDIAN
ABILITIES:
Corridor Travel
Translation
Superb Healers
MAGIC – *None*
IQ – *Excellent*
BATTLE SKILLS – *Limited*

BATTLE RANKS
CIRCLE OF EVIL

DESTROYER
ABILITIES:
Identity Transfer
Power Allocation
Animation of Environment
MAGIC – *Impenetrable*
IQ – *Advanced*
BATTLE SKILLS – *Tactical Brilliance*

SHADOW WARRIOR
ABILITIES:
Corridor Travel
Invisibility
Weapons Construction
MAGIC – *Exceptional*
IQ – *Superior*
BATTLE SKILLS – *Excellent*

SLAYER
ABILITIES:
Corridor Travel
Limitless Energy
Blinding Speed
MAGIC – *Good*
IQ – *Poor*
BATTLE SKILLS – *Superior*

KEEPER
ABILITIES:
Corridor Travel
Cell Construction
Imprisonment Specialists
MAGIC – *Limited*
IQ – *Good*
BATTLE SKILLS – *Limited*

Conor
and
The
Crossworlds

Book Five: The Author of All Worlds

PANDEMONIUM

CHAPTER ONE

"Preposterous!" boomed the Lord of All Life. "No one commands that much power. If this council meditated for a thousand centuries it could never approach the type of cataclysmic force you describe." The crimson aura flared as the supreme councilor threw out his hands in disgust. "I refuse to believe it. Your findings must be flawed."

"The precision of the mathematics cannot be disputed," answered a calm and reserved Mr. Hikkins. "The sequence I am illustrating for the council is occurring even now. I cannot speak as to the source of this phenomenal power, but I assure you my figures are correct. Not only is the entire system in jeopardy, but also I believe Conor's world may be in the most immediate danger. If my calculations prove reliable, earth will be wiped away from its galaxy in approximately twenty-two days."

"This is madness!" shouted the first councilor, rising from his floating seat and slamming an open palm against the table. "Entire worlds disappearing without a trace? Do you realize what you are suggesting?"

"I am *not* suggesting," replied Mr. Hikkins through clenched teeth.

Arriving two days prior to his session, the soft-spoken but determined seeker had demanded an immediate audience with the Council of Seven. Merely stating a request so boldly would keep most visitors in the gardens for weeks, but Mr. Hikkins had always been something of an enigma to the creators. His intellectual capabilities had never been questioned, but his decisions left some on the council suspicious of his motives. Indeed, the crafty seeker had solved many of the most perplexing dilemmas during his service, including the final calculations for the protection packet used by Conor in his first battle with Seefra. But his judgment often troubled some of the council members. His decision to travel constantly instead of dedicating himself to the realm had not sat well with the Lord of All Life. The council debated whether to restrict his movements many times, but in the end they understood the overall value of his contribution. Mr. Hikkins, on the other hand, had never allowed his relations with the council to hamper his precious responsibilities. He preferred close contact with the beings under his guidance. He enjoyed traveling through the corridors acting as mentor to the Crossworlds' most valuable inhabitants.

He discovered the anomaly in the system almost by accident. Staring up at the stars one evening, he noticed a tiny discoloration appear and then disappear in deep space. He thought nothing of it, until a few days later he spied an identical shift in the pattern of the night sky. His disciplined mind would not accept a random occurrence repeating itself in such a short period of time. He began investigating the phenomenon immediately. He contacted most of the preeminent mathematicians and astronomers in the Crossworlds system. He ran simulations in his mind and constantly jotted down bizarre sets of equations. Most he threw away, but the few that remained began to form a most interesting model indeed.

The result, when he had finally dismissed all other possibilities, astounded him. He didn't feel fear or dread; instead he appreciated the purity of the strategy. The Circle of Evil couldn't possibly annihilate every planet in the Crossworlds system. That would take too long and they wanted immediate revenge. Instead, they had devised a formula that depended on random selection based on calculated odds, slating worlds for destruction while shaving the probability of selection error to less than five percent. It was brilliant and deadly, and unless the creators could decipher the source of their power, Conor would have to be notified at once.

"There is no mistake, first councilor," repeated Mr. Hikkins. "I haven't determined the physics of the weapon, but I have deciphered the pattern of their attack." The seeker waited a few moments, allowing the reality of his account to settle in with the council. When he felt he had their collective attention, he dropped the one statement he knew would ignite controversy. "The situation leaves us no choice. We must notify Conor immediately and inform him of the circumstances."

"No," said a soft, delicate voice. It came from the rear of the chamber. The Lady of the Light stepped forward, announcing her presence to the members of the council. Up to this point she had listened quietly while Mr. Hikkins delivered his account. Preferring not to become directly involved unless absolutely necessary, she had held her tongue as long as possible. This, however, must not be allowed.

"We cannot turn to him again so quickly," she continued. "He has established a life for himself back on earth. He and his companion have worked tirelessly to pick up the pieces of their shattered lives and move forward again. They have established a path for their futures, and we must not intervene and disrupt their progress."

"We appreciate the zeal with which you defend your Champion," interjected the first councilor. "Let me remind you, however, that your presence here is only tolerated so long as you observe and remain silent. You may not interrupt the proceedings no matter how strongly you feel about the subject matter."

The Lady of the Light gently lowered her chin in submission, but did not retreat to her former position. Her silver aura flared briefly, highlighting her apprehension.

"My Lady, if I may," began Mr. Hikkins, "you must know how deeply I care for Conor and Janine. After all, I spent a good deal of time with both of them during Conor's first year of high school. I do not wish to disturb their happiness, nor do I find the prospect of throwing the young man into another journey appealing. However, you must understand the complexity of the situation and grasp the mortal danger we all face."

Mr. Hikkins turned to face the Council of Seven directly. "The ability to wipe away the existence of an entire planet has never confronted us before. Due to your design and the collective power of the system, the Crossworlds has successfully existed for untold millennia. What I tell you now I say with the support of empirical evidence. Earth will not be the final target for the Circle of Evil. I believe they will continue their offensive after destroying the birthplace of our latest Champion. Then they will turn the focus of their mighty weapon against the glade of Champions and the realm of the creators. I do believe, first councilor, they intend to destroy every world that holds positive dominion over the system itself."

The council chamber exploded with comments and argument. Mr. Hikkins accepted a barrage of challenges to his suppositions. He stood silently while accepting the flood of criticism. He knew better than to try and debate the council, especially after delivering such a shocking message. Even under intense scrutiny, however, he felt comfortable with his conclusions. After all, he held the conviction of his science and a consummate belief in what he put before them. In his opinion, they could only come to one conclusion. To be certain of the outcome, though, he allowed the council to exhaust their conversations before delivering the final blow.

"May I remind the council," he stated quietly, waiting for the last points to be aired before continuing, "that we haven't touched upon the most important aspect of their strategy."

"And that is?" demanded a clearly exasperated supreme councilor.

"The corridors, my Lord," answered Mr. Hikkins without hesitation. "Imagine if you will, the network of portals connected to the combined energies of just one world."

The chamber went completely still. The council members froze in place, none of them uttering a sound. They stared at Mr. Hikkins for what seemed like the first time. Their expressions softened towards him, as if their opinion of his intelligence climbed a notch or two. As one group, they changed their posture, looking directly at him with open minds.

"Yes," continued the brilliant mathematician. "Not only are the complex organic connections throughout the system in jeopardy, but consider this, esteemed council members. If we do not act, and act promptly, we may not be able to recruit Conor and his companion at all. We may be cut off from them permanently. What's more, if the portals that bond the glade of Champions to the realm of the creators are severed by the elimination of a symbiotic world, then you will be without the services of your most powerful protectors."

The Council of Seven sat in stunned silence. The Lady of the Light placed her head in her hands, sighing deeply. All present in the chamber now began to grasp what Mr. Hikkins already knew as fact. The Circle of Evil, whatever remained of them after the great battle with the Champions, had devised one last deadly strategy to destroy the Crossworlds forever. The desperation of the tactic confirmed their depleted state; Mr. Hikkins had said as much when he referred to the random aspect of their attack. They were gambling that the worlds they wanted to eliminate would fall within a projected line without touching their own provinces. The first councilor had spoken the truth, for the plan *was* madness. The Circle of Evil had decided to gamble with a weapon strong enough to erase an entire galaxy from existence. There appeared to be only one logical course of action, as distasteful as some in the chamber found it.

"How soon can we contact Conor?" asked the Lady of the Light.

"Preliminary calculations have already been arranged," replied Mr. Hikkins.

"Proceed then," commanded the supreme councilor. "My Lady, I assume you wish to travel to the glade?"

"I will leave immediately," she answered with a slight bow of her head.

"Then let it be so," stated the Lord of All Life. "Let this be the final battle between the creators and the Circle of Evil. I will hear no more about them after this journey."

"I assure you, my Lord," said Mr. Hikkins. "One way or another, this will be our final confrontation."

CHAPTER TWO

Gribba walked among the trees of his simple estate. Holding hands with his mate, he inhaled the fragrant smells from the budding fruit walls climbing up from the ground all around them. Each scent reached his nostrils in its own time, dancing around his powerful senses before making room for the next distinct aroma. The giant ezuvex guardian strolled along at a gentle, relaxed pace. He took his time enjoying what life offered, and he would not rush through this peaceful moment. Having lived for over a century, Gribba knew how important it was to savor the morsels of simplicity life so rarely afforded him.

It had been almost two years to the day since the battalion of ezuvex warriors had returned to their planet from the hideous world of the Circle of Evil. They had annihilated the shadow warriors, losing only a few of their own to death or serious injury. They had returned home to a hero's welcome. Nearly every inhabitant of their considerable world turned out to greet them after they emerged, row by row, from the corridor drawn forth by the Lady of the Light. The celebration had lasted nearly a month, with dancing, story telling and prediction challenges between younger and older generations. Gribba had smiled and laughed along with his extended family of ezuvex, happy to encourage their frivolity.

For him, though, the proceedings masked a more somber mood. He had happily returned to his home, but he brought with him a disdain for all things unpleasant and bitter.

He had relished the destruction of the shadow warriors; even he could not dispute that. They were another race of beings, however, and no matter how repulsive, they represented life. All life, mused the ezuvex leader, deserved a chance to thrive and live as they desired. He could never arbitrarily judge another race of beings no matter how different or peculiar they might be. He had fought to save his friends and his kind, to avenge the slaughter of his world by the Circle of Evil. If called upon he would do so again. He would not, however, take personal delight in the destruction of life. Keeping his beliefs to himself, he wandered through the crowds of revelers, grasping hands and exchanging smiles. He would not dampen their joy, but some day, his beliefs would be displayed openly for future generations.

"May I intrude upon your thoughts?" asked Shim, Gribba's mate of almost half a century.

The huge bear creature shook himself mentally, bringing his mind back to the present. He inhaled again, smiling as the dreamy scents in his garden drifted into his nostrils. He turned his head, looking at the greatest joy in his life. Shim had given him twenty offspring, strong sons and daughters who had prospered from their combined guidance. Determined and attractive, their offspring had excelled in every aspect of life. Mostly grown now and spread far and wide around the planet of Wilzerd, Gribba and Shim rarely saw the entire group of them together anymore. The battle with the shadow warriors had at least marshaled a half dozen of them under the banner of Gribba's forces. Four sons and two daughters had come home from the war to stay with their parents for a short while. Joined by a handful of their brothers and sisters during the celebration, the group brought many days of happiness to their parents. Now and then, Gribba looked over at his mate and saw the contented smile she wore. If there was anything greater than that sight, he could not fathom it.

"You may always ask, Shim," answered the towering ezuvex without turning to meet her eyes. He walked a few more steps before answering. "The battle with the shadow warriors crowds my mind."

Shim grabbed her mate's arm with both hands, resting her head against his huge shoulder. She couldn't comprehend war. It held no logical outcome. She wouldn't allow her soul to be corrupted by it. If her family was threatened and war offered the only recourse, then so be it, but she would never approve of it. She said nothing in response to Gribba's remark. Instead she simply crushed her body against his, hoping the touch of her love would soothe his tortured soul. He reciprocated, putting a giant, furry hand against her cheek.

"Do not worry, Shim," said the guardian, softly. "Everything passes with the soothing flux of time. Before long the memories of the battle will be a distant disturbance, and the two us will be harvesting baskets of fresh fruit to enjoy before our morning walks."

She held her mate tightly, believing what he said. He had never failed her, not once in the fifty years they had paired their affections. For some reason, though, on this day, the touch of his furry shoulder troubled her. She had never sensed this feeling in her mate in all the years she had known him. Through every trial they had suffered together, Gribba always maintained a strong exterior, even when inside he felt fear or indecision. This afternoon, however, he seemed altogether different. The fear she sensed deep within his soul pressed its energy outward to the very hair along his skin. She could feel it, sizzling like a slice of meat on hot rocks. He did his best to hide it from her, but she knew her mate well enough to know something was terribly wrong. She could feel the onset of some horrible event, but she could not pinpoint it or describe it.

She knew better than to pressure Gribba into revealing what troubled him. He would inform her when the time was right. As a mother, though, she feared for the safety of her children. If some tragic event loomed ahead, she wanted desperately to know so she could warn them. They may not be able to escape it, but at least she would try to give them the chance. A tear emerged from one of her eyes. She blinked once, causing it to drip down onto her cheek. She pressed her face against Gribba's strong arm, smashing the tear into his fur. She squeezed his hand again, pulling herself into his body and matching his stride.

She knows, thought Gribba. He hadn't mentioned a word to anyone and yet she knows. Thus is the beauty of a long companionship, where one person knows the other's thoughts without question. Gribba loved his mate, and he did not wish to worry her if his feelings proved wrong. After all, that is all they were, just feelings, judgments about strange phenomena he saw occurring in the night sky. Even he could not discern the meaning of the shifting pattern of the stars, but he believed nothing good would come of it. Something told him the disappearing lights in the sky represented a devastating development for whoever lived so far out in space. As long as it remained distant he held out hope that the bizarre occurrence might pass them by on its way to another galaxy.

The previous night, however, had shattered those hopes forever. A square of light as big as his fingernail had flashed in the sky before vanishing completely. Seconds later the night sky looked the same as it had only moments before, minus the planet that had previously occupied that region of space. He wanted to tell his wife immediately after the incident, but decided against it. The creators would understand the phenomenon. They would know what to do. He would seek their counsel in a day or two, and then call the leaders of Wilzerd together if need be. Until then, he would house his fears within his own mind. Tonight, after Shim went to bed, he would come outside and watch the sky again.

CHAPTER THREE

In the deep, frigid regions of space, a tiny, glittering rectangle of light traveled a linear course toward a preset destination. Although organic in composition, the pulsating object held its course without a conscious thought or feeling. It had been given life and purpose, and now it would fulfill its assignment without pausing to ponder the moral question of whether its function was healthy or destructive. It lived, and its designers had issued their orders. It would carry them out efficiently and without pause. When it completed its mission, it would dissolve into the energy from whence it came, hoping only to be drawn forth again at another time for another objective.

The object traveled through the Gulserian galaxy, passing stars and planets by the thousands. Its trajectory carried it along a straight line, except when that course intercepted one of the large celestial bodies blocking its path. Only then did it deviate from its direct track, hopping around the distraction and then returning to its original path.

The counter placed in its sensory organ registered the halfway point in its journey. The object blinked at a constant rate every one point five seconds, counting off the light years between its launch point and target. One more galaxy to overtake and then the next would contain its objective. It would not fail its assignment. Its designers had placed within it an overwhelming drive to complete its mission. Its existence depended on its ability to finish what it had been sent to accomplish. The small rectangle sailed along through the infinite reaches of space, blinking methodically while preparing to execute its orders.

Gribba stood outside of his estate, inhaling the cold air from the winter winds. He loved the night, for its quiet as much as for its mystery. Only the bravest of creatures ventured out at night and Gribba saw or sensed very few on this particularly cold evening. After scanning his fields and ascertaining his safety, the great ezuvex leader lifted his eyes to the heavens. He stared straight ahead for ten or fifteen minutes before moving his eyes first to the left and then slowly in the opposite direction. He inspected every inch of the night sky, and after he finished a complete sweep he reversed course and examined it again. He stayed out under the stars for roughly three hours, a solitary creature scanning the sky for an answer to a riddle he couldn't understand.

He felt insignificant and unworthy, because whatever was occurring above him seemed beyond his control. He couldn't reverse its course by any method known to him. If the phenomenon moved toward Wilzerd, he would only be able to stand by impotently and witness its destiny. Squeezing his eyes shut, he cursed himself for his inability to conquer the strange enemy. He uttered a silent message to the Lady of the Light, asking for her guidance in case the worst of his fears came to pass. The council would come to their aid. They had to; it was written in the ancient code. Besides, Gribba's people had destroyed the shadow warriors. Surely they would do everything in their power in light of their recent victory over the Circle of Evil.

The ezuvex guardian raised his chin, looking up to the stars again. Where a benign, passive sky existed before, something that caused his entire body to shiver with fear loomed above. The breath of life left his lungs as his heart leapt into his throat. He tried to call out to Shim but found he couldn't. He felt as though he was having a nightmare of the most horrible sort, the kind where your mouth opens but no sound emerges. He tried to scream, to call for his mate, but nothing escaped his lungs. He clutched at his neck, trying to free up his vocal chords. He stared at the stars and scratched out the only words he could whisper. It would be the last statement ever uttered from an inhabitant of the planet Wilzerd.

"Mind of the Creators!" he wheezed, before running toward his estate.

Three short blinks in rapid succession informed the glowing rectangle that its journey had come to an end. The target lay directly before it. The rectangle hummed, beeping softly while scanning the gigantic world for exact dimensions, density and molecular composition. The information was rapidly filed and collated:

Wilzerd: eighth planet in a galaxy of twenty one with three stars – Tillon, Elitte, and Venefin.

197,648 kilometers diameter
2.229×12^{26} kilograms mass
3.164 grams/centimeter^3 density

Planetary composition: 28.6% Iron, 39.5% Oxygen, 9.2% Silicon, 9.7% Magnesium, 5.5% Nickel, 1.9% Sulfur and 5.1% Titanium.

Indigenous life forms: air, ground and water
Population: approximately two million
Homo erectus, plus or minus ten thousand.

Approximately twenty two billion years old with one hundred fifty billion kilometers^2 total area.

Another three quick blinks informed the rectangle that data collection was complete and successful. The device could now commence operations.

A flash of dark auburn light raced around the perimeter of the rectangle. The corridor sent by the Circle of Evil began expanding. At a distance of less than 400,000 kilometers from the planet Wilzerd, the small rectangle grew as it rapidly spread from all four corners. As its size increased, the speed with which it grew accelerated as well.

On its way to full capacity, the mushrooming corridor encountered all manner of stars and space debris. Because it had altered its structure before resizing itself, it consumed everything it touched with little or no effort. Where once it had been a completely benign, silent traveler, its new matrix had given it the capabilities of one of the Circle of Evil's most devastating weapons. Nothing could stand before it, even at a marginal size, and when the corridor had reached its full dimensions not even a world the size of Wilzerd would be safe.

The portal measurements soared past 150,000 kilometers length and 125,000 kilometers width. The membrane suddenly flashed, illuminating a blood-red, milky substance that quickly solidified, attaching itself firmly to each side and corner of the corridor. Stars and smaller satellites began flowing toward the immense portal, ripped away from their gravitational fields by the all-consuming strength of the membrane. The indistinct and much smaller corridors, those attached to the world facing the giant portal, flew away from Wilzerd and were swallowed into the endless morass. In an instant, any possible escape for Gribba and his race had been withdrawn. Every corridor connected to the planet now resided within the massive membrane of the ever-expanding portal. No flash, fire or explosion occurred when they encountered the organic passage; they simply disappeared into the crimson pool without a trace. It looked exactly like a black hole, except anyone with a rudimentary knowledge of orbital physics would know otherwise. This entity was a killing machine, and although organic at birth, it would obey its programming to the letter.

The expansion ceased. The gigantic corridor now measured 250,000 kilometers length and 215,000 kilometers width. As if checking every component before initiating final instructions, the boundaries of the portal flexed and stretched. In doing so, they checked the tautness of the membrane against the perimeter of the corridor. The milky passageway also ran a series of checks on itself. Allowing a number of electric charges to pass from one side to the other and from top to bottom, the membrane established a measure of consistency along the massive face of the corridor.

Satisfied that everything was in order, the immense window in space flashed one final time, illuminating the membrane with a fiery blast of titanic energy. The entire corridor burned with a controlled fury, and as the intensity accelerated, the portal began moving toward Wilzerd. Its pace remained slow and determined. As it progressed to the target world, it calibrated its advance ever so slightly. It wanted to please its masters, and it would, by consuming its largest objective to date. It would do so flawlessly, living up to the reputation its kind had enjoyed since the inception of the Crossworlds.

Chaos reigned on the surface of the planet. The ezuvex tribes ran in every direction. They looked for valuables, for relatives and for any possible means of escape. The elders and wizards of the tribes, confounded by the loss of their corridors, cursed themselves for not finding the ability to draw forth new passageways. Ezuvex by the thousands crowded around them, screaming for deliverance. They offered everything they had, wealth, children, servitude for life; they would give anything for a way off their doomed world.

Gribba hugged his weeping mate, keeping her cheek close to his heart. Shim had raced around the estate for close to thirty minutes after learning the truth from him. She ran from room to room, gathering things together as if preparing to evacuate to a shelter. She frantically tapped the communication device surgically implanted in her cheek, ordering the computer to contact each of her children. Most of the servers had expired, but she managed to reach a few of her offspring. She demanded they contact their brothers and sisters and come to the estate immediately. They had arrangements to make if they were going to survive the attack. She cried and pleaded with her children, begging them to come home. When she finally gave in to her intellect, understanding that the distance between them would prevent a reunion, she collapsed onto the floor in a puddle of tears. Bewailing the idiocy of warfare, she cursed the creators, her mate, the shadow warriors and the Circle of Evil. She fought against Gribba's attempts to help her to her feet, screaming and scratching against his huge, furry body. Finally, after exhausting her frustrations, Shim fell against his muscular chest and wept loudly. She squeezed her arms around his neck harder and harder with each passing moment until she relaxed into a mantra, repeating a phrase over and over directly to her mate's heart.

"I love you, Gribba."

"And I you, my sweet Shim," answered the ezuvex leader.

How would anyone respond to the realization that they would perish within the span of one or two hours? Gribba felt strangely calm about the entire incident. Possibly because he had always known after the battle with the shadow warriors there would be some retribution for their destruction. Standing in a pool of dark blood and mangled bodies in the chamber of caves, Gribba had sensed even then a future response to their stunning victory. He envisioned an attack by a platoon of destroyers, or a biochemical assault against Wilzerd, but the total destruction of their world using a passageway that for all time had enjoyed serving the tenants of the Crossworlds?

What power had the Circle of Evil been saving in reserve for this day? Were other worlds at risk? What of the realm, and the glade, had they already been destroyed? It was too much to grasp, so Gribba did the only logical thing he could think of doing – he grabbed his mate and held her until her suffering ceased. Holding her tightly in his arms, he led her outside, past the main entrance to the estate.

They looked to the east, where the suns usually hovered for most of the afternoon and evening. On this day, however, a corridor so massive it defied description had eclipsed the natural stars that usually warmed Wilzerd.

"Mind of the creators, Gribba," said Shim softly, turning her head just far enough to allow her right eye to glimpse the devastating phenomenon. "What is it?"

"It is a corridor, my love," he replied. He refused to shade the truth for her. He loved her and wanted to be honest, but he also realized that if he tried to conceal any aspect of it, she would know instantly. A brilliant physicist in her own right, Shim would sense the fabrication and deduce the truth on her own. "It is a portal large enough to swallow an entire planet. It was sent by the Circle of Evil, of that I am sure. I don't know the extent of their plans. Unfortunately, we will never know. I fear, though, that if they have found the power to construct one corridor of this size, it stands to reason there might be more. I fear for the creators and for the Champions of the Crossworlds. There can be no defense against this. Once the portals for Crossworlds travel have been wiped away, as ours have been, then the Circle of Evil will truly have dominion over any world they care to destroy. There will be no escape for anyone."

Gribba escorted his wife to the main reflecting pool in front of their estate. Uttering a small incantation, he summoned a water wall for his mate. As it emerged from the pool, sparkling and willing to serve, he felt Shim's delicate but strong hand grasp his wrist.

"I know what you intend," she said, "and I thank you for considering me. But I wish to stay with you and wait for the end together. Can we not sit with our feet in the warm water of our reflecting pool? Can we not reminisce about our long, happy life together?" She pressed her palm against his wrist, turning him toward her. "Will you embrace me one last time, my love?"

The massive, bloody membrane intercepted the eastern edge of the planet Wilzerd. Without any cataclysmic sound or display of energy, the gigantic corridor began consuming Gribba's world. The portal moved methodically, capturing every molecule of the planet. Nothing remained on the far side of the immense passageway. The Circle of Evil would not only eliminate the world of Wilzerd, it would erase its existence from the long history of the Crossworlds. When the corridor had completed its work it would be as if Wilzerd never existed. In the cold silence of space the lunar and solar gravitational fields would be updated as the heavens reordered the small section of the galaxy.

No one could speculate about the future of Gribba and the ezuvex race. As the giant membrane passed the halfway point of the planet, continuing to swallow it whole, not even it could fathom the final destination for the giant world. Understanding was not in its coding, it merely carried out its instructions as efficiently as possible. Its limited memory cells informed it of the progress of its mission and nothing else. If the planet suddenly exhibited characteristics beyond its initial assessment, it would calibrate the membrane in order to accommodate for the anomaly. The procedure was commencing as ordered. The corridor, pleased with itself, moved forward to the more populated segments of the world.

The fiery portal raced across the surface of Wilzerd like a hyperactive wildfire. In deep space, its movement seemed slow enough to be almost imperceptible. Across the countryside and through the cities of Wilzerd, however, the blinding speed of the attack overwhelmed everything in its path. Ezuvex inhabitants barely had time to shriek with terror before the bloody membrane overtook them in a flash. The bear-like creatures ran in all directions, instantly vaporized as the corridor swept through city after city. Entire regions of the planet were swallowed up in seconds by the relentless onslaught, and still the membrane rushed forward. Nothing remained behind the moving wall of the slaughter except the quiet anonymity of space. Two million inhabitants of a benign world would be erased from existence in less than nine hours, and Gribba, the leader of the ezuvex, could do little more than watch.

He sat quietly with his wife, watching the mind-numbing events take place. Shim had long since accepted their inevitable fate, and she too sat mesmerized by the magnificent creation as it moved toward them like a tsunami. They held each other fiercely, and for her, that served perfectly as a parting gift to their world, to her and to her husband. She turned to him, looking at his intelligent face, his huge brown eyes, and his tiny little nose.

"Do you suppose any of us will survive?" she asked.

"I don't know, Shim," he answered. "I am comforted by the fact that the end came quickly for our race. Our children did not suffer, and I believe we will encounter them in another place, possibly in another form. Who can say? Who knows the mysteries of the creators' ultimate design?"

"May they suffer an identical fate," replied Shim.

"Do not wish a similar catastrophe on any being," said Gribba.

"Keep a positive and warm thought in your soul, my mate, for the corridor approaches."

The two ezuvex, bonded together for over half a century, sat calmly on the edge of their reflecting pool with their feet and legs dangling in the water. They listened as a titanic wall of fantastic energy surged toward them. As soundless as a morning breeze, the portal whisked through the estate, consuming everything in its path. At the last second, Gribba held up a furry right hand, fingers and thumb extended in defense. It was his last act as a living being, an insignificant gesture in an attempt to deny their imminent demise.

Ignoring the tiny appendage placed before it, the corridor charged through Gribba and Shim on its way toward the western edge of the planet. Checking its headings one last time, the portal made two tiny course adjustments before devouring the remaining tenth of the immense world. After completing its task, the membrane disappeared, the rectangle contracted to its former size and readings were projected back to its source. It would then quietly dissolve while awaiting another chance to serve its masters.

CHAPTER FOUR

Maya opened his eyes, lifting his head away from his crossed forepaws. He blinked a few times, focusing his vision on the beauty of the glade before him. The peaceful surroundings of their home gave all the Champions the opportunity to rest at any time, day or night. As cats normally do, Maya and his brothers slept most of the days away, lying around in the sun, warming their fur and soothing their muscles while dreaming of fresh water and delicious meals.

The nights served as calls for slumber as well, but rarely for cats. The Champions spent at least half the lunar cycle awake and prowling around the glade. At times during the night the giant cats would play hunting games, stalking each other silently until one would rush madly through the foliage toward another. Thousands of pounds of snarling fury would collide somewhere in the trees, and a brief scuffle would ensue before breaking off without any blood drawn. In some cases the cats would part, only to begin the exercise again. At other times the idle Champions would join the two combatants for a midnight briefing, reliving the mock battle and making suggestions for improvements or alternate combat strategies. After all, they were the guardians of the Crossworlds and victory in the shadow world or not, they had to keep themselves in prime fighting condition.

Maya smiled coyly, remembering the last pre-dawn skirmish

between Eha and Surmitang. The great Sumatran tiger had stalked the wily cheetah for close to an hour, determined to take him down without a lengthy charge. Eha had walked calmly through the forest for almost five miles, stopping every once in a while to sniff another cat's marking, dig lightly under a log or stoop down for a quick drink. It always seemed that at the precise moment when Surmitang appeared ready to strike, Eha would scamper away, intent on something else up the trail a bit. When Surmitang finally made his move, he did so forgetting the cardinal rule of pursuit – always leave yourself an alternate line of escape. Eha had positioned himself next to a pool bracketed by three monstrous stone walls. To any predator, it would appear to be a golden opportunity, and Surmitang wasted no time with his attack.

As soon as Eha heard the big tiger crash through the shallows, he sprang straight up in the air twenty feet above the pond. Just as his paws cleared the space over Surmitang's back, the huge tiger crashed headfirst into one of the rock slabs surrounding the pool. Stunned but still proud, Surmitang turned, swiping at anything he thought might be lying in wait for him. He looked like a drunken cub, staggering in and out of the pool and swiping his huge paws through the air whenever he could manage to stand up straight.

The force of the impact finally got the best of his traumatized brain. Three thousand pounds of bristling ferocity collapsed in the murky water. Eha, gripping a twisted clump of tree branches and watching the whole scene from above, almost fell beside his brother from laughing so hard. He finally plopped down next to Surmitang, convulsing with uproarious laughter while ascertaining the tiger's well-being. When he determined that Surmitang still had steady breath in his body, he sat down on his haunches, spitting shouts of laughter so loudly that the rest of the Champions entered the forest to see about the ruckus.

When Surmitang finally regained his senses, he had to recall the stalk and attack sequence for the others to assess. Eha listened to ten words of the story before exploding in a fit of laughter again. When the poor tiger finally reached the end of the account, Therion, Purugama and Maya threw their heads back and roared with delight. Even Surmitang, prickling with bruised pride, eventually let go of his strident control, laughing right along with the rest of them. Maya silently blessed Eha, the true prankster of the group. He had given them all laughter again, something they sorely needed after returning from the shadow world.

It had been nearly two years, and they missed Ajur terribly. Even the Lady of the Light hadn't fully recovered from their loss, and for the first six months after returning, the Champions took great care to see to her every need. They didn't want her to face anything else so soon after their unforgettable journey. Their constant attention slowly brought her spirits back, and soon she began telling her stories again. She even told the Champions about her confrontation with Zelexa on the outer worlds of the shadow realm. The cats had been silently thrilled to see a healthy creator again. They all loved her, maybe not as deeply or as genuinely as Ajur had loved her, but they loved her nonetheless. They wanted nothing for her but a life of extreme happiness and contentment.

Maya's thoughts returned to the present moment. If what he felt in his soul was authentic, then his Lady must be on her way to the glade this very moment. Some terrible event had occurred recently, and in Maya's estimation, the journey of two years ago paled in comparison to this present incident. He couldn't discern the precise nature of it, but he could feel nothing good coming from his heightened senses. He knew someone close to him had suffered a horrible tragedy.

The Lord of the Champions pressed his body to a standing position and loosed a mournful wail into the early evening sky. Every time his breath expired, he inhaled, repeating the exercise again and again. The call wasn't deafening by any means, but the pitch and tone of Maya's voice cut through to every corner of the glade.

One by one, the immense Champions of the Crossworlds emerged from their respective napping quarters. Surmitang rudely parted the trees, making an opening for his great striped bulk to exit the forest. Eha rolled back and forth in a large patch of dirt, scratching his back and coating his fur with the smelly soil before hopping down the mountain toward Maya. Therion, long a king of his earthly realm, rose from his position next to the large lake in the glade. It seemed as though he always guarded the water as he did his sparse watering hole back on the plains of Africa. He rose, taking a direct line toward his Lord. Purugama, staying mostly by himself since returning from the shadow world, lazily flew across the lake from his solitary resting place.

When the Lord of the Champions saw his brothers making their way toward him, he ceased yowling and walked to a clear place in the center of the glade. He watched silently as the four massive cats assumed the protective rotation; Therion to his rear, Eha in front, and the powerful tiger and cougar on his left and right. After facing outward, making sure that nothing threatened their Lord, the four cats turned and faced him.

"What is it, Maya?" asked Purugama, his giant wings softly flapping. "What troubles you?"

"I cannot say for certain, great cougar. There is one thing I do know, however. We shall see the Lady of the Light very soon."

"She's on her way here, now?" asked the huge tiger, worried that his appearance might be a shade from perfect. "We must prepare the glade for her arrival immediately!"

"Then make haste with your preparations, Surmitang," counseled the leader of the Crossworlds Champions, "because our Lady approaches as we speak."

CHAPTER FIVE

Conor scooted down the lush green athletic field. The Baker College defense formed up front of their net with calculated precision, making the prospect of a goal extremely difficult. For now, the defense ignored Conor, allowing him a free path down the right side of the field. Redwood State's winger drew the Baker defense toward him with a mad charge down the center of the field. To every player in the match, it looked as though Morales would take ball on side himself and drive through the defense for a shot on goal. As the Baker players rushed ahead to close off his path, Morales' feet flashed and the ball shot out to the right. He led Conor perfectly with a blistering pass.

Conor took the ball in stride and faked the first Baker defender right out of his shorts. He sent the ball left of the next defenseman, changing directions so fast he sent a spray of turf toward the sidelines. The Baker goalkeeper positioned himself at an angle to deny his opponent as much of the net as possible. But at this stage of Conor's charge, it was all but over. Redwood State's star player altered his course three times before sweeping the ball in front of the net. After causing the goalie to tangle his feet together in a desperate attempt to deny the freshman a hat trick, Conor hammered home his third goal of the game. Before his players could mob him in a congratulatory celebration, Conor had rushed back to help the Baker goaltender to his feet. After making sure he was uninjured, Conor ran away from his cheering teammates, leading them down the field in a mad rush toward their bench. Only then did he allow them to dive all over him, ruffle his hair and pound his back in a screaming salute to his performance.

The Baker College men's soccer club had won the NCAA II title four years in a row. They had been Redwood State's nemesis for the last twenty years. Their program had produced more professional soccer players for national and international play than any other college in the nation.

As soon as he heard Conor had returned to Northern California, Baker's coach had hounded him for weeks to come play for the Barons. He offered him a full scholarship, room and board at his own home if he wanted, and a starting position in his first year. Conor had politely declined his offers, along with all the others flooding his parents' home from all over the country. As much as he appreciated the attention, he wanted to attend Redwood State. His mother and father had received their degrees there, a few of his friends from Mountmoor were already attending, and, of course, Janine had already enrolled. It would take all the forces of the Crossworlds to pull him away from that particular university.

The two coaches met at midfield after the game. "You've got yourself a player, Walt," said the Baker coach, pumping the Redwood State coach's hand vigorously. "No one's ever made our goalie work that hard."

"He's a wonder," replied Coach Rumsey. "I had him for two years down at Mountmoor. I'm sure you remember. He broke nearly every high school record in the section while only playing his freshman and senior years."

"Keep him healthy and you'll win state this year for sure," said the Baker coach as he waved his final goodbye.

The two teams shook hands and left the field for their respective locker rooms. Conor walked around Redwood Stadium, cooling down a bit before hitting the showers. He loved the calming environment of Redwood State. No place on earth could be better for the soul, he felt. He walked around the track craning his neck at the towering trees rimming their field of play. He inspected the giant sentinels surrounding the facility, the thick burly bark lining the trunks, the fern carpet covering the healthy brown soil, and the lush green branches shooting out from the highest reaches of the trees. In a strange sense, it reminded him at times of the forest of forever, the infinite woods where he almost spent the rest of his life. This environment was so different, though. It seemed friendly and welcoming, and Conor enjoyed running through the forest whenever he could spare the time from his studies.

The college was built right next to an old-growth redwood forest, a place so magical and soothing that many students rushed into the mystical woods whenever they had a break from school. Some used the area to escape from reality. Others came simply to meditate. Conor visited the forest to wonder at the beauty of nature, and to imagine his brothers surprising him by appearing from behind one of the trees. As huge as the Champions were, even they could hide their bulk behind one of the massive trunks of these great redwoods.

Conor would trek deep into the forest, sometimes alone, and sometimes with Janine. The two of them would play games, trying to locate the one place where the Champions could be waiting for them. At times, Conor would leave his girlfriend, sneaking away before she could notice. He would move from tree to tree like a cat, completely silent and undetectable. Then, from the shadow of a massive redwood, he would gruffle, chuff or call out in Eha or Purugama's voice. Janine would join in by asking her Champion to reveal himself. During some of these playful encounters, she remarked to Conor that his imitations had been so strong she almost expected one of the big cats to walk out from behind the tree.

After showering and hanging out with his teammates, Conor took off on a quick jog through the main campus. He passed Founder's Row, a series of buildings almost a century old, and skipped down the many sets of stairs leading to the main quad. He ran by the bookstore, the library, and down the hill past the parking lot to the science labs. He knew he would find her there, as he had almost every day since the semester started. She took her program very seriously, spending more time in the lab as a sophomore than most seniors. She had already awed her professors with one of her compounds. After replicating her research, they entered the formula in a state competition for autonomous student achievement. She had placed second, gaining instant notoriety amongst the physical science faculty.

Conor had mixed feelings about her achievement. While he felt extremely proud of her, the newfound celebrity status had robbed them of precious hours they could share with each other.

"Is there an overworked teaching assistant anywhere around here?" he asked, after swinging open the heavy metal door.

Janine looked up from her electron microscope. Smiling coyly, she placed a finger against her lips. After cautioning Conor to silence, she called him over with a wave of her delicate hand.

Janine had blossomed since returning from her captivity in the shadow world. Conor felt his knees go weak every time he saw her, even as she stood in the lab wearing her chemistry trappings.

She had grown about three inches, placing her final height at just over five foot seven. Her figure, once a healthy, athletic build, had reformed itself into the type of stunning shape that turned heads everywhere she went on campus. The male students at Redwood State couldn't stay away from her; she constantly received invitations to dinner.

Janine accepted all of it as a part of life. She resigned herself to the fact that she couldn't do anything about it. She demurely declined invitations from all hopeful suitors, repeating time and again that she had been in a serious relationship for many years. In every case, she flashed a dazzling smile that removed any pain of rejection from the student in question.

Defying Conor's strong protest, she had cut her hair and dyed it a rich brown with deep ruby highlights. The first time he saw her after the change, his heart nearly stopped beating. He suddenly couldn't breathe. He told her repeatedly how great she looked. Just as he did when he first saw her at Mountmoor High School, he developed a serious crush on his girlfriend of four years.

Conor was a lovesick puppy and he relished every second of it. But he knew something that the students and faculty didn't understand about his girlfriend. Janine certainly was physically stunning, but that wasn't what drew him to her in the first place, and it still ran a close second to the quality that made him finally notice her back in high school. He had known Janine quite some time, and he still found it hard to find the right adjective to describe her best attribute.

Special didn't quite define it, but it was as close as he had been able to get so far. She just appeared so comfortable with herself all the time, in any situation. She helped professors without being asked. She signed for deaf students when their interpreters failed to show up for class. She usually raised her hand first during most discussions just to help teachers get the ball rolling. She had a magical ability to make every human interaction a happy and positive connection for both parties. Conor had learned a great deal from her through the years. When he asked her about her natural glow, she honestly dismissed any knowledge of a special aptitude for human relations. She would say she just tried her best to be happy all the time.

"Take a look," she said, motioning toward the microscope. "I've isolated a new microbe. I'm going to present it to the committee next week. If I get lucky, I can enter it into the next state competition."

Conor moved past her, placing his forehead close to the eyepieces of the scope. He neither saw nor sensed anything after that, however, because one whiff of Janine's scent removed all rational intellect from his brain. He mumbled a soft congratulatory statement before reaching out and grabbing her around the waist. She struggled against his strong arms, but not that hard, and soon the two college students held each other in a long, loving embrace. They clutched each other closely, the memories of their incredible journey to the shadow world still fresh in their minds. Conor moved his left hand up Janine's back, tracing her spine before reaching the nape of her neck in one fluid motion. He grasped a handful of her luxurious hair, clenching his fist and drawing her head back. He held her head still with his left hand while inhaling her scent over and over again. His other hand followed the curve of her right side, down her rib cage and around her delicate waist. Sensing no obstruction, he deftly pulled the lab coat aside.

She broke away from him abruptly, wiping the corner of her mouth with the back of her right palm. "No you don't, Conor

Jameson," she said, breathing deeply. The way Conor overwhelmed her during their intimate moments drove her absolutely wild. It felt like she was engaging a wild animal or, as she often said, one of the Champions of the Crossworlds. She had no idea how much power the creators had bestowed on him, but feeling it come alive during their private moments both frightened and aroused her. Sometimes while just standing close to him she could feel the energy bristling from his pores. "A few more seconds and we'll have to lock the doors and turn down all the blinds," she joked.

"So?" Conor answered, arms up in the air. "Let's lock it down for half an hour. Who's going to notice?"

"Professor Grubin, that's who, and I won't damage professional relationships with any of my immediate faculty," she said, regaining complete control as she briskly tidied her clothes and hair. She removed her lab coat and shook it vigorously many times before donning it again. "Now, if you don't mind, I have some data to enter."

Conor smiled. He knew what was coming next. "See you for dinner later?" he asked innocently.

She turned her head slightly, lancing his heart with the most devastating pair of eyes in all the Crossworlds. "Get some rest, Conor," she said, letting the corner of her mouth turn up slightly. "I'll see you in a few hours."

Anyone noticing Redwood State's star soccer player bounding through campus during the next half hour would have sworn the young man was drunk or high on something. Conor ran circles around everyone he saw, zigzagging all over the place and jumping up onto benches, walls and anything else that looked challenging. As he passed the library entrance, he almost accidentally revealed some of his uncanny abilities. He felt so happy he couldn't help himself. He saw an awning in front of the library, six steel poles supporting an extended ceiling roughly twelve feet above the patio. Without even thinking, Conor skipped up onto the bicycle rack, flicked his right foot and shot up above the awning. Realizing suddenly that no human could ever hope to accomplish such a feat, he forced himself to fall back to the walkway. It looked as though he hit the ground pretty hard, and he certainly played the part to the hilt. After deferring calls for assistance from many students, Conor shook himself off and went about his way.

Careful not to attract any more attention, he ran up the walkway toward the social science building. After entering the main floor and greeting the sociology secretary and a few faculty members he knew from his classes, he crashed through the stairwell doors that led to the computer labs in the basement of the building.

Conor liked these labs better than any of the others on campus. For some reason they weren't very well known, so he never had to wait for a seat. The other thing he liked was the surreal quality of the building itself. Redwood State was an old campus, one of the oldest in the California system. Its walls and hallways held memories of thousands of students. Conor could almost hear the voices speaking to him when he descended into the depths of buildings like these. He loved the movie-like atmosphere of the ancient hallways. He expected Seefra or one of the other destroyers to confront him during one of his forays to the computer labs.

He plopped himself down in a chair in front of a computer in a room farthest from the stairwell. Only three other students occupied the lab – two women working together on their senior project and another male student perusing the Internet. It had been raining for over a week, and the musty odor of aged concrete and redwood burl filled Conor's nostrils as he entered his login and password. He waited the customary one to two minutes for the server to recognize his information and boot up the computer. The screen finally flashed, showing a familiar column of icons down the left side.

Before doing anything else, he pulled up the Internet, activating his favorite online game. He played for a few minutes to settle his mind, continuously getting eliminated at the same level. After closing the game he opened his campus email program and clicked through his inbox. He quickly marked and deleted the spam and then moved through the mail from students and team members on campus. Some of the forwards he laughed at, most he deleted without opening. He never opened emails that had been forwarded to him from people who didn't send him any personal correspondence. He figured if he wasn't important enough for a short note every now and then, he didn't care to be clogging up anyone's distribution list.

After responding to a half dozen emails from close friends on campus, he left the e-mail program active and moved the mouse down to the task bar. He activated the word processor and retrieved a small flash disk from his pocket. He inserted it into the appropriate drive, pulling up a paper he wanted to finish. Just as he began editing the first page, he saw the blinking envelope at the lower left corner of the monitor. Another email had popped into his inbox. He almost ignored it, thinking it could be spam or an email from another long lost friend. Something made him look, however, and when he switched screens he saw a name he never thought he'd see again, at least not in this context. The notification posted the following terse message:

From: Mr. Hikkins
To: Trolond Tar
Subject: Request Immediate Meeting
Body: Conor, extremely important we meet at once.
              Reply with preferred location and time.
              Yours, Mr. Hikkins

Conor read the brief message over and over again. He checked the sender and receiver lines a dozen times, focusing particularly on the title "Trolond Tar." Purugama had mentioned that name at the close of their last journey. The meaning of the title still puzzled Conor.

"No!" he said aloud to the computer screen, causing the other three students to look up from their work. All three turned to check on him, decided he wasn't in any immediate danger and then returned to their own tasks.

Conor couldn't believe it; he just couldn't believe this was happening. *What could possibly be occurring that would force a seeker like Mr. Hikkins to contact me again so soon? It hadn't even been two years!* He and Janine had settled into a life they loved, they had set a course for their future believing that the threat to the Crossworlds had been eliminated for all time. He wouldn't allow their lives to be disrupted again, or at the very least, Janine's. He might be convinced to go with them under the direst of circumstances, but she would stay right here where she belonged, where her safety was assured. That was one condition he would never negotiate.

The more he thought about it, the more he realized that what he wanted most was to stay here with Janine. He wanted both of them to complete their coursework, obtain their degrees and start a life together somewhere far from the glade of Champions and the realm of the creators. He loved Purugama and the rest of the cats, and he owed a debt of gratitude to the creators and the council, but in his opinion, all obligations had been settled. They were even.

It wasn't so much that Conor didn't want to help them; he just felt that he and Janine had done their part. He wanted his life back, at least more than two years of it at a time. He came to a conclusion right then and there. The creators and their Champions would have to solve their latest dilemma on their own. Janine deserved better, and besides that, they were happy together. He certainly didn't want to interrupt that aspect of their lives. Yes, he would give his newest family his sincere regrets, informing them that he had rejoined the human race and planned to stay there. He grabbed the mouse and clicked the reply icon.

From: Conor Jameson

To: Mr. Hikkins

Subject: re: Request Immediate Meeting

Body: Mr. Hikkins, please inform my Lady, the council and the Champions that my services are no longer available. I have committed myself to my studies, my girlfriend and my life here on earth. I'm certain the combined magic of the Council of Seven will overcome any potential threat to the Crossworlds. Sincerely, Conor (Trolond Tar?)

Conor stared at the send icon for a full minute before moving the mouse pointer over it. He clicked to send the email, feeling a great pang of regret and guilt about not rising to the challenge once again. A mental skirmish began, with one side hammering his decision and the other side supporting him. *After all, they were quite capable in their own right, weren't they?* Even without Ajur, the Champions presented a formidable threat to anyone foolish enough to assault the glade or the realm. He couldn't understand how their situation could be so dire that they would call upon him again.

And what had become of the Circle of Evil, he wondered. *Hadn't they been utterly destroyed on the plains of the shadow world, in the chamber of caves and in the chamber of cells? Didn't the Lady of the Light destroy her twin sister, the leader of the traitorous protection forces?* Conor couldn't accept that there might be another level to the Circle of Evil, or another gargantuan force arrayed against the creators. He wouldn't allow his imagination to run wild, giving rise to images of the Lady of the Light disappearing, or the Champions being eliminated one by one. He wouldn't allow his feelings to reverse the course he had set. He wanted to stay here with Janine, his friends and his family. He wanted to finish the soccer season and win a state title for Coach Rumsey. He wanted to eat hamburgers and pizza, get into food fights with Beau and his other friends. He wanted to be an eighteen-year-old teenager and enjoy his young life. After what he had been through in the last eight years, he wanted as normal a life as possible right now.

He decided not to tell Janine about Mr. Hikkins' email. More than anything else, he didn't want to worry her or bring back any of the stressful memories of her time in Seefra's Cell of Crystals. Janine put up a very strong front, but he could see from time to time the ill effects of her captivity. The master of darkness had left his mark on Janine, a stain that would never fade, and as much as she tried to ignore it, she would always carry the memories outwardly for Conor to see. He had worked very hard trying to ease the pain of her recollection, and he sure as fire was not going to allow the creators to add to those memories by sending them both on another dangerous and unpredictable journey.

Finally convinced he had done the right thing, Conor closed his email program. He tried to continue editing his paper, but the new development would not allow his mind to focus. Ultimately, he saved his changes, retrieved his flash disk and logged off. He hadn't even noticed the other three students' departures, and when he looked up at the clock he couldn't believe his eyes. Three hours had passed since he entered the lab. He had sat there mulling over his decision for so long, the time had just slipped away.

He stood and slid his chair back. The metal tabs scraping across the linoleum floor awakened something in his mind, something he couldn't quite understand. Then he looked at the clock again, realizing the significance of the time. In five minutes he was supposed to call on Janine for their Friday night date. Slapping his forehead with his hand, he raced down the row of computer stations, knocking one of the chairs over as he turned toward the door. The chair clattered into the trash and recycle cans, careening off the receptacles in a loud, echoing chorus. Although usually conscientious about cleaning up after his mistakes, Conor left the clutter behind as he raced up the staircase and out the door of the social science building. He had five minutes to rush home, shower, shave and dress, and then scoot across campus to Janine's house. As he used Eha's cheetah speed to scamper up the trail next to the walkway, he looked around for any sign of other students who might see his abnormal pace. When he felt assured that he had no company, he kicked it into high gear, arriving at his house in less than a minute.

CHAPTER SIX

The Champions hastily put the glade in order. Using their particular magical qualities, they addressed each of the natural aspects in turn, making them shine and sparkle brilliantly. Therion spoke to the lake, his personal watering hole, asking it to become calm, to glisten softly for the Lady after she arrived. Surmitang stalked back and forth in front of the forest, growling and chuffing at every branch and leaf like a staff sergeant preparing his troops for parade. As the massive tiger walked along the lengthy assortment of flora, each individual tree or bush seemed to straighten or spread its limbs a little wider. Every leaf extended its grainy fibers as much as possible, blanketing the forest in a lush green façade.

Purugama soared over the central meeting area, carrying clouds in his wake and positioning them perfectly along the horizon. Inhaling great volumes of air, he rearranged the clouds, blowing those that detracted from the overall beauty of the sky to the far side of the lake. Only when he felt satisfied with the look of the afternoon sky did he float back down to rejoin Maya. The three Champions gathered around their leader at the base of a mountain of volcanic rock.

Maya and his brothers watched a manic Eha sprinting around the glade, hastily trying to tidy up the grounds before the Lady arrived. The big cheetah flew this way and that, patting down select areas of the grounds with his giant, fluffy tail. He appeared to be talking as he worked, giving encouragement to himself as he frantically sped from location to location. The humorous aspect to the whole ordeal lay in the fact that he was making more of a mess by rushing everywhere than he was as he tried to clean up.

When Maya could stand it no longer, he mumbled a short spell, freezing Eha in place. "Easy, Eha," said the Lord of the Champions. "The Lady will love you no matter the condition of the glade. Take your time with each aspect of your tasks, and you'll find yourself a much more efficient servant."

The giant cheetah tried desperately to move, but found he could only turn his head toward the Lord of the Champions. Even though he was frozen in place, the happy Champion smiled widely at Maya's instruction. When Maya released him, Eha padded around the glade softly, checking that every rock and grain of sand was in place. The cats moved carefully to their protective locations around the central courtyard of the glade. Maya put his head down, closing his eyes for a short nap in case the Lady's transition was delayed. The other four Champions stayed wide-eyed and alert, hovering over their Lord as they always did, daring any force to make a threatening move against him. They awaited their Lady quietly, and the news she bore, with a great sense of urgency.

Maya napped for only a few minutes before the dust and debris in the center of the courtyard began swirling. The Lord of the Champions opened his eyes, but did not immediately raise his head. He had seen this phenomenon for many years. What he expected to happen would happen again as it always did, quietly at first and then with much greater force.

The churning particles began to sparkle and crack with a frenzied form of electricity as the perimeter of the corridor appeared in the middle of the Champions' circle. An instant later, every bit of natural debris flattened to the ground in a spasm of noise and magical thrust. The debris pulsed with a heady vibration as the first images of the corridor appeared in the glade. Sizzling, silver energy exploded at the base of the portal, splitting into two identical rods of intense power. The mirror images of the Lady's immense energy parted from each other, moving outward to form the base of the corridor frame. At the same moment, both bars of energy shifted direction, moving upward toward the completion of the Lady's passageway. Again, they changed direction, moving toward each other with perfect accuracy. Upon meeting at the close of the frame, the silver membrane flashed once inside the portal's perimeter. Almost vanishing completely, the filmy center reappeared with a much healthier consistency. The membrane locked together with the sides of the frame, coalescing into a perfectly healthy corridor.

The portal settled itself, appearing to sense the importance of the traveler within its confines. Seconds later, the membrane loosened its hold on the frame, allowing its substance to grasp the Lady's hand and help her through the doorway. The Lady of the Light's figure appeared in the center of the corridor, enveloped by the silvery essence of the membrane. Even the strands of her hair were lovingly caressed by the magical transference as the Lady made the voyage from the realm to the glade of Champions. After only a second or two, Athazia stepped through the corridor, treading softly on the freshly swept ground of the glade. The membrane, certain of her successful arrival, recoiled back into the frame of the portal. The corridor stood ready to transport another traveler, but when it sensed its services were no longer required, it slipped silently into the ground just behind the Lady's feet.

"My Lady, how may I serve you?" asked Eha after sidling up next to her and offering a flank for her to balance herself.

"A strong shelf where I might rest," she answered, her pale face revealing the weight of her concern.

"My Lady," offered Purugama delicately, as Therion rushed to her side, opposite Eha, "you do not look well. Perhaps corridor travel was not the most advisable course at present."

"Please," chimed in Surmitang, "allow us to serve you, to remove that which troubles you through mirth or valor."

Maya watched his Champions quietly, stifling any concerns of his own for the moment. He knew in his soul what the Lady would say when she finally found her voice. He had known the instant he awoke from his afternoon nap, and now he could see it in the lines on her perfectly formed face. *She hadn't just been crying. No, she had been passionately weeping for someone or something, or maybe both.* Her eyes, always so pure and clear, vibrated slightly with fear and uncertainty. She swallowed repeatedly, as if trying to ingest something her body wouldn't accept. Her anxiety seeped through Maya's fur, traveling right into his bones. The great leader of the Crossworlds Champions felt an emotion he hadn't experienced in centuries.

If one of the creators could be so severely shaken by a series of events, then who were the Champions to hope to remedy anything? Their combined power was insignificant compared to the awesome strength of just one of the creators, and here before him sat one of those supreme beings, clearly terrified. He didn't know what to do. He hadn't any idea how to approach her. He couldn't think of a way to dance around the situation, so he did as he always had when addressing her. He crouched to the ground and pawed his way over to her. Putting his huge black and white face directly in her line of sight, he locked eyes with her.

"Speak, Lady," he said, while staring into her soul.

The Lady of the Light took in a long, slow breath, held it while closing her eyes, then exhaled smoothly. "Gribba's world is gone," she replied weakly, barely able to complete the statement. "Wilzerd has disappeared from the Crossworlds system."

"What?" asked Therion, suddenly focusing on her every word. "Are you certain of this?"

The other Champions joined in the query, all except Maya, who sat staring into the Lady's silvery, multi-hued eyes. She returned his gaze, preferring the sight of his calm countenance to anything else at the moment.

"We are certain," she continued. "Actually, it is our seeker who certified the findings. He came to us not long ago with an incredible theory regarding a destructive force unknown to anyone in the system." She continued staring at Maya, drawing strength from the Lord of the Champions. "We refused to believe at first, but the seeker remained persistent. He finally convinced us of the danger, and I was on my way to the glade when I felt the greatest sensation of loss I have ever experienced."

Maya recalled the feeling he woke with earlier that day.

"I rushed back to the council chamber to verify my suspicions, and found the Lord of All Life crumpled over a chair in obvious physical pain. The remaining council members frantically addressed his needs, and when he saw me waiting at the portal outside the chamber, he bellowed through the intense agony ravaging his body." Athazia placed a weary hand to her stomach as she continued to relay the events.

"And so I have come to collect the great Crossworlds Champions. We must stop the devastating weapon sweeping through our system."

Maya blinked his eyes once, never removing them from his Lady's red-rimmed field of vision. "Who, my Lady?" he asked steadily. "Who has the power to release such a force?"

"It can only be the inner element of the Circle of Evil," she replied.

Surmitang growled his frustration and disbelief. "But we destroyed their armies, decimated the shadow warriors, and put down Seefra himself. What can be left of their union except a frazzled array of misguided individuals? They cannot exist, I won't believe it!"

"No, great tiger, the seeker speaks truth," stated the Lady firmly. "This is the ruling body, minus my sister, of course. Our seeker has confirmed the source of the weapon, and the council agrees with his assumptions. Destructive corridors larger than entire worlds are originating from somewhere deep within a far corner of the Crossworlds, sent forth by the Circle of Evil to annihilate any planet allied with the creators. We've no doubt that other worlds have been wiped away, but Wilzerd was the first to impact us so deeply. Gribba and the ezuvex –all of them – are gone, gone."

The Lady lowered her forehead into her hands, weeping openly. It was the first time she had ever shown such deep emotion to the entire assembly of Champions. It unnerved the great cats. To see such a powerful being, one they loved so dearly, reduced to such a state was difficult. All five of them, Purugama included, crowded around the Lady, offering her the only assistance they could, their warmth and love. They might have stayed there for all eternity had Athazia desired it. Instead, she hugged all of them in turn and stood, wiping her tears away for the last time.

"I thank you, all of you," she said warmly, looking at each cat individually. "However, we must get started. We have plans to make."

"Yes," growled Surmitang. "Let us travel through the corridors and surprise the last of this inner element and annihilate them once and for all! Let us be done with them, for I grow tired of their endless stalking."

"Save your aggression, Surmitang," said Maya softly. "You're sure to find an outlet for it at some future date."

"Yes, my lovely tiger," said the Lady. "Maya speaks wisely. The inner element of the Circle of Evil will not easily be located, and their predatory corridors appear in space once every three days. We have precious little time to plan, much less execute a strategy."

"Your pardon, my Lady," interrupted Purugama, always very deferential to his creator. "What of Conor and his companion, Janine? What part will they play in this new journey?"

The Lady of the Light looked up at the giant cougar with his golden, leathery wings at rest beside his muscular body. She reached out to him, remembering that it was he who visited Conor the first time on that lonely mesa so many years ago. She could understand his concern for their newest Champion, especially in light of the loss of Ajur. Ajur had truly been Purugama's brother for all his life, and Conor, well, he would always be like a son to him. After all, Purugama had practically raised him during their first journey together.

"Conor will be fine, I assure you," replied the Lady. "Our seeker has contacted him, and as I fully expected, Conor refused to meet with him. Of course he has no knowledge of the terrifying nature of the danger facing us, but nevertheless he has informed Mr. Hikkins that his services are no longer available. If you want my honest opinion, I applaud him for refusing."

Purugama smiled inwardly, showing no outward emotion at all. "We will be traveling to earth, then, to collect him?"

"The arrangements have already been made. Therion will

accompany our seeker and meet with Conor directly. The rest of you will follow me through another corridor. We will return to the realm of the creators for a tactical conference. We have less than three weeks to marshal our forces against this new threat."

"Why so little time, my Lady?" asked Eha.

"Our seeker has calculated the pattern of the predatory corridors. The destruction of Wilzerd confirms his findings. Conor's world lies in a direct path facing the stream of killer portals. We believe one will strike and consume the earth within nineteen days."

"Then let us away," snarled Therion. "We haven't a moment to spare. Set us on our new course, my Lady. Send me to the seeker at once so we can fetch Conor and bring him to the realm."

"Yes, we must leave immediately," she answered. "But you must all be aware of something before we depart. The corridor structure has been damaged by the disappearing worlds. Every time a predatory portal consumes a planet, the attached corridors vanish as well. We've no idea exactly which corridor linkages have been damaged and where the corresponding links might exist. Be careful how you travel, and watch the membrane of any portal closely as you enter. You may find yourself at the entrance of a corridor with no exit."

The five cats sat quietly, listening intently to their Lady. Even Maya couldn't suppress the look of concern on his face.

"That is correct, my Champions. If you enter a corridor with no exit and do not retreat quickly enough, the portal will close behind you, cutting you off from any possible escape. You will be imprisoned as surely as if you had been sentenced by the council itself. It might be centuries before we locate you again." The Lady of the Light looked at each of the Champions in turn, sensing their collective apprehension. "Just be careful, please. We desperately need every one of you.

CHAPTER SEVEN

Conor and Janine lay next to each other in front of a glowing fire.
An assortment of odd-sized, colorful pillows lay scattered around
the living room. Some they used to brace their posture, others had
been cast aside. Janine's roommates had left for Wilson Creek earlier in the day, off on another backpacking and hiking venture in
one of the many parks surrounding Redwood State. The two of
them had the house to themselves for two days and two nights,
and they decided to make the best of it.

After Conor arrived to pick up Janine, fifteen minutes late as
always, they had walked from campus down to the adjoining town
of Markinson. They hustled through a light rain and an assortment of street peddlers and panhandlers, to make their way across
town to one of the local coffeehouses. After they checked in at
the counter and ordered a couple of warm drinks, they greeted a
few friends and then squeezed into a small space on a community
bench.

The place overflowed with people, students mostly, as it did on
most nights. In a far corner by a sparkling fire, a group of musicians
played a handful of odd instruments. The Celtic tunes complemented the peculiar little coffeehouse perfectly. It was a warm place with
good people and good music; all housed in an interior of seasoned
wood and delicious smells of assorted teas and baked goods.

After singing a few songs and laughing with friends for a while, Conor checked in with the counter again. He accepted his key, towels and robes from the staff member, motioned to Janine to meet him at the far door, and said goodbye to their friends. One of his teammates, an exchange student from Germany, patted him on the shoulder, asking him how he ever got to be so lucky.

He and Janine walked through the garden area outside the coffeehouse, light raindrops sprinkling their cheeks. After arriving at their bathhouse, they quickly changed into their swimwear and entered the steaming water in the deep, Swedish tub. Conor submerged immediately, wiping his wet hair back over his ears. Janine kept her head above water, preferring to keep her freshly washed hair away from the scented pool. Instead, she closed her eyes, inhaling the eucalyptus fragrance into her sinuses.

She loved coming to these baths. There was something about dipping her body into hot water that allowed her to forget nearly everything on her mind. She focused on every tiny part of her body, even down to the pores of her skin. She felt her toes accept the trickling water at every point where the skin made contact with her nails, likewise with her fingers. She felt the solid teak siding of the tub on her back, and as she arched slightly, she could feel the rivulets of water seeping down her bikini. She focused on her legs, her stomach and her arms as the soothing warmth penetrated everywhere, releasing her from any worries she might have carried into the tub with her.

Keeping her eyes closed, she felt the lightest touch of Conor's index and middle finger against her belly. He left it there, against her stomach for almost a minute, and then began lightly tracing a circular path above and below her belly button. She smiled widely, still keeping her eyes closed but enjoying her boyfriend's playful attempts to arouse her. She let him continue for a while before teasing him a little.

"You can wait until we get back, Conor," she said coyly. "Besides, if you're a good boy, I've got a surprise waiting back at the house for you."

Conor leaned over, kissing her neck lightly. "I thought I was being a good boy." He released his two fingers and started rubbing her shoulders and neck, pushing the hot, scented water into her skin. "So what's the surprise?"

Janine opened her eyes and smiled playfully. "I guess you'll have to be on your best behavior if you want to find out."

Back at Janine's house, they had started a movie and watched it impatiently for roughly thirty minutes. They finally decided to turn it off and listen to the fire instead. Janine disappeared into the bedroom for quite some time and when she returned, Conor forgot all about the fire, the Swedish baths, the state soccer title, their degrees, Mr. Hikkins' email, and anything else that wasn't standing a dozen feet in front of him.

The two of them lost themselves in each other for over an hour. The fire cooled but their passion didn't, and when they finally pulled away they stared into each other's eyes, gasping for breath and any explanation for what had just occurred. They loved each other deeply, and, with each passing day, their fondness for each other increased a thousand fold.

"The fire's about to go out," said Janine without looking away from Conor's radiant blue eyes.

"What fire?" replied Conor, his mouth twisting into a devilish smile.

"Please, Conor," she answered. "I'd like to stay here for a while, but I'm getting cold. You don't want me to go put something on, do you?"

That was all the motivation Conor needed. He stood and threw on a pair of jeans in one fluid motion. After telling her to stay put, he padded across the room and ripped open the back door. He flicked on the outside light, running barefoot out into a light rain while keeping the woodpile in sight with every step. He gathered a generous pile of logs into his arms and turned back toward the house. About halfway to the back door he suddenly stopped, splashing his right foot into a squishy puddle of rain and mud. His eyes had locked onto the western sky out over the ocean.

Forgetting all about the weight of the logs, he approached the light switch outside of the door. Flicking it off, he backed up a few steps, lifting his eyes up toward the sky again. It was still there, a strange blood-red dot among the stars. Conor couldn't tell how far it might be from earth, but nevertheless it stood out like exactly what it was – a completely unique phenomenon floating in the sky. At least at this distance it seemed as though it hovered innocently. He looked a while longer until Janine called out to him, telling him to close the door before she froze to death. He did so, scraping the mud from his feet before entering the house again. When he returned to the living room, he fielded questions from his girlfriend as he placed a few logs on top of the glowing embers.

"Do you have another girl stashed outside by the woodpile?" Janine asked playfully. "I didn't think you'd become bored with me so quickly."

Conor gave her a look that said she had truly lost her mind. "The sky looked different tonight. I just wanted to check it out a little longer, that's all."

Janine sat up, pulling a few pillows together for support. "Different how?"

"The colors mostly," said Conor. "There seems to be a giant red star out there, deep red, like the color of blood."

"Show me," said Janine excitedly, standing up with a blanket around her torso. "Where is it? Can I see it out this window?"

"It's gone," answered Conor, not telling the truth entirely. "I watched it for about fifteen or twenty seconds before it started to fade out." To be honest, he didn't think it had disappeared, but Janine wouldn't be able to verify it unless she went outside. He didn't think she'd like the cold all that much, so he counted on her desire to keep close to the fire.

Something about the red star troubled Conor. He couldn't place it, but seeing that strange light so soon after receiving Mr. Hikkins' note unnerved him. Perhaps he shouldn't have blown off his old teacher's appeal to see him so easily. Maybe there was more to it than a simple request for an audience. Anyway, there was certainly nothing he could do about it tonight. Perhaps next week after class he could find the email and respond to it again. For right now, however, the room was getting warmer and Janine was snuggling close to him again.

"Know what I want to do tomorrow?" she asked innocently.

"What's that?" replied Conor, throwing a blanket over the two of them.

"Let's go for a walk in Redwood Park, behind the school. Let's take lunch and go for a really long hike. We can play our game together, the one where you disappear and start mimicking the Champions. We haven't done that since regular practice started for the soccer team."

Conor selected a strand of Janine's chocolate brown hair and tucked it behind her ear. "You know I'd do anything for you, don't you?"

"Anything?" she asked, nestling in closer to his strong chest. The fire roared again, giving Conor and Janine the warmth that matched their passion. Both of them couldn't think of any other place they'd rather be than right there together, wrapped tightly in a loving embrace.

CHAPTER EIGHT

The following morning was a rare, rainless day in Redwood County – at least for the time between the months of November and July. The residents of the small county always claimed that if one could survive the constant rain during winter and spring, Redwood County became a virtual paradise between August and October. After months of continuous rain, the entire county glowed with an emerald green carpet that extended from the ocean all the way through the forest. The gigantic redwoods, massive and strong in late summer, stretched toward the sky as if they too had waited for the sun to finally greet them again. Large, puffy cumulus clouds dotted the bright blue sky every day during those three months, perfectly content to remain in Redwood County until the rain returned in November.

The people who lived in the towns dotting the Pacific Coast this far north took full advantage of the summer weather. Outdoor activities were the norm, and people engaged in all sorts of organized sports and many unorganized events as well. One of these elective activities was hiking the many trails that were weaved throughout the redwood forests. There were hundreds of miles of managed trails, starting at the extreme northern border of California and extending a hundred or so miles south of Redwood State. One of the most popular, and indeed Janine's favorite of all the trails she and Conor had explored together, was the Fern Canyon trail just south of Crescent City. At a little over ten miles, it not only provided an excellent workout, but it gave individual packs of hikers ample opportunity to isolate themselves. There was nothing better than standing amidst a column of gigantic redwood trees alone, holding your breath and listening to the sounds of the forest. There was no doubt that even while surrounded by hundreds of creatures, if they preferred, you would never know they existed.

The sun glistened far above the two hikers as it tried desperately to penetrate the redwood canopy three hundred feet above the ground. Conor and Janine saw the tiny beams of sunlight flicking against their eyelashes. The rays flashed across the rustic trail in front of them while they looked out across the endless fern-covered floor of the forest. They felt decades of redwood burl shavings grinding and squeaking beneath their feet as they ambled along the Fern Canyon trail. Every few seconds both of them would tip their foreheads back as far as humanly possible, craning their necks to look straight up at the tops of the massive trees. The sun, although brilliant up above the foliage, appeared to be perfectly filtered by the giant canopies of the redwoods. Conor and Janine could stare endlessly toward the heavens and receive nothing more than an assortment of glistening streams of sunshine in return.

Janine noticed that Conor hadn't spoken much since they entered the forest. Usually he ran all over the place for the first mile or two, excited by the prospect of communing with nature once again. He loved to explore his heightened senses – smelling, touching and tasting everything before stopping dead in his tracks to watch and listen. Today, however, he seemed strangely preoccupied. The change was subtle, and if Janine hadn't been so close to him for so long she might not have noticed. He definitely had something on his mind. She could see it as clearly as if he had a sign around his neck.

"What's wrong, Conor?" she asked innocently while gliding her fingers through the curls of a fern branch. "Why so quiet?"

He looked up quickly, a young man caught with his hand in the cookie jar. "Nothing's wrong. I just feel quiet. I want to listen to the forest for a while."

Janine walked over to her boyfriend, taking a stance directly in front of him. He gave a weak attempt at walking around her, but she quickly cut him off. Blocking his path, she stared into his eyes for a second or two before twisting her mouth into a crooked grin. "I said what's wrong, Conor?"

He was done before he had the chance to take another breath. He couldn't hide it from her any longer, so he decided to let her in on everything. He told her how he really felt about the strange red light in the sky he saw the night before, and how it held particular significance due to the fact that he had received a terse email only hours before from someone they both knew quite well. He told her about rejecting Mr. Hikkins outright, and how he now felt maybe that wasn't the best response he could have given. Finally, he explained his terrible feeling about the strange red light, and while he couldn't explain it to her completely, he somehow knew that it spelled trouble for the Crossworlds.

Janine lowered her head, holding Conor's arms with clenched fists. She began to visibly shake, most evidently around the shoulders and neck. Her head, rocking back and forth randomly at first, quickly assumed an unwavering pace, clearly denoting her displeasure with the entire affair.

"No, Conor, I won't. I will not go back there!" She spat the words into Conor's chest, wanting to implant her feelings into her boyfriend so he would never forget them. "We've given enough of ourselves for their cause; well, you certainly have. I won't have our lives delayed or destroyed again just because some cosmic force decides to include us in another one of its adventures.

"Besides, the Champions destroyed their enemies," she continued hopefully. "Isn't that right? Weren't Seefra and his servants defeated at the chamber of cells?" Tears began to well up in her eyes. Conor could see that Janine was visibly disturbed by the news. He felt the same overwhelming desire to protect her that he did when he finally found her again outside of Seefra's laboratory. Moving closer, he gathered her up in his strong arms, pressing her cheek against his chest. A small group of hikers suddenly appeared on the trail just east of them. Conor greeted them as they passed by, and then waited until they disappeared around the next bend in the trail.

"Janine," he started, "I don't even know why Mr. Hikkins contacted me. For all we know it's a reunion party for the Champions, or a coronation of a new supreme councilor. I'll go back to the lab tonight when we get home and send him another email. Maybe I can find out what he wants."

Janine inhaled and clinched her arms around her boyfriend's waist. She would not be put off so easily. Her intuition about the series of events felt too strong. She blasted the wind from her lungs and squeezed Conor with all her strength.

"I can't take another imprisonment," she breathed. "It took everything I had to keep going while Seefra kept me in that cell. I saw so many creatures fall to their deaths, so many tortured right in front of me. I took everything Seefra dished out and did my best to stay strong for you, Conor, but I can't be captured by them again. I won't be. Do you understand?"

He held her close to him for the longest time. He wanted the warmth of his body to soothe her pain away. He felt such a blinding rage whenever he recalled her captivity. He hated Seefra, the Circle of Evil, and most of all he still blamed himself for allowing her to be taken from him. He would never allow that to happen again, even if it meant his own life. He increased the compression in his arms, holding her even closer. When he finally sensed her breathing pattern returning to normal, he eased her away from him, grinning at her.

"Let's head off the main trail for an hour or so, get really deep into the forest. We'll find a place to play our game together. What do you think?"

Janine pressed the palms of her hands against her eyes, wiping away any remaining moisture. "Yes, I'd like that."

For the next thirty minutes Conor and Janine ran through the chest-high ferns laughing and screaming like a pair of five-year-olds. Sometimes Conor would run low toward one of the larger redwood trunks, collapsing behind the chunky base, listening for Janine to stop and seek him out. Following her every step with his heightened sense of hearing, he planned his attack with meticulous cruelty. Waiting until the absolute last moment, he would spring from behind the tree, roaring like an enraged tiger. Usually Janine would merely slap his hands away before running away through the forest. Sometimes, though, Conor would time his pounce so perfectly that he'd catch her with her back turned and scare the daylights out of her. It was then that he received the worst reprisals. She would tackle him to the ground and pound against his arms and chest with everything she had. A session of tickling and teasing usually followed, with the two of them finally helping each other up and sharing a few well-deserved kisses.

When they finally paused to rest and get their bearings, Conor admitted to Janine that he had no idea where they were. They stopped all movement, listening to the forest, attempting to seek guidance from the giant redwoods all around them. Conor noticed that the stream of sunshine from above had shifted quite a bit, telling him it was late in the afternoon. A dense redwood forest was not the place to be overnight, so Conor decided to climb one of the huge monoliths and find a way back to the trail. After placing Janine at the base of the tree, he scaled the first hundred feet in seconds. He looked around for a bit, checked the tree, and scampered up another hundred feet. At just over two hundred feet in the air, he spotted the trail about five hundred yards away. He also saw the tips of the ranger station's radio antennae roughly five miles to the east. They would be okay after all, and Conor smiled as he looked down toward Janine. He opened his mouth to call down to her and his grin quickly diminished. He saw a huge animal heading right for her.

A brown bear, a big male, was nosing his way toward a smell he obviously picked up while lumbering through the forest. *He probably followed her scent for miles,* and now he's about to surprise Janine. Conor could see she had no idea what approached her through the thick ferns. She stood quietly at the base of the tree, waiting for him to come down and lead them out of the forest.

Conor had less than a minute to decide how to handle the situation. The bear, all eight hundred pounds of him, would be confronting Janine within seconds. He couldn't call down and warn her. She couldn't climb trees the way he could, and if she tried to run, the bear would catch up to her before she ever hit her stride. If he yelled at the bear from this height, it probably wouldn't register any threat at all. No, the big brown had Janine on its mind, and if

Conor didn't get down there immediately it was going to go badly for her.

Letting go with his hands, Conor allowed gravity to pull his body away from the trunk of the giant redwood. He turned in mid-air, falling face first toward his girlfriend and the bear. As he passed the fifty-foot mark, he saw a shiny, black nose poke through the last stand of ferns near Janine. He watched it wrinkle as the bear sniffed, determining her closeness.

Grabbing a low-hanging branch about twenty feet above the ground, Conor swung his body like a gymnast under and around the tree, breaking his momentum while slowing his fall. He landed gently next to Janine, legs crouched and fingers splayed on the ground in front of him. Even with the extra physical strength and agility given to him by the creators, Conor knew he'd never stand a chance against one of the largest land mammals in the world. He had to get Janine out of there, and fast. He had one big problem, though – bears could climb trees, and this one looked hungry. If it wanted to, it could follow them right up the base of any one the trees in this forest. They couldn't outrun it, and they couldn't climb their way out of trouble. Conor stood silently, backing his way into Janine.

"Don't make a sound," whispered Conor, "and don't move, or try to run away."

The bear, upon hearing Conor's quiet instructions, snuffled a little louder, blasting debris toward the two college students. It pressed through the ferns, exposing its eyes and ears. Then its entire head came through. It stared at Conor and Janine, coughing out a few warning growls.

Conor grabbed Janine's hand while placing his other arm around her waist. Together, they backed away from the bear, circling to the right around the base of the giant redwood. Conor kept his eyes glued to the bear's movements, watching for any sign of a charge. Its ears still stood casually forward, showing no sign of stress or anger. Conor took that as a good sign, and he continued leading Janine away from its line of sight. *Maybe,* he thought, *they could give way to the bear's path and let it pass.*

The bear hadn't tracked Janine for miles just to give her up. He pushed his way through the ferns with an angry growl, scraping the ground a few times with its huge claws, challenging Conor. The fluffy ears that once made it look as innocent as a child's teddy bear were now slanted straight back. The mouth expanded as it turned its head in a ferocious growl. The game was over. Conor knew his strategy had failed.

"Janine, when I push you, I want you to run as fast as you can in the direction I send you. Keep running and don't turn around. Don't look back until you reach the ranger station."

She started to protest. "But what about…?"

"No time, Janine," said Conor. "No time for that. Now, get ready."

The big brown emerged from the far side of the giant redwood, ears back, fur down and all business. It growled one last time as it charged the hikers. It came at them so quickly that Conor barely had time to send Janine on her way. He stood his ground, not knowing exactly what he would do. The only thing he knew for sure was that he would sacrifice himself for Janine, no questions asked. He bellowed at the charging bear. He picked up the biggest rock he could find and hurled it with all his might. He watched as it bounced harmlessly off the right forepaw. Conor had a flashing thought that maybe he wouldn't have to respond to Mr. Hikkins after all. He stood his ground, waiting until the last moment before running in order to lead the bear away from Janine.

A thunderous roar blasted through the fern forest. It was so close and so loud that Conor found himself shocked by the sound. He turned his head quickly from side to side, disoriented, looking for another bear. The deafening roar repeated itself as Therion crashed through the redwood forest toward his brother Champion. With a mighty leap, he landed directly between Conor and the charging bear. He turned violently, throwing his great, chocolate mane toward his opponent. Snarling viciously, he opened his huge mouth, exposing the giant fangs of a five thousand pound African lion. His voice boomed across the expanse toward the bear, causing it to halt his charge in mid step. Everything stopped for a few seconds, long enough for all parties to assess their positions. The only sound in the forest was the diminishing echo of Therion's vocal warnings.

The bear stood on its hind legs, unwilling to give up its prey so easily. Lifting its body to provide maximum size and intimidation, the bear growled menacingly at Therion. Swiping its great paws a few times at the giant lion, the bear returned to the ground, advancing a few steps toward the Crossworlds Champion. Opening its mouth in a threatening posture, the bear returned Therion's warning by baring its own set of lethal jaws. Its huge paws flashed out toward the giant lion, scraping the ground and throwing rocks and bark to either side. It took a few more steps toward its rival, daring the immense cat to defy his authority in the forest.

Therion's lips peeled back in a snarling expression of disdain. *How dare this puny creature delay this journey for even a moment?* The huge Champion stepped toward the bear, lashing out with a muscular forepaw. With claws extended, he slashed the trunk of the nearest redwood, making sure the initial impact hit the bark head on. The base of the tree exploded, with huge sections of burl flying in every direction. The bear cowered under a shower of jagged pieces of redwood bark. It growled loudly, sounding its frustration after traveling so far for what it hoped would be an easy meal. Therion advanced again, slashing another tree and sending even more wooden shrapnel toward the bear. He did not wish to hurt it; he knew this animal was a predecessor of the ezuvex race and someone to be venerated. All the same, he certainly would not allow Conor or his companion to be harmed. He stepped toward the cringing bear one last time, slashing the ferns directly in front of it with his razor-sharp claws. A shower of confetti rained down onto the brown bear. After one last display of defiance, it followed its instincts and backed away from Therion. Turning in the opposite direction, it trudged away, snuffling the ground for perhaps another scent to follow. Conor watched the rolling shoulders pass through the ferns until the bear finally disappeared.

Therion immediately turned to address his brother. "Are you alright, Conor? Did the bear injure you before I arrived?"

"No," said a clearly shaken young man. "I mean yes, fine, I'm uninjured. You came at exactly the right moment, Therion. Thank you."

"Any of us would have done the same," replied the big cat. "The Champions protect each other, always." The giant lion raised his furry head, sniffing vigorously in many directions. "Your companion, Conor, I do not sense her presence close by. Should we not look for her and ascertain her well-being?"

The question jolted Conor from his stupor. He had sent Janine off into the forest when the bear charged. He had no idea where she was now, or if she had found safety anywhere. He called out to her, again and again, and when he heard nothing in return, he ran to Therion and jumped on his wide shoulders with one quick skip off the ground. Grabbing a hefty chunk of Therion's mane in one hand, he pointed with the other toward the direction he wanted the huge lion to proceed.

"Go, Champion," he ordered. "Find my companion, now!"

Therion crouched, preparing to leap over a giant redwood that lay prone in the forest directly ahead of them. Just as he tensed to jump, the soft, frail ferns to their right slowly parted. Janine passed through first, followed by a very dignified but uncomfortable Mr. Hikkins. The seeker brushed his clothing meticulously, trying to look as normal as possible. He despised the outdoors, "a messy and unpredictable place" in his estimation. Very difficult to keep one's station while constantly looking after one's appearance. Satisfied with his work, at least for the moment, the former high school math teacher presented himself to his student. He waited a few moments, of course, while Conor and Janine enjoyed a breathless reunion.

"Good afternoon, Mr. Jameson," said the seeker, as if greeting a student in one of his classrooms. "I trust your adventurous spirit hasn't left you in too much disarray."

"Mr. Hikkins," said Conor, gasping for breath, half from his and Janine's narrow escape and half from seeing his former teacher in the middle of nowhere. "Thank the creators you showed up, but how did you know about the bear, and how did you get here so fast?"

"Our intervention into your unfortunate affair was simply fortuitous, Mr. Jameson. Therion and I had come to speak to you about your rather abrupt response to my recent email. Upon locating you and arriving in this forest, we happened upon your impending altercation just in time."

Conor lowered his head for a moment. "I'm, eh, sorry about my note to you. I meant no disrespect."

"Think nothing further of it," answered Mr. Hikkins, turning to Janine. "Are you quite well, my dear? No lasting effects from your ordeal?"

"I'll be alright," she said, but her eyes reflected the deep, dark memories she had of the living nightmare. Forcing herself to forget once again, she turned to Therion. "Thank you, lion. Your bravery has saved us yet again."

"It is an honor to serve the Keeper of the Keys," cooed the great Champion. Therion lowered his immense head, nuzzling against Janine's shoulder for a moment. She reached up to scratch the huge mane, finding a large ear in the midst of the rich, brown fur. She began rubbing and massaging it. Soon the entire area hummed and vibrated with the overwhelming sound of Therion purring like a kitten under Janine's spell. The giant lion let his head fall into her grasp. She rubbed his cheeks, his ears and his neck in appreciation for saving their lives.

Mr. Hikkins had seen quite enough. After all, they had come on an urgent journey. The Lady of the Light would be awaiting their return. "Conor," he began with hands clasped behind his back, "something of the utmost urgency demands that you return with me to the realm of the creators. I had hoped the email I sent you would prompt a positive response. Since it did not, the Lady sent Therion to accompany me to earth. She commands an audience with you, and we have been charged with delivering you to her presence without delay."

Conor looked over at Janine, whose hands had fallen to her sides. Therion had dropped to the ground beside her while staring coolly at Conor. Janine had an expression of quiet desperation masking her usual calm composure.

"We haven't much time, Conor," said Mr. Hikkins squarely.

Conor looked back at his former teacher, who returned his gaze without any judgment at all. If he could fathom the uncertainty in Conor's soul, he certainly gave no indication. His mind was ruled by logic and rational outcome. He viewed all situations as equations to be solved. There was no room for emotionalism, which in his estimation only clouded one's decision-making. "What's the nature of the problem?" he asked Mr. Hikkins.

"Earth will be annihilated in less than nineteen days," answered the seeker. He stared at the young Champion, gauging his reaction to the news. He watched as Conor looked again at Janine, his eyes conveying the deep fright and pain suddenly coursing through his body. Mr. Hikkins flicked his line of sight over to Janine for one moment, seeing an identical response in her eyes.

"We discovered the strategy only a few weeks ago," he continued, explaining as quickly as he could the phenomenon of the predatory corridors. "Although the random aspect of their attack has been verified, we still cannot locate every single world that might suffer an onslaught by one of these portals. After calculating the quantitative nature of the pattern, I realized early on that earth had also been designated as one of the initial targets."

Conor interrupted his former teacher. "What do you mean, 'had also been designated'?"

Mr. Hikkins didn't delay his response for a moment. Clasping his hands behind his back again, he pressed against his instep, elevating his body another half inch from the ground. "The world of the ezuvex disappeared from the Crossworlds system less than three days ago."

"What?" shouted Conor. "Gribba, destroyed?"

"Their entire race, obliterated. Their world, Conor, consumed by a corridor large enough to devour one hundred planets the size of the earth."

"But by whom?" Conor gasped. "Who would use the corridors for such a purpose, and why would...?" The young Champion stopped, a look of disbelief and horror bleeding down his face. He turned to Janine, who had fallen against Therion for support. The giant lion continued to stare at Conor, giving him nothing but a placid expression.

"No!" he shouted at no one in particular. The small group stood quietly listening to his objection echo down the Fern Canyon trail. "We destroyed them, all of them! Therion? Tell the seeker what you saw at the chamber of cells. Speak truth, lion. Ajur gave his life for us on that journey. Speak!"

Therion sat quietly without blinking an eye.

"Apparently, the inner element of the Circle of Evil remains," remarked Mr. Hikkins. "The craftiest and most powerful lords of their domain, having nothing left with which to attack the creators, have decided on a strategy that could ultimately rebound against them. I have constructed various models supporting that theory. Nevertheless, they have embarked on a serious offensive maneuver against the creators. Wilzerd has been destroyed. Make no mistake about it, Conor, the earth sits in direct alignment with the linear progression of these predatory corridors. It will suffer the same fate as Gribba's planet. We need every resource we can call upon, including you. You are Trolond Tar, after all, and you must return to the realm with us. Immediately."

"I'm Conor Jameson!" bellowed the young man. His patience had run out. He relished his life now; he wanted nothing to interfere with his or Janine's happiness. "I belong here on earth, a normal eighteen-year-old college student enjoying his life, his girlfriend and his friends! I gave my entire adolescence to the creators and the Crossworlds, asking nothing in return. I defeated shadow warriors and destroyers single-handedly during the journeys you sent me on, and what I want now more than ever is to be left alone!"

Conor stomped his right foot on the ground like a spoiled child. "I want my life back! I want Janine to live and be happy without the constant reminder of her imprisonment! I wish I'd never called forth Purugama in the first place. I wish I'd never penetrated the Crossworlds dimension. It seems like my association with you will never end!"

Mr. Hikkins calmly waited for the storm to abate. As he had thought before, emotions only got in the way of sound reasoning. He would give his Champion the space he needed, and then direct him toward his only course using the discipline of logic.

Therion watched his brother closely. Although he held his own emotions in check, he certainly understood Conor's frustrations. He could feel the friction emanating from the young man's shoulders. After all, it was this exact difficulty that led the giant lion to betray the creators and kidnap Conor only a few years before. Therion had silently plotted against his benefactors for decades, always questioning their decision to remove him from his pride on earth. It nearly destroyed him, and in order to successfully endure the separation, he devised a plan to strike back at them, taking away the one thing they cherished most in all the Crossworlds. The big cat searched Conor's soul, wondering if a similar spark existed within Trolond Tar. *Now that would be a remarkable battle,* he mused, *especially when Conor finally grasped his true nature, realizing the kind of immense powers he could command.*

"Conor," offered Mr. Hikkins, "I appreciate your aggravation, as does the Lady of the Light and the Council of Seven. We want nothing more than to leave you here with your companion, living a life of undisturbed tranquility. You have, however, become an integral component in the arsenal the creators need to combat forces detrimental to the system. You cannot deny your destiny. Just as I must embrace mine, and Therion has ultimately welcomed his vocation, you must also join with your true self and embark upon this final journey."

"How do I know this will be the last time?" demanded Conor. "What if the Circle of Evil can't be destroyed? What if they always have another hand to play, another device to wield, or another way to threaten the Crossworlds? Is my life to be held hostage for all eternity? Tell me now, seeker, and speak truth. I can barely tolerate another journey, and certainly no more after that, and I will not put up with dishonesty, especially from a servant of the creators."

Therion's massive eyelashes closed for a split second. The big cat blinked involuntarily, and at a time when he was trying so hard to remain dispassionate about the proceedings. For a split second, Therion had seen Conor become a different person. At any time before this, he never would have treated the seeker with anything but extreme deference. He had done as much earlier in this conversation when apologizing for his harsh reply to the seeker's message.

Could it be? wondered the giant lion. *Could the ancient prophecy of the oracle actually be materializing? Could the Lady of the Light have spoken truth all this time?* Conor had looked more than uncomfortable at the mention of his true name, on this day and on many other occasions. Therion remembered the day the group of seven had been ready to penetrate the Lady's corridor and advance into the shadow world. She gave Conor the garments of battle she had been holding for centuries. The headband she placed on Conor's head had designated him as none other than Trolond Tar.

When she introduced him to the Champions, Conor smiled sheepishly, without any idea of his true identity. He cringed emotionally when anyone ever mentioned the name, expressing his discomfort for everyone to see. But today Therion saw something that caused him to uncharacteristically flinch with excitement. Conor the young man had departed, and in his place emerged Trolond Tar. A proud and demanding warrior had awakened through Conor's frustration, a warrior accustomed to giving orders and having them followed without question. Trolond Tar questioned the seeker not as a boy requesting information, but as a man, a warrior, demanding information from a peer, or maybe even a servant. The transformation awed Therion, but as soon as it manifested itself, it vanished, once again leaving Conor alone in his body.

"Conor, listen to me," instructed Mr. Hikkins gently. "There can be no other course for you. You must return to the realm at once. Say your goodbyes, here and now, and come with us. We shall ensure your companion safe passage back to her home."

"I will follow you back to the realm, Mr. Hikkins," answered Conor, "on two conditions. Give me until tomorrow to say my goodbyes, and swear by the life of the creators that you will personally see to Janine's safety."

The seeker stood placidly, assessing Conor's demands. He

knew he would be honored to guard the Keeper of the Keys under any circumstances, but he had his misgivings about leaving Conor here for another day. *What if the Circle of Evil had omitted a vital piece of information about the predatory corridors, a minute segment of the equation that might alter his findings?* It was always possible that due to their devious nature, the schedule for earth's destruction might be beyond his understanding. Allowing Conor that one extra day might mean the difference between success and failure. In the end, however, the seeker understood Conor's nature better than anyone else in the Crossworlds, except for Purugama, of course. Once Conor came to a decision about something, an entire division of shadow warriors would never be able to change his mind.

"Agreed," stated Mr. Hikkins, "as long as I set the time and location of your corridor transmission." Conor's former teacher had a knack for an economy of words. Wasting no time, he stated his terms plainly and directly. The only thing Conor could do was accept the offer.

Conor stepped forward to shake Mr. Hikkins' hand, as he had done many times in the past when he thought he was a simple high school teacher. As he grasped the weakly-offered palm of the seeker, a voice cut in to their transaction.

"I haven't given my approval yet," said Janine with more than a bit of irritation. "Don't I have a say in my own destiny, or are the three of you determined to arrange things without my input?"

Conor sputtered a few apologies. Mr. Hikkins raised his hands from his sides in a gesture of submission. Therion didn't move a hair on his coat, but he marked the event for a story-telling session with his brothers at some point in the future. Humans reacted much like those in the animal kingdom when confronted by an angry female. If you weren't directly involved, it certainly made for interesting theater.

"I have my own affairs to attend to, and I will access the corridor at the appointed time tomorrow. But I want assurances from the council. They must use their magic to return us to the exact time and place of our departure. I want them to swear by their very existence that this will come to pass. Conor and I must be able to walk back into our world as if nothing at all had occurred. If our lives are to be interrupted once again, then the creators must promise to return us to our precise starting point. I won't have another period of our lives taken from us."

"As you wish," replied Mr. Hikkins.

"Seeker," commanded Conor, once again emerging as Trolond Tar. "What if we fail? What if we cannot turn back the portal?"

Mr. Hikkins glanced once at Therion before responding. "Then the earth and everyone you know will be wiped clean from the galaxy. Your world, your home, will disappear forever."

Trolond Tar answered with a quick nod of his head. "You two better find your way back to the realm. I can hear trackers within a mile of us. I'm sure the rangers heard Therion's challenges to the brown bear. They'll be here in a matter of minutes."

"Until noon tomorrow, then?" confirmed Mr. Hikkins. "Be at the entrance to the crab pier in Trinidad."

"We'll be there," said Conor. "I'd advise you to send the corridor and nothing else. I don't think a lion the size of an army tank would go over too well with the locals."

"Well said, Trolond Tar. The portal will appear at precisely twelve o'clock. I will inform the Lady of your impending arrival."

Conor placed his arm around Janine's shoulders. With his free hand, he reached out to Therion, scrunching his jowl harshly.

The giant lion gruffled, pulling his cheek from Conor's grasp. The young man looked back at the Champion as he and his companion disappeared into the fern-covered forest. Therion said nothing further, but he noticed a glint in Conor's eye that told him the warrior had come to the right decision. The group of seven would rise again, even without their bravest member. They would always refer to themselves as the group of seven, as the great jaguar would run with them toward every destination, toward any enemy they faced, for all eternity. Just as Purugama had risen after falling in his battle with Drazian, and he himself had returned to the glade of Champions, so too would Ajur always run with the Champions. Even if the huge jaguar's spirit was all that remained, that was more than most could provide in physical form. Therion blinked his golden eyelids twice and then again while reminiscing about the lost Champion. Ajur meant something unique to every cat in the glade. They would never allow his memory to fade.

The big lion chuffed once before turning to fall in step with the seeker. Mr. Hikkins waited for the massive cat to turn and walk abreast of him before taking his first step. When traveling with any of the big cats, he always walked one step behind their nearest forepaw. He held the Champions in great esteem, and this gesture allowed him to show his everlasting respect for their accomplishments. Walking alongside the largest of the Champions, the seeker silently marveled at the heavy footsteps of the animal. Therion's footprint displaced more than fifty times the amount of trail than his puny little shoe. He listened while the fern leaves and redwood burl littering the trail groaned under Therion's tremendous bulk.

The seeker allowed a momentary flash of emotion to pass through his mind. He felt the slightest pang of jealousy, imagining Conor battling the Circle of Evil side by side with these majestic warriors. He entertained the thought for only a second before re-turning his mind to the rigid discipline he always maintained.

A sizzling corridor opened up before them. As the portal solidified, the redwoods and ferns came alive around its perimeter. The giant trees strained to press their trunks and leafy branches a little closer to the bristling portal. The ferns seemed electrified by its presence. The curling leaves springing from the young branch-es stretched themselves toward the perimeter of the passageway. They danced a lively jig as they contacted the outer edge of the corridor, pulling back slightly before timidly reaching out again. Local birds and animals of every breed appeared from everywhere to see and feel the energy of the creators' portal.

Just as the two travelers were about to enter the membrane, Therion turned to see a group of rangers bursting through the ferns behind them. They all stopped, mouths agape, watching a man fearlessly walking next to a lion as large as an elephant. Be-fore they could do or say anything, the peculiar pair stepped into a doorway unlike anything the rangers had ever seen, disappearing from earth without a trace. The corridor, still holding the native flora and fauna enthralled, closed quietly, first by height and then by width. With a silent pop, it too vanished from sight. The rangers stood still, eyes bulging and completely speechless.

CHAPTER NINE

Conor and Janine arrived back at her house a little after dusk. They hadn't said a word to each other during the drive back from Crescent City. For over an hour, Conor simply gazed out the window at the uncanny beauty of Redwood County. His mind drifted in and out of various stages of reality. *The entire planet, destroyed, exterminated, wiped away?* He couldn't even fathom it. He looked at the passing scenery, trying to wrap his mind around the immensity of the earth. Here they were, driving down a single road in one county in one state of a vast country, on one of many immense continents the world over. The gigantic land masses he thought about represented only a fraction of the planet he called home. The oceans covered far more of the earth than any of the continents. It became daunting for him to think about the earth as a mass of living surface area, whether land or sea.

He began thinking about the many forms of life existing in their world, right then, at that moment, just as he and Janine traveled down the serene highway together. Mammals, birds, insects, rodents, and all of the diverse life in the oceans, everything could be wiped out, along with a few billion humans. *Could humankind and their paltry weapons thwart an enemy as powerful as this? Not a chance,* he thought. With all their mighty technology, the population of earth would only be able to stand by and witness the annihilation of their world.

The more he thought about it, the angrier he became. Human beings may be fallible, but they didn't deserve to perish in a solar holocaust. Conor's anger welled up from a deeper place, however. As he looked out the window of Janine's car, he saw countless examples of living nature. Imagining the extermination of the flora and fauna in just this region of his world made his blood boil. He looked out toward the endless tips of the giant redwoods, seeing elk and deer randomly spotting the highway, hawks and seagulls sharing the clean air of the northern coast and a host of lesser rodents scampering along the side of the road.

Conor loved all animals deeply. He didn't require his strange alter ego, Trolond Tar, to help him summon the anger and strength he would need for this latest journey. If the Circle of Evil wanted another shot at him, threatening the inhabitants of earth's ecosystem was not a healthy way for them to begin their assault.

Seeing just one defenseless animal abused or destroyed would send Conor into an uncontrolled rage. He couldn't even grasp the depth of the fury he would feel, or the punishment he would exact upon the architect of such an assault if the entire ecosystem was wiped away because of a feud that earth's animals had no part of. His body shook involuntarily as he thought about such a shocking outcome.

As they pulled into the driveway of Janine's rented home on the outskirts of campus, Conor tossed a strange puzzle around in his mind. He loved Janine with all his heart. He loved his family just as much, but in a different way of course. His friends from his hometown and those he had made here at school enriched his life to no end. He wondered, though, when it came down to it, whether his true motivation would come from a defense of human life, or of the animal life on his world. The thought consumed him so deeply he failed to notice the car stopping or the engine shutting off. He barely felt Janine's touch, something that always sparked his senses no matter what the occasion.

"Hey you," said Janine softly, squeezing his arm. "We're home."

Conor turned and looked at her, the word home freshly implanted in his mind. Up to this point it had been a meaningless expression, but now it possessed an immeasurable worth even he couldn't judge. He turned his face to her, smiling and squeezing her forearm. He exited the car, walking around to her door and opening it mechanically, just as he had done a thousand times before. He offered his hand; she took it and rose from the driver's side. She pecked him on the cheek while grabbing his hand to lead him toward the house. After entering, she asked him to start a fire as she dropped her coat onto the couch.

As Conor stacked the logs appropriately in the fireplace, adding some kindling and a few crumpled sheets of newspaper, he heard the bath begin to run in the other room. *How like her,* he thought, *everything can be solved with a hot bath.* He smiled, breaking from his reverie for the first time since they left the ranger station. He sat in front the fireplace coaxing his small creation to life. When he felt certain of its strength, he closed the screen and removed his boots. Padding across the living room, he removed his sweater and thermal shirt and dropped them on the couch next to Janine's overcoat. Balancing himself against the edge of the couch, he removed his socks, leaving them on the floor next to the wall. He rounded the corner into the master bedroom and found Janine lounging in a large Jacuzzi tub while the steaming water continued to spill into the basin. Smiling at Conor, she crooked a finger and motioned for him to join her in the bathtub.

After removing his jeans and boxers, he stepped gingerly into the water, seething at the intense heat. His girlfriend taunted him a little.

"The great Trolond Tar," she said while looking up at him, "afraid of a little hot water. Why they chose you to save the world again I'll never understand."

She seemed so at ease with the whole thing, as if she had battled with the idea, realized the logic behind their involvement and then simply accepted it. *It's one of the qualities you love about her,* Conor silently told himself. He shook his head, kneeling down into the water at her feet. "It's not as though I have much choice. One of those corridors is on a collision course with earth, and we have less than three weeks to intercept it."

"I don't like it any more than you do, Conor," she said, soothing his strong arms and shoulders with a sponge soaked with the burning water from the bath. "We only have until tomorrow noon. Let's make the most of our time together."

Conor forgot all about the intense heat of the water. "Mind of the creators, Janine, I love you so much."

"I know, Conor. Believe me, I know. I love you with all my heart. Promise me we'll be back on earth before too long."

"I promise," he said while nudging his body tightly against hers in the bathtub. "But then again, I'd promise you anything."

THE INNER ELEMENT

CHAPTER TEN

"We have decreased our margin of error and accelerated the overall process by nearly one percent," reported one of the three beings seated at the triangular table in the dimly lit room.

"What affect will that have on the trajectory of the device?" asked the handsome but callous-looking leader of the inner element.

"Earth will be consumed in fourteen days, a condensed application of our original estimate. The Council of Seven will not be able to decipher the new calculations in time to correct their current course of action. If all proceeds as planned, we should have a clear path to the glade in less than thirty days."

"What chance for any collateral damage?"

"The probability of error includes an impact with two worlds formerly in league with our forces," replied the lesser being. "They possess no knowledge of our current activities, however. Perhaps their imminent destruction might be blamed on the creators and their Champions; something to consider should our strategy play out to our utmost expectations."

"Culpability poses no problem," answered the absolute ruler of the Circle of Evil. "Let the planets be destroyed, their inhabitants annihilated. Soon there will be no one alive to condemn us. Earth holds the key. When it vanishes from its galaxy, the greatest Champion in the history of our struggle will be erased from existence. After Trolond Tar perishes, the others will follow easily. Perhaps Maya might end up giving us more than his share of trouble, but I will see to his torture and termination personally. Mistakenly, he feels his magic cannot be countered. That proved true on the battlefields of the shadow world, but against one as powerful as Shordano, he will taste his final hours."

The supreme leader slid his ancient chair back slowly, grating the metal legs against the floor of their chamber, their last chamber, converted into a staging area for the final assault against the Crossworlds creators. Shordano left his chair and walked over to the hastily-cut opening in the high wall of the enclosure. He looked out onto the ruined lands of the shadow world, his home for ten thousand centuries.

They had left mangled carcasses on every battlefield, a reminder of their hideous loss to the Champions and their leader, the Lady of the Light. He thought of Athazia, how lovely she was, how stubborn and unwilling to grasp the truth. Unlike her sister, Athazia kept her covenant with the Council of Seven, serving their every need her entire life. She hadn't found the strength to leap into the shadow world with all of her heart to serve the true masters of the Crossworlds.

Her sister had been a willing servant. Without the genetic decoration of a creator, however, the benefit of her association had contained severe limitations. If only he could have convinced Athazia to cross over, what a powerful combination they could have become. Shordano turned from the window to face the third arc of the inner element.

"Has the assassin been released?" he asked softly.

"Final preparations proceed as we speak, my Lord."

"You assured me the beast would be on its way as of this meeting!" roared Shordano. "Explain the delay in your duties!"

The third arc of the inner element neither struck back mentally nor raised his voice. He glanced once at his seated associate before responding. "I ask you one last time, my Lord. Repeal this order. Remove this tactic from the overall plan. You cannot possibly comprehend the damage to the Crossworlds if the destroyer accomplishes this goal. With one fatal strike, it is quite possible that your servant will end all life within the Crossworlds system and quite possibly everything beyond the boundaries of all we understand."

"I am aware of that!" bellowed Shordano. "Send the destroyer this minute! I will not tolerate any further discussion. We must have a contingency plan in case the Champions and the creators overcome our predatory corridors before they complete their assignments. The assassin will be our final answer. There is no defense against its ruthless nature."

"But my Lord..." interjected the third arc.

"Keep your silence, Wolbus," ordered Shordano. "I see your thoughts written on your face. Do you not think that I comprehend our immediate danger? I most certainly do, but I will not yield or give final victory to those we have struggled against for countless millennia. If the corridors fail, then the Crossworlds be damned. If that means our destruction as well, then so be it. Who could find a reason to continue living in a world where we would be nothing more than servants to the creators?"

"By your command, my Lord," answered the calm, soft-spoken Wolbus, "I will implant the image of the Author of All Worlds into the psyche of the assassin. It will be released at the sun's disappearance this evening." Wolbus raised his eyes to the ceiling of their chamber. "And may the Crossworlds be remembered by any who survive your futuristic Armageddon."

"Pah," answered the leader of the inner element. "Come, Jek, let us see what can be done to improve upon your excellent work with the corridor calculations. Perhaps we can squeeze another day from their trajectory. I want to be rid of Trolond Tar as quickly as possible."

Pausing momentarily to make eye contact with his associate, Jek followed his master through the door, away from the staging area toward the makeshift laboratory. They left a silent, thoughtful Wolbus leaning forward on his elbows, which were propped against the hard, grainy surface of the table.

The principal orator of the Circle of Evil allowed his forehead to slip idly into his hands. Saying nothing, yet thinking so loudly he felt Shordano might hear him, Wolbus began making mental calculations for the release of the most horrible destroyer the Crossworlds had ever encountered.

How many times had he proposed its destruction, if only for their safety, he sat, wondering. The hideous creature had escaped confinement once during his tenure as their servant. It had taken *two companies of shadow warriors* and all the magic of the inner element to recapture it. Most of the shadow warriors had been brutally annihilated. One high-level member of the outer circle had also perished during the onslaught.

The creature lived to stalk and mutilate, the only purpose it had ever known. Unlike Drazian, who had become what Purugama ultimately destroyed, this creature, if it could be called such, started life in its predetermined, hideous form. It had never changed, never been altered by the creators or by the Circle of Evil. The

Council of Seven wouldn't go near it; they never allowed even the most remote discussion about capturing and containing the creature in the forbidden corridors. It was simply too deadly, too dangerous. They decided to give its destiny over to the Circle of Evil, if they deemed the hazard worth risking.

Wolbus pondered the putrid nature of the destroyer for almost ninety minutes. He tossed a few scenarios around in his mind. None arrived at the outcome he desired. If he refused to release it, Shordano would destroy him and discharge the monster himself. If he gambled for more time, his Lord might just throw him into the pen with the destroyer, making him a target. It wasn't as if Wolbus feared death. He did not, but he could not countenance needless slaughter.

Once the destroyer left its cage, it would pursue the Author of All Worlds relentlessly. Nothing could halt its advance. No one, at least to this day, had ever been able to stand in its way. The powers it wielded remained unknown to even the most advanced scholars in the Circle of Evil. They were formidable indeed; it controlled every element known to the Crossworlds in its most basic and violent form. It could instantly combine any number of these with magical and physical experimentation, producing components so deadly that no creature, Champion or Destroyer, could withstand their impact.

It maintained a devastatingly hostile attitude toward everything placed in its path. Wolbus had never witnessed anything like it in all his long years. It acted as though it detested every other creature it saw. It used that hatred to fuel an already boundless aggression. When it attacked, the sight of its violent actions terrified others so deeply they eagerly welcomed their own death. Nothing could stop its advance or slow it down for one moment.

Wolbus had heard tales of worthy opponents standing fast against it, even hacking away pieces from its body. To their horror, the dismembered segment bounced from the ground, attacking the opponent along with the suddenly wingless creature. The assassin would repay its foe by slicing it to pieces, forcing some into the mouth of the dying opponent while consuming other parts itself. When certain of its enemy's impending death, it would flatten its face with a foot as heavy and solid as granite. By the time it turned away from another vanquished foe, the sliced limb had returned to the destroyer's body. Within seconds, the creature resumed its former shape, looking for its next victim with a sadistic eye that missed nothing.

Wolbus' body shook from the horrible memories. Just thinking of the assassin sent chills down his spine, cold sweat streaming down his temples. He did not relish his task, for even he could not predict the ultimate outcome. He had dissected his duty in every way possible, and it appeared he had no alternative but to release the creature. His one encouraging thought lay in a tiny alteration of the plan, his own modification even Shordano wouldn't understand until far too late. He would buy some time – how much he couldn't estimate – but he would give the predatory corridors every opportunity to complete their mission. Perhaps then Shordano would consider calling the assassin back.

He pressed against the arms of his chair, standing slowly and stretching his legs. He looked out the lone window of the chamber, taking in the devastation that at one point in time represented their kingdom. *How could it have come to this? Hadn't the Circle of Evil started as just an opposing force, something offering an alternative to the creators' designs? Hadn't the protection forces aligned themselves with Zelexa to avenge what had occurred during the first struggle beneath the equinox?* He shook his head and turned toward the door of the chamber. "Let us survive this strategy," he whispered. "Let us survive our own foolhardiness."

Wolbus walked through a corridor of his own making. He just as easily could have floated down the crumbling stairwells into the bowels of the shadow world, but they weren't entirely stable these days. When Athazia had returned for the four keys and to destroy Seefra's monster, she had been a little too fervent with her powers. While obliterating the chamber of cells and the deep chasm beneath, the Lady of the Light nearly destroyed every remaining compartment left to the inner element. *Had she known how close she had come to opening the cell containing the assassin, would she have halted her onslaught?* Wolbus pondered this for a moment, finally concluding she would have continued her attack, possibly daring the beast to face her in what remained of the chamber. Her grief would have been her undoing that day. The assassin would have annihilated her. *Not before an intriguing battle, however,* thought Wolbus. Extremely distraught over the death of her favorite Champion, she would have overestimated her abilities and walked into a conflict she couldn't possibly have survived. *Unfortunate about Ajur,* thought Wolbus. He was always a favorite of the inner element, probably why they had set Seefra against him so early in their skirmish with the creators. *If they could have coaxed him over to their side, well, what might have happened then?*

Wolbus exited the corridor, clearing his mind of all distractions. It may be their cell, but the surrounding environment belonged to Nemelissi. The putrid stench flowing through the sparkling bars of its cell nearly toppled Wolbus. He quickly raised a portion of his cloak, covering his nose and mouth with the soft fabric. It did little to salve the sensory assault.

The principle orator placed his free hand on the wall to steady himself. He quickly yanked it away, brushing the acidic paste from his fingers. His hand burned with a mysterious, fiery pain. Uttering a quick spell, he momentarily soothed his smoldering fingers.

From somewhere within the mists came a sickening cackle. It sounded to Wolbus like a retching animal. As quickly as it began, the laughter vanished, leaving him alone again in the swirling vapor.

After almost fainting from the wretched odor, Wolbus raised his eyes and looked into the mists. He could barely make out the bars of the cell due to the putrid smoke emanating from the assassin's body. He heard the alternating heat and cold spiking up and down and across the thin organic bars. *The keepers truly outdid themselves with this one. Nothing synthetic could have held this creature for an instant.* They had used the organic composition of the corridors to construct a cell that reacted to whatever its captive used to enhance its attempts to escape. Energy met equal energy, brute force with brute force. Transference or invisibility would be countered with an opposing spell, eclipsing the energy used by the prisoner. The cell could not be breached by anyone, or anything, known to the Crossworlds.

Seefra had argued against using it to house Nemelissi. He claimed that Conor of Earth should be placed within its impenetrable bars. Wolbus considered this for a moment, finally understanding the master of darkness' reasoning. Trolond Tar had escaped from the cell of shadows with the help of that meddlesome seeker, Hikkins. Seefra had not only been right, he had paid the ultimate price for their miscalculation. Everything had gone poorly from that moment forward. All they had left was a desperate gamble, one he felt they had little chance of surviving.

Suddenly, the mists in the small cubicle parted like a ragged curtain, revealing the assassin, who crouched facing the wall in one corner of the cell. The chalky smoke previously drifting through the area now streamed directly toward the creature. Set in motion by silent command, the dense fog returned to its master, seeping into its skin through pores suddenly appearing on Nemelissi's back.

With the cubicle now clear, Wolbus stared through the bars at the assassin, a gruesome monster straight out of every child's most terrifying nightmare. He could see the creature breathing evenly, giving no reaction to his presence. He waited for what he knew would come, standing as far back from the bars as he could. He knew Nemelissi well, better than others who had taken it for granted in the past. He watched, waiting for the attack.

Breathing shallowly, he saw the inky sledge that had poisoned his hand streaming along the walls toward its place of origin. The pores on the destroyer's back opened wide, accepting the magical seepage. Once the walls were clear and the liquid acid gone, the skin on the monster's back closed up. The assassin flexed its powerful muscles, appearing to enjoy ingesting toxic chemicals into its blood.

The attack came as Wolbus expected, with no warning at all. Nemelissi flung its body toward the bars without any physical exertion at all. It seemed to spring toward Wolbus using some unknown source of energy. It crashed violently against the cage, rocking the cubicle's foundations. For a moment, Wolbus believed this time the creature would break through. The ferocity of its attack shocked the principle orator anew, causing him to fall back against the far wall. He placed both hands up against the cool stone for support. Wolbus had no idea where he would escape should the creature actually break free. Calling forth a corridor would take too long, and climbing eighteen hundred feet of stone wall certainly was out of the question. Even so, the sight of the assassin lashing through the bars, and the thought of how he would perish at the hands of Nemelissi, caused him to lean against the wall for some semblance of support. He just couldn't help himself.

The cell fought back. Taking only a fraction of a second to examine the chemical nature of the destroyer, the bars lost their rigid shape, collapsing around the body of the creature. Separating from the walls on either side of the cell, they formed a second skin around the assassin. The cell forced the creature's arms and legs to return to their original positions. A series of smaller bars clasped around its mouth, closing off any further attempts to howl at its captor. Nemelissi could barely move at all. It certainly couldn't move toward Wolbus. The walls on either side of the creature shimmered with a golden light as pure and powerful as any corridor in the Crossworlds. These energy points weren't designed for travel. However, they held the bars in place as if they were physically connected to them.

The assassin struggled tirelessly, gaining strength from the sight of another kill so close at hand. Its eyes burned with a hatred so fierce they nearly popped out of their sockets. Wolbus, comforted by the cell's reaction to the attack, brushed the palms of his hands together while taking a tentative step forward. He began reciting the spell that would summon the creature's corridor. He looked down for a brief moment to check his hands for any remaining residue.

Nemelissi, groaning with a mighty effort, surged forward out of its cell. The bars sparkled with an equal amount of reverse energy, but the monster would not be denied. As Wolbus reeled backward, crashing against the wall again, the assassin's hair follicles, the one thing left dangling by the cell bars, arced over the top of the creature's head. Instead of trying to reach their target, however, the follicles shot a series of needle-tipped darts toward Wolbus.

Hundreds of projectiles shot forward. With less than ten yards of distance to cover, they would be inside Wolbus' skin in a flash. The principle orator's eyes went wide. He raised his hands in an impotent attempt to shield himself against the oncoming horde of poisonous pinpricks. He placed the bottom of one shoe against the stone wall, thinking that might allow him some respite against the attack. He closed his eyes, waiting to die a hideous death.

The bars of the cell flashed once, sending a stream of golden spikes across the expanse between the assassin and the principle orator. The spikes overtook the needles instantly, swallowing the offensive weapons just before they reached Wolbus. As each spike consumed one of the needles, it fell to the floor of the cubicle, seemingly expired from the completion of its duties. Wolbus watched the spikes drifting toward each other, one by one, and pressing together to form a large spear. With each additional spike, the spear expanded, ultimately becoming a formidable weapon.

Once whole, the spear slowly rose from the floor. Elevating, it levitated at eye level with Wolbus. The principle orator could see the streamlined golden spear in his immediate vision, almost eclipsing the assassin in the background. Then, the spear shot forward toward the monster, aiming directly for its head.

The impact drove Nemelissi back into the original area of the cell. The golden spear disintegrated in a flash of blinding light, and in the midst of the explosion, the bars of the cell fought back against its captive. Changing their composition, they delivered a brace of frigid cold into the body of the monster.

Nemelissi bellowed anew, this time with pain beyond comprehension. Wolbus watched as the creature's body coloring shifted toward the icy blue of intense, freezing cold. Its mouth froze in a mute expression of terrible agony. The eyes stopped moving as well, but they stared at Wolbus with a defiance that shook the principle orator down to his bones. The cold dissipated, followed by an agonizing wave of extreme heat.

Wolbus heard and smelled the creature's skin sizzling under the intense radiation of the cell. The monster shrieked like all the devils of the shadow world under the intense, searing heat of the attack.

The high temperature of the cell bars singed away a few layers of skin, pausing between each one in order to deliver the maximum amount of agonizing pain. After what seemed like a lifetime to Wolbus, the bars contracted, squeezing the creature's body into a misshapen jumble of limbs, eyes and hair. The cubicle convulsed violently, spitting the assassin against the rear wall of its cell. Smashing against the stone wall, the monster flopped onto the floor, unmoving. Wolbus would have thought it was dead, if not for the sickening laughter coming from behind the bars. Nemelissi, beaten and bloodied, wanted its jailer to understand it would rise again momentarily. Someday, maybe, it would pass through the bars and exact its revenge.

"Do you not understand?" asked the principle orator while taking a few tentative steps toward the cell. "I've been sent here to release you."

The laughter ceased. Slowly, the gruesome head turned in Wolbus' direction. Golden pupils, surrounded by deep blue sockets, latched onto its jailer's eyes, squinting once or twice for effect. The destroyer made no move toward the bars of its cell. The eyes continued their vigil, however, holding Wolbus' stare without interruption.

"Yes," he continued. "I have been ordered to unchain you, to free you from this cell." Wolbus stepped closer to the bars, holding the creature's eyes in his gaze. "It appears you have one more journey to undertake, one more enemy to vanquish. You will be a willing dupe in your own destruction, should you succeed. Can you comprehend this, I wonder? Do you see that by completing your task you will destroy not only the Author of All Worlds, but everything you've ever known as well? Your world will cease to exist, you will move beyond oblivion into an abyss you will never escape."

Wolbus now stood a little more than arm's length from the bars of the cell. The assassin began flexing its muscles again, stretching its limbs as the strength returned to its body. A low rumble radiated from its entire being, and Wolbus' eyes flared as he witnessed the pores on the creature's back open wide again. A putrid gas wafted up from cavities in the monster's skin, causing Wolbus to wince and gag. He quickly lifted his robe and placed it over his nose. The principle orator's eyes watered as more of the pores exuded the sickening smoke. If the assassin could not break through the bars and massacre his jailer, he would certainly make his life miserable in the interim.

"No, I suppose you wouldn't know or care," said Wolbus. He stepped back a few paces, centering himself between the two walls of the cubicle. Focusing his sight on the back of the cell, he began chanting the incantation that would call forth the corridor. As he spoke the words, the stone wall behind the creature melted into a golden mass of intense energy. The perimeter of the portal flashed, freeing the rear wall from its connections to the rest of the cell.

The membrane, a sickening yellowish gold, failed to emerge completely, which was by Wolbus' design. He couldn't set the assassin free without an objective. Doing so would put every life form in the Crossworlds in severe peril. *That might be the creature's sole endearing quality, a mindless obedience to achieve any task assigned to it. It must have been a source of pride for Nemelissi.* It had been born a killer. It understood its role perfectly. It took great care to perform its duty with a single-minded motivation, to find and mutilate whatever its masters set before it.

Wolbus returned his gaze to the creature's eyes. He focused his thoughts on the Author of All Worlds, creating an image in his mind for the destroyer to duplicate. After a second or two, the golden eyes of the creature opened wide. It began thrashing around inside its cage, but not with any harsh intentions toward its jailer. It had been given a task, and it eagerly awaited its release. Its reason to exist had been validated once again. It wanted nothing more than to flee the cell and begin its journey.

After confirming the identity link, Wolbus broke contact with the assassin's mind. He returned his attention to the partially completed corridor. Reciting the final phrase for activation, the principle orator stepped back as the membrane congealed into a flawless transmission device. He watched as the destroyer checked the portal for consistency. Although a bloodthirsty assassin, the monster refused to be reckless. Its intelligence would not jeopardize its safety no matter how eagerly it wanted to begin its journey. When it sensed the composition of the corridor had reached a secure point, it looked back one last time at Wolbus. No expression marked the creature's face; it merely locked on to Wolbus' eyes one last time. Then, with the same violent energy it used in its earlier attack, it sprang through the portal and disappeared.

The principle orator stared at the empty membrane. He didn't care for the look the destroyer gave him just before departing. It could have been an expression of appreciation, it might have been a threat, or it could easily have meant nothing at all. *That is the most frightening aspect of its existence,* he thought. No one could ever tell what it was thinking. Its every move surprised even the most skilled strategists. Wolbus considered its objective, shuddering with the image of what would happen when the monster found the Author of All Worlds.

"At least you will be long in finding him," he said under his breath. "You will understand this upon emerging from the portal. Our primary strategy must be given time to work. We must reserve the right to recall you in case your particular services are no longer necessary. May the shadows grant us that very outcome."

Wolbus turned from the cell. He started to generate another passageway for himself but abruptly halted his incantation. He pressed a series of stones on the wall to the right of the cell bars. A door opened, revealing a stairway that rose eerily into the abyss above him. He stepped on the first slat, glancing one last time at the destroyer's cell. Closing his eyes tightly, he rocked his head slowly back and forth. He opened his eyes again, stepped into the stairwell and looked toward the infinite climb above him. *It would take more than a day to ascend from these depths,* he thought, *but no matter.* He wanted time to think before facing Shordano again. His shoes clapped against the hard stone slats as he completed the first rise. He turned toward the next set as the rusted doorway closed behind him.

CHAPTER ELEVEN

Conor entered the Redwood State athletic building early the following morning. He knew his coach's schedule as well as anyone, so he wasn't the least bit surprised to find him hunched over his desk before seven o'clock. Coach Rumsey was a stickler for details. He believed in the basics, sound fundamentals that formed the foundation of a good soccer club. Anything beyond that in his opinion was a gift from the creators. Conor Jameson had been such a gift. From the first moment he saw the high school freshman dancing around with a soccer ball, he knew his coaching career would change forever. The boy had incredible athletic ability. Sometimes when he ran at full tilt, the coach would swear he was floating down the field on a cushion of air. He made opposing players look almost foolish, at times it even seemed like he was backing off in order to save the other player some dignity.

Coach Rumsey guided Conor through his high school career without ever asking him where he had disappeared to during is sophomore and junior years. The explanation Conor offered had been brief and pained. The coach saw no need to drag anything more out of the boy. He wanted to help Conor mature as a man and develop as a player. He wanted a few college programs to take note of his team's progress.

By the middle of his freshman season, half the schools in the country had contacted the coach about his star player. After he scored seven goals in the second game of his senior year, the stands at Mountmoor High entertained more than their share of college recruiters. Coach Rumsey protected Conor like a newborn babe, fielding questions and helping him with recruitment offers. While shepherding him through the entire process, Coach Rumsey became something of a minor celebrity, accepting dinners out with his wife and children on a weekly basis. After all, it wasn't against the rules for a coach to accept gratuitous offerings.

Even when becoming chummy with division one recruiters, he never forgot his primary focus. Conor's happiness was all that mattered to Coach Rumsey. The boy was a thrill to be around. His parents, and whatever extra influences he may have enjoyed while growing up, certainly did a wonderful job raising him. He was polite, eager to learn and always helped other players in any way he could. The coach really enjoyed Conor's sense of humor. He laughed a lot, at himself as much at anyone else. He couldn't have loved him more if Conor had been his own son.

When Redwood State's soccer coach left during Conor's last year of high school, it didn't surprise Coach Rumsey one bit to reach into his mailbox and find his own recruitment letter. A few meetings with the athletic director followed, and after much hand shaking and back clapping, the offer had been made, with one very obvious caveat. Unless Conor Jameson came along as part of the deal, Mountmoor High School would retain its head soccer coach for the immediate future.

Coach Rumsey had been completely honest with Conor about the situation. He told him Redwood State would not provide the exposure of a major college program. He could get him a full scholarship, and their preparatory programs for what Conor wanted to pursue were not bad, but any future soccer career would depend on the highlights he could generate on the field. No major television crews were about to brave the Redwood Route for two hundred miles to cover a secondary sport like soccer. He told Conor to spend some time talking with his father, maybe some other players and his girlfriend. He assured him of his complete understanding. He would support any decision Conor made, after all, his future was riding on it.

Conor told him right then and there he would attend Redwood State. He didn't care a whole lot about national exposure or a future in professional soccer. After what he and Janine had recently experienced, he just wanted to be close to home and family. Coach Rumsey was a good man; he deserved a bump in his career. He had taught Conor a great deal about the game, he felt comfortable around him, and if he could help him move up he would certainly do it.

He stood outside his coach's door for a second, not quite sure again how he would break the news. The Crossworlds had already taken two years of their friendship, and he was about to inform him of another separation. At least he didn't have to tell him that the earth might be destroyed in a little over two weeks. If Mr. Hikkins stayed true to his word, their conversation would be academic anyway. He knocked on the door lightly with the knuckles of his index and middle fingers.

"Conor, boy," said Coach Rumsey with a smile, "come in, come in, I was just going over our lines for the game against Cal next week. You'll have your hands full with their defense, son. They know all about you, and I hear from my sources they've devised a special scheme just to stop you. I've half a mind to use you as a decoy for the first half. I might give our other strikers a chance to score a few goals."

Conor's eyebrows arched up as he looked at his coach's player sheets. "Looks like you've got a good strategy for the game. What would you say to putting Morales in at striker? You know he's been itching to play my position. He's done everything you've asked. Heck, he plays defense like a demon. Why don't you try him out at practice this week, see how he does?"

Coach Rumsey went pale as a ghost. He dropped his pencil, stared at Conor like a man with an unknown disease. "You're leaving again, son?"

"I'm sorry. I know we're in a great position to win state this year. Believe me, if I could work it out another way, I..."

"Don't worry yourself, boy," said the coach, smiling. "I didn't get to be this old without understanding a little bit about life. Is it your family again?"

"Something like that," responded Conor. "All I can tell you is that it's important. I have to go away for awhile. I don't know how long I'll be gone."

"You'll be careful, though, won't you?" asked the coach, patting Conor's shoulder lightly.

Conor felt a strong pang of affection for his coach. He had just delivered a deathblow to the man's soccer season. Without him on the field, Cal would be all but impossible to beat. Their team received national exposure, so the caliber of player reporting to training camp remained consistent every year. On top of that, Redwood State had three tough games right after Cal, and there would no rest for Coach Rumsey's team following those games either. State playoffs would begin almost immediately. Conor's team had a good enough record to get in no matter what happened during the rest of their regular season, but if they lost even two of their last four games, their seeding in the tournament would be murder. He couldn't help but feel guilty.

"Yes," he said, putting on a good face, smiling for his coach. "I'll come and see you as soon as I get back. Good luck against Cal, and don't forget what I said about Morales. He's a better than average player, and he'll show his appreciation on the field if you give him a chance."

"I'll have a look at him," responded Coach Rumsey as he stood. He moved around his desk, extending his hand to Conor. "Remember what I said, son. You be careful."

Conor clasped his coach's hand tightly. He felt a brief moment of surprise as the man he'd known for almost six years pulled him forward into a tight bear hug. Conor squeezed back, burying his chin into Rumsey's right shoulder. He sensed a peculiar wisdom in him, almost as if he knew precisely where Conor was headed. The coach broke off the embrace, holding him at arm's length for a few seconds. Conor saw a tiny bit of moisture around the man's eyes. He blinked back a tear of his own, nodding once before leaving the room. He felt Coach Rumsey's eyes on his back all the way down the hallway.

Janine sat alone in the dark laboratory, peering into a microscope with an unblinking eye. She stared into the prism with perfect focus, looking for the one microbe that would prove her theory. If she could isolate a particular cell, she could easily win the next student science competition. She might even land a job with one of the bioscience companies in Southern California. *Having them foot the bill for the rest of my education wouldn't be bad at all,* she thought. After a few more seconds of inspection, she removed the slide from the microscope, inserting the next one from her collection.

She enjoyed working in a dark laboratory. It helped her to see things more clearly. To her, the light brought distractions she didn't need. She knew she was close to a major discovery in chemical biology. She hadn't even told Conor everything about her work. Only her thesis advisor knew the depth of what she was trying to accomplish. Originally, she'd been working on something entirely different. One day while mixing her reagents she decided to do away with the school's rituals and try a completely innovative protocol.

Janine had always been a very precise woman. Even as a little girl her actions were always measured; defined. It took an excessive amount of courage for her to venture out on the edge, especially in the laboratory. It had paid off, though, giving her a leg up on most of the bioscience students in the nation. She had developed a mutated cell, one with the ability to examine other cells and mimic their composition, or in the case of her research, alter its own form to reflect the polar opposite of what it encountered. Her cell could react with other cells in one of two ways – by joining with them or by destroying them.

The opposing composition didn't really tear down other cells; it merely rendered them inert by canceling out their active biologic processes. She had yet to confirm the action, which explained why she spent countless hours staring into a microscope. Her endless examination provided a look into the activity of the cells, one pair at a time. When she finally found a slide that contained neither her cell nor the original cell, just a bland configuration of both, she would consider her work a success.

She wanted desperately to prove her theory before she and

Conor left. In fact, after Conor kissed her goodbye late the night before, she grabbed her jacket and ran straight to the laboratory. Her advisor had given her a set of keys long ago. She had free reign in her office, any of the labs and in all the supply rooms. She had been standing in front of this particular microscope for close to eight hours. With her mind closed off to everything but her slides, she barely noticed the soft music playing through the ear buds resting snugly in her ears.

She heard the door to the laboratory squeak angrily as someone pulled it wide. She saw the ancient overhead lights flicker to life all around her. A new day had dawned at the college; students began filtering in to the laboratory with experiments in hand. Janine leaned back from her microscope. She resigned herself to the fact that her discovery would have to wait.

She tried desperately to convince her advisor to put one of these electron microscopes in her office for Janine's personal use. The woman had adamantly refused, telling Janine she isolated herself enough as it was. She wouldn't have her ignoring human contact completely, even if she were on the brink of a discovery that might challenge the roots of chemistry forever. Until she had her own facilities, her advisor commented, she would just have to work alongside the rest of the world.

Janine removed the current slide from the microscope, delicately placing it in the right column of her specimen carton. In this particular series she still had fifteen slides left to examine. After pausing for a moment's thought, she did a most peculiar thing. Taking a specimen envelope from the container, she inserted each of the fifteen slides into a separate sleeve. Gently, she placed them in the interior pocket of her coat. She couldn't say exactly why she kept the tests, but she felt compelled to remove them from a path of imminent danger. If the earth was destined for destruction, she wanted to keep her work safe.

Placing everything else into the lockers in the back of the lab, she locked her section of the shelf and turned to go. She saw one of Conor's friends enter the laboratory, someone they both knew from their days at Mountmoor High.

"Beau," she called out. "Up kind of early this morning, aren't we?"

"Hey Janine," he answered weakly. "What's up?"

"Not you, from the way your eyes look. Another all-nighter?"

"Yep," replied Beau. "Quantitative methods mid-term today. Crosbie's really laying it on thick. He keeps referring to the test as the widow-maker."

Beau plopped his backpack into a chair. Leaning over, he typed his login and password into the keyboard. "Where's Conor been? I haven't seen him anywhere since last Friday."

"He's around," answered Janine. "In case he doesn't get a chance to tell you, though, we're going away for a while."

"Both of you?"

"Yea," said Janine, buttoning her coat. "Something about his family, I guess. He hasn't given me all the information, but we're leaving at noon today."

Beau typed in a few commands. "Who's going to take care of his room, and for that matter, his rent? I hope he finds me and gives me some advice about what to do."

"I'm sure he will," responded Janine. "Just in case, though, my lab partner needs a room for the rest of the school year. She just found out today that her roommate is transferring to another campus."

"You mean Monica?" asked Beau, suddenly smiling from ear to ear.

"That's right," said Janine. "She asked about you the other day, by the way. Why don't you drop by later tonight and talk with her about it. I'll tell her you're coming by."

Beau returned to his keyboard, typing commands with a renewed vigor. "Tell her I'll be by around seven or seven thirty."

"Okay. Well, I guess I'll see you around." Janine leaned down to peck Beau's cheek. He stood suddenly, knocking his backpack onto the floor. Ignoring his clumsiness, he wrapped Janine up in his arms.

"You guys be careful," he said. "Tell Conor I appreciate him leaving his room open for Monica."

Janine squeezed Beau right under his rib cage, causing him to jump backward, yelping at the same time.

"Don't do that," he ordered, smiling at her playful gesture. He tried to return the favor, but Janine was already at the door of the lab. She flashed a stunning smile before disappearing into the hallway.

Beau looked at the door for a second after she vanished. "Conor, you are one lucky guy," he said, shaking his head.

CHAPTER TWELVE

From the deepest reaches of the Crossworlds, a tiny rectangle of
pristine light emerged from a cavernous crater located on what
appeared to be a frozen, dead world. After breaking free from the
confines of its rocky prison, the light around the geometric form
began blinking at an even pace. As it penetrated open space, it
seemed to breathe deeply while accelerating to mission speed. A
system check reaffirmed earth as its target destination. Distance
to objective, six hundred fifty million kilometers, plus or minus
one hundred thousand. The rectangle expanded slightly, tripling
its size while reinforcing its perimeter energy. Boundary density
increased by a factor of ten, giving it the ability to blast through
anything but the largest planet. It would no doubt encounter thousands of obstacles along its way. Those it couldn't avoid it would
merely penetrate, escaping through the other side with no loss
of efficiency. With mission speed accomplished, the rectangle of
light estimated its arrival. As ordered, the corridor performed
a few minute calibrations in order to reduce its projected travel
time. At present speed, it would reach its destination in less than
thirteen days.

CHAPTER THIRTEEN

The town of Trinidad on the northern shore of the California coast was so sparsely populated, one could easily miss it from the highway. Only a small sign denoted its presence, very small and insignificant, just like the town itself. It almost appeared as though the residents of the tiny crab-fishing village didn't really care to entertain visitors. The small amount of retail commerce in Trinidad served the locals nicely, and aside from a smattering of restaurants, no other tourist trappings existed. If it hadn't been for the unmatched beauty of the coastal environment, the residents in the tranquil town might have been left alone. The proximity to the school had been its downfall. Only fifteen miles from the Redwood State campus, it was easily accessible and a great place for stressed out students to enjoy leisurely strolls along the beach.

The shoreline of Trinidad rivaled any ocean panorama in the world. A line of giant redwoods guarded the water's edge like a battalion of imposing sentinels. Huge multicolored rock formations broke away from the trees, jutting out into the sea, providing centuries of captivating seats for travelers of every sort. Some of the stone outcroppings had captured the seeds from the coast, forming a base for a handful of redwoods to grow to maturity. The sea crashed endlessly against the immobile rocks and their redwood towers, giving each of the giant boulders a unique and intriguing face.

The students of Redwood State visited the Trinidad beaches frequently. Natural walkways had been worn into the tops of the rock watchtowers, providing easy access to the extreme edges of the boulders. Many students arrived here before dawn, scrambling along the pathways like crabs, feeling their way out to the best viewpoints atop the rocks. As the sun approached, they sat quietly in their perches watching night turn to day. Fortunately, even with all the years of nocturnal rock climbing, not one student had ever fallen into the sea or sustained any type of injury. It almost seemed as though the ecosystem of Trinidad protected the explorers who entered its confines. One found it hard to think otherwise when walking along the ten mile stretch of stunning shoreline.

Trinidad's ancient, undersized pier stretched out toward the ocean like a petulant wooden tongue insulting the beautiful coastline. Although it was a small pier, barely two hundred yards long, it had served a small community of crab fishermen for almost a dozen generations. It also retained a picture postcard charisma, with its worn pilings, slick deck and small group of crab boats clustered around the far end. Great bins lined the top end of the pier, sometimes empty, sometimes teeming with crab. Those on the bottom of the pile squirmed under a hundred pounds of their fellows, waiting for the truck to take them to market. Those on top, however, sometimes managed to crawl across the gathering to the edge of the bin. Once stationed at the edge of their temporary cell, they waited, hesitating for a moment, unsure of their decision to leave the pack. Ultimately, they would creep over the side, bounce off the rotted boards of the pier and fall twenty or thirty feet to the water below. Students or other travelers, witnessing the escape of one or two crabs, cheered wildly upon seeing one rejoin the sea again. The crab fishermen took no notice of them at all. They worked the same way their fathers had before them and their father's fathers before that time. If their labor provided a latent measure of enjoyment for the passing public, they marked it off as a bonus.

Janine pulled her car to the curb by the lighthouse. No signs existed defining any type of parking enforcement; she figured if the car stayed quietly on the street for a while it wouldn't be touched. She leaned across the driver's seat to plant a kiss on Conor. The two of them exchanged glances, lost in the comfort they found in each other's company. Their eyes lingered a bit longer than normal. They wanted one last measure of peace in their own world before embarking on another journey with the Champions. Here, in the little town of Trinidad, they would swim in each other's souls for a brief moment before leaving their world again, possibly for the last time.

"I love you," said Conor, touching his forehead to hers.

"And I you, Conor, always," she replied.

"What time is it?" he asked.

"Eleven-forty," said Janine, looking at her watch quickly. "Twenty minutes to go. That is, if we're hooked into Crossworlds time.

"Conor," she said, pleading. "Don't leave me this time. Don't let them take me, no matter what happens."

The young Champion dropped his chin for a brief second, ashamed to look his girlfriend in the eye. He quickly recovered. "I swear I won't leave you unless it's the only way we can overcome the threat."

Janine looked at her boyfriend with a worried expression. "You know something, don't you? You don't want to tell me because you know I'll worry. What is it, Conor? What do you know that I don't?"

Conor gathered his small bag from the back seat. "Come on, it's nearly time. We'd better get to the pier."

"Conor," Janine growled, "don't you do this to me."

He cupped a warm hand around the back of her neck. "I promise you'll understand when we get to the realm of the creators. We have to go, we have to be there when the corridor activates. Do you want some local fisherman to walk through the portal and end up standing face to face with Surmitang?"

Janine grabbed her small bag, leaned against the car door and stepped out of the car. She closed the door a little too harshly, letting Conor know she wasn't the least bit pleased with his little surprise. She walked around the car and stopped by the trunk, waiting for Conor to join her.

Conor took off toward the pier, turned and waited for her to catch up. When she did, he nuzzled her, made faces, tickled her, trying anything to break her mood. Within a couple minutes, she slapped his muscled stomach as hard as she could while gaily stating that he could charm the horns from the devil himself. She loved him so much she couldn't imagine life without him, and here they were preparing to walk into the unknown again. She wouldn't lose him, not for any price in the world. As much as she detested the thought of another imprisonment, she'd give up a thousand lifetimes in Seefra's dungeons if it meant she could always return to him.

As they walked past the lighthouse toward the pier, she looked up at him, his strong face, broad shoulders, and his capable athletic stride. Yes, she loved him all right, right down to her bones.

Since the crab boats wouldn't return for another four or five hours, the Trinidad pier was relatively deserted. A few old-timers hung out in front of the Seaview Restaurant, waiting for a bowl of chowder or if they were lucky, a few stray crab legs. Those with less were treated differently this far north of the big California cities; if they were hungry, a private citizen or even a restaurant would always chip in and help out.

A few restaurant employees bustled about in the Seaview, getting ready for another weekday lunch shift. Only three workers occupied the restaurant – two waitresses and a cook. Since only a few people frequented the Seaview during weekdays in the fall, providing any more than a few workers would have been fruitless.

Conor and Janine bounced off each other's hips as they ambled down the cement walkway to the pier. Once on the deck, Conor slid his feet back and forth on the wood slats, running his shoes along the slimy remains of crab, bait and seagull droppings. They approached the restaurant, hailing the men lounging outside on the benches. Janine waved at one of the waitresses looking out at them through the window. She recognized her from one of her biochemistry classes. Conor enjoyed a vibrant conversation with the old fishermen, laughing out loud when one of them would crack a joke about the way things used to be in the old country. The men had become a fixture since taking up residence in Trinidad a few years earlier. Janine rejoined her boyfriend, greeted the men after Conor introduced her, and fell into his ploy as soon as she recognized it.

"So," said Conor, "have you noticed the peculiar lights today?"

The men offered up a confused expression.

"Sure, haven't you heard?" he continued. "Something about the sun this time of year, the angle toward the earth, it produces a strange radiance with seawater. Sometimes it almost looks like the heavens are opening up right in front of you. We've seen it twice today, haven't we?"

Janine answered quickly, following Conor's lead. "Oh yes, once over at the bottoms and again here, up by the lighthouse."

"Yer daft, boy," said the oldest of the three fisherman. "I been comin' 'ere since nine'een and eighty seven, and I ain't never seen nor 'eard of such a thing as you describe."

"Aye," remarked another in the group. "Once the sun was so bright on the water I thought me eyeballs would melt right outta me 'ead, but tha's only far out to sea. Nuthin' like tha' ever happens so close to shore." The speaker nudged the third fisherman with an elbow. "Wha' you say, William, are they any bright lights about, up 'ere on the pier?"

William tossed his head from side to side, shifting his rump slightly on the bench. After refolding his arms, he lowered his head and resumed sleeping.

"It's true, gentlemen," said Conor. "Our professors at school gave us the information just this week, told us to watch out for the strange lights if we happened to be close to the shore. We didn't believe it either until we went to the bottoms yesterday afternoon. A brilliant light, as big as a church door, standing right on the land close to the water. We've never seen anything like it."

"Augh!" chimed the two fishermen. William licked his lips and snorted.

"He speaks the truth, gentlemen," added Janine. "We saw it happen again, right over there by the lighthouse. A flash of brilliant light, about as big as the window on that restaurant appeared right in front of us. After a few seconds it vanished, but it was there, I swear it."

"You're a looker," said the first fisherman. "A beauty a man would sail the seven seas to find, tha's a fact. And smart, too, one can tell that by hearin' you speak. Him I don' know abou', but you, lass, why would you fill our heads with such rubbish? Us wit'out a speck o' lunch in us yet, I'd expect more from a lass like you."

Conor smiled from ear to ear. He loved these old guys. He had come to the pier off and on during his time at Redwood State just to joke with them and ask them about their lives back home. As he listened to them talk, his whole world shrank into a microcosm of the three men. If he and Janine had to risk their lives defending the earth for only these fellows, he knew he would do it. In that instant he didn't need any other reason. He looked around the pier, stared at the lighthouse, checked the restaurant workers one last time, and flipped the cover of his cell phone up to check the time. Eleven fifty-nine. *Less than a minute to go.* He watched Janine entertain the men on the stone bench for a few seconds more. He smiled again, suddenly loving the earth more than he ever had in his life.

A brace of wind swept around the front of the restaurant, carrying a small parade of disregarded trash and discarded fishing line along with it. The men on the bench, all but William, grabbed their hats and held onto anything not buttoned down or zipped up.

"Look 'ere," remarked the first fisherman. "Now where's tha' big wind coming from? Somethin' like tha' only comes round late in the afternoon, and it's barely mid'ay yet."

The pier became silent again, but only for a second. The wind rambled away, dragging its possessions with it. All seemed safe and quiet. Then right before their eyes, a corridor began forming on the pier. The perimeter brightened with such intensity that young and old alike shielded their eyes from the visual onslaught. The membrane flashed, liquefying into a swirling mass of textured silver. As the center congealed, the border illumination lessened, finally taking on the characteristics of a strong, fluorescent light. The men on the bench, all but William, lowered their hands, glaring into the mind-boggling sight before them. The first fisherman looked around, hoping to find anyone who might confirm the strange sight. The restaurant workers were nowhere to be seen, however, and no one else was on the pier.

"We're in for it, now," said the man to his mates. "Iss one o' those alien kidnappin's, tha's what it is! Look inside there, Kenny, ain't that the dammest thing you ever saw?"

The second man couldn't move at all. He tried to answer his companion, but found nothing escaping his throat except a raspy gargle. His left hand was clamped around his mate's right forearm. Somehow that gave him a measure of comfort, knowing that if they took him, his mate would have to come along. Until the bizarre event concluded, they wouldn't be able to separate the two men with a blowtorch or a sledge hammer.

Conor stepped in front of his new friends. Smiling warmly, he grabbed Janine's hand, bringing her within view of the men as well. She was smiling also; sending a wave of relief over them. Conor tossed his cell phone to the first man on the bench, telling him he could do what he wished with it. Then he applied his index finger to his pursed lips, winking to them as if sharing a confidence. Taking Janine's arm in his, he turned in unison with his girlfriend and walked into the silvery membrane.

They vanished without a trace. As soon as the last bit of physical evidence certifying their existence disappeared into the corridor, the perimeter brightened. The men covered their eyes, fearful of what might occur next. Through their shaded vision they watched the portal dismantle itself.

Thirty seconds after the two students disappeared, the corridor vanished, heading back to the one who had commanded it to find Conor and Janine and transport them to the realm of the creators.

The fishermen held their hands over their faces, too fearful of the outcome should they drop them to their waists again. The first man, the boldest of the three, finally peeked through two split fingers. He pulled his hands away from his face, encouraging his mate to do the same.

"Blimey," said the oldest. "'Ave you ever seen the like? Those two kids up an' poofed righ' into tha' light. I ask you, 'ave you ever?" The man looked past his frozen second mate. "William, lad, did you ever see anythin' so odd in all your life?"

William never even opened his eyes. He smashed his right palm to his face, rubbing away a pesky itch. He hitched his pants up a little before refolding his arms and settling back into his nap.

CHAPTER FOURTEEN

After pressing through the familiar sensations of extreme cold and heat, Conor and Janine stepped into the beauty of their benefactors' birthplace. The realm of the creators had never looked more stunning. Colors of every hue coated the landscape. The lush gardens and walkways invited the two travelers to forget their concerns in favor of a long afternoon stroll. An assortment of liquid instruments dotted the realm, giving anyone who wished more spiritual nourishment than they could ever imagine. Indeed, as Conor and Janine took their first few steps among the emerald grass and colorful array of flowers, a pair of water walls quietly emerged from beside the pathway. Beds made of the softest soil, thickly carpeted with jasmine and honeysuckle, offered their services to the newest guests of the realm. As they walked by the living walls, Janine reached out, placing a soft hand among the flowers on one of the beds. She inhaled deeply, drinking in the potent aroma of jasmine. It had always been her favorite scent; she felt more than tempted to lie down and allow the water wall to perform its magic.

"Greetings, Champion," spoke a familiar, humble voice. "Welcome, Keeper, it is good to see you both again."

Conor and Janine turned, simultaneously looking over their shoulders. Maya, Lord of the Crossworlds Champions, sat calmly a few feet behind them. Holding his head high, his lean shoulders erect, the leader of the Champions quietly held the two travelers in his golden gaze. Conor finally broke the silence, rushing over to greet one of his greatest mentors.

"My Lord," he said, greeting the noble cat formally. Seconds later he left all decorum aside, jumping into the thick black and white fur. He hugged Maya around his long, supple neck for almost a minute, inhaling the wonderful scent of a clean, well-groomed cat. He finally broke away, keeping his right hand latched around the back of Maya's head. Placing his forehead against Maya's, he uttered a soft plea for Gribba's race of ezuvex.

"I'm deeply sorry for our loss, Maya. Gribba saved my life more than once. He was a wonderful, kind creature. I'll miss him more than I can say."

"I echo Conor's words, Maya," said Janine, coming up behind them. She grabbed a handful of fur, rubbing the big cat's cheek vigorously. "May our combined efforts ensure that no one else suffers the same fate."

"I thank you for your sentiments," offered the Lord of the Champions. "All who gather here feel a profound loss over the destruction of Wilzerd. Had we known of the phenomenon earlier, perhaps...." His words trailed off, as did his eyes. Maya stared off into the beauty of the realm, seeing none of it. Any loss of life affected the Champions and creators deeply, but the destruction of Gribba's race had nearly destroyed their collective mood.

"Unfortunately, two more worlds have been annihilated," said Maya, regaining his voice again. "Apparently, the inner element accelerated the frequency of their attacks. We know of six more predatory corridors currently staging themselves somewhere within the system. The ultimate aim for five of the projectiles is unknown to us. We do, however, know the destination of the sixth."

Without hesitation, Conor said, "Earth," sending chills up his own spine.

"Yes," said Maya. "Earth. The seeker has calculated its speed and course, giving us arrival estimates twice a day. Unfortunately his reports change from time to time. He now believes we have little more than a week to devise a strategy to deflect or destroy it."

"One week," said Janine, suddenly realizing why Conor had kept his secret to himself. Images of her home flashed quickly through her mind; her family, friends, favorite places, her pets. *This couldn't be allowed to happen,* she thought. "What steps have been taken to provide protection for our world?"

"Beyond the constant vigil to find an organic barrier against the corridor, nothing," said Maya. "Our seeker works around the clock hoping to find a solution. He believes he has solved part of the equation, but the remaining elements elude him."

"What about the people of earth?" asked Conor. "Shouldn't they be warned? I mean, isn't there someone we can tell?"

"What would you have us say?" replied Maya, "Excuse me, everyone, but a monstrous, interstellar cloak will consume the earth in less than a week. Should we announce that everything everyone has ever known and loved will cease to exist in a matter of days?"

Conor thought about Maya's comments. The Lord of the Champions was right, of course. Even if the numbskulls in charge of making decisions on earth believed them, they'd never have time to execute any sort of meaningful plan. Not that anything could help them, anyway. The entire planet was about to be consumed by a gigantic sheet of energy, and no one, no matter how wealthy or powerful, would be able to escape it.

"Would you have me explain to the people of earth the danger they face?" Maya continued. "Should we make clear to them the fact that they have little time left, that their days are numbered? Can you imagine, Conor, what would occur on a planetary scale should that knowledge become universally known?"

"Chaos," said Conor. "Absolute pandemonium. The world would fall into a state of complete anomie."

"That is correct," said Maya. "Anarchy would rule the cities of your world. If we fail to stop the predatory corridor, then the people's condition would hardly matter. But if we successfully defend earth against this weapon, a return to normalcy after such a transformation would be difficult without instituting a lengthy period of martial law."

"I see your point, Maya," said Conor, grabbing his girlfriend's hand, squeezing it tightly. "We'll do whatever we can to help the council arrive at an appropriate strategy. Perhaps we should...."

"Conor!" a happy voice shouted as the branches riffled to Janine's left. Eha exploded from the brush, hitting Conor broadside in midair. The young Champion released Janine's hand so she wouldn't be pulled along into the scuffling ball of spotted fur. Eha landed on his side, protecting Conor as he rolled over in the grassy area next to the path. Laughing with delight at seeing his old friend and brother, Eha swatted Conor's face a few times with a softly padded paw. Every time Conor tried to push away the huge feet, Eha would let him achieve a measure of success before smacking him with another paw. The giant cheetah wrapped his forepaws around Conor's head while tickling him wildly with his hind paws.

Conor laughed like a two-year-old for close to a minute. Then he turned his body to the right, grabbed Eha's midsection and flipped the big cat over on his back. Straddling him while wedging an elbow underneath his chin, Conor began tickling Eha just below his ribcage.

The cheetah cackled like a hyena, laughing hysterically at Conor's prompting. "I give!" he shouted, losing his breath by the second. "You win, Conor. Let me up and I'll behave. I promise!" Another round of hilarious laughter followed his pleas for mercy.

Conor jumped up, ceasing his torment. He watched Eha tumble over on one side, still laughing as he attempted to regain his breath. At length the big cheetah looked over at Maya, who sat patiently without emotion. The expressionless gaze gave Eha all the instruction he needed. The giant cheetah rolled over, stood and shook the debris from his fur with one smooth, brisk vibration of his body. Smiling like a child, he sprinted over to Janine, facing her with head held low.

"Greetings, Keeper," he said, showing a far greater amount of deference to Conor's girlfriend.

"Oh Eha," replied Janine, squeezing the strong neck against her cheek. "It's so good to see you. If all creatures enjoyed your playful personality, the Crossworlds would be such a happy place."

"I thank you," said the cheetah. Eha looked over Janine's shoulder at his Lord. He understood Maya's unspoken comment perfectly. "Come, we must take you to the council chamber at once. The creators await you."

The four of them moved off in a coordinated progression. The picturesque path seemed to swallow them as they walked through the perfectly groomed environment of the realm. Maya led the way, conversing with Conor and Janine briefly from time to time. Eha instinctively fell in behind them, protecting the pair. Although the huge cheetah smiled broadly while escorting the young Champion and his girlfriend, his eyes and ears remained fully alert.

The Champions looked upon their tasks very seriously, and Eha certainly was no exception. The Lady had instructed them to bring Conor and Janine to the council chamber straightaway. With the trouble in the Crossworlds, she said, they had little time to find a solution. Smiling at Maya and Eha, she sent them on their errand with a soft pat on the rump.

The small group rounded a corner next to a bristling group of palms. The pathway widened a bit, allowing for an easier climb up the short hill to the council chamber. As Maya set his paw down on the first measurable rise in the trail, a thunderous roar echoed down the pathway. Galloping down in its wake, Therion, the largest of the Champions, charged forward to confront the procession. The giant lion stopped about thirty feet in front of Maya, challenging the leader of the Champions directly.

"Go no farther, cat," Therion threatened, "until reciting your name and the words agreed upon earlier this day."

"Mind of the creators, Therion," said Conor. "Let us pass. Can't you recognize friend from foe? Do you not see the Keeper of the Keys, or me, your fellow Champion? Can you not look upon your own brothers and recall your challenge?"

Maya slapped his tail on the ground directly in front of Conor. He rotated his head only long enough to hiss a fast warning. The Lord of the Champions turned back to Therion, addressing him in the old language. "Give way, lion. Why must we be required to present credentials for the right to pass? We are well above your station; I command you to escort our group to the council chamber."

Surmitang vaulted forward from a different perch, landing directly left of the small procession. He challenged Maya personally, snarling wildly while keeping a tight watch on Conor, Janine and Eha as well. This was no game; the group would not be allowed another step until Maya gave the correct response and password.

Although amazed by the ferocity of their attack, Conor saw something in Therion and Surmitang's eyes that troubled him a great deal more. He saw fear in the depths of the Champions' souls, something he never imagined creatures as fierce as these would ever feel. Combined with the dream he remembered from the previous night, the sensation disturbed him greatly. *If these proud and brave cats knew what I learned from the bizarre visitor from my dreams, would they even have the courage to show their faces this day?* He pondered this while waiting for Maya to clear their way into the council chamber.

"Heed my words, brave cats. I am known as Maya, Lord and leader of the Crossworlds Champions, special counsel to the Lady of the Light and first mentor for countless guardians of this system. My password is this: 'Ajur lives forever in the soul of the Crossworlds.'"

Therion and Surmitang immediately broke away from their confrontational posture. They visibly relaxed, walking toward Maya with an almost submissive gait. Conor noticed the obvious relief in both of them; they almost fell at Maya's feet upon hearing the password. Therion reached his Lord first, touched noses with him, further identifying his leader. Surmitang followed suit, sniffing around Maya's cheeks and ears for any foreign scent. After the two Champions stepped aside, allowing Maya and Eha passage into the chamber, the two massive cats stood fast waiting for Conor and Janine to approach them.

"Our apologies, my brother," boomed Therion in a low gruffle. "The creators are most concerned. We are to guard the entrance to the chamber until they say otherwise. We shall let no one pass, even if they depart and return but never leave our sight. I hope our enthusiasm did not unnerve you."

"Keeper," said Surmitang in greeting while pressing his nose a little too near to Janine for Conor's liking. The young Champion stepped a bit closer as he listened to the great tiger's breath gusting forth into his girlfriend's face. "You're looking well."

"Thank you, Surmitang," said Janine, showing less discomfort than Conor. She grabbed a handful of the multicolored fur, pulling the tiger's face even closer. She kissed his nose four times briefly, accentuating the smack on the fifth peck. Releasing his jowl, she almost laughed out loud as the huge Champion reared back with a look of disgust. "As always, tiger, you are the very picture of beauty. Your handsome presence outclasses every other Champion."

Surmitang tried to speak, but found he could not. His sudden silence came partly from Janine's magnetism, partly from her passionate greeting. He had hoped to frighten her into submission; instead she had overcome his ploy and gave him a dose of her own medicine.

"Not an easy one to deal with, eh, proud tiger?" asked Conor, smiling. He ruffled Surmitang's chin, grabbed a tuft of fur, and then reached over and grabbed a hunk of Therion's mane. Lifting himself off the ground, he pulled both cats toward him. He gave each a bear hug around the neck, nuzzling a cheek here and there for effect. "It's great to see you guys."

"And you, Champion," said Therion without delay. "Even in times such as these, where all who serve the creators must be summoned forth to do battle again; it is still gratifying to lay our eyes upon you."

"Aye, Conor, *first protector*," added Surmitang, bowing low in mock salute. "It is good to look upon you again. You've grown, young one, and quite large at that. You might show promise in the games at the glade later this year." The huge tiger took a playful swipe at Conor, which the young Champion easily side-stepped. The second one, however, an instant behind the first, took Conor cleanly underneath the knees. He went down in a heap, his body's impact kicking up a small cloud of dust.

Therion whacked Surmitang on the nose with the tip of his tail. "Stop with your nonsense. Do you want the Lady to see your foolishness and come out here and blast us into a forbidden corridor for all eternity?" The giant lion turned to Conor. "Come, boy, and you too, Keeper. You must enter the chamber without delay. The Council of Seven has gathered. The Lady and Maya are also present, as is the seeker, or Mr. Hikkins, as you refer to him. We'll stay out here and make sure you're all safe."

Conor stood, brushed himself off and grazed the big tiger's chin with a lightening-fast round kick. Surmitang shook his huge, multicolored head, worked his mouth from side to side before licking his lips once or twice. He actually smiled at Conor, acknowledging a decent attack. Obeying Therion's wishes, he did not strike back at the young Champion. Therion started to turn, but Conor grabbed his mane and stopped him.

"Where is Purugama?" he asked.

"Searching the realm from border to border for any sign of intruders," answered Therion. "We haven't seen him in over a week."

"The creators ordered it," added Surmitang. "Our Lady fought against sending one of us out alone, but the council quickly over-rode her."

Conor looked up into the sky, searching for the tiny speck that would be his mentor. He hoped to see him soon. He couldn't wait to join him on his excursions. Powerful and fierce though he may be, Conor did not like the idea of him flying alone, separated from the other Champions. Concluding that nothing could be done at the moment, he turned to follow Therion.

He noticed that Maya had already gone inside. Eha had taken a position outside the corridor, with the obvious intention of standing guard with the other two Champions. He winked at Conor and Janine as they climbed the last of the stairs toward the gleaming passageway that would take them into the council chamber. Janine looked back at the cheetah, giving him a dazzling smile.

Out of all the Champions, Eha was far and away her favorite. He had such a happy personality, he always saw the positive in any situation, and he made her laugh, just as Conor did. As the corridor flashed, changing its intensity, she reached her hand out toward the huge cheetah. He quickly extended his nose, sniffed a few times and then licked her palm once. She smiled again and caught Eha's grin just before following Conor through the portal.

The council chamber vibrated with a mixture of sights and sounds. Most of the Council of Seven stood in a tight pack around the transparent, floating conference table. The room was animated with heightened, anxious excitement. Most of the council members spoke at the same time, determined to make their points heard above all others. The Lord of All Life, supreme councilor and creator emeritus, experienced little success trying to facilitate any semblance of courteous discussion. At times he would throw up his hands, spewing a lush, ruby aura about the chamber as he stepped away from the disorderly debate. After a moment or two of quiet meditation with Maya, he would again try to coordinate the group's efforts.

Resplendent in her formal gown, the Lady of the Light stood apart from the roiling madness of the gathering. She kept her own council, mostly, but now that Maya had entered the chamber, she held regular brief conversations with him. The two of them would listen to the council battle it out – at times silently observing, at other times discussing their particular points of view.

Mr. Hikkins, Conor noticed, hadn't wasted a moment of his time speaking with anyone. In one of the most remote corners of the chamber, the seeker stood perched over a podium that also served as a computer terminal. He stared at the screen like a zombie, willing his latest calculations to bear fruit. He acted as if he were the only person in the chamber. His focus was absolute; nothing mattered to him except his figures.

Conor took Janine's hand, leading her into the center of the chamber. As they moved farther away from the passageway, the intense light of the portal dimmed. Others in the chamber began noticing them, none more immediately than the Lady of the Light. Leaving Maya's side, she rushed over to greet the two travelers.

"Conor, Janine," she said warmly, clasping their outstretched hands in each of her own. "My joy at seeing you is tempered only by my sincere apologies for our having called upon you again."

Conor wanted to respond right away but found he couldn't. The Lady had that effect on most men she encountered. Janine certainly was exciting and beautiful, but the Lady of the Light was simply exquisite. Her gown shimmered with perfect silver light. She truly was an elegant Goddess.

"My Lady," offered Conor, giving a quick formal bow.

"Lady," said Janine, slightly uncomfortable in the presence of such an intimidating figure. She and Conor had heard about her final visit to the chamber of cells. While Janine enjoyed the idea of Seefra's laboratory being blown to bits, she did feel somewhat awed by the actual creature that had performed the deed. She bowed her head low, looking at her toes for a second before raising her self back up.

"Please," said the Lady, "neither of you need show deference to anyone in this chamber." She looked them up and down, smiling as she did so. "You both have grown into fine-looking adults. I am pleased by what I see. After the council session, if time permits, perhaps you might tell me about your current exploits back on earth."

Conor inquired about the proceedings. The Lady of the Light explained that the predatory corridors had increased their effectiveness, thereby speeding up their schedules. The creators had less than a week to design a counterattack to throw against the portal. If they did not, and earth was destroyed, key elements of the Crossworlds corridor alignment would be irreparably damaged. Such an event would reduce their ability to combat the inner element. The Circle of Evil, or what remained of it, would have the rest of the system in a virtual stranglehold.

Conor listened to the Lady's description. He also took in everything else around him as she continued speaking. He watched the boisterous arguing occurring around the council table. He saw Janine, Maya, and a few creators he didn't know standing silently in the background. He glanced momentarily at Mr. Hikkins, deeply in sync with his mathematical formulas. He barely noticed the Lady's voice trailing off. Without hesitation, as soon as she left an opening for him to speak, he blurted out his question before he could imagine the consequences of the spoken words.

"My Lady," he said quietly while watching the shouting match heat up at the council's conference table. "Who is the Author of All Worlds?"

The raucous sounds in the room abruptly ceased. The battling voices crumpled to the floor of the chamber, disintegrating into small clouds of verbal dust. Every head in the room, except that of Mr. Hikkins, turned in Conor's direction. Even the normally stoic Maya lost his composure for a moment. Stunned, he looked directly at Conor, his discerning stare becoming more acute as his ears traveled to the top his head.

Although Mr. Hikkins maintained his focus, it was obvious that he had become quite interested in the conversation.

"Where did you hear that name?" demanded the Lord of All Life. "Even the creators dare not whisper it in public."

Conor was at a loss for words. He didn't know how to handle his mistake. He had obviously upset everyone in the chamber, including the Lady of the Light, who stood gaping at him as though she had never met him before. Maya had regained control of himself, but the golden eyes never left Conor for a second. It seemed like the big cat knew exactly what would fall from his Champion's lips in the next few moments. The Lord of the Champions steadied himself, preparing for the next statement.

Conor took one step forward. In deference but also showing an element of strength, he looked directly at the council members. "I asked, 'Who is the Author of All Worlds?'"

"Be silent!" commanded the supreme councilor. His aura flared brightly, signifying his desire to continue speaking. Conor cut him off without showing any consideration for his position.

"Someone is after the Author of All Worlds," he said forcefully. "Who is the assassin, Nemelissi, and why did we not face him in the battle against Seefra's forces?"

This time, even Mr. Hikkins turned to look at Conor. The room became even quieter than before. All sound disappeared from the chamber. Eyes wide with terror, no one dared breathe after hearing the name Nemelissi the assassin.

CHAPTER FIFTEEN

The assassin wrenched itself free of the portal's grip. Falling through the membrane, it collapsed in a heap at the foot of a large structure. Instantly righting itself, it stood on two extraordinarily powerful legs. Maintaining an eerie silence, it took in its immediate surroundings. It instinctively knew that gauging the battlefield was always the first step when entering a strange environment.

It listened patiently as it scanned the streets of the large city. Hearing nothing that signified life, the assassin placed one of its huge hands on the brick surface of the building. It began tapping the brick with its strong, sharp claws, sending the signal throughout the city in a steady, repetitive beat. Using its magic, it amplified the sickening sound of tapping and scraping to an ear-splitting level. The entire area would be able to hear the noise, so if any life existed here, it would surely come to investigate the commotion. No one disturbed the destroyer's strange little concert, however, and after a few minutes Wolbus' strategy became clear in the creature's mind. With a terrible roar of frustration, Nemelissi reached back, slashing at the brick edifice with all its might. The ancient red stone shredded, exploding in all directions.

The creature itself took the brunt of its own attack. Huge pieces of razor-sharp stone pelted its face and body. Sickening wounds oozing strange, milky blood closed soon after disgorging a small amount of fluid. The assassin lashed out again and again, bellowing at the huge inanimate object in front of it. It almost felt compelled to travel back to the inner element and dispose of its jailer. Imprisonment was one thing; downright deception was another, especially when the creature had completed every mission they had designed for it since the beginning of time.

Wolbus had called forth a very specific corridor, sending the creature as far from its objective as possible. Nemelissi understood this perfectly. The world it occupied had been dead for centuries. The suns above it burned weakly, showing their distance from the planet and their incredible age. The principle orator wanted to buy time, wanted the predatory corridors to be given a chance to do their work. It would take the destroyer many days to find its way to the Author of All Worlds. That was Wolbus' last gift to the Crossworlds.

Nemelissi watched the building as it began teetering on its unstable foundation. It pondered taking a few more swipes just to watch the abandoned structure crumble. The image of its objective returned to the forefront of its mind, however, forcing it to leave the building to its own demise. It turned, bounding up the street with uncanny speed and agility. Using all of its senses, it raced around the city searching for the next corridor.

CHAPTER SIXTEEN

"Nemelissi!" screamed the first councilor, panic-stricken at the thought of the Crossworlds' most formidable destroyer. "We are doomed! After the assassin annihilates the Author of All Worlds, it will descend upon us with an insatiable fury. It will reduce the realm to ashes. It will shred us into a billion particles and scatter us throughout the outermost galaxies. We will become nothing more than floating debris."

"If Nemelissi achieves the objective assigned to it," interrupted Mr. Hikkins, "it will hardly be able to continue on toward the realm. If the Author of All Worlds is eliminated, we will all cease to exist immediately thereafter. At least in that event you will not suffer a horrible death at the assassin's hands, my Lord."

"Mind of the creators," said Maya. "Have they lost their souls? What could the inner element hope to gain by destroying everything we've ever been, our lives, our history, even our ultimate purpose?"

"Please," interrupted the Lady of the Light. "We must not suffer the fate of our own speculation. If Nemelissi is loose, then we are all in terrible danger. We know that to be true. But we have no way of knowing when and where the creature will be released, or how long it may take for it to find the Author of All Worlds. The predatory corridors must remain our first concern. We have concrete information about their power, when they will arrive and how important it is for us to save the Conor's world. Let us not yield to the sickness of terror. I, for one, will not end my existence wailing like a newborn cub in search of my mother's nipple."

"How dare you speak to this gathering in such a manner," exploded the first councilor. "We have every right to...."

"Silence," ordered the Lord of All Life, halting every speaker in the chamber. "Our Lady's words should be heeded. We haven't the luxury of time anymore. The predatory corridors are within striking range. They must continue to be the focus of our combined energies." The supreme councilor turned to the lonely figure in the corner of the chamber. "Seeker, have your calculations given you any hope for a defense against the portals?"

"Unfortunately," answered Mr. Hikkins, "there has been no breakthrough as of yet. I will continue, however, until we either succeed or suffer the same fate as Wilzerd."

"If I may," offered Janine, stepping forward. "I might be able to assist the seeker. I'm willing to try, anyway."

"You, Keeper?" asked the first councilor.

"Yes," she replied. "I believe I might have found a unique approach, something I'm certain Mr. Hikkins, I mean, the seeker, has not yet attempted."

"Please," instructed the first councilor. "We appreciate your zeal, young lady, but we are working on important matters here. If you would just take a seat and...."

The Lady of the Light's aura flared brightly, almost exploding in the first councilor's face. "Why shouldn't she be allowed to assist? Are you saying a young girl is of no worth in our struggle, that she has nothing to offer? Do you judge another's offer of assistance as insignificant without inquiring as to the nature of her strategy?"

The Lady stepped forward, directly challenging her superior. "I would heed her advice over your council every day for a thousand millennia!"

"How dare you!" responded the first councilor.

"Enough!" barked the Lord of All Life. "Athazia, your enthusiasm is encouraging but misplaced. You will apologize immediately. Maybe then we can return to our respective duties." Turning toward Janine, he began to offer an explanation for his co-council's behavior, but when he turned to look at her, she wasn't there. He looked toward the seeker and found Janine standing next to him. The two of them were deeply engaged with each other. The supreme councilor decided to let that be the end of the confrontation.

"Conor," requested the Lady of the Light, "would you accompany me outside the council chamber for a moment? Maya, you as well, if you don't mind."

Conor glanced once at Janine and Mr. Hikkins, who were lost in their technical discussion. It appeared as though his girlfriend had hit upon something worthwhile. Conor had never seen Mr. Hikkins as animated as he was at that moment. As he left with the Lady and Maya, he noticed that Mr. Hikkins had even given his terminal over to Janine so she might better explain her findings. With her safety assured, the young Champion gave way to Maya, allowing his Lord to leave the chamber in front of him. He followed close by, instinctively guarding both his and the Lady's path.

The three of them passed through the portal without incident. In seconds, they emerged outside the chamber with the other three Champions. Four giant cats, Conor, and the creator who guided their every move stood quietly together in the beauty of the realm. The lady motioned Maya and Conor to take a seat next to the pathway leading toward the council chamber. She glanced at Surmitang, ordering him to the same side of the path with a flick of her silver eyes. The massive tiger moved without making a sound. He even crossed the path without once touching it. As the big cats and Conor began finding places to settle for what appeared to be a lesson from their creator, water walls emerged from the ground beneath their feet. They rose to different levels, accommodating each Champion. When all had settled into comfortable positions, the Lady summoned a small water wall, seating herself. Daintily, she pressed her gown forward and sat facing the Champions. When she felt comfortable in her position, she spoke to the group gathered before her.

"Surmitang," she began quietly. "Perhaps you can tell us about the Author of All Worlds."

The huge tiger squirmed in his prone stance, showing his discomfort. To speak of such a personage was not encouraged in any company, much less that of a creator.

"Speak freely, prince of Sumatra," requested the Lady. "Our young Champion needs to know why he will be risking his life to save him. Please, tell us about the Author of All Worlds."

Janine accessed the disk she brought with her from the lab at Redwood State. She almost jumped back after inserting it into the bizarre terminal Mr. Hikkins offered her. The port seemed to come alive. It grabbed at the disk hungrily, like a cybernetic mouth craving a source of nutrition. Her folders instantly popped up on the terminal screen and, after reclaiming her composure, Janine called up her samples and case histories. She first showed Mr. Hikkins the literary review and the theoretical premise of her experiments.

The seeker, extremely interested in her work, nodded his head occasionally without asking a single question. He smiled during some aspects of her presentation, seeming to grasp the suppositions of her clinical trials. He waited patiently for her to finish her background material and set up the discussion for future research. He understood the excitement a researcher feels when on the brink of an important discovery. He didn't want to rob her of any part of the process, even though he assumed he knew the rest of her presentation even before she finished.

"Here is where I always seem to run into then same roadblock," she explained patiently while showing him pictures of individual slides. "Apparently the cell construction holds during the transformation, but the new matrix fails to render the original structure inert."

Mr. Hikkins removed his glasses as he looked at the progression of the slides. He respected the fact that Janine gave him the time he needed to think, rather than prattling on like most students. Finally he spoke, more to the terminal than to her. For him, it was enough. "Perhaps the composition is based too much on chemical compounds and not enough on the synergy of organic chemistry and physics. The corridors are living beings, but they also exist according to certain physical principles. Let me show you a few of the calculations I've been manipulating. Perhaps you might offer a fresh perspective on how they might be combined with your cells. I think between the two of us, we might be able to present a working model by nightfall."

Janine smiled at the diminutive man. Conor was right. Although a bit odd, he was courteous, helpful and brilliant. She could certainly benefit from his assistance once their journey had ended. She stepped aside, giving the seeker full control of the terminal. She watched as his small hands flew over the keyboard. In seconds, equations Janine never knew existed popped up on the screen in front of them.

"I'm supposed to save him," said Conor, his body involuntarily moving forward, "with that thing coming after him?" Conor remembered the horrified looks on the faces of every creator standing around the conference table the instant he uttered Nemelissi's name. "If the assassin is as powerful as everyone says it is, how am I supposed to stand in its way?"

"Nemelissi is indeed powerful," said the Lady of the Light. "It is not invincible, however. The Circle of Evil managed to capture it not once but twice. They kept the assassin deep within the confines of their fortress for centuries. So you see, Champion, it can be captured and killed."

"You said they captured it twice," said Conor. "What happened? Did it escape? How many of their warriors did it take to recapture it?"

"It escaped, yes," answered the Lady without emotion. "It rendered the best cell the keepers had created up to that point utterly useless. Before they managed to return it to a new cell, Nemelissi slaughtered two companies of shadow warriors and one member of the outer element." The Lady stared at Conor after completing her report. She gave away nothing, not a whisper of emotion, not a single secret she might have been hiding behind those glorious silver eyes.

"With all respect, my Lady, Maya," said Conor, trying to grasp the situation being thrust upon him, "how do you expect me to do battle against something like that?"

"Because," she replied, smiling now, with her eyes and face. "You are Trolond Tar, chief protector of the Lady of the Light and all the Crossworlds."

Conor wanted to scream or jump up and run away. Anything would be better than sitting there at that particular moment. He wanted so badly to find out just what the connection was between him and this great warrior they all kept mentioning. He was a human being from earth, a soccer player and a college student. He happened to fall into an amazing adventure, that was true, but beyond that, he couldn't understand what they kept referring to. He kept his tongue, however, and his seat. He settled himself, showing his Lady he was prepared to hear more.

"Surmitang," requested the Lady of the Light, "if you will continue, please."

"The Author of All Worlds cannot be measured by any standard known to the Crossworlds," began Surmitang. "As far as any of us know, he has always existed. But no one, not even the Lord of All Life, has ever seen him."

"How can we be so certain he lives without concrete proof of his existence?" asked Conor.

The huge tiger's immaculately colored head swiveled on its strong neck and shoulders. No other part of his body moved, except for his eyes, which took in Conor as soon as they were able. "How do you know *we* exist?" asked Surmitang. "How do we know *you* exist, Trolond Tar? With the magic available to any one of us seated here, how can you be sure that you presently sit within the realm of the creators?"

"That's different," returned Conor, ready to continue speaking. Surmitang cut him off cold.

"There is no difference whatsoever," stated the big cat. "You either believe what your mind tells you, or you do not. Whether you possess corporeal evidence makes no difference."

Conor opened his mouth to speak, but Surmitang held up a huge paw. None of the other cats came to the young Champion's defense, so he settled back down into his seat, waiting for Surmitang to continue.

"Let me ask you something. Think about before you came to know us, before your journeys with us. If someone had told you that a group of gigantic warrior cats protected an infinite number of worlds with their physical and magical prowess, and that if you wished to meet them, all you would have to do was walk through a corridor burning in the wall of your bedroom, would you have believed them?"

"No," replied Conor. "Not in a million years."

"And yet," continued Surmitang, "here we sit, together, along with the creator that bound us to our calling."

"Yes," said Conor quickly, "but you said only moments ago that any of us could be a figment of each other's imagination, so even the proof of your existence does not necessarily confirm reality."

"A good point, Champion," answered Surmitang. "You forget one important ingredient of our discussion, however. No one is forcing you to believe in us, or us to believe in you. It is a choice we all make – a conscious choice. It is the same with the Author of All Worlds. I know he exists, because I believe he exists. It is the same with every other cat gathered around you, and also for the Lady and the other creators."

Conor listened without interrupting again. He absorbed everything Surmitang said about the peculiar being that seemed to hold dominion over everything in the Crossworlds and beyond. He couldn't help wondering, though, about a soul so powerful it could dictate the existence of everything known to it. *If it truly enjoyed that much incontestable power, why would it allow anything distasteful to occur in any of the worlds it created?* It didn't make sense to Conor, but he preferred not to question Surmitang further. He merely listened, gaining as much knowledge as he could.

"The Author of All Worlds resides somewhere within the Crossworlds system," continued the huge tiger. "No one but the Lord of All Life knows exactly where he lives, or which planet he calls home. We do know he inhabits one of the worlds he created, however, and in that knowledge lays the danger to his existence.

"If the inner element of the Circle of Evil has determined the location of his home, then it is only a matter of time before Nemelissi completes his mission. If the Author of All Worlds is annihilated, we will all immediately cease to exist. All that the Crossworlds ever was, is now and ever will be will instantly disappear. It will be as if we never existed."

"None of you?" asked Conor. "The realm of the creators, the glade of Champions? Nothing will be left?"

"That is correct," answered Surmitang. "The creators, the Champions, your world and all the worlds in the system will vanish without a trace."

Conor shook his head in disbelief. It seemed his long journey within the Crossworlds system would never end. No matter what he did, no matter how many armies he helped destroy, the evil in the Crossworlds continued to threaten all that was good. He turned to the Lady of the Light, asking for her guidance while trying not to offend his brother Champion. "My lady, tell me truthfully, if we defeat this assassin, turn back the predatory corridors, and vanquish the inner element, will the journey be complete? Will the threat to the Crossworlds finally be ended?"

The Lady of the Light turned to Surmitang, asking silently for his permission to respond. When he didn't object, she turned back to Conor. "Yes, Trolond Tar, you can be certain that if what you propose comes to pass, the Crossworlds will be rid of their arch enemy forever."

Conor watched as the other Champions, one by one, nodded their great furry heads in unison. Even Maya, normally noncommittal in discussions of this sort, signaled his agreement. The young Champion turned his gaze back to his mistress, the creator who initiated his adventure nearly a decade ago. He had made his decision, once again choosing to throw himself into the struggle.

"Tell me about Nemelissi," he said to the group gathered in front of him.

"I am pleased with the results of your work, Miss Cochran," pronounced Mr. Hikkins. "The cell cultures you brought with you from your laboratory may prove to be the difference in our fight against the predatory corridors. I will be happy to write a commendation letter on your behalf when you and Conor return to earth."

"I had a feeling they might be valuable," replied Janine, who had been standing quietly next to the seeker for the last thirty minutes. She had patiently watched his fingers dance around the keyboard, designing models, making calculations, adding and subtracting frames of estimates. She felt so awed by what she witnessed; she hadn't dared breathe a word during his ruminations. At length, she began to recognize some of his efforts. She decided to inquire about them. "What exactly are you working on now, sir?"

"I am attempting to build a linear model for our mode of defense against the corridor. First, however, we must calculate a very thin margin of error for our regression estimates. In effect, Janine, we are going to use their own strategy against them."

"You're going to give us as much of a chance as we can hope for," she reasoned. "Is that it?"

"Precisely," said the seeker. "By combining the organic attributes of corridor composition into your excellent work with chemical reactive agents, we might be able to expand our defensive reach by adding a small amount of statistical modeling. The interplay of the three disciplines poses some complexities I haven't yet been able to solve. I'm having difficulty constructing a model that will accept the summation of our three-tiered attack."

"May I try?" asked Janine.

"By all means, my dear," answered the seeker.

She changed places with Mr. Hikkins, watching him station himself a respectable distance from the workstation. The smallest things about his mannerisms reinforced her affection for the man. He stepped back in order to give her room to breathe and to think. Very few people would be so kind or so aware.

She leaned toward the screen, looking at the array of numbers and formulas highlighted in front of her. She found the active window and gazed at the output for a few moments. She had guessed right, he was trying to develop a linear model that would accept close to a dozen variables in a set of symbiotic analyses. Even for someone as brilliant as Mr. Hikkins, she knew as well as he that with that much input, the procedure would rarely produce a significant model. She stared relentlessly at the figures on the screen, willing her mind to come to a conclusion. She switched her focus to the windows with the organic and chemical conclusions and then focused back on the model again. Something nagged at her from the deep recesses of her mind, something from an introductory statistics course she took as a freshman at Mountmoor High School. She nearly scolded herself for her inability to remember, when suddenly it all became clear to her. The answer seemed to grow right out of the screen like a spring flower. She turned excitedly, her eyes wide. She couldn't wait to include Mr. Hikkins in her discovery.

The four cats blinked nervously as they waited for someone to respond to Conor's request. None of them appeared very eager to speak about Nemelissi, as if doing so might stain their souls. The mere thought of such a wicked creature turned the stomach of anyone who dared speak of it. Maya, after witnessing the discomfort of his Champions, decided to spare them the painful task.

"There has never been a destroyer such as Nemelissi," he began, staring at the ground intently. For some reason he didn't feel comfortable looking Conor in the eye just then. "No one knows its sex, whether it is a he or a she, or whether the distinction exists on whatever world produced it. No one who has ever seen Nemelissi has been able to discern that fact and return with the knowledge. No creature, no matter how massive or formidable, has ever returned alive after a confrontation with this assassin."

The leader of the Champions continued his tale. "Nemelissi possesses a poisonous revulsion for any creature it encounters. It kills with a passion unknown to any other being in the Crossworlds. Even the shadow warriors, with their hideous methods of torture and execution, cannot come close to Nemelissi's wickedness.

"It has been known to slash an opponent to ribbons with a calculated attack that produces intolerable pain without the blessed relief of death. It then lashes what remains of the body onto its back, carrying it for days as it slowly and agonizingly oozes every bit of anguish from the ragged shell.

"Sometimes Nemelissi consumes the wasted corpse. Under other circumstances it might shred the remaining body parts, casting them about in whatever environment it presently occupies. It is a ruthless killer, Trolond Tar, merciless and without fear. It knows no natural enemies within the Crossworlds, and it relishes that fact. It maintains the role of the predator in every altercation. The opponent is merely another fatality in a long line of massacred enemies."

Conor shook his head slowly, exhaling lightly so no one could hear but the Lady, who stared at him lovingly. "Does it have any weaknesses?" he asked. "Has anyone ever heard of anything that might help in a battle against it?"

"Unfortunately, no," replied Maya. "As I said previously, no one who has faced Nemelissi has lived to report any useful information."

"Understanding the creature as we do," interjected the Lady of the Light, "it would be logical to assume it attacks without planning or reason. Any creature, no matter how powerful or vicious, would leave itself open to retaliation as it charges blindly into battle."

"Yes," added Therion, animated for the first time since the discussion began. "One might believe that such a creature could be lured in for the kill, or for some debilitating assault on its vital organs."

"That, at least," said Maya, "you have in your favor. When you finally meet Nemelissi, prepare for an immediate attack. It lives for the hunt, and I believe it is hunting the Author of All Worlds as we speak. When it sees you, it is liable to charge without delay.

Wherever your travels take you, act as if the destroyer will be waiting for you around every corner."

"Even with its savage nature and astonishing control over shadow magic, you will possess the weapons you need to defeat him, Trolond Tar," said the Lady. "It will be up to you to find them, but rest assured they are there for you should you choose to use them."

"When should I leave?" asked a reluctant but resolved young Champion.

"As soon as we can call Purugama back from his reconnaissance flights," replied the Lady. "We will need to fit the saddle to his shoulders and replace your clothing again. I believe we have your warrior garments here at the realm."

"Purugama is coming with me?" asked an excited Conor.

"Of course, Champion," answered the Lady of the Light. "What did you think; we would send you against Nemelissi without your mentor?"

Conor smiled as sweat dripped down his relieved forehead and cheeks. Hideous destroyer or no, he suddenly felt a thousand times better knowing the great cougar would be alongside him during this journey. He stood, gathering the few items he carried with him from earth. Dropping them into his jeans, he suddenly remembered he wouldn't have any pockets soon. Janine would be able to care for his things. He would give them to her just prior to leaving.

Janine. *What would she say after finding out about his latest undertaking?* He had promised her they wouldn't be parted during this last journey. Well, not really, but mostly, he had given her his assurances. Now he would take them away, along with her trust in him. He pondered the possibility of not revealing Nemelissi's vile nature to her, but quickly discarded the thought. First, he didn't want to add to her misery by lying to her. Second, she had an almost uncanny ability to see through him whenever he withheld something.

No, he would tell her tonight, tell her everything and then hold her while she cried and cursed him for being so dear to her and so valuable to the creators. He looked down at his feet, feeling the sting of having to hurt and disappoint someone who meant so much to him. He felt the pads of a large, feline paw clamp down around his shoulder. He looked over at the spotted fur, smiling a little, knowing that Eha had come over to comfort him.

"Don't worry," said the big cheetah. Eha smiled as wide as he could for Conor. "All we have to do is halt the progress of a killer corridor that's bigger than the earth's diameter, overpower a destroyer who has never known defeat, and then overcome the inner element of the Circle of Evil. Heck, I've done more than that before breakfast."

Conor elbowed the big cheetah in the ribs. "Then you go face Nemelissi and I'll supervise the displacement of the predatory corridor. I'll be sure and save most of the work on that front for when you return."

"Sorry, Champion," replied Eha with a comically mournful expression. "You get all the glory again. We wouldn't want you to go back to earth with no stories to tell, would we?"

Conor grabbed two handfuls of spotted fur and began wrestling with Eha. The huge cheetah overpowered him quickly, throwing him to the ground and licking his face raw. Conor got a few punches and kicks in, but he did little damage to the lithe, powerful cat. Eha held him down easily, laughing as he smothered him with his giant body. The big cat laughed and laughed, and the Lady allowed their scuffling to continue unchecked. She wanted them to release some tension before returning to the council chamber. Had it been a few centuries ago, she might have jumped into the fray herself. Instead, she merely smiled at the sound of Eha's laughter. She hoped they would hear it for many years to come.

CHAPTER SEVENTEEN

The blinking rectangle surged ahead, long past the mid-point of its journey. Rechecking its calibration to ascertain trajectory and distance to target, it effected minor adjustments in its course heading. It blasted through small stars in its path as if they didn't exist. Nothing would stand in the way of its objective. The mission would be completed and afterwards it would calmly return to its source for another assignment.

As ordered, the predatory corridor began reviewing the data in its memory banks. It quickly collated the files pertaining to its objective. Earth, third planet from the star referred to as Sol, approximately five billion years old, with one natural satellite, protected by five layers of atmosphere, with the exosphere the first to be contacted during penetration. Once contact is achieved, five layers of planetary core must be successfully breached in order to consume the world's mass. The crust and upper mantle would provide little resistance. The inner core, however, will force the portal to focus its energies precisely. Plant and animal life, although quite dense in selected areas, should not impede the membrane to any noticeable degree. The rectangle believed the process of earth's elimination would occur without incident.

It reflected momentarily on the earth's lone satellite. Since the orbital period was less than 30 days, it might be able to consume it along with its mother planet. After a period of study, it decided the moon would be destroyed rather than absorbed. Too much vital energy would be used in the conversion process, and earth remained its primary objective. The rectangle would plan an approach opposite the orbital trajectory of the moon, intercepting it if it interfered with primary target contact.

The rectangle blinked in perfect cadence as it deposited the information back into its memory banks. Increasing its speed again, it felt a measure of pride. Thus far, it had carried out its mission with tremendous precision. Continuing on, it silently sailed through space toward its objective.

CHAPTER EIGHTEEN

Conor lifted himself off the ground, using Eha's furry bulk for leverage. He straightened his clothing while slapping the cheetah on the ears a few times for fun. At the Lady's urging, he lifted his eyes and looked far off into the horizon. First, a tiny speck floated along, tracing a lazy pattern across the sky. Then it appeared to turn on a purposeful course, heading directly toward the small group gathered in front of the council chamber. The image grew with every passing second.

Soon Conor recognized the immense form of his mentor, Purugama. The great cougar flapped his leathery wings every few seconds, riding along on the back of the strong winds of the realm. Conor looked at his big friend without blinking, holding a wide smile the entire time. He loved Purugama with all his heart. Just seeing the giant cat soaring through the sky filled him with a great amount of hope. He looked so formidable, so intimidating. Conor thought about starting yet another journey with the huge Champion of the Crossworlds. He couldn't help but feel a charge of excitement race through his body. Dangerous, yes. Life threatening, absolutely. But all the same Conor couldn't deny his enthusiasm.

Purugama achieved pattern altitude, rocketing over Conor's head at more than seventy miles per hour. The young Champion could smell the cougar's damp fur as he raced by him. His hair twisted and flew about his head as the wind following Purugama hit the group waiting on the ground. The big cat let out a guttural snarl as he reversed course a hundred or so yards away. With three robust swipes of his great wings, he steadied himself, touched his paws to the ground and jogged lightly toward his mistress. He sneezed twice, two mighty blasts that would have blown Conor off his feet had they been pointed in his direction.

Instead of greeting his longtime apprentice, Purugama walked straight to the Lady of the Light. Lowering his head, he gingerly approached her.

"My Lady," he said.

"Tell us, great Champion," she replied. "What have you seen at the extreme edges of the realm?"

"Happily, I saw nothing," said the winged cat. "I traversed the four corners at least a dozen times over the last few days. The area is calm and undisturbed. For now, that is."

"That is good news, Purugama, and couched by an astute observation. It is only a matter of time until the final confrontation penetrates the realm."

The great cougar nodded his head once in agreement before turning to greet Conor. Purugama smiled (if brandishing a double row of lethal fangs could be called a smile). He looked Conor up and down from his position beside the Lady of the Light. "You've grown, boy. You're a man now, and a strong one at that." The big cat chuffed a few times, urging Conor to acknowledge him.

"It warms my heart to see you. You look somewhat older, but still capable I suppose."

Eha chuckled under his breath. Surmitang gruffled noisily. Maya and Therion sat stoically, observing the reunion. The Lady began turning toward the council chamber, but stopped when she heard Purugama speak again.

"A thousand centuries from now, Trolond Tar, I will still be teaching you combat strategies and battle tactics. It would take a dozen just like you to wrestle me to the ground, magic or no magic. Maybe I should turn upside down in mid-flight to see how well you fly without me."

"You would, wouldn't you?" asked Conor as he walked over and jumped onto Purugama's back. "You'd do it just to see how long I could hold out without panicking." He grabbed the scruff of fur under the cougar's chin, shook it back and forth vigorously. "You'd never let me hit the ground, though. We both know that, don't we? How could you ever hope to survive without me?"

Surmitang huffed again, this time with greater emphasis. The rest of the cats chimed in, throwing disgusted chirps and chuffs in Conor's direction. The Lady of the Light smiled and shook her head. How she ever got this group to act in accordance with her wishes was beyond her comprehension. She loved them all, though, and frequently allowed their lapses of decorum.

"Come, Champions," she said, calling them to attention. "It is time to meet with the council. Our last planning session is upon us. We mustn't keep my Lord waiting."

CHAPTER NINETEEN

Nemelissi emerged from the fourth in a series of geographically controlled corridors designed to guide the assassin toward its goal. It had become angry after exiting the second portal. The third passageway caused it to boil over with intense hatred.

For some bizarre reason it could not fathom, its jailer had placed a variety of obstructions in its path. If he had wanted the image in its mind destroyed, then why not call forth a corridor that led directly to it? The rage in Nemelissi's irrational mind had increased with each irrelevant stop along the way. It had nearly brought down an abandoned building at the first location. At the second and third stops it had done just that, obliterating entire cities with its destructive magical spells.

Here, at the fourth location, it saw something new – living beings inhabiting a city. A good size population milled about in the buildings and on the streets below. Even if the Author of All Worlds didn't live here, at least the destroyer could satisfy its bloodlust before passing through the next portal.

Nemelissi raised its thick, powerful jawbone, sniffing the air. It recognized most of the scents of this world, but something else drifted into its nostrils as well. The Author of All Worlds lived elsewhere, it felt certain of that. He was close, though, very close indeed. The assassin felt certain it would find its target lurking beyond the next corridor. The realization fed its mad desire to destroy. Blind rage combined with a positive step in its mission caused it to grow extremely ferocious.

It fell to the ground, scraping huge chunks of cement into its calloused fingers and filthy claws. Its feet, constructed as a mirror image of its hands, used the opposing thumbs to crunch the hard ground into dust as it sought out its first victims. After scraping the sidewalk into rubble and flexing its huge muscles, Nemelissi bellowed his warning to every creature within earshot. The call continued for over a minute, becoming more hideous and terrifying with each passing second.

The sickening cry pouring from the destroyer's lungs boomed through the huge city, freezing the inhabitants in their tracks. Every face within a thousand yards turned and looked at Nemelissi. When they saw the source of the awful sound, fear gripped their bones, shaking the sense from their souls. Many of them lost consciousness. Others lost all bodily functions and relieved themselves where they stood. Those correctly responding to the fight or flight quandary ran for their lives. Those that didn't fell back against the nearest wall, frozen and waiting for their impending deaths like rabbits surrounded by a pack of hungry coyotes.

Nemelissi reached back with one muscular arm. It threw the appendage forward with a grunt, splaying the fingers on its hand to their maximum width. A shower of sparkling energy rocketed forward from the tips, cleaving the nearest building at its midpoint. The magical discharge sliced through the structure so cleanly it didn't seem affected at first. Then the top half of the building slowly slid toward the inhabitants on the sidewalk. Cement and steel screeched, breaking apart as the upper half of the giant building toppled over onto the unfortunate victims.

Those on the street ran in all directions, trying to escape the thousands of tons of debris falling from above. Nemelissi, hoping to increase their fear to the fullest, ordered a series of barriers to emerge from the streets and sidewalks.

The fleeing mob soon found their escape routes blocked. They tried to climb over the obstructions, but the barricades increased in size every time someone scrambled a little higher. Doomed to their fate, they uttered their last thoughts before being buried under a thunderous wave of structural wreckage.

The destroyer gurgled quietly, a momentary compliment to its first assault. It looked beyond the area of immediate destruction, finding more residents fleeing the large city. It launched itself in their direction.

The screams of the damned fueled Nemelissi's depraved lust. As it advanced toward its second target, it thought about a number of possible attacks. Discarding every sensible strategy, it allowed its fuming mind to run free. Whatever occurred would be the result of a random psychosis. When it came within fifty feet of the terrified beings, it jumped forward at a dizzying speed. Elevating itself slightly, it came after them at more than fifteen feet above their heads.

The assassin convulsed violently, vomiting a bellyful of boiling, acidic sewage toward the cringing masses. The molecules of the discharge divided in midair, causing the mass of deadly filth to expand rapidly. By the time it loomed over the roiling mass of inhabitants, it covered an area larger than an acre. When it hit the fleeing masses, a sound like raw bacon slapping against a sizzling frying pan rose up from the crowd. A second later, a chorus of horrified screams blotted out the sounds of cooking flesh.

Burning bodies ran wildly about the street. Hundreds of

calls for aid went unheard as everyone tried desperately to save themselves. Blinded by the powerful acid, dozens of inhabitants smacked fiercely into one another, knocking each other down in the street. Some wallowed on their backs, kicked in their rotting faces by those madly running about, or serving as stumbling blocks for others. In the end, a large pile of half dead corpses lay in the crowded street. A few continued to call out for help. Some cried for salvation. Others cursed the creators. All eventually died.

Wrapping one huge arm around a sturdy metal staff, Nemelissi hung from a flagpole at a corner building. It watched the result of its work with great interest. Held captive for so long by the inner element, the destroyer had spent its time devising different extermination techniques. It had never used one of the new methods before this day.

Droplets of its vomit dribbled from its lips. Rolling its wart-infested tongue outside its mouth, it gathered up the remaining poison. Swallowing the sewage, it filed the attack away in its vast catalog of execution strategies. It smiled while watching the last of the city's inhabitants rot away and die. It thought of its objective, the author, and how it might best prolong his suffering. If the acid were applied first to the non-vital areas, the Author of All Worlds might live for days. A horrible, extremely painful existence, yes, but the assassin's jailer had not given it instructions regarding the type or length of death. He merely said they wanted him eliminated. The horrible creature widened its smile, imagining the torture his quarry would endure.

Nemelissi released the flagpole, falling to the ground with a harsh thump. It jerked its head immediately at the sounds of additional life. Prancing up the street with an animated gait, it launched itself toward a bridge spanning a small river. Using its hands and feet like powerful clamps, it scurried to the top of the structure in seconds. At the far end of the river, in the southernmost section of the city, the last remaining inhabitants seemingly raced to safety. Some ran on the streets, while others overloaded a streetcar, arms and legs poking out of every window and door.

The assassin shrieked with delight, salivating over another kill so close at hand. Letting itself fall from the bridge, it disappeared into the water with a surprisingly nimble dive. The river water barely moved at all, giving way to the creature without a struggle. A single line of rising bubbles heading in the direction of the escaping crowd marked the only sign of Nemelissi's existence.

Wolbus reached the top of the endless stairway. In the pitch-black silence of the Circle of Evil's inner sanctum, he expressed his hope that the creators might find it in their hearts to spare at least some of the inhabitants now under assault by Nemelissi. He uttered the mental appeal, ejecting it from his mind quickly after his recitation. If Shordano suspected even a hint of mutiny, he would feed him to Nemelissi himself. He closed his eyes tightly, squeezing off the last of his petition. He would never forgive himself for what he had done, however necessary it may have been.

Wolbus knew by counting the stairs under his feet that the assassin would be at a specific location at precisely this moment. He shivered at the thought of what Nemelissi might be doing. He clamped his jaws together, as if by doing so he might close off some of the shame he felt for casting the inhabitants of that world to their fate. He had found no other way but to send the destroyer on a path directly through that solar system.

He knew Nemelissi would not allow any of them to survive.

That fact would buy them the precise amount of time they needed, should the creators follow the correct course. By now, Trolond Tar would be reunited with Purugama, the last warrior to briefly hold Nemelissi at bay. Maybe this time the confrontation would turn out differently.

Possibly, however, the other might seize the opportunity and lay Nemelissi low once and for all. Everything appeared to be falling into place. Wolbus lifted his foot to access the final step. He stopped and set it back down. He let his forehead fall into his right hand. He sniffled once, asking for the creators' benevolence one last time. The image of Nemelissi's carnage dismissed all other thoughts from his mind. Wolbus grimaced with intolerable pain. After regaining himself, he carefully stepped up and through the doorway into the chamber of the inner element.

A strong, scaly hand emerged from the river. The immense claws drove into the hard concrete wall, creating a natural handle for Nemelissi's arms and legs. Before the gruesome head emerged, the other arm, dripping with filthy water, broke through the surface and created another hold in the wall. With a powerful grunt, Nemelissi pulled its muscular body from the water. Leapfrogging over its arms, it landed on the sidewalk facing away from the river. It shook itself like a dog emerging from a pond. Then it looked back toward the city, toward the last group of inhabitants heading its way.

Swimming under water, Nemelissi had covered more than two miles in as many seconds. The planet's inhabitants had no idea their worst nightmare now sat patiently awaiting their arrival. They moved toward it in a large, concentrated pack, either on foot or by vehicle. They couldn't have presented an easier target for the destroyer. By spreading out, they might have delayed Nemelissi's departure by an hour our two. Staying together gave them a sense of safety, as if their numbers would intimidate their enemy. They wouldn't stay alive long enough to realize their mistake.

The assassin waited until the last possible second. It wanted the crowd close, and sitting as long as possible allowed it to enjoy the anticipation of the kill. Staying completely still and waiting patiently gave it the frenzied sensation it would call upon to ruthlessly demolish its target. Its body shook with excitement. Seeing the first of the crowd break through the city into open ground, it couldn't hold off its ferocious desire any longer. Nemelissi yowled like a sick wolf, exploding toward the inhabitants in a puff of cement and dirt.

Any of a thousand weapons would have completed the task in short order, but the assassin wanted to finish this massacre with its own hands and feet. Fifty yards from the first wedge of the crowd, it sprang into the air, flaring its hair and arms out for everyone to see. It crashed down onto one of the strongest inhabitants, smashing the large man to a pulp in front of his fellows. The others recoiled at the hideous display of aggression, taking their eyes from the mutilated body just long enough to recognize what had entered their midst.

Nemelissi ripped into the rest of the first group, using hands, feet and teeth to tear the fleeing bodies to shreds. Some of the remnants it swallowed, others it stuffed into the mouths of terrified onlookers before decapitating them. It approached a particularly obese man and ripped his arms from their flabby sockets. After the remainder of the man fell to the ground, it used the beefy limbs to bludgeon the rest of the inhabitants into an early grave.

During the horrible melee, Nemelissi gained strength and ferocity with each kill. It moved faster, lunged more powerfully, and grew more perverse with every passing second. A city of a hundred thousand would certainly have fallen before such an onslaught.

The assassin, soaked with blood, muscle tissue and shredded skin, moved toward its next objective. Three vehicles, bursting with occupants, raced through the city streets. In moments they would move beyond it into the safety of the hills. Nemelissi crouched low to the ground, clamping down into the turf with all four appendages. Shaking its hair free, it mumbled a garbled incantation.

The assassin's hair shot forward. Assaulting the lead vehicle first, it penetrated from front to back like a swarm of living needles. No sound emerged from the slowing bus. It coughed a few times, still in gear but traveling too slow to maintain the engine. Finally it stopped, sagging on its right side. Pools of blood seeped from cracks in the sheet metal, dripping onto the pitted street below.

Nemelissi called its hair back, yanking it free from the vehicle. The door of the bus slipped open a second later, letting two of its occupants roll out onto the street. They looked perfectly normal, except for the thousands of tiny pinpricks dotting their bodies. The insertions were so clean only tiny amounts of blood dribbled forth from them. Even the eye sockets had been penetrated multiple times. The two inhabitants lying on the ground stared at their slayer through stippled pupils.

It turned to look at the other two vehicles. Thinking for a moment about sending the needles forth again, the assassin decided on a more physical solution. Disappearing under the sidewalk with a loud crunch and an explosion of gray dust, it traveled underground toward the lead vehicle. Feeling for the vibration of the engine and tires, Nemelissi burst through the ground, carrying the gigantic streetcar into the air. The destroyer balanced the huge trolley above its head like a toy. The terrified passengers wailed in a long continuous plea for mercy. They seemed to know Nemelissi's plan. They looked down to the ground, watching the other streetcar racing toward them. Those who could grabbed each other's hands, screaming together as their trolley fell from the sky.

Nemelissi slammed the two streetcars together with a hatred no one riding on either trolley would ever come to understand. It appeared as though it wanted to drive some of the demons from its soul with the impact. Perhaps it believed that obliterating everything in its path might give it a moment's respite from the terrible chaos occupying its mind. Every move had to be crueler than the last, every death more gruesome. There could be no other explanation for such a sadistic display.

The two streetcars crashed together in a steaming pile of twisted metal and glass. Nemelissi, unfazed and unhurt, watched the debris and body parts moving swiftly in every direction. It blinked its eyes once. A stream of white-hot fire, like a blowtorch, shot forth from its pupils. The assassin sat there calmly, waving the flame back and forth over the mass of wrecked trolleys and carcasses.

The intense heat melted the glass into pools of liquid fire. Nemelissi ordered these flaming puddles to assault the passengers that were still alive. It smiled while listening to their terrifying screams. Bringing the torch flame to its highest degree, the assassin cooked the rubble into a gleaming monument. The blistering flames receded back into its eyes. It stretched broadly, as if just awakening from a long afternoon nap.

It stood, rotating its head and scanning the surrounding

environment. *It must be here*, it thought. *The next corridor must be within reach.* The assassin sniffed the air again. Beyond the immediate pungent smell of bodies and metal, it recaptured a familiar scent – *the Author of All Worlds.* He lived close by, perhaps only a world away. Even if it were an entire galaxy, Nemelissi knew in its foul heart that the next corridor would be a direct conduit. The inner element had held it back long enough. The objective was at hand, and the assassin felt primed to execute its prey.

Jogging back to the edge of the river, it looked at the rippling surface, trying to decipher any unnatural changes in the vast volume of water. It turned, briefly looking back at the city. Seeing nothing but death and abandoned territory, the assassin decided to depend on its first instinct. It dove into the river, gobbling up great sections of water with its huge arms and legs. With no need for oxygen, it swam underneath the surface fluidly, seeking a source of light that could only mean one thing – a corridor waiting to transport it to its final destination.

It held itself to the bottom of the river, hoping to find the portal attached to the sandy bottom. If it existed closer to the surface, Nemelissi would be able to spot it easily from this vantage point as well. It pushed itself forward with its powerful legs, grasping sturdy boulders along the way. With these, it propelled itself toward its objective even more quickly. As the river bottom's depth increased, a murky darkness overtook its form.

CHAPTER TWENTY

The chamber barely held the entire assembly. The Council of Seven stood quietly around their conference table. The Champions – Purugama, Therion, Eha and Surmitang – sat on the other side of the chamber, guarding the Lady of the Light. Conor and Janine hovered over Mr. Hikkins' computer, discussing the model he and Janine had designed.

The Lord of All Life looked around the chamber, noticing the tight quarters and how cramped the Champions seemed. With a simple wave of his hand, he enlarged the chamber to three times its original area. The big cats, especially Purugama, silently thanked the creator for his kind consideration. They spread out, giving themselves more breathing room. Their posture around the Lady never altered, however. The cube of defense remained locked about her position.

"Let us begin," commanded the first councilor. "Seeker, your report, if you please."

Mr. Hikkins stepped forward. "My latest estimate shows the predatory corridor reaching the earth's exosphere in one point two five days."

"Estimate?" repeated the first councilor, his yellow aura flaring briefly.

"One can never provide a precise calibration," answered the

seeker. "I trust in my calculations, however, and believe my *esti-mate* to be worthy of the council's trust."

"Continue," barked the first councilor.

Mr. Hikkins spoke to the council as a group, favoring none of the creators individually. "If we hope to intercept and hold the predatory corridor at bay, we must leave no later than midnight tonight. This will provide ample time to stage our defense and bring the power of the council to its fullest potential."

"You would have us leave the protection of the realm?" said the first councilor. "You must be mad, seeker, if you think the Council of Seven could be coerced into such an act."

The Lord of All Life opened his mouth to object. Instead, he stared at the seeker calmly. *Such a peculiar man,* he thought. *How many times he had performed beyond their expectations, only to be questioned again at the next opportunity.* Odd but brilliant, the seeker had never requested any reward for his many deeds. Here he stood, accepting ridicule with the same bland expression he always wore. Perhaps after this is ended, the Lord mused, he might sit for a while with this unassuming man. Much could be learned from such a conversation.

Mr. Hikkins waited for the first councilor to finish his protest. Without moving a muscle, the seeker stood with hands locked behind his back. When he believed his turn to speak had arrived, he showered the first councilor with logic and facts. "Therefore, my Lord, there is only one way to thwart the power of these immense corridors. The Keeper has given me the one ingredient I was lacking to construct a model powerful enough to hold the predatory corridor in check."

Mr. Hikkins waited for another interruption. When none surfaced, he continued. "In order to call forth an energy source potent enough to match the strength of the inner element's predatory corridors, we will need the combined powers of every creator, every available Champion, and even those seekers who can be encouraged to participate. With the exception of Conor and Purugama, everyone in this chamber must travel to earth tonight."

Janine's head snapped up from Mr. Hikkins computer screen. She looked at Conor right away, found his big blue eyes staring back at her. Her boyfriend said nothing; he just stared at her silently. They shared a quiet moment in each other's minds. She pleaded for an explanation and he wished he could provide one that might ease her soul. He had promised her, yes, but with a small caveat, and now she understood. They would separate once again, and deep in her heart she would worry herself sick until he returned to her.

She feared for her own safety, but next to the thought of losing Conor again, that emotion faded away like a morning mist under a rising sun. She wanted to say something. She wanted to reach across the console and slap him as hard as she could. She wanted to throw her arms around him and never allow anyone to take him from her.

She did none of these things. She merely accepted him, accepted the situation while tamping down emotions that struggled to reach the surface and burst from her eyes in a torrent of tears. Conor reached out to her, his strong hand hovering above the console. She took it in her delicate fingers, squeezing it softly. She understood. She agreed with the fact that he had a duty to perform. She realized that her boyfriend was more than he appeared to be. Whoever this Trolond Tar was, he might be Conor after all. If she wanted him in her life, she would have to invite the warrior in as well. She smiled weakly, accepting the unspoken response as a comforting symbol of his love.

The argument between the creators shook her from her reverie. She released Conor's hand, turned to see the source of the commotion. Apparently the first councilor did not appreciate Mr. Hikkins' tone.

"How dare you order the creators about! Do you believe us to be minions, underlings awaiting your every command? You will apologize at once and beg the council's forgiveness."

"I will do no such thing," replied Mr. Hikkins, clearly irritated with the creator. "Every second you delay means another few thousand miles in the predatory corridor's journey toward earth. I have described precisely the nature of the weapon and how rapidly it will destroy any world it locates as its target.

Without the appropriate defense, the weapons will destroy planet after planet in our system.

"The organic life that constitutes these corridors has been irreparably altered. While still a living being, their new programming instills one directive only – to seek out and destroy whatever world has been assigned by the inner element."

The first councilor opened his mouth to interject. Mr. Hikkins cut him off cleanly, staring directly into the creator's eyes.

"May I remind you that five additional predatory corridors presently wander about the Crossworlds. We have yet to successfully determine their targets, because our efforts have been predominately directed toward earth. Any one of them could be heading for the glade of Champions, or even for the realm of the creators. This is occurring as we sit here bantering about your station, and whether or not we can call upon the council to travel to earth this evening. I assure you, first councilor, we have no choice but to act immediately."

Mr. Hikkins held the creator's gaze. He stepped forward quietly, moving closer to him. The first councilor's yellow aura flickered slightly. He held his ground, however, and did not challenge the seeker.

"I believe you all realize, before you make your *choice* whether to accompany us to earth, that our model will not be one hundred percent reliable. The Keeper has provided an excellent component to its design, but I will not deceive you. We obviously have had no opportunity to test the model, with no similar anomalies threatening the Crossworlds in the last, oh, two thousand centuries. I assure you of two things, however. One, I believe it will work, and two, we simply have no other choice. Unless of course you feel safe enough here, that is until Nemelissi arrives."

The creators grimaced at the mention of the assassin's name. The first councilor's fear of Nemelissi reached so deeply into his psyche that his aura all but disappeared.

Janine looked at Conor, a pleading, confused glance that asked for an explanation for the strange name Mr. Hikkins uttered. She saw cold fear sweep over the faces of every creator at the table. She glanced quickly to the Lady of the Light but gained nothing by examining her expression. Now she held her boyfriend's gaze steadily, grasping his hand for emphasis. She knew instinctively that Conor and Nemelissi would cross paths. She didn't know how, but she knew it as surely as she knew the sun would fall in the sky that evening. Conor waved his other hand subtly, asking for patience in a chamber where so much tension already existed. She granted it, but he saw her determination. She would know soon enough; she would see to it.

"Your points are well taken, seeker. We will arrange for departure at once," said the supreme councilor as he looked toward the rest of the council. "Unless there are any more objections."

The first councilor backed away from Mr. Hikkins. He turned, joining the other creators as they used their individual portals to exit the council chamber. Each had their own preparations to make, their own inner deities to call upon for assurance and guidance. After all of them had vanished, the Lord of All Life turned to Athazia and the Champions.

"I am afraid we must call upon you again, brave warriors of the Crossworlds. Trolond Tar, you have served us bravely in the past. Now, I fear, you must face the deadliest test of all. I wouldn't order my worst enemy to battle Nemelissi, and yet we ask you to face it, alone, with your mentor, Purugama. We will do whatever the seeker asks of us on your home planet, but understand this – if you fail in your task to rescue and protect the Author of All Worlds, nothing we accomplish on earth will make any difference. The Author must be protected at all costs. Do you understand this?"

"I understand," said Conor. "He will be protected, I swear it."

Purugama walked up behind his apprentice. Without even seeing him, Conor reached up, grasped a handful of jowl and pulled the great cougar's jaw against the side of his face.

"We will not fail you, my Lord," rumbled Purugama.

"Very well," said the supreme councilor. He reached out with his arm, extending two of his fingers toward Conor and Purugama. A glorious filament of ruby energy streamed out from the tips. It swam over Conor and the cougar, altering their appearance in front of everyone remaining in the chamber. When the sparkling fiber disappeared, Conor stood clothed in the warrior outfit of Trolond Tar. It was the same leather pants and vest he had worn while battling Seefra's armies. The Lord of All Life pointed his index finger at Conor's forehead. The golden band materialized, encircling the crown of Conor's head. An insignia with the letter C emerged just over and between Conor's eyes. The band fit tightly around Conor's head, but not painfully.

The young Champion reached up and touched the smooth, glistening metal. He traced his fingers around the crown of his head and found the band to be completely seamless. Then he touched the insignia. It too felt perfectly smooth, flawlessly shaped by some unknown metallurgist. He felt as he did the first time he had donned the outfit of the great warrior – somewhat awed, but not at all unworthy. Something about the clothing and the head-band felt entirely familiar to him, and not just because he had worn it previously.

He looked up at Purugama and saw the leather saddle placed about the great cougar's neck and shoulders. Although it had been cleaned, Conor saw the permanent marks of their previous battle against Seefra and the shadow warriors. Everything seemed to complement the situation, reassuring Conor that he, the saddle and his powerful mentor had successfully returned from a previous battle. They had overcome great obstacles together and would do so again. This journey to find the Author of All Worlds would be the closing chapter of a long, triumphant relationship between man and beast, mentor and apprentice, comrade and companion. Purugama gruffled quietly, signaling his confidence to Conor. Now that he understood their assignment, the big cat was eager to depart.

"You must leave immediately, Purugama," said the Lord of All Life. "We cannot say precisely, but we feel Nemelissi has closed the distance between itself and the Author of All Worlds. It may be only minutes from finding him. The Lady of the Light will draw forth a corridor that will take you directly to his current location. May your journey be swift, cougar, and your wings remain strong."

Purugama said nothing in return. He merely turned, made

brief eye contact with his brothers, bowed his head to Maya and the Lady, and crouched down so Conor could climb aboard. The young Champion declined, turning to his Lady.

"A moment alone, please, with my companion?"

"A brief moment, Trolond Tar," she answered. "We have little time."

Grabbing Janine's hand, he led her over to a somewhat isolated corner of the council chamber. He drew her close to him, feeling the warmth of her body, her love penetrating his soul. Holding her still for a minute, the two of them quietly communicated their love to each other. Breaking away finally, he held the back of her head in a strong, capable hand.

"I'm sorry," he said. "I told you we wouldn't be separated again."

"As long as you come back to me," she said. "Please, Conor, whatever this thing is, don't let it take you from me. I don't want to live the rest of my life without you."

"You won't, I promise." He kissed her lightly on the lips, pressed his cheek lightly against hers, and whispered into her ear. "I love you, Janine. If any thought takes me through this journey, it will be knowing that we have a lifetime to look forward to together."

"Conor, you mean everything to me. I love you so much."

"Do whatever it takes to survive, Janine. No matter what, we must come back to each other."

"Conor," said the Lady of the Light. "It is time."

The young Champion kissed his girlfriend again. He looked deeply into her eyes, searching her soul for the one place they shared without intrusion from the outside world. He smiled. She smiled back. They returned to the small gathering of Champions and creators.

Conor jumped into the saddle, placing his sandals into the snug, leather stirrups. The wall behind the Champions dissolved slowly, giving way to the beauty of the realm. A soft wind blew lazily through the trees, giving the entire area a surreal quality. It seemed impossible that anything could threaten such beauty.

Athazia stepped away from the group of Champions. Lifting both arms in front of her, she uttered a small incantation, calling forth the corridor that would transport her two Champions to the first stage of their journey.

Maya stood facing Purugama. The two cats appeared to communicate silently for a few moments. Afterward, Maya lifted his black and white head, holding Purugama's golden eyes with his own. "Remember the order of your allegiance, cougar. Crossworlds first, creators second, followed by your brother Champions. Consideration for your own safety always comes last."

Purugama chuffed his consent. He touched Maya's nose lightly before looking up at his passenger. "Are you ready, Trolond Tar?"

"One second," replied Conor. He saw Janine running to his side. Unhooking his foot from the stirrup, he leaned down to hug her one last time. After the embrace, he placed his forehead against hers. They closed their eyes, feeling the pulse of their love for each other. Enjoying one last moment together, they separated with Conor's hand lightly touching her cheek. He released his girlfriend into the care of the Champions, calling out to the cat who gave his life for Conor half a dozen years ago.

"Surmitang," he said, riding high on Purugama's shoulders. "She is in your care. I trust you will return her to me safely."

"Aye, Champion," said the huge tiger. "We'll all look after her as if she were our own cub. Go now, and be confident in your choice. My life stands before hers."

Conor smiled at the Champions, bowed to the Lady of the Light, and gave Maya one final look. Turning toward the blazing corridor, he patted the great cougar's shoulder a few times. "Well," he said, "it looks like it's the two us again, Purugama."

Strangely quiet, the big cat gruffled his agreement while approaching the corridor. Without a word to any of the group assembled behind them, he sprang forward into the swirling membrane. Conor and Purugama disappeared into the portal, which quickly dissolved into thin air. The finality of their departure affected even the Lady of the Light.

Janine swallowed a huge lump in her throat. She would not cry in front of the Lady and the Champions. She blinked away a solitary tear and let it roll down her cheek, hoping no one had noticed. Athazia watched the moisture seep down the girl's face. She placed a warm hand around the nape of her neck. Pulling Janine's head to her breast, she gave a small, hopeful comment.

"Don't worry, child. Once he realizes his true identity, he will have all the strength he needs to defeat Nemelissi."

"But what if he doesn't?"

"In that event," answered the Lady of the Light, "we are surely doomed."

CHAPTER TWENTY-ONE

The blinking rectangle entered the Milky Way galaxy. Racing through space at maximum velocity, its sensors registered the planet farthest from the sun. Silently speeding by the body formerly known as Pluto, it sent out organic probes to collect samples as it passed.

It would not allow any mistakes during the performance of its mission. It would carefully sample and catalog each world on the way to its primary objective. Registering the next planet in the system by its molecular hydrogen atmosphere, the rectangle soared along the outer reaches of Neptune.

Using the proximity of the two outer planets and its present rate of speed, the corridor calculated that earth should be within range in ten point two seven hours. Shutting down all non-essential functions, the rectangle poured every ounce of its reserve into its organic engines. If it could shave a few more valuable seconds from its travel time, perhaps its masters might call upon it again to perform another mission.

Blasting through space debris and most of the smaller stars, the rectangle chimed its way toward Uranus and Saturn on the way to its objective – earth.

CHAPTER TWENTY-TWO

The creators assembled just outside the council chamber, very near the location where Conor and Purugama departed only moments before. The Lord of All Life, the first councilor and five other robed creators convened nervously among the giant Champions and their mistress, Athazia. With the exception of the supreme councilor, none of the creators had ever been called upon to do battle for the Crossworlds. The Champions intervened if the need ever arose, as had the protection forces before them.

They considered themselves above such common altercations. Their duties fell within the sphere of design and administration. Warfare and armed confrontation did not suit those bred for and raised in privilege. That was why the protection forces were given certain powers and the Champions wielded such formidable magic. They had made a mistake with the protection forces, which ultimately grew too powerful, too ambitious. Their rebellion had cost the creators dearly. If the Champions hadn't been quickly assembled they might never have defeated Zelexa's armies during the devastating equinox war.

The Lady of the Light, the Champions, the seeker and Janine waited somewhat impatiently for the small host to gather in the staging area. When the entire company appeared ready to leave, Mr. Hikkins stepped forward to address them.

"We will be arriving in a vast forest very close to where Conor and Janine attend school," he began. "After calculating the trajectory of the predatory corridor, I have determined its initial atmospheric penetration point. Within an acceptable margin of error, the planet destroyer will touch down very close to latitude forty degrees north and longitude one hundred twenty-four degrees west. If we construct our defenses anywhere within Redwood County, we should be able to focus our attack directly into the heart of the predatory corridor. I have chosen the old-growth forests near Willow Creek as our staging area."

"Seeker," asked the Lord of All Life. "Exactly what is your plan? How can such a small company defeat a force capable of annihilating an entire planet? I am eager to hear your strategy."

"We have no time, my Lord," said Mr. Hikkins. "I can only tell you that we will need every ounce of magical energy available to us. Everyone gathered together here – creators and Champions alike – will have to summon the depths of their reserves in order to fuel the reactive portal the keeper and I will unleash against the inner element's weapon. Any lapse of concentration, any seed of doubt entering anyone's mind for a fraction of a second will result in our instantaneous destruction. The end will take place so quickly none of us will even register its occurrence."

"Please," said the Lady of the Light to the council. "I trust our seeker, and we simply have no other choice. We must *all* trust him and Conor's companion. I do not believe the Crossworlds has existed this long only to be wiped away by a desperate effort put forth by the inner element. We *can* defeat the Circle of Evil one last time. We *will* defeat them; I believe it in my heart."

Therion, Surmitang, Eha and Maya all moved a step closer to

their mistress. In a show of solidarity and adoration, they displayed their unshakable belief in her statements.

"Very well, then," ordered the supreme councilor. "You have my allegiance, Athazia. I am certain you have the others' as well. Draw forth a corridor, and let us travel to this Redwood County. I am eager to rid the Crossworlds of the inner element forever."

The Lady of the Light drew her hand across the horizon, chanting a few mystical phrases as she did so. A peculiar sensation swept over her as she watched the perimeter of the corridor take shape. She realized this might be the last portal she would ever summon. Over the endless stream of centuries she had served the Crossworlds, she must have drawn forth thousands of passageways. Now, as the milky membrane congealed in front of her, she looked at the corridor lovingly, as a mother looks upon one of her children.

It was she, after all, who had designed the first of the organic portals. Up to that point, all corridor travel had been through synthetic passageways. They worked efficiently enough, but no relationship existed between the portals and their passengers.

The organic corridors embraced their travelers, coating them with a protective skin. The thin film acted as either a conductor or a repellant of any sensory energies generated by traveling through the passageways. When using the synthetic corridors, one might actually need a period of rest to recuperate. The organic portals, however, protected the travelers, leaving them with only a brief touch of extreme cold and heat.

Athazia stood close by as the corridor flashed, signaling its eagerness to transport the creators and their passengers. It beamed proudly with the understanding of its assignment. No other being in the Crossworlds could be more proud. The Lady of the Light thrust her hand into the membrane, feeling the immense power pulsing through the liquid energy. She closed her hand into a fist, allowing the membrane to squirt through her fingers. Closing her eyes briefly, she made a silent plea for their safe passage. Pulling her hand free, she turned to the small assembly.

"The corridor is ready, my Lord." With that simple statement, she walked into the membrane as casually as one walks through an archway. The rest of the group followed. First, eager to protect their Lady, the Champions followed her. Janine and Mr. Hikkins walked closely behind. Reluctantly, the Council of Seven followed. Even the first councilor, always critical of the seeker's work, followed the rest of his company into the corridor. The massive portal checked to see that everyone had passed through, closed up like an elevator, and left nothing behind but the tranquil beauty of the realm.

The assassin explored the depths of the strange river. Clinging to the rocks and debris at the sandy bottom, it pulled itself along while kicking rhythmically with its powerful legs. An inky blackness surrounded it now, signaling to Nemelissi the depth of the lake's bottom.

Nemelissi felt the pressure of the fathoms trying to break through its tough skin. Each time it sensed a breach, it altered the molecular composition of its cells. In this manner, it fortified its body against the river's attempts to crush it outright. For a while, Nemelissi even swam with its eyes closed. It was either that or blindly stare at darkness, and it saw no need to look upon the inky blackness.

Far off in the distance, a faint light appeared at the bottom of the river. Nemelissi swam toward it without knowing of its existence. After ten minutes of blind swimming it opened its eyes, seeing the tiny blades of light streaking toward the surface. Excited at the prospect of finally reaching its goal, the assassin pulled itself ahead, fortified by an aching anticipation. Closing in on the source of the light, it closed one set of gills on the right side of its neck. It would use the set on the left to survive underwater, but it wanted to prepare itself for the sudden shift to an oxygenated atmosphere, where it would breathe normally with the right side of its body while restoring the left lung. Satisfied with the transformation, it focused on its target. The light's intensity grew as Nemelissi approached the portal.

The assassin swam over the top of the corridor, placed precisely at the extreme depths of the river. A perimeter glistened, the membrane seemed intact, but something about the passageway puzzled Nemelissi. For some reason it didn't seem accessible. The membrane, while intense, didn't possess the brilliance of an ordinary corridor.

Then the destroyer realized the problem. It fumed at its jailer once again. With its own energies it placed Wolbus' image firmly in the recesses of its mind. After disposing of the Author of All Worlds, it would indeed pay his jailer a visit. Making it find its way through a sequence of corridors was one thing, stacking multiple portals on top of each other was quite another.

Nemelissi would have to determine the correct sequence in order to enter the passageway. No doubt his jailer had devised an impossible method for extraction as well. Once inside the maze of portals, it would have to brave the cold and heat while trying to solve the mystery of Wolbus' design. It could take a hundred years, or it might occur spontaneously, according to whatever plan the jailer had devised.

Nemelissi would not wait for blind chance. It decided to dive in head first, taking the layers one at a time. If it injured itself in the process, then so be it. The mission was all that mattered. Besides, the quicker it found and disposed of its prey, the sooner it would be traveling back through the sequence of portals to find Wolbus. He would make quick work of his jailer, and eliminate the two others in the inner element as well. With them out of the way, Nemelissi would be free to pursue any targets he wished. Happily, maliciously, the destroyer dug its way into the first layer in the stack of corridors.

THE AUTHOR OF ALL WORLDS

CHAPTER TWENTY-THREE

The bright sun spilled down from the sky, warming the swaying trees beside the two-story home. No clouds appeared anywhere above the neighborhood, anywhere along either horizon for that matter. It was another flawless day, marked by seventy-five degree perfection. Warm, clear ocean water invited everyone to the beach, which could be heard from only a few miles away.

A few swallows hastily built their mud nests on the side of the home near the window to the study. They darted to and fro, collecting materials while others huddled inside the nest, shaping and grooming. Nature appeared to be in full bloom; the world beamed with happy anticipation.

The author sat in his semi-comfortable chair, tapping away at a keyboard perched upon his oversized desk. Every minute or so, he leaned forward, leaving his keyboard silent so he might see the words on his computer screen. A few of these he changed, most he left alone. The hardest part, he kept telling himself, was to allow his mind to write freely, forbidding the logical half to determine when and where he should stop and examine his work. *After all, that's what my editor is for,* he thought. He seemed to fluctuate around a happy medium, sometimes writing with abandon and enjoying his rampant creativity and other times fighting against the internal professor who demanded perfection even in the first draft.

The author's wife entered his study. Grasping three different bags, she kissed her husband while announcing dinner would be somewhat late due to her busy schedule. He returned the kiss absentmindedly, looking at his screen, mentally playing with three different versions of his protagonist's latest escapades. She stayed close after the kiss, waiting for recognition. The author noticed her proximity, finally turning after he typed another sentence. They smiled at each other, a game played often during their seven plus years of marriage. He loved her deeply, although he wished she could appreciate his work. She couldn't share the joy of a particular passage in his books, or a direction that a character had suddenly taken. Her interests lay elsewhere.

He accepted the differences in their tastes, content with the knowledge that his writing gave them a comfortable life. He watched her walk through the door of his study, pleased with the sight of his wife, almost fifty years old and still a striking woman. She had not allowed her features to melt away like so many others. It was a source of pride for her; after all, in her business one had to present an attractive image.

The author settled back into his story. As best he could, he released his mind from any outside influence, allowing the words to randomly spring from the keyboard.

The story seemed to be going well, although for some unknown reason the author couldn't quite connect with it in the same way he had with his last book. Perhaps that journey had taken so much from him emotionally; he had yet to recover sufficiently in order to completely give himself over to the present tale. He reached out his hand without focusing on its target. Grasping the switch of the desk fan, he turned it to the lowest setting. He felt the cool breeze push lightly against his skin and allowed the story to continue falling from his fingertips.

Suddenly, a bizarre noise startled him. He turned around, looking outside the small window of his study. No car alarms, no loud music, no sounds of construction or emergency vehicles assaulted his ears. He saw nothing out of the ordinary, save a tiny spasm of light dancing around the parking area. Believing it to be nothing more than a fluke from the approaching equinox, the author disregarded it. Pulling the blinds away, he slid the double-paned window shut. *This will reduce the noise level would fall considerably,* he thought as he turned to finish his daily writing.

Although the words came easily on this particular day, the author couldn't expel a nagging thought from his mind. He knew he had always been successful at resolving such issues, mostly by letting things work themselves out, but this particular aspect of the story troubled him. If one of the main characters exerted complete control over the outcome of the journey, then how would the author explain the character's predicament? Perhaps another individual could wrest control away from him, adding an element of unpredictability. Maybe the influential character could be seen as schizophrenic, or perhaps he might be subject to the whims of others, or a greater power than himself. It puzzled him, and the author did his best to lock that quandary away in a safe place in his mind. After all, he still had three pages to write, and the story was beginning to show promise on many other fronts.

Another sound caught his attention, and then another. The second sound had come from the front of his home. It sounded to him like trees limbs crashing together. The author turned around again, checking the driveway first. He saw no one – no moving cars, no reason for any disturbance. He began to turn away, ready to save his work on the computer before investigating the front yard, when a flash of light from the parking area caught his eye. He turned and gasped, pressing his face against the window. Something out of the ordinary was occurring, but for the life of him he couldn't determine the cause. A variety of lights danced around the middle of the driveway. It definitely wasn't sunlight, and it couldn't have been some peculiar collection of mirrored reflections. *Strange,* he thought as he watched.

An urgent pounding on the front door startled the author. Someone was obviously desperate. *Now what,* he wondered, *another kid selling oversize candy bars?* He pressed two keys on his computer and watched the tiny icon flash on the taskbar. Satisfied with the safety of his work, the author carefully descended the fifteen stairs to the first floor of his home. He reached for the door handle, watching the door and the frame shake under the assault from his unexpected guest. A passing thought occurred to him, but he bypassed the peephole. Instead, he ripped the door open like a madman, hoping to scare the candy-selling youngster away.

As he looked through the screen door he found he couldn't breathe. A young man, tall, strong, wearing a strange leather warrior's outfit and a golden headband stood at a respectful distance from the screen. The young Champion bowed silently, dropping to one knee at the foot of the stoop. The author was so taken aback by the sight of Conor he fumbled for something to say. At long last he unlocked the screen, opened it wide, waiting for some kind of exchange.

"I apologize for disturbing you," said Conor with great deference, his eyes still focused on the ground at his feet. "I have been sent by the Lady of the Light to retrieve you."

"I know…." stumbled the author. "I mean, thank…." He couldn't possibly know what to say. *How could this be happening? It couldn't be. It must be a dream, some subconscious manifestation of my thoughts.* The boy kneeling before him was a figment of his imagination, a character in his stories, and yet he *was here*, as real as any person he had ever met. The author stood there, dumbfounded, speechless.

"Your pardon, sir," said Conor, finally looking up. "We must leave immediately. Your life is in grave danger."

The author started to protest, but something stayed his words. He suddenly comprehended the horror of the situation. If Conor were truly here, then somehow his story had…. *No, it couldn't be.* His blood went cold.

"Come in," said the author. "I need to get a few things."

"We have no time," protested the young Champion politely.

"You don't understand," returned the author. "And I don't have time to explain. Trust me, if I leave without my work, there's no telling what might happen."

The two of them raced up the stairs into the study. A loud crash sounded from the author's driveway. Two terrifying screams followed, and then another thunderous crash. Conor looked out the study window into the driveway.

"We have to go, *now*."

The author grabbed two laptops as he slapped a flash drive into the front of his desktop computer. Ordering the device to copy his book files onto the external drive, he sidled over to Conor and looked out the window. In the space where the display of lights occurred only minutes ago, a distorted corridor now appeared in mid-air. Even before the membrane congealed, a pair of powerful limbs broke through the portal, pushing their way to freedom.

One side of a hideous looking face emerged from the passageway as well. The author gasped as he looked upon it – the ugliness, the twisted sense of evil purpose.

"What the hell is that?" he said to no one in particular.

"That," answered Conor, "is your creation, and it's been sent here to kill you."

"Nemelissi," gasped the author.

CHAPTER TWENTY-FOUR

Sensing proximity to its target, the blinking rectangle dismissed the remaining propellant in its engine. It used the inertia of its progress to close the final distance between itself and earth. As it sailed by the moon at more than twenty-thousand miles an hour, the predatory corridor began cataloguing the physical characteristics of its target. When it arrived, it wanted to be ready to commence operations immediately. If it could please those who programmed its function, perhaps it might not sit idle for too long after returning to its launch point. The rectangle quietly began collating data.

Earth: third planet in a galaxy of nine with one star – Sol.

12,742 kilometers diameter

5.9736×10^{24} kilograms mass

5.515 kilograms/mass^3 density

Planetary composition: 34.6% Iron, 29.5% Oxygen, 15.2% Silicon, 12.7% Magnesium, 2.4% Nickel, 1.9% Sulfur and .05% Titanium

Atmospheric components, primarily nitrogen 77%, oxygen 21%, roughly 2% remaining trace elements
Indigenous life forms; air, ground and water
Population: approximately six point five billion
Homo erectus, plus or minus two hundred fifty thousand

Approximately four point five billion years old with five hundred ten million kilometers^2 total area.

Reducing speed as it passed the halfway point between the moon and the earth, the rectangle blinked three times, signaling its readiness to begin the conversion process. It took no notice of the moon at this stage of operations. Considering the gravitational relationship between the earth and its satellite, the rectangle calculated a seventy-nine percent probability that the moon would be irreparably harmed by the annihilation of earth. Deciding not to collect data on the moon at present, the predatory corridor began positioning itself for an assault on its primary target.

CHAPTER TWENTY-FIVE

The author grabbed his disk, shoved it in his pocket and flew down the stairs with Conor in the lead. He saw a picture of his family resting on the television as he hit the first floor. He stopped suddenly, astonishing fear burning in his gut. He called out to Conor, who stood in the doorway holding the screen wide.

"My wife. Our sons."

"It won't touch them," the young Champion answered. "I promise you. You are its only concern, its only target. Now we must go, *please!*"

The author placed his palm against the filthy screen door, holding it open so he could pass. A thousand thoughts slammed against his head at once. He watched the ground as he ran, trying to focus on some aspect of logical recourse. He never even saw the gigantic golden forepaw standing in his way. He ran headlong into it, smacking his forehead against strong muscle and hard bone, and falling back on his rear end. He dropped one of the laptops, shook his head and looked up. The anxious face of a three thousand pound cougar stared down at him.

"Greetings, author," rumbled Purugama.

"Holy *shit*," said the dazed man in response. He started to push himself up from the lawn when he felt a huge set of teeth grip the back of his sweatshirt and lift him from the ground.

"My laptops," shouted the author. "I must have them!"

As the great cougar lowered him to the ground to let him collect his possessions, Conor threw the saddle around Purugama's shoulders. After strapping it tightly around his mid-section, he looked warily in every direction.

A horrendous shriek rolled over the house from the driveway. A chorus of different screams followed, coming from terrified people running for their lives. A crunching noise occurred even closer to Purugama and his two companions. It was the sound of roof tiles being crushed into pebbles.

Purugama looked up to the top of the author's house and watched Nemelissi pull himself over the ridge of the roof. The assassin took one look at the Champion, opened its mouth wide and bellowed again. The force of the blast blew the trees bare, every leaf sailing away as if frightened by the horrific apparition.

"Go cougar, *now!*" ordered Conor, turning to secure the author's position behind him. Purugama ran through the trees, looking for an opening where he could spread his wings and take flight.

Nemelissi used all four appendages to launch its powerfully-built body toward the three travelers. It focused solely on the Author of All Worlds, lunging madly at the man as Purugama raced by. The crazed assassin crashed into a studio across from the author's house, smashing a door to splinters, the concussion breaking nearly every window in the home. It bellowed its insane desire to finish its target quickly while jumping away from the wrecked structure. In a flash it climbed to the highest branch in the trees outside the author's home.

Spotting Purugama's wings hastily beating a path straight up into the sky, Nemelissi threw its right hand toward the great cougar's tail. A flaming net shot forward from the destroyer's palm, hurtling toward Purugama with incredible speed. Nemelissi watched hungrily, waiting for the cage of fire to complete its task.

Turning to see the hideous assassin standing atop a huge eucalyptus tree, Conor urged his mentor on. As soon as Nemelissi jerked its arm in their direction, he noticed the burning web flying through the sky directly toward them. He guessed the netting would overtake them in less than five seconds. He turned forward, issuing a command to his mentor.

"Keep flying in the same direction, Purugama. I'm going to call forth a corridor and place it immediately ahead of us. Don't turn around, or do anything that might reduce our speed. Just keep flying forward."

The great cougar didn't answer. He didn't want to. He focused every ounce of his strength into his powerful wings. He pumped them frantically, trying to squeeze out every ounce of speed he could muster. Although he wanted to turn and see what might be behind them, he dared not take the chance. To be honest, seeing Nemelissi closing in on them would do more harm than good.

The Champions always showed a great deal of courage, proving themselves time and again, but the assassin was something else altogether. To a cat, they feared it because it was something they couldn't understand. Drazian, Fumemos, even Seefra annihilated worlds for a purpose – to gain power, destroy a key enemy, or obtain a vital resource. Nemelissi killed for pleasure and nothing else. It had developed the craft of death to the deepest extent, using dark magic in ways unknown even to the inner element of the Circle of Evil. Purugama knew that any Champion in the glade would fight it if forced to, but they all knew their efforts might provide temporary safety for another being and not much else. Only one Champion had ever stood his ground against Nemelissi, and he had paid for the decision with his life.

A brilliant light splashed against the sky directly in front of him. A silver corridor, borders and membrane solidifying rapidly, opened up in front of the giant cat. Purugama snuck a quick look behind him just before disappearing into the safety of the portal. He felt sick as he watched the cage of fire in its final stage of transformation zoom in, trying to grasp one of his hind legs. With one last powerful lurch of his wings, the Champion yanked his leg away from the flaming net. Purugama and his two passengers shot into the corridor, disappearing from the sky over the author's house.

Instead of howling his frustration at losing his target, Nemelissi watched as the cage of fire collapsed around the corridor. The organic passageway fought to complete its task and vanish without a trace, thereby prohibiting any pursuit. The fiery bars held it fast, however, drawing it down toward the tree where Nemelissi eagerly waited.

Its progress was slowed by the almost human stubbornness of the corridor. It used all its remaining power to thwart the desires of the cage of fire. The destroyer gave its instrument the time it needed, for it knew the struggle was a forgone conclusion. While awaiting its arrival, Nemelissi checked its present whereabouts. No one walked about the property. All who lived here had apparently taken refuge inside. The assassin toyed with the idea of leveling the author's home and massacring everyone who ran from the devastation. Its stomach boiled with the poisonous lava. Its arms throbbed with a dozen possible spells it could use to pummel the buildings into rubble. It decided to wait, however, until it finally caught the Author of All Worlds. It would allow the fever to build, for the longer it stayed trapped inside, the more gruesome it would be when finally released.

Nemelissi turned his attention back to the sky. The cage of fire had won the battle with Conor's corridor. It dragged the silver membrane down to within Nemelissi's grasp, hovering in place quietly. The destroyer waved a clawed hand across the face of the fiery webbing. It disappeared instantly, leaving the huge corridor helpless in front of Nemelissi. Plunging one powerful arm into the swirling mass, the assassin focused its mental energies on the sensations it received from the portal. It tracked Purugama, Conor and the Author of All Worlds to their new location, understanding the landscape perfectly. It noted their current direction, selecting the appropriate place where it might intercept them. Signaling to the corridor its desires, the assassin stood boldly on the treetops outside of the author's house. It would surprise them, hack the Author of All Worlds to pieces, and then eliminate the other two Champions as a bonus to its jailers.

Just before stepping into the portal, Nemelissi noticed a line of strange carriages racing up the driveway. All bi-colored, all shrieking horribly, the bizarre vehicles slid to a stop just under the tree. A series of creatures bearing a resemblance to each other stepped out, all of them screaming at the assassin. One fired a crude weapon at it, stinging its arm momentarily. Nemelissi sneered at the men, allowing the poisonous vomit to rise in its throat. *Perhaps the Author of All Worlds will roam free a while longer,* it thought while descending the uppermost branches of the tree. It stared down at the closest man, focusing the trajectory of its mouth directly over the officer's body.

CHAPTER TWENTY-SIX

In the inky black of night, a glistening silver light flashed deep in the forests of Redwood County. The corridor formed quickly, emitting a shimmering brilliance for its passengers to use while traveling through its confines. As each traveler stepped out into the vast gathering of gigantic sentinels, the portal beamed proudly. If a certain member of the Council of Seven found refuge on a large boulder or a fallen tree, the corridor pointed a special beam of light in their direction. It kept the membrane perfectly still as everyone stepped forward toward their destination.

When everyone had been transported safely, the Lady of the Light stepped through the blazing passageway. She looked every bit the goddess she was, as beautiful as a fall sunrise, as regal as the redwoods that surrounded her. Most of the council, far from the comfort of the realm of the creators, leaned on her for spiritual support.

Always generous and caring, she held no animosity toward any of them for past differences. She simply couldn't keep anything within her except positive energy. She gave of herself to everyone and everything. She cared for the other creators as if they were her own children. Helping each of them find a comfortable spot, she waited for the seeker to enlighten them about their strategy.

Maya and the other Champions waited quietly around the

perimeter of the gathering. As they always did when traveling with their mistress, the four giant cats took up their protective positions around her. They used their acute senses to track anything moving in the strange forest.

None of them had spent a great amount of time in a place so powerfully built. If a single tree fell it could crush the entire group before any of them knew it. Even Therion's great bulk could easily be hidden behind one of the massive, burled trunks.

Both he and Surmitang kept a wary eye around their encampment. If this strange forest reminded them of anything, in the black of night it looked uncomfortably similar to the forest of forever. A shiver traveled the length of Therion's spine as the giant lion peered down the endless rows of trees in the misty darkness.

The corridor blinked out of existence. Not a trace of light remained, save the brilliant stars lounging in the moonless sky. The Lady of the Light snapped her fingers three times, allowing individual globes of silvery light to appear in the palm of her hand. These she sent to the three edges of their encampment, where they provided ample illumination for the group of anxious travelers. She visually checked the assembly, counting heads and inspecting faces. She smiled at the Champions. Eha returned the expression, causing her to love him even more. No matter what, the happy cheetah always gave her reason to feel good about their chances.

The creators, all seated except for the first councilor, looked apprehensive but capable. They merely wanted to return to the realm, where everything was beautiful and serene. They would perform their function, maybe not selflessly, but at least the passion for their home would keep them strong.

She shifted her eyes to Janine, who sat with her hands clasped and her elbows holding her knees in place. Athazia could see the sickness in her soul. She worried after Conor, and with good reason. She loved him deeply. That was apparent; something the Lady knew would serve her Champion well after he completed his journey. After his battle with Nemelissi, Trolond Tar would need the soft touch of a caring woman for many months. If he returned at all, that is.

Athazia held her emotions in check; she did not want Janine to read in her face what she knew in her heart to be true. There was no more capable a warrior than Trolond Tar. Nemelissi, on the other hand, was terrifyingly unpredictable. She believed in her Champion, but still....

Finally, she glanced at the seeker. Mr. Hikkins stood staring at her, completely detached. He had a task to perform. For all the excitement he showed, he looked like a teacher waiting to enter a classroom.

"Seeker," she asked, finally breaking the silence. "What day is the morrow?"

Mr. Hikkins raised his voice so everyone gathered in the forest could hear his reply. "Tomorrow, my Lady, marks the anniversary of the creators' victory over the Circle of Evil in the equinox war. It also introduces the tenth turning of the two thousand year cycle."

The Lady of the Light allowed the comment to settle around the shoulders of those sitting near her. The equinox war, the ultimate conflict between good and evil in the Crossworlds, was barely won by the benevolent forces of her father's army. The Circle of Evil had been driven away, battered and defeated on the ceremonial battlefield. The day held tremendous meaning for all who allied themselves with the Council of Seven. Beyond that, it was said that the tenth turning opened a mystical door allowing certain magical ancestors to provide assistance to those in dire peril, as they had during the equinox war. Athazia closed her eyes briefly, thanking her father for all his years of expert guidance. She raised her eyelids, speaking to the seeker again.

"Begin your explanation. Tell us of our respective roles in your strategy."

Mr. Hikkins commenced his lesson as any high school teacher in a modern day classroom might do. He explained the physics of the model in its most basic form. Following this, he outlined the organic interaction between the predatory corridor and their defensive shield. He deferred to Janine at one point during his description, giving her the opportunity to elaborate on her addition to his model. She performed beautifully in his estimation, confidently playing the part of a true scientist. She kept strictly to the facts, logically defining the principle components of her work in the laboratories of Redwood State. She then carried her audience to the next level, illustrating how her experiments would be translated to a gargantuan scale in order to contact and absorb the destructive energies of the predatory corridor. She also briefly described the nature of the statistical model she and Mr. Hikkins had designed as a framework for their counterattack.

"The most vital aspect of our strategy," she said, a grinning teacher standing slightly abreast of her, "will be our flexibility. The model assumes a confidence level of nearly ninety-nine percent. While this yields an extremely low probability of error, it is not perfect. And since we have no data on the nature of the predatory corridor, we must prepare ourselves for the inevitable fluctuation in its energy pattern. At a moment's notice, and under the most extreme circumstances, we must be prepared to alter the tender balance of our combined energies.

"The magical fusion from every living source must at all times be at a premium. It must maintain maximum output every second. One dent, one glitch in our concentration, is all it will take for the predatory corridor to use the one percent error window to overtake and destroy the earth. And us along with it."

The creators no longer lounged around the thickly-wooded forest. All seven of them stood at attention, clearly daunted by the task they were being asked to perform.

As emotional as they might be at times, the creators were certainly not dense. They realized perfectly what the seeker and Conor's companion were asking of them. They also understood their chances, and they began rebelling against the strategy that brought them there.

"You have sentenced all of us to an early grave, seeker," boomed the first councilor.

"Would you wait a few more days to meet the same fate at the realm?" replied Mr. Hikkins evenly.

"At least there we might perish with peace in our souls," added the creator who commanded the skies.

"Yes," added another luminescent being, standing in the rear of the group next to Maya. "Return us to our home, seeker. I command you."

The comments raged on for many minutes. Even the supreme councilor vented his frustration more than once. At length, the seeker's arguments won the day.

"Will you abandon another of the great planets in the Crossworlds system, all for another few days lurking around the realm, awaiting the inevitable?" He looked around the gathering of creators. "If it is the wish of the council, I will restrict my efforts. Command me and I will turn away and allow the Lady to escort you back to the realm. Before you go, however, look to the stars behind you; see the fate that awaits you at the realm. Nothing can save you. *Nothing.* You will stand and fight, here on earth, or you will walk toward your last living act, a cowardly retreat instead of a magnificent victory."

The supreme councilor turned his head, following the direction of the seeker's eyes. What he saw froze the blood in his veins. The other creators heard him suck a cold breath into his lungs, so they also turned, looking up into the star-filled sky. As they caught sight of the expanding blood-red corridor, their anxious reactions peppered the silent forest. Even the Lady of the Light's expression involuntarily flinched when she saw the gigantic portal in the sky. Only the Champions maintained their composure, for their primary purpose lay in their Lady's safety. They would never allow anyone or anything to alter the course of that directive. If the end of all things danced in the sky behind them, then so be it. The Lady would be protected until the last second. The Lord of All Life turned back to Mr. Hikkins with a mixture of fear and resolve painted on his face.

"We understand now, seeker," he said. The supreme councilor checked the eyes of all the creators emeritus. Seeing no dissent in any of them, he stepped forward. "Apparently we've run out of time. Inform us of our respective duties."

CHAPTER TWENTY-SEVEN

Shordano paced about the chamber, fighting to control his emotions. Squeezing his hands behind his back, he looked out the fractured window onto the sparse lands that at one time had been a paradise. The bulk of the area had been converted into Seefra's dreaded chamber of cells, but they had always intended to return the region to its natural beauty. The Champions of the Crossworlds had ruined those plans, however. Together with the accursed Trolond Tar, they had beaten their armies handily, nearly driving Seefra and his disgusting monster back into the inner element's headquarters in the process. Now, however, everything appeared to be proceeding as planned.

Something gnawed at Shordano's mind. He couldn't dismiss the idea that some aspect of their strategy had been overlooked. They couldn't allow even the smallest mistake this time. If they blundered, the creators would finish them for all time.

"Jek," the leader of the inner element called out, still looking out the window. "Has the primary corridor reached its destination?"

"Yes, as ordered, Excellency," answered the third arc of the inner element. "It successfully reduced travel time by eleven percent; I believe we might use this particular corridor again for the next...."

"Has the conversion process begun?" interrupted Shordano, spitting the words out in frustration.

"The expansion is underway, my Lord. If the corridor's examination of planetary composition was precisely executed, evaporation should begin within the hour."

"Thank you, Jek," said Shordano. "You have performed brilliantly. Report to me immediately upon completion. I wish to know the exact moment that the portal finishes consuming the accursed planet."

The leader of the inner element watched through the corner of his eye as his servant bowed deeply before departing. He released the grip on his hands and turned to look at Wolbus, who sat at the council table with an alarmed look on his face.

"How is the progress with the Author of All Worlds?" he asked his second in command. When he didn't get an immediate answer, Shordano placed his palms on the table directly in front of Wolbus. "Answer me!" he demanded. "How fares the assassin?"

Wolbus' lips twitched a little. A sad smile spread across his face, followed by a terse laugh. "He fares very well, Shordano, but I assure you, it is no longer our destroyer. After it finishes the Author of All Worlds, it has every intention of coming back here to exterminate us." Wolbus looked up at his superior, his smile increasing to its fullest extent. The laughter came with some difficulty at first, but then it rolled from Wolbus' belly in great waves. He knew what he had done by sending the assassin on a lengthy chase for its objective. He had infuriated it, caused it to lust for revenge against those who had imprisoned it. It would carry out its orders, but after that, if anything still existed in the Crossworlds, it would return to the inner element and exact a horrible price indeed. Wolbus only hoped he would live long enough to see Nemelissi dismember his superior.

Wolbus felt the back of Shordano's hand smack against his cheekbone. The principle orator flew from his chair, smashing against the far wall with a sickening thud. He felt his body rising from the floor as Shordano used his dark magic to confront his comrade. Wolbus' limbs stretched out in all directions, pulling against the joints, tendons stretching to their limit. The principle orator wanted to continue laughing but found he couldn't. The pain of his buckling joints forced a terrified scream from his lungs.

"You cannot escape it, Shordano," panted Wolbus through the pain.

The leader of the inner element bit his words off precisely. "Has the assassin made contact with the Author of All Worlds?" He increased the pressure on Wolbus' limbs, smiling when the principle orator shrieked again in pain-induced horror.

"Yes! Mind of the creators, yes! Less than an hour ago, Nemelissi broke through the layered corridors and found its target. It is only a matter of time, now." Wolbus felt his body slump to the floor as soon as he spit out the last words.

Shordano had removed the spell. While his limbs no longer seemed ready to split in two, he couldn't move them. He sagged over to one side, watching Shordano walk across the room, open the door and leave without a backwards glance.

CHAPTER TWENTY-EIGHT

The predatory corridor's perimeter expanded rapidly. With the glorious bluish-green coloring of earth in the background, the massive portal raced to achieve the chosen dimensions. The vast reaches of space silently witnessed the bizarre transformation as the once tiny corridor reached its immense proportions. Any debris, smaller stars or planetary bodies that happened to stand in the way of the expansion were summarily destroyed. The frames of the corridor grew both in size and mass. In order to encase and control a membrane with a width larger than the diameter of the earth, the boundaries of the portal had to be fantastically dense. As the perimeter grew in length and width, the framework bulged into a heavy border capable of holding the deadly, swirling passageway.

Soundlessly, the gigantic frame slowed its progress. Locking all four corners together with an organic substance stronger than any adhesive known, the perimeter of the corridor halted its expansion.

Floating in space directly between the moon and earth, the predatory corridor seemed like an immense picture frame awaiting some celestial portrait. It looked utterly harmless, a silent wall bearing no inner core. The moon continued its daily route around the earth, unfazed by the monstrous but inactive portal standing between it and its master. The earth looked beautiful, unharmed, infinite, as it always had before. It was a mother cradling billions of inhabitants, caring for them with a deep, giving heart. Except for a handful of visitors in a forest thousands of miles from the corridor, no one on earth had any clue about the titanic event about to occur. In less time than it takes to attend church, take a mid-term exam, have lunch or win a needless argument, earth would cease to exist. Unless the creators could succeed in turning back the destructive power of the predatory corridor, a planet's population would roil with the madness of total anarchy.

The membrane flashed, beginning with the center of the barren space between the borders of the portal. A murky cloud, blood-red in color, swirled in the middle of the corridor. Tendrils, acting like the appendages of a living being, stretched out toward the four corners of the perimeter. They snaked their way toward the edges, not exactly cutting a precise line. First the upper left connected, then the lower left. After contacting this side of the boundary, other tendrils sped toward their respective targets. Latching on hungrily, the appendages signaled their success to one another. With all four corners bonded together, the corridor flashed again, this time with much greater intensity. The entire membrane took form, stirring to life and swallowing energy from small stars in the immediate vicinity.

The crimson membrane finally occupied the entire passageway. If sound were audible in space, one would have heard a deep, rhythmic pulse pushing outward from the center of the corridor. As the membrane thickened, the sound fell octave by octave, humming evenly as the portal gained strength and substance.

As the transformation concluded, the membrane spilled over the edges of the immense corridor, solidifying the bonds and signaling its readiness to proceed. Flashing its bloody core one final time, the predatory corridor surged forward toward its target.

The moon, puzzled by the gravitational disconnection to its host planet, began swirling in and out of orbit. Once it passed the edge of the killer portal, it locked on to its orbital plane again. The damage had been done, however, and it couldn't reestablish the symbiotic relationship with its host planet. Peculiar phenomena began occurring all over earth, including a location a few hundred miles north of San Francisco. The tides and currents of the great oceans of earth, moderated for all time by the moon, had dislodged themselves from its control.

CHAPTER TWENTY-NINE

"Mind of the creators," said Mr. Hikkins quietly as he prepared to assemble the creators and Champions in their respective locations. The sky had fought a losing battle with the churning membrane. It looked as though a giant crimson sheet had appeared among the stars, completely blocking all light. Even the stoic seeker fumbled spiritually at the sight of it. He did everything he could to produce moisture for his mouth so he might be able to speak. He too, upon seeing the gigantic predatory corridor, doubted their ability to defend the earth. It just seemed too massive, too immensely powerful. He looked down from the sky, saw the ocean roiling, spitting its giant waves against the bluffs of the northern California coastline. *So little time,* he thought, beginning his instructions.

"Quickly now," he said, "the Council of Seven must form an occupied triangle." He turned to the supreme councilor. "You, my Lord, will act as our spear point. Take your position at the head of the creators. All of the combined energy will flow through your aura, then outward toward the corridor. Take up your position at a point at least thirty paces from the trees, with the first councilor standing directly behind you. The other creators will form the wedge, yes, two of you behind the first councilor, then the last three behind those two."

Mr. Hikkins assisted the nervous creators to their respective posts. He bade them to look forward, directly at the terrifying sight coming straight at them. Ordering them to wait patiently for his signal, the seeker began positioning the Champions. This he accomplished by placing them in a diamond roughly ten feet behind the creators. Eha stood closest to the rear line of the council. Therion and Surmitang stood behind him, side by side about twenty feet apart. Maya formed the rear of the triangle. He would be closest to the trees, and also the initial contact for the energy flow.

"Miss Cochran," announced the seeker. "You may begin."

As Janine worked the keys on the makeshift workstation provided by the Lord of All Life, Mr. Hikkins approached Athazia. He guided her to her place in the formation, equidistant between the Champions and the creators. "You will be the conduit, my Lady," said the seeker. "The magical energy flowing from your Champions will filter through your aura before surging forward toward the council. You must distribute the energies equally, never infusing too much or too little into any one creator. The forces channeling through you will be greatly amplified by the chemical changes brought about by Miss Cochran's formula. It will give us the power to deflect the predatory corridor, but it may also exterminate anyone unfortunate enough to encounter too much at one time. We will begin slowly, pouring in more components of her procedure as we build toward our target rate. You may stand if you wish, but I respectfully submit that you might want to kneel or sit. The onslaught will be tiring for you, my Lady. We may be here for quite some time."

"I understand, seeker," replied the Lady of the Light, already assuming a defiant posture. She seemed ready for battle, for she had collapsed all other emotions in preparation for her role. "I will stand proudly with the other creators, through life or death, defeat or victory. Tend to your calculations, and see to it that no harm comes to Janine."

Mr. Hikkins bowed slightly, and then moved to the rear of the peculiar arsenal. He stood in front of Maya, bowed, and delivered his final instructions. "The formula for the organic chemical reaction will flow first through you, Maya. You must endeavor to blend the elements of the reagent with your magical energies. Do not allow the mixture to remain within your body any longer than necessary. Pass it forward to Surmitang and Therion. They will send it to Eha, who will guide the stream toward the Lady of the Light, and so forth. Do you have any questions?"

Maya shook his finely groomed black and white head once. Leaning forward, he whispered a brief comment to the seeker, who in return patted Maya's cheek. It was a small consideration, exchanged by two beings very different from one another, who knew in their hearts this might be their last stand.

"Miss Cochran," asked the seeker, "are we ready?"

"Power levels at one hundred percent," she answered. "The model is holding steady with the increased intensity. Cell manipulation and reformation looks good, even on a massive scale. We're ready."

"Proceed."

Janine typed in the final instructions.

Maya closed his eyes. He made certain his body pointed directly forward before doing so. Now he sat rigidly, like a statue waiting for a sculptor to apply the final chips and scrapes to his masterpiece. The great Lord of the Champions accepted the strange energies as they entered his body. He allowed access without wavering in the slightest. He channeled his own magical force, commanding it to release itself freely. The power sensations felt odd, but not at all threatening. Janine and the seeker had done their work well.

"Remember," shouted the seeker so everyone could hear, "do not hold the energy within your bodies. Allow it to mix with your magical capabilities before passing it to the next recipient. With each successive stop, the fusion will become more powerful and somewhat more difficult to control. After the entire chain is flowing with the combined energies of all participants, we will increase the spectrum of our model. You might experience some odd sensations. Your primary concern is to never impede the energy flow. Allow it access to your auras, inject your own content, and let it escape to the next recipient."

No one moved or answered. Mr. Hikkins took this as a sign of complete understanding. He nodded his head to Janine, asking for an elevation of power. He looked over at Maya, checking to see that his Lord had suffered no peculiar effects as yet. He watched as the Champion received the increased flow from Janine's computations.

Maya kept his eyes closed. He couldn't identify the feelings coursing through his body. The bizarre mixture of organic chemical compounds raced through his insides, searching for some sort of departure point. Maya could feel the energy building in intensity every second it stayed within his spirit. Far away on some mental journey, the great Lord of the Champions discharged the full nature of his magical powers so they might intertwine with the foreign energy stream. An instant after merging together, the powerful mixture surged forth toward Therion and Surmitang. The immense energy blast blew Maya's fur forward toward the two Champions. He stayed in his pristine position, completely calm, totally quiet and lost on some spiritual path that would allow him to perform his task without interruption. The energy sought out its next portals, slamming into the two cats in front of Maya with an almost human aggression.

"Back it down a small amount, please," said Mr. Hikkins to Janine.

Therion and Surmitang performed their task equally well, allowing the raging storm to slide in and out of their bodies easily. They added their magic to the mix as well, creating an even larger stream for Eha to contend with.

The diminutive cheetah accepted the energy with the same elated attitude he reserved for everything else in his life. Giggling at first, he soon began laughing like a little child getting a good tickle from his parents. Eha took the intense energy blasts from both sides, converted the flow by adding his own magic and sent the new combination forward to the Lady of the Light.

Athazia nearly collapsed when the first blast hit her shoulders. She expected a strong impact, but nothing like what she experienced. She quickly recovered from the disturbance, her aura shining like a silver beacon in the dark forest. She let the cosmic miasma swirl around her body, adding a degree of magic here and there to assure herself of its stability.

Finally, after pointing her fingers toward the Council of Seven, she released the whole of her magical force into the mixture. Her body convulsed once, then again as the immense power sought an avenue of escape. Traveling the length of her arms, the power erupted from her fingertips toward the rear line of the council. The Lady kept her eyes wide open, focusing on the stream, dividing it equally among the three creators at the back of the triangle.

The thrust of overwhelming power hungrily sought out new vessels to inhabit. Instead of halting this time, the energy blast went right through the first line of the triangle. It seemed to gain momentum as the power hungrily overtook the next two creators.

In the face of their uncertainty, the Council of Seven wavered under the strength of the assault. The beam of their combined forces surged forward into the first councilor, consuming him completely. The energy burned with manic intensity, swallowing the first councilor inside its womb. The power remained around him, rendering him invisible, yet unable for some reason to travel any further.

Fascinated, Mr. Hikkins watched their creation amplify with each additional being it encountered. *The progression has worked almost perfectly,* he mused while observing the triangle of creators shudder as the power swarmed over and through them. *Interesting,* he thought, *that the first councilor held the ability to halt the flow within his body when the others before him could not.*

"Increase power injection by twenty-five percent," he said to Janine. She followed his instructions quickly, without question.

He had kept one vital piece of information to himself during the initial planning. He knew the power flow would react differently with each recipient in the progression. Everything hinged on his ability to balance the organic chemical flow for each Champion and creator, so the outcome would be beneficial and not detrimental. The mixture had to be designed so that each of the recipients would deliver the most potent energy possible, yielding the maximum power output from the Lord of All Life. The trick, and this was Mr. Hikkins dirty little secret, was riding a fine line between life and death. He had to give everyone in the progression precisely as much as they could handle or the shield would never hold its own against the predatory corridor.

Too much energy or the wrong mixture might cause instant death to one of the Champions or creators. He had already seen his Lady buckle once because of the power coming from the Champions. They had only been operating at a little more than twenty-five percent at that time. He surmised correctly that once the power flow had invaded the recipients, increasing the injection level would not cause undue harm. Of course, that was only in theory.

The first councilor released his magic into the mixture. The power exploded from his torso like a flood bursting through a weakened dam. No time elapsed between the release and the impact on the supreme councilor. The Lord of All Life fell forward, catching himself with a well-placed right foot. He stood, letting the stunning energy flow blister his skin as it enveloped him. Bellowing with the pain, he straightened his body, reclaiming his former position as the spear point in the progression. The power seemed ready to blow him apart, but he held his position with a defiant strength.

Seconds before he might have vanished in the stream of relentless energy, he released his formidable magic into the mixture. His body arced forward as the power streamed forth into the sky. After a few seconds, he breathed normally, now as part of the overall mechanism instead of the main recipient of an unpredictable power flow.

"Increase injection flow by an additional thirty percent," said Mr. Hikkins to Janine. She responded smoothly, manipulating the keys on the workstation.

"Power surge now leveling off at seventy-seven percent," she reported. She heard no response from Mr. Hikkins. When she looked up she understood why. The sight before her eyes took her breath away. Instead of individual power stations, which each of the creators and Champions resembled at the outset, now they all appeared as one organic apparatus. None of the recipients showed any sign of distress or pain whatsoever.

The energy pattern flowed through them at a speed faster than any human eye could fathom. They stood there, all in a state of composed bliss, allowing the power to flow freely through their bodies. She felt so moved by it she almost missed the seeker's next instruction.

"Alter the composition of the power flow," he said. "Adjust the chemical injection to match your clinical experiments. If we observe no harsh reactions among the participants, increase power to one hundred percent and lock in the model."

Janine followed his instructions to the letter. After executing the chemical changes, she waited roughly five minutes before increasing the power output to its highest level. She inserted the code to lock in her changes, stepped back a few feet to take a breath, and then moved forward again, grasping the seeker's arm.

"How can they stand that much energy?" she gasped.

"The key, as I said before, is never to impede its progress," he answered. "As long as the power flow moves through them without interruption, they will not be harmed."

"So when the energy finally reaches its target," she asked, watching the awesome power surging in front of her, "its ability to proceed no further will halt the predatory corridor's advance?"

"Precisely," replied the seeker. "I'm certain that will be something to see."

The force of the energy surging through the small group seemed too powerful to describe. Janine watched as the beam rocketed through the Lord of All Life out into space. It rushed toward the corridor with an almost human purpose. The tip of the beam had assumed a pointed shape, no doubt a tiny extra added by the supreme councilor. Now hundreds of miles away from the coastline, Janine felt certain it would impact the giant membrane any second.

In truth, the beam had many thousands of miles to travel before encountering its objective. It seemed to understand its purpose, feeling eager to engage its opponent. It wanted to serve its masters and mistresses well, to fight with them against the killer corridor. It all seemed so surreal to Janine, who moved a little closer to her old high school teacher. The two of them stood together, watching the fruits of their labor operating perfectly. Mr. Hikkins smiled at a passing thought.

"Do you suppose," he said quietly to Janine, "the national student science symposium would give you first prize for this little project?"

Maya sat completely immobile, a statue. The fur all over his body vibrated wildly, but the leader of the Crossworlds Champions kept his eyes closed and his spirit far away. Where he traveled no one could have followed. His soul meandered in a different place, seeking the assistance of those would might provide the final burst of organic power needed to overcome the massive portal hurtling toward earth.

The energy flowed through his body perfectly, his own magical qualities combining easily with the power source. His absence did not disturb the progression in the slightest. As the Lady had said so many years ago, the Lord of the Champions possessed powers even the creators did not fully understand. He remained, physically, with the other recipients while roaming the heavens in spirit. He would not return until his quest had been completed.

CHAPTER THIRTY

Purugama burst through the corridor membrane, wings pumping at a furious pace. Putting distance between Nemelissi and his passengers drove his every thought. He knew the Author of All Worlds would be easy prey for the assassin. Even he, with all his great powers, would not be able to hold it off forever. Their only course was to lose Nemelissi in a maze of corridor passages. That might give them the time to try and determine some sort of strategy to use against it.

They had emerged over an expansive rock-strewn desert. Some foliage appeared here and there, but for the most part the entire area seemed blighted. A steady breeze danced around the desert floor, picking up intermittent wind funnels swirling with sand. The entire area, an outcropping of solid rock no more than fifty miles wide, ended in a sheer cliff face that dropped five hundred feet into a lazy, tepid pool of water.

A single stream, tiny, almost a trickle compared to the massive landscape surrounding it, ran the length of the grounds to the edge of the cliff. There, the water dribbled over the side, tumbling toward the pool below. Its fall was so slight that the water barely gave the droplets notice as they entered the small lake at the base of the cliff. Purugama looked at the tiny river and marveled at how it seemed to run in a flawlessly straight line. It looked like an engineer had drawn the river's course with a precise instrument before inviting the water in.

The great cougar noticed one other thing – the location of the stream. It appeared to cut the landscape in two. It sliced a precise line right down the middle of the vast desert.

Purugama lowered a wing, lazily soaring down toward an area with a large stand of leafy trees. They would find shade there at least. The big cat gave an extra effort to land softly, knowing that his new passenger might need the consideration. He walked up to the trees, flexing his wings in and out, happy to be at rest after such a tiring flight. After folding them in a final time, he crouched down so his passengers could quickly disembark.

Conor swung his right leg forward over Purugama's head, falling to the ground easily. He grabbed the author's laptops, cradling them while offering his other hand to help the man slide off the golden perch.

"May I offer you anything?" asked Conor, bowing slightly. "Are you well?"

The author looked at Conor, bewildered. He looked up at the giant cougar, also leaning forward with head bowed, and found himself speechless again. His mind whirled with a thousand questions at once. These two beings were alive, but they were nothing more than creations from the depths of his imagination. He still felt as though he must be dreaming, but he put that thought aside for now. He would accept the bizarre course of events until something more rational presented itself.

"Is there somewhere I might work without interruption?" he asked.

Conor glanced up at Purugama, who flicked his eyes toward the shady part of the oasis. "Please," he said to the author, "this way."

After situating him, Conor reversed course and walked back to where Purugama rested. He stopped briefly on the way, silently parting a thick branch. He watched the author unfold both of his laptops, turn them on, and retrieve the flash disk from the pocket of his jeans. After the computers had cycled, he inserted the disk into each one, downloading the additions to the final book of his series into each hard drive. He closed one of the laptops, securing it next to him, and began typing into the other. Conor witnessed the man's single-minded purpose with a bizarre fascination. The author seemed to forget where he was, or who he was for that matter. All he seemed to focus on was his story. Strange, thought the Champion, even when life existed all around him, this man sought to create new worlds for others to occupy.

The author banged away at the keys like a madman, writing furiously, page after page. No matter what appeared out of the sky, he wanted to alter the course of the story. He would not allow Nemelissi to harm Conor or Purugama, nor would he stand by while a predatory corridor of his own creation wiped away everything he knew and loved.

Conor let the branch slide across his palm until it returned to its natural position. Without making a sound, he backtracked to the place where Purugama awaited him. He found the great cougar sitting on his haunches, preening himself.

"How much time do you think we have?" asked Conor while walking up to his mentor.

"A day, a minute, maybe no time at all," said Purugama. "Nemelissi exists only to annihilate. He will not dawdle near the author's home for long."

"How can he find us so easily?" asked Conor.

"Nemelissi possesses powerful magic. No doubt you saw the cage of fire racing through the sky toward us?"

"Yes," said Conor. "It seemed to spring directly from where he sat in the trees."

Purugama gruffled slightly, chewing on his haunch for a moment. He examined his work momentarily before continuing. "It came from *Nemelissi*, Trolond Tar." The great cougar chuffed, looking at the shock and surprise on Conor's face. "It commands an infinite number of weapons, including a vast array of cells. It forced a very talented group of keepers to turn over nearly every cell design they owned. Seconds after they delivered their most ingenious inventions, it tore them to shreds without a moment's hesitation."

"We escaped it, though," said Conor, hopefully. "We blasted through the corridor before the cage of fire reached us."

"It was never meant to reach us, or capture us," said Purugama.

"What?" said Conor, puzzled. "What do you mean?"

"Nemelissi can alter the composition of anything it wishes," answered the great cougar. "He threw that particular cage of fire so it would ensnare the corridor before it could consume itself. With enough power, the cage of fire can hold the membrane intact as well. With that organic information, Nemelissi will be able to pinpoint our location exactly."

"Then why hasn't it arrived?" asked Conor.

"I don't know," said Purugama. "That is what troubles me. Perhaps the assassin looks for a port of entry he can use to surprise us. Perhaps it is resting because it knows our chances of escaping it are very slim. Perhaps it is developing new weapons to use against us."

Purugama lifted his golden head. He stood abruptly, raising his nostrils high above Conor. His muscles tensed, his wings flared out as if preparing for flight. The bronze eyes squinted as the nostrils flared again and again.

"What is it, Purugama?" asked Conor. "What do you sense? Has Nemelissi arrived?"

The giant, golden tail whisked back and forth, giving tempo to the big cat's inspection. After five or six minutes, Purugama sat down again. The sense of alert no longer caused the small oasis to hum nervously. The danger appeared to have passed. "No, it has not arrived yet. I thought perhaps I smelled the unmistakable foulness. When it comes, Trolond Tar, you will know by the pungent stench. It is truly unbearable. Nemelissi thrives on it. Perhaps it enjoys such aromas. I believe it understands the effect it has on its opponents, so it does its best to develop its putrid scent."

"Could this get any better?" said the young Champion. "Now I have to deal with some psychotic monster that smells like a cesspool and appears to enjoy it."

Conor removed the headband for a moment. Passing his right hand through the opening, he cradled it in his elbow while using both hands to brush his hair back over his ears. Flattening his palms against his forehead, he mashed the beading sweat away from his face. As he wiped his palms against his tunic, his right elbow sang out with a stinging pain. He ripped the headband away from the affected area, placing it back on his head immediately. As if it never existed, the pain vanished, his elbow seemingly unharmed. Conor adjusted the headband, tucking a few strands of hair away from his face. He looked over at Purugama, who had been watching him closely.

"I wouldn't take that headband off for too long," said the cougar. "Once removed, it will believe you to be dead, and it will react accordingly."

"What will happen if it thinks I've been killed?"

"That depends on the situation," replied Purugama. "Just as your clothing contained magical pellets during the battle against the shadow forces, your outfit and headband contain a great amount of magic. Only the Lady of the Light can know the precise outcome from their use, since she initially designed the uniform."

Conor adjusted the headband one last time. He felt a question banging against his brain, fighting hard for recognition. It had bothered him for the last two years, and now seemed like as good a time as any to release it again. If anyone would tell him, his big friend would. After all, they had known each other close to ten years.

"Purugama, you called me Trolond Tar after the battle in the shadow world, and here you continue referring to me by that strange name. Can't you tell me about him? Can't I know anything, or do I have to wait for some sign to tell me what I want to know?"

Purugama crouched down, taking up a sphinx-like position. He stared at Conor for quite some time. It seemed like the big cat wanted to give forth some information, but couldn't. "It is not for me to say, Trolond Tar. However, you are in the company of the one person who can give you the information you seek. No one can tell you what you wish to know with greater skill than the Author of All Worlds."

"I don't dare disturb him," said Conor. "He seems quite involved with his work."

"His work?" replied Purugama with a short gruffle. "He writes the story of your life as we speak. He tells the tale of all our lives, the Champions, creators, the Crossworlds, everything. The Author of All Worlds brought all of us into existence. He is the father of the Crossworlds – of earth, Wilzerd, the Glade of Champions, even the Realm of the Creators. Every time he writes, you speak, or another being speaks to you. Without the Author of All Worlds, everything you and I know would perish."

"He wrote the battle between the Champions and the shadow armies?" asked Conor.

"Yes," said Purugama. "Anything that has ever happened within the Crossworlds system came from his mind's eye."

"He allowed the destruction of Wilzerd?"

"Yes."

"Then he is a horrible man," said Conor. "One without compassion or love, he is as bad as Nemelissi or Seefra."

The big cat growled abruptly, deep and menacing. "You would claim to be more knowledgeable than the one who brought the Crossworlds into existence?"

"I claim nothing," answered Conor, angry at the author and angry at himself for arguing with Purugama. "I see what is in front of me, and that's all. Perhaps if the Author of All Worlds felt some of the pain he inflicts on others he might think twice before letting his thoughts ruin our lives."

"Are you so certain he has not?" said the great cougar, chuffing the comment from between clenched teeth.

Conor looked down at his feet. He didn't know what to feel. His mission was to protect the author from Nemelissi. He would do that to the best of his ability. If they survived this madness, he would surely pose some questions to the man. Ajur's death might be a good place to start. *How could such a noble beast be put down so harshly?* Conor fished through a hundred other questions in his mind. He couldn't understand any of it anymore. His mind began to spin.

"I will speak to him, then," he said to his mentor. He noticed when he looked up that Purugama had closed his eyes. The huge flank rose and fell evenly, signaling a short nap for the big cougar. *How like a cat,* thought Conor. Even in the face of mortal danger, a cat will catch a quick nap whenever and wherever it can. Conor smiled at that, stepping away softly so he wouldn't disturb Purugama.

He located the Author of All Worlds in the exact spot where he left him. The man sat cross-legged with one of his laptops rocking back and forth on his thighs. He typed furiously; hurrying to finish one part of the tale. *Perhaps he was writing Nemelissi out of the story,* thought Conor. *Maybe we can simply head home, dismiss the predatory corridor out of hand and return to Redwood State without any knowledge of this latest journey.*

He waited for a lag in the author's work. When he saw the man pause in his typing, Conor stepped forward. "Excuse me, sir," he said with as much respect as he could, "may I talk to you for a moment, please?"

The man looked up from his laptop, perplexed by something. Conor couldn't understand why the author looked at him so strangely. Perhaps he still didn't believe in his existence, or maybe he needed to shake the story from his mind before he could converse with another living being. The puzzled expression remained until Conor stepped forward into the clearing.

"Have you a moment to speak?" he asked.

A smile wiped away the author's skeptical look. He looked at Conor, shaking his head and grinning. "It's uncanny. You look exactly as I imagined, a strong but lanky young man. Capable, but not supremely coordinated and always enjoying life with a ready smile." The author's grin widened; he felt pleased by what he saw. He stared at his creation for quite some time, feeling emotions he could never describe. After a time, he collected himself and offered Conor a seat. "What is it, then?" he asked. "What's on your mind?"

Conor crouched down across from the author. Never taking his eyes from him, the young Champion brushed away a few small sticks and leaves from around his feet. He found the base of a sturdy tree and sat against it. He moved a few dangling leaves away from his face, placing them behind stronger branches. He did this while staring at the author, a man as common as any he had ever seen on earth. Except for the eyes, which expressed an equal amount of pain and love, the author seemed quite ordinary. He looked to be about Conor's height, although heavier, and with the same hair coloring. A few streaks of gray peppered the author's hair, mostly on the sides and in one spot near his forehead.

His eyes tell a million stories, thought Conor. He could see the type of crow's feet that only arrive after years of laughter, but he could also see an incredible accumulation of grief and sorrow. He had seen eyes like those before. Some of his father's friends, and yes, even his uncle Jake had similar markings on his face. A small pang of yearning passed through Conor, a remembrance of a relative who passed away more than ten years ago. The young Champion smiled, swimming in the memory of his uncle until the author broke the silence.

"You said you wanted to talk."

"I have a question I need answered," said Conor.

"Speak then," replied the author. "What is it you wish to know?"

"Who is Trolond Tar?"

The author paused briefly, and then answered. "He is you, Conor."

The young Champion protested. "I'm only one of many people

from the planet earth. I have been given certain powers in order to complete my journeys for the Crossworlds, but beyond that I have no special nickname."

The author looked at Conor, showing a wry smile. "How do you know you were 'given' the powers you describe? Is it because someone told you, perhaps Eha, Maya, or the Lady of the Light? Did it ever occur to you that those powers might have existed within you the entire time, that maybe they lay dormant within you since before you were born?"

Conor shook his head. "I never felt any supernatural powers while growing up. Nothing ever leapt out of me; I couldn't feel anything boiling inside me, nothing like that at all. I never experienced any kind of extra special abilities until I met the Lady of the Light and the Champions at the glade."

"Would you have comprehended the power as a young child? You deny it even now, after many journeys wielding unspeakable forms of magic. You may think the power was a gift of the creators, but I assure you, it has always been within you. You only needed the proper motivation in order to find it."

Conor lifted his eyes from the author's gaze for the first time since he sat down. He looked up into the bright sun, squinting as his line of sight circled around the star. He felt the tickle of a wayward branch grazing the back of his head.

It couldn't be as this man says, he thought. *But then, maybe it could be. After all, the author wrote all of them into existence. He could give any of them a wide assortment of powers just by deciding to do so.* He dropped his eyes and looked back at the man sitting across from him.

"Okay, so I'm Trolond Tar," he said. "That still doesn't tell me anything about who he is or was."

"Trolond Tar is the greatest warrior the Crossworlds system has ever known," said the Author of All Worlds. "He existed long before the Champions. He served the creators even before the time of the protection forces. He was first warrior and consort to the Lady of the Light. No creature could stand against Trolond Tar in battle, that is, until the equinox war."

"What happened during that battle?" asked Conor.

"Trolond Tar encountered a horrible opponent, a vicious beast with powers even greater than his," said the author. "The creators were devastated by the loss, terrified that a creature that dominant existed within the system. It was then that they contacted the first of the protection forces."

"Seefra," said Conor.

"Yes," said the author.

"And who was the creature who killed Trolond Tar during the equinox war?"

The Author of All Worlds gave Conor a grim look. "I'm sure you know the answer to that."

"Nemelissi," said Conor, his face turning pale.

The man sitting across from Conor shook his head in the affirmative. A pained expression contorted his face. "Yes, Nemelissi, a creature I designed with horrifying powers. Its strength seemed to grow every time I introduced it into another part of the Crossworlds. I wish I'd never created it. It represents the worst in all of us."

Conor didn't know what to say. He had to, though, so he just blurted it out before he lost his nerve. "If you hate Nemelissi so much, why don't you just write him out of our lives?"

The man stared at Conor with a bizarre expression. It looked like frightened anticipation. He didn't answer him right away.

"You're the Author of All Worlds," pleaded Conor.

"I'm just a man, Conor, not much different from you."

"That can't be true. You're revered on every world within the system. The creators don't even speak your name aloud unless absolutely necessary. You have dominion over everything in the Crossworlds. Please, open the tale of our lives and make the changes."

"I can't," said the author. "I tried, but something has gone terribly wrong."

"What do you mean?" asked Conor.

The author closed his laptop, listening for the soft click that clasped the two sides together. "That's what I've been trying to do for the last half hour. I wrote an entire chapter, eliminating Nemelissi completely."

"That's great," said Conor. "That's what we want, isn't it?"

"Yes," replied the author. "But there's a problem."

"What?" asked Conor.

The author picked up both of his laptops, wiping a little dirt from the bottom of one of them. "I never wrote anything about you and I having this conversation. It shouldn't have happened."

Conor stared at the man, mouth wide open. He tried to speak but nothing came out. He had fought monsters and magical demons, conquering all of them for the great cause of the Crossworlds. None of that made any difference now. He didn't know how to fight something as mysterious as this.

"I think we'd better leave this place right now," said the Author of All Worlds.

Conor nodded once, taking the author by the arm. He guided him back to the other side of the oasis, calling out to Purugama as they approached. When they reached the far side of the trees, they found nothing but undisturbed ground. Purugama had vanished. Conor looked around, his heart beating out of his chest. It looked as though the cougar had never been there at all. There wasn't any kind of bodily impression in the sand, and Conor couldn't see one paw print anywhere around where Purugama had been resting.

"We're in trouble," said Conor.

"This is incredible," said the author. "I wonder if anything I write from now on will affect the Crossworlds at all. Is it possible someone else is contributing to the story by some form of magic unknown to us?"

Conor heard the unmistakable sound of a corridor coming alive somewhere out on the cliffs. The activation sequence occurred rapidly, telling him that a strong signal had been used to bring whoever the passenger was to this place. He knew it could be no one other than the assassin.

"Mind of the creators! What next?" he said.

"Nemelissi?" asked the author.

"Without a doubt," answered Conor, hastily. "Look, Purugama can't help us now. Only the creators know where he's gone. I'm going to call forth a corridor that will hopefully take you to a safe place. When you get there, you must continue writing. Don't give up, no matter what happens. Maybe some of what you write won't occur, but maybe some of it will. That's what I'm counting on, anyway."

Conor drew the perimeter of a large, silver corridor directly in front of the two of them. The membrane flashed, liquefying in seconds. The portal silently awaited its passenger, its destination clear in its mind.

"Quickly," urged Conor.

"You're not coming?" the author asked, concerned for his character.

"I understand my destiny now," replied the young Champion. "I have to stay here and try my best to stop Nemelissi."

The author grasped Conor's right arm and looked deeply into his eyes. "Remember, your powers have always been yours to command. That was written in the beginning, so no one can change that now."

Conor had been looking over his shoulder during the author's last comment. After making sure Nemelissi wasn't lurking around, he turned back to the author. "Keep writing no matter what."

"I'm proud of you, Conor," said the Author of All Worlds. "Your uncle would be proud as well." The two of them locked eyes for a moment. The author released Conor's arm, tightened his grip on the two laptops and stepped into the corridor.

CHAPTER THIRTY-ONE

Seventy-thousand miles from earth, the energy stream created by the defenders of earth slammed full-force against the predatory corridor. The portal reacted to the strange beam not by slowing its progress, but by examining the contents of the invading entity. The stream of energy, flattening against the surface of the corridor upon impact, splayed out rapidly across the face of the portal. Like a pail of fresh paint poured onto a sidewalk, the bristling energy streaked outward in all directions. It worked rapidly to cover the surface of the predatory corridor as quickly as it could.

Once it had achieved its first goal, the power in the beam altered its composition. Using the continued input of the seeker's energy stream, the beam pressed against the center of the membrane. By doing this, it slowed its progress significantly, bringing the predatory corridor almost to a complete stop. The beam continued battering the face of the portal with an endless stream of powerful magic.

Instead of reacting impulsively, the corridor analyzed its vulnerability to the invading power source. Allowing the energy beam to bring it to a standstill, it began collating information about the invading power. It realized this process would add precious minutes to its task, but it knew that challenging an intruder without knowing its composition was poor strategy. The corridor rested in space, slightly more than sixty-five thousand miles from its target.

"We've done it," said the elated seeker. "The predatory corridor has halted its advance. The power beam is holding it in place."

Janine's excitement overtook her sense of decorum. She hugged Mr. Hikkins around the neck, whispering her thanks for his brilliant work. Both she and the seeker kept a close eye on the creators and Champions during the initial impact with the killer corridor. Even with the excitement of the moment, neither of them ignored their benefactors for too long. They both returned their eyes to the recipients in the formation.

Everyone along the line seemed to be holding up well. The Lady of the Light, standing at the focal point, continued to distribute the magical energy flow evenly to the three creators in front of her. The first councilor allowed the intense rush of energy to flow evenly through his body, giving the Lord of All Life everything he could handle and more. Mr. Hikkins had been quite concerned about the supreme councilor in the beginning. No one, not even one of the creators emeritus, could stand that much of a barrage for too long without buckling. Up to this point, however, his Lord had performed admirably, taking the stream from all those behind him and delivering it forward in a concentrated ray of immense power.

The Champions had all fallen into a trance-like state, much like their leader, Maya. Only the fur on their immense bodies moved regularly, undulating in random directions as the energy flowed around and through them. The only sign of life came from Eha, who, while standing like a sleeping statue, giggled every now and then as the awesome power stream flowed over his body.

The seeker examined his instruments again. Everything checked out, all numbers were perfectly in line. He asked Janine about the cell conversion sequence one last time. He felt ready to implement the next phase of their plans.

CHAPTER THIRTY-TWO

Fighter jets roared to life at military bases all along the west coast of the United States. Edwards, Vandenberg, Travis and Beale Air Force Bases had scrambled jets the instant the predatory corridor appeared in the sky. Soon after an unknown energy source originating from earth had impacted the gigantic bloody curtain, the jets soared into the skies above central and northern California. Their orders were to observe and report back to base the nature of their sightings. Under no circumstances were they to engage the anomalies.

There was no official word from Washington regarding the strange light show in the skies above the continent of North America. The president appeared on all major networks, stating he could neither confirm nor deny the existence of an anomaly billions of people were seeing with their own eyes. His speeches were a useless gesture, delivered poorly by a bumbling fool reading a teleprompter instead of talking to people from the heart.

News stations all over the world had streaming video of the incident. They kept it on their screens constantly, fearing that a moment without the images might lose them a few indispensable viewers and the advertising dollars that came with them.

Thousands of reporters lined the coastlines of California, Oregon and Washington. Freshly dressed with hair perfectly cemented to their skulls, the talking heads of the media tried their best to tell the story with an intriguing angle. Nothing they could say, however, changed the obvious fact that the earth lay in the path of a devastating force. Advancing at a steady pace, nothing in mankind's arsenal of weapons would be able to stop it. The reporters tried their best to come up with flashy bylines for their stories. *"Finally, the answer to what's beyond the wall in space" …. "Almighty God is preparing to wipe the earth clean" …. "Immortality or oblivion, you decide!"* Even as they witnessed the apparent end of humanity, the news stations tried to one-up each other.

Even after the president's statement, many cities fell into a state of anarchy. Those situated on the western hemisphere fared the worst. The populations in those areas saw the predatory corridor expand right in front of their eyes.

It didn't really matter to them that another power source had launched an attack against the giant portal. All they saw was something out in space big enough to swallow the earth whole, and it drove them into a passionate fit of unbridled madness. They believed they had only hours to live, so they reacted as any society tumbling into a state of anomie would. Riots broke out everywhere. People who once abided by the norms of everyday society suddenly relished the experience of doing anything they wished. The institutions of law and order soon evaporated, leaving cities and towns the world over in total chaos. Those who could pack their belongings and their families in a car or truck headed for the mountains. Others congregated in local places of worship, praying to their deities for deliverance from the terrible force hell bent on consuming them. Many people wandered the streets trying to sell the precious items they owned, as if money might stave off the oncoming catastrophe.

The lead squadron from Vandenberg Air Force base topped out at forty-five thousand feet. They looked utterly insignificant racing alongside the energy beam coming from the forests of Redwood County. They held their course perfectly, zooming toward the predatory corridor at over nine hundred miles an hour. When they reached maximum altitude, flight leader Sampey pulled his hornet into a six-G turn, banking away from the energy beam. The five hornets in the formation followed his lead, flying directly across the face of the killer portal.

"It looks like soup," Sampey said into his headset. "Blood-red, thick soup. Or like spaghetti sauce."

"Say again, squadron leader," said the general stationed back at Vandenberg. "Repeat and describe more effectively."

"The face of the anomaly looks to be alive, sir," said Sampey. "I can see the other beam's plasma all over the surface of the curtain, or whatever it is, but it seems very light compared to the red surface. As far as I can tell, the borders of the anomaly are rigid. Inside the perimeter, however, the material is pliable, almost liquid."

"Understood," said the general. "Return to energy stream and head back. We need positive confirmation of where that other beam is originating. Do you copy, squadron leader?"

Sampey stared wide-eyed at the immense predatory corridor. If he tried very hard, he could locate its edge. Mostly, though, the membrane seemed to take up his entire field of vision. He exhaled slowly, wondering how they would ever do battle with something like this. "Roger that, sir," he said, "turning now."

"Falcon formation," ordered Sampey. "Follow my lead back to the source of the energy beam. We'll go to max speed as soon as all birds fall in line. The first to target the coordinates of that beam's origin gets a case of Boddingtons."

The falcons streaked toward earth at Mach one point six five. One of the pilots remarked to the others how strange it felt to be flying that fast next to a beam of energy that obviously was traveling five times that speed in the opposite direction. It seemed almost surreal. One pilot swore she could see something within the stream of energy flowing beside her jet. Staring at it for quite some time, she finally shook herself back to reality. She checked her instruments, making sure her ride performed at maximum efficiency. North America lay directly ahead, the beam of energy emerging from somewhere within that land mass.

After giving directions to his team, flight leader Sampey took his falcon on a wide circuit across northern California. It was easy enough to see the source of the energy stream. It blasted forth from a redwood forest some three or four miles inland from the coast. *Old-growth for sure,* thought Sampey, looking at the thick groves of majestic redwoods lining the valley of the Hoopa Indian reservation.

"Flight leader to base," he called after closing his mask again. "Cannot say for sure, but appears beam originated from within Hoopa Indian lands, roughly seventy miles south of Oregon border in northern California."

"Roger that, flight leader," replied the general in charge of operations. "Can you see the source of the beam, or the type of machinery they're using to generate that kind of power?"

Sampey veered left and reversed course. Sweeping down through the valley again, the flight leader squinted as they passed close by the beam. "Sorry sir, we must be moving too fast. All I can detect is a small cluster of people, but no machinery that I can see.

They must have it buried underground or maybe they have it hidden in the trees somehow. Recommend sending helicopters for a closer look. Flight leader out."

"Copy that. Bring your squadron home, colonel."

The general immediately ordered two teams of apache helicopters to the area inside the Hoopa reservation. "Damn, this could get dicey." He didn't relish the idea of violating sovereignty, but in this case it couldn't be avoided. He knew the tribal chairman personally. He'd put a call in to him in just a few minutes, but for now he needed to coordinate his strategy. He looked out the window of base headquarters, seeing nothing in the sky but a massive red curtain taking up the entire horizon. He kept his mind focused on his duty, but what he really wanted was to drive straight home and gather his family together around him.

CHAPTER THIRTY-THREE

"Commencing alterations now," said Mr. Hikkins as he depressed a slide located on the right side of his workstation. The energy stream flowing into Maya changed colors almost immediately. Instead of a bluish flow the color of the ocean at midday, a dark, murky fluid began pouring into the Lord of the Champions. Maya absorbed the new power without flinching. He kept the pathway open, adding his magical energies to the mixture and pushing it forward. The rest of the Champions did the same, finally throwing the blackish beam at the Lady of the Light. She also accepted the new formula without incident, feeding it forward to the other creators in the triangle. It rushed through the entire group, finally surging around the Lord of All Life and out into the sky. The color change looked remarkable. What was once a powder blue column had now become a perfectly black cord of extreme chemical emissions. The new color zoomed along the beam, overtaking the bluish hue at an astonishing pace. When it finally impacted the predatory corridor, the chemical reaction created a light show the earth would remember for a thousand centuries.

CHAPTER THIRTY-FOUR

"What do you mean the portal cannot move?" bellowed Shordano. First, he thought, *Nemelissi had not dealt with the Author of All Worlds, and now the destruction of earth has been delayed?* "What is the nature of the obstruction, Jek?"

"Apparently the seeker has rallied the creators and Champions," said the third arc. "They have somehow combined their magical capabilities, thereby creating a synchronous being. The seeker and someone whom I cannot identify have managed to construct a beam of considerable power. It has impacted the predatory corridor and is now holding it in place, some sixty thousand miles from earth's outer atmosphere. I cannot tell exactly, but it appears they have launched another attack through the stream of magical energy. I will need time to determine the nature of their latest counter-offensive."

"Time?" bellowed the leader of the inner element. "We have no time. Earth is the key! If we destroy the home of Trolond Tar we can recall the destroyer. The Author of All Worlds and everything he designed will remain alive and we will have our victory."

"Are you so sure you can order the assassin back to its cell?" asked Jek. "If you recall, we have no army of shadow warriors to sacrifice. Nemelissi will exterminate us as easily as a pack of pigeons standing by a seawall."

"It will do as it is told," said Shordano. "Besides, we may not have to use our own resources against it. Trolond Tar will sacrifice himself to save his precious creator. Perhaps this time the outcome will be different."

"Perhaps," agreed Jek. "However, I think your celebration might prove premature. No one even knows the true abilities of the assassin. It has never been defeated in combat, and for all we know, it's knowledge of weaponry and magic has increased a thousand-fold."

"Then they will both be destroyed," mused Shordano. "Wouldn't that be a delicious outcome?" The supreme leader of the inner element strolled away from Jek's workstation, casually moving up to the window of the council chamber. He looked out upon their wasted lands, the decimated home he had known for millennia.

Because of the Champions, and the creators who sent them, his home had been obliterated. The Champions, the creators, all of them together on a world called earth, using their combined powers to thwart the greatest weapon ever designed in the Crossworlds. Together, all of them, earth. A thought blasted through Shordano's mind. His eyes went wide as he understood his good fortune. He turned from the window and walked back over to stand behind Jek. The credit for the demise of their enemies would be his and his alone.

"Increase corridor acceleration to maximum," he ordered.

Jek's fingers stopped moving, resting over the last keys. He didn't know exactly how to respond to Shordano's command. He had suspected his superior's insanity when he commanded Wolbus to release the assassin. Now he had no doubt whatsoever. His leader, a being he had served faithfully for longer than he could remember, had lost his mind. He would risk everything for victory, even their world. If Nemelissi killed the Author of All Worlds, they were finished. If they didn't perish immediately, the assassin would come back and make them beg to die.

Now Shordano wanted to add another mode of extinction into the mix. The predatory corridors' organic composition kept them stable to a certain degree. Passing a certain energy level presented all kinds of hazardous outcomes, the worst of which lay in the possibility that the portal will no longer be under their control. Once energized to maximum power output, the predatory corridor became an entity unto itself. It would remember its primary duty, but unseen developments could always arise. Jek did not like the idea of relinquishing control of the portal.

"I advise against that," the third arc cautioned. "You aided in the design of these monstrosities. You know better than anyone the danger of infusing that much energy."

The supreme leader exploded, pushing Jek onto the floor with a brusque wave of his hand. "Must I explain everything? I said bring the corridor to full power!" Shordano held his left hand over the screen, sensing in his mind the changes he desired. The numbers changed, a few lights flashed here and there, and seconds later a new configuration rose up from the depths of the machine's memory.

Jek placed his hands on the floor of the chamber, pressing his body up into a standing position. He leaned forward, analyzing the changes on the screen. Once he comprehended the full meaning of Shordano's efforts, he gasped while placing a hand against the console. "Fool," he hissed. "You have doomed us all!"

"I may have, at that," said Shordano. "Someone has to be brave enough to take the chance. The predatory corridor will destroy earth. We will have Nemelissi back under our control and the creators and Champions will be no more. Then, Jek, you will understand why you served me for so many years. We will build another paradise, one that will stand forever without opposition."

"You're mad," said Jek. "Don't you realize what you've done? The corridor will never respond to another of our commands. If it malfunctions we will be powerless to stop it. There are a billion potential outcomes, and we've never released a portal with this much energy. We have no idea what might happen."

Shordano's eyes stared straight through his subordinate. "Then make certain the corridor retains its purity, Jek. I will not tolerate failure. If the creators survive and our corridors fail, I will personally destroy both you and Wolbus before we meet our collective fate. See to your duties, and report to me through the mind link on the hour."

CHAPTER THIRTY-FIVE

The sky smoldered on the horizon as the sun fell from the heavens. The equinox would occur in less than an hour. On a day where light and darkness shared equal time, the earth's immense star would shine brightly along the equator, giving the planet a surreal atmospheric veneer.

Architecture had been designed to capture the mind-numbing qualities of the equinox. Faith-based organizations thrived on the meanings of its significance. Thousands gathered by the western oceans of the world each year, collapsing into collective trances during the brief interlude between the solstices. It was said that the equinox contained magical powers beyond comprehension. No one within the Crossworlds system had ever been able to extract even a fraction of the energy in the mystical occurrence. The equinox came and went so quickly, not even the creators had ever successfully breached its secrets.

They were not the only party interested in its powers; it had been an ongoing obsession with Seefra. He felt if the code of the equinox could be cracked, the Circle of Evil could use the overwhelming power to confront and defeat the creators. That was precisely why the Lady of the Shadows demanded the equinox war be held on a specific fall day so many centuries ago. She believed in Seefra's plan. She fought feverishly during the preliminary skirmishes in order to give her servant the time to penetrate the enclave of the equinox.

Unfortunately for her, it had never happened. The master of darkness, in all his great wizardry, could not command the natural phenomenon to release its secrets. The forces of the Circle of Evil had ultimately retreated, as the sunlight had retreated before them, leaving nothing behind but a cold, dark battlefield.

Back at the oasis, Conor stood by the silver corridor until nothing remained. He gave a silent plea to the creators for the author's safe journey. Afterwards, he lifted his eyes to the sky, inhaling the bizarre scent suddenly wafting through his small sanctuary. It smelled of jasmine, but the soft wind brushing by his cheek spoke otherwise. The scent seemed entirely foreign to him, different, but enjoyable all the same. He inhaled deeply through his nostrils, consuming the wonderful aroma again and again.

Suddenly, a completely different odor entered his nostrils. Tears formed in the outer regions of Conor's eyes. His face contorted as he slapped his hand over his nose and mouth. Neither action made any difference, for the smell entering the oasis from the cliffs penetrated any defense he could raise. It was without a doubt the most putrid, offensive stench Conor had ever encountered.

He gagged and fell to his knees, retching streams of vomit as his insides spilled their contents to the ground. The gruesome odor made it almost impossible to breathe.

He collected himself, breathing shallowly through his mouth for a few minutes. He stood, slowly straightening his muscles. After a bit he finally found himself able to inhale without trembling. He closed his eyes, keeping his breathing short and controlled. By doing so he adapted his senses to the hideous smell. At long last, he felt he might not only survive, but he may even be able to fight under such deplorable sensory circumstances.

A spine-tingling shriek broke the silence in the oasis. Conor felt the tiny hairs on the back of his neck stand up straight. Again, and then again the assassin screamed its challenge for Trolond Tar. If the reeking odor wasn't bad enough, Nemelissi's otherworldly bellowing tripled Conor's sense of dread. It seemed to understand every intricacy of battle.

Believe in your ability to win. Make your opponent believe in his inability to win. Be patient with your physical attack. Assault your opponent's spirit first, rendering him emotionally incapable of fighting. After every pre-fight strategy has been employed, pounce upon your enemy with savage intensity, leaving no possibility for defense or counter attack.

Conor braced himself against any of these potential strategies. He walked around the trees, away from the oasis just as the sun began touching the horizon. He found the small river, the one cut into the surface of the cliff. He walked alongside the liquid channel, noticing that the stream ended at the precise midpoint of the sun's position in the sky. The cliffs, split in two by the strange canal, accepted the sun into their midst almost as an altar preparing for some bizarre rite of passage.

As he walked toward the cliff edge, Conor watched the gigantic sun setting against the astounding background. He felt overwhelmed by the beauty of the equinox. Even though he saw the outline of the assassin in the distance, he felt no fear. The repulsive stench seemed a thing of the past. His stride remained strong and fluid. He felt nothing but peace and adoration for himself, his world, and the Crossworlds. His journeys of the past eight years replayed themselves in his mind, and he realized who he really was, why Purugama had come to him when he was a boy, and why he had been selected to serve as a Crossworlds Champion. He felt as though the equinox had chosen him to be here at this very moment. He was at one with the worlds, the sun and the immense energies flowing all around him.

As the sun's pattern of descent reached the midpoint of the cliffs, it ceased moving altogether. Conor's universe came to a sudden stop. Even Nemelissi looked almost like a caricature of itself. It stared at Conor, but not even a scaly finger moved toward him. It was difficult for Conor to understand. The assassin did not look to be trapped by any force, but then again, it wasn't making any threatening sounds or moves against him.

As quickly as he noticed this, his mind began drifting away from Nemelissi. It had not been a conscious decision on his part, but Conor felt his attention drifting toward the sun, which lay directly ahead. The star consumed the entire horizon, its stunning brightness reaching out to Conor. It wanted to take him into its bosom, caress him gently, like a long lost child.

The young Champion stared directly into the fiery sphere, the life giver that sustained innumerable worlds within the Crossworlds system. His retinas should have fizzled away in seconds, but instead Conor found he could look directly into the center of the sun without injury.

As he stared at the source of limitless energy, something wonderful and strange began to occur. Conor's peripheral vision opened wide. He began seeing the equinox in its entirety. The sun balanced itself against the cliff walls. The river, the tiny stream of life-giving elements, drifted calmly toward the sun, dribbling over the side of the cliff in what seemed like a completely harmless act.

The tiny brook could have been a raging torrent for all it mattered, because size no longer seemed important. The elements of life were all that mattered during the equinox. The sun gave heat and light, the land, essential minerals and stability. Water was the elixir of all life, combining all other elements together into an enduring organism that lived according to the mystical properties of the universe.

The sun enveloped Conor. The soothing warmth of the star washed over its disciple, leaving the young Champion in a state of complete hypnosis. He breathed slowly, evenly, suddenly discovering the final element that gave existence to every living being.

Life needed air to live. In one form or another, everything needed the molecules of oxygen – air, water, land, heat and light. Conor heard his mind repeating the elements over and over.

His body had become one with the sun. Only his mind continued to function, if only on a basic level. Conor had never felt so relaxed and aware in his life. At that moment the secret of the equinox became known to him.

The sun split into two equal portions, leaving a small opening between the upper and lower halves. The river, previously falling to the bottom of the cliffs, streamed straight outward toward the blazing star. Chunks of land at the top of the cliff broke away, flying directly at the void in the sun. The air all around Conor rushed forward as well. As they sped toward the giant star in the sky, the elements converged into a single entity. Conor wanted to reach out and participate in the event, but all he could do was stand and watch in wonder.

Suddenly, the inward flow of the elements ceased. The water dropped to the floor of the cliffs again. The air settled. The lands became calm. The sun repaired itself, leaving only a tiny cavity in its very center.

Conor watched the blazing orb intently. Although just a spectator, he knew something would occur within moments. He blinked his eyes once, a momentary flash of inattention. When his eyes focused again, he saw a beam of power streaking toward him from the center of the sun. He squirmed slightly, a natural reaction upon seeing the elements of life racing toward him.

The beam hit him square in the solar plexus, but did no harm. At a speed too rapid to calculate, the energy of the elements poured into Conor's soul at the precise moment of the equinox. To Conor, the power insertion seemed to last for hours. In reality, the beam burst into his spirit for less than a second. It felt like a thousand fingers caressing every muscle in his body.

He collapsed into the mystical embrace, allowing it total freedom to do whatever it wished. The warmth of the sun swarmed over his skull, sweeping into his eyes and ears, even deep into his throat.

When it contacted his brain, Conor blacked out. Before he comprehended his unconsciousness state, he awoke again. Still, all he sensed was the tremendous intensity of the sun. It washed over and through him, inserting an unfathomable power into his body. From the depths of his mind, Conor became aware that the energy of the equinox would be his to command.

When the infusion ended, the sun sealed itself, beginning its slow descent once again. The air, water and land all returned to a sense of normalcy. The scene became as it always had been, the tail end of a yearly equinox on a planet deep within the Crossworlds system.

Conor gathered himself. He did not fall, but instead he

stretched, placing his hands along the joints of his body. He looked around the expansive cliffs for a sign that might have appeared during the bizarre exchange with the elements. Seeing nothing out of the ordinary, he looked back toward the edge of the cliffs. He saw the river, trickling toward the overhang, splitting the giant rock formation into two equal halves.

With a bolt of shocking recognition, he saw Nemelissi squatting by the edge of the precipice, staring down at the depths of the canyon. Somehow, Conor had been propelled forward some distance during his brief interlude with the equinox. He now stood barely fifty feet or so from the assassin. He looked at the creature, alarmed by its appearance. Conor had never seen anything so hideous or intimidating in his life.

Nemelissi jerked its huge head around, its spindly hair following the rotation of its skull. Instead of surging forward in a mindless attack, it stared at Conor silently.

The assassin uttered its first words in over ten thousand years. The greeting rasped forth from a throat blistered by countless attacks with fire, lava, and poisonous gas. Even with the recent mystical transformation, it pierced Conor's soul like an icicle falling from the roof of a frozen cavern.

"We meet again, Trolond Tar."

CHAPTER THIRTY-SIX

"What is it?" asked Janine, leaning forward to scan the surface of the workstation. "Why isn't the transformation occurring? The formula has to work!"

"Calm yourself, my dear," said Mr. Hikkins. "The empirical pursuit is often fraught with obstacles. Apparently the inner element has decided to fight against our defenses with stronger magic than I had anticipated. I knew they would eventually bring everything they had to bear. It was only a matter of time. My failure was not accepting the gravity of their circumstances. Our task now is to understand their new strategy and prepare our response accordingly."

"But the creators, the Champions," she said, pointing frantically. Look at them!"

"I am aware of their condition," answered the seeker. "Please refrain from any further excitable gestures. They need our help, Janine. We are the only ones who can save them. Emotional outbursts will do nothing to better their situation. Have I made myself clear?"

Janine nodded nervously. Stepping back a pace, she gave Mr. Hikkins the room he needed.

What she saw happening in the forest made her sick with fright. The creators, even the Lord of All Life, twitched wildly at random intervals. It appeared as though energy from the predatory corridor was forcing its way back through the stream and into the prism. She watched the bizarre exchange while a dozen terrifying scenarios danced through her brain. *What if they were all killed by the battling energy streams? What if the predatory corridor sucked them into its beam, drawing them into the bloody membrane?*

A deafening sound shook Janine from her train of thought. Ducking down out of habit, she recognized the booming roar of fighter jets breaking the sound barrier. She instinctively looked up into the sky, even though she knew the jets would be long gone by the time her eyes saw the clouds. She kept her neck bent, however, listening for the telltale sounds of a reverse flight pattern. The supersonic jets faded, turned and roared back in her direction. This time no thunderclap followed behind them.

They must be trying to pinpoint our position, she thought. *Mr. Hikkins has to know about this.* If the air force had become interested enough to send fighters, then other forms of intrusion wouldn't be too far behind. She expected ground forces within an hour. That would not bode well for what they were trying to accomplish.

She looked back at the disturbing sight. There had been no improvement. The creators, and periodically, the Champions, shook violently from time to time, as if some negative power source had entered their bodies. Looking at them scared the life out of her. She could see everyone in the line fighting to keep their posture. Even the Lady of the Light, the most powerful being Janine had ever met, looked painfully uncomfortable. The Lady fought bravely against the reverse injection. Janine watched her, willing her own strength to her. Then she turned to look back at Mr. Hikkins.

Something caught her peripheral vision as she swept her eyes across the grounds. She'd been so consumed by the group, she never noticed the one recipient unaffected by the new development.

"Mind of the creators!" she gasped.

The Lord of the Champions stood firmly in place without trembling at all. While the other Champions and creators suffered mightily, Maya seemed completely at one with the energy stream. With his hooded head held high and his eyes tightly shut, Maya sat calmly, totally unfazed by whatever disturbed the others. Although still a part in the union with every other recipient, Maya had disconnected himself from the entire assembly. Somehow he had managed to escape the carnage attacking his brothers and the creators.

Maya had mentally elevated to a different plane entirely. Walking on a dozen worlds at once, the great leader of the Crossworlds Champions looked at the gigantic trees shadowing the infinite trails he traveled. He spoke softly to a hundred different species of flora, as if enjoying a casual conversation with old friends.

They *were* his friends, for the great variety of trees on all worlds enjoyed a wonderful unity. They all lived together as one family, the *fingers of the forest*. Maya spoke respectfully to every tree he encountered, sometimes even stopping for a while when one held his interest with an enticing topic. During these times he sat comfortably by the side of the pathway, reminiscing with an old friend.

Maya understood so much about the Crossworlds that others took for granted. While most creatures and beings believed that trees and other forms of non-corporeal life were indeed alive, that appeared to be the sum of their appreciation. Some grew to empathize with the great forests of their worlds, even fighting to save them from those who would destroy them for a moment's profit. Others realized the physical value of trees, knowing for a fact that without them, the breath of life would disappear from their planet. In the simplest form, some people knew the value of a good tree, the shade it provides, the whistling of its leaves when a strong breeze passes through a grove, or the branches it provides for a swing or a hammock, or even just for climbing.

Maya's comprehension went much further than that. He spoke to the trees, maybe not aloud, but the exchange was just as real, just as warm. After many centuries of deep communion with the trees of many worlds, Maya realized that trees were not, in fact, separate beings at all. All trees shared the same soil, the same molecules, and, in effect, the same root system with all other trees. In a world ten times the size of earth, every tree on the planet communed with one another. Like an enormous family, all trees were spiritually connected.

When a new sapling pushed out of the ground, the trees of the world rejoiced. When an ancient tree finally perished, tumbling to the ground like a fallen sibling, the remaining trees celebrated instead of mourning their loss. To the trees of the world, the residue of one of their own would someday rise again. Their lives were everlasting; they constantly rejuvenated themselves as new members of their immortal family.

And so, on a stellar plane even the creators couldn't fathom, Maya traveled to countless worlds. He talked to the trees residing in all these places, merely conversing about their health, their family and well-being. He told the trees stories about the great Champion, Conor Jameson, who had returned as Trolond Tar after centuries to help the creators vanquish their enemies. He gave accounts of all the Champions, telling the trees about the demise of Ajur, the bravest and most beloved of all the big cats. The trees listened quietly, for they enjoyed a well spoken tale.

After Maya had finished his host of stories, the trees reciprocated, sharing information with Maya. The trees contributed so much history about their worlds that it became difficult for Maya to grasp everything. It pained the Lord of the Champions deeply when they told him of the horrible damage done during the uprising, when beings of all sorts decided the trees had only one use. Ripped from the ground or cleaved at the trunk by the millions, trees of every world began believing their time was at hand. So many of them disappeared. The link had even been broken for a time, that is, until the beings that began the butchery realized the folly of their actions. With their help, the trees repopulated, covering the worlds with fresh air, shade and their mystical connection to nature.

Maya sat quietly in much the same posture he held back on earth, listening to the trees with eyes closed, showing his contentment with a soft rolling purr. After the trees finished speaking to him, he thanked them for their kindness. He offered his counsel and assistance whenever they might find a need for his services. On every world he presently occupied, the great leader of the Champions bowed deeply before fading from view.

He returned to his own body, feeling the inconsistency in the power flow at once. Opening his eyes, he watched his brothers, his Lady and the rest of the creators vibrating under the attack from the predatory corridor. He did nothing to save them or alter the situation in any way. He merely closed his eyes again.

If anyone in the forest could have possibly understood the big cat's mind, they would have realized his intent. As it was, Janine and Mr. Hikkins could only watch Maya as he seemed to fall into another trance. Janine wondered after him, worrying all the while about everyone else in the line.

The seeker seemed worried as well. He knew Maya better than most of the creators. If the big cat found it easy to rest during such a trying time, there must be a reason for his complacency. Still, he had no idea how long the others could hold out.

He had withheld one small item from Janine after the predatory corridor went on the offensive. The portal had begun closing the distance between itself and earth again. The movement was slow but steady. If the corridor continued to advance at this speed, it would hit the exosphere in less than six hours. He wondered about the stamina of the creators. Not only were they infused with all the power he could give them, they were also repelling the magnified force of the killer portal.

Although doubt entered his mind at times, he did his best to maintain a logical and rational outlook. He knew there was nothing else to do. The model had been constructed and put into place, and the creators had done extremely well to this point. He understood the danger should one of the recipients in the line falter. If just one of them fell away of the configuration, the rest would overload in a matter of minutes. Even the Lord of All Life, with the immense power reserves he held, could never stand alone while channeling that much raw power.

He didn't give a passing thought to the Champions. Eha was the slightest of them, and the seeker knew the cheetah would lose the skin off his back before he allowed any harm to come to the Lady of the Light. All the Champions adored her. That fact, coupled with their massive physiques, gave them the edge over the creators. Eha showed a few signs of distress, but nothing worth a moment's concern. Surmitang's fur bristled repeatedly, but his intense pride would never allow him to show the slightest discomfort at all. Therion sat abreast of the great tiger, looking like a brick wall. At better than five thousand pounds, it would take a great deal more than what the inner element was dishing out to cause the giant lion any irritation at all.

He glanced at Maya. The seeker felt certain he was the key, but he couldn't imagine in what way. *Maya must be up to something,* he thought. He believed the Lord of the Champions would reveal his strategy very soon. He watched Maya drift in and out of his self-induced bliss. He stared at him as long as he dared. Every other second he devoted to his screen. With the new configuration of the predatory corridor, he had to constantly monitor the power flow going out and coming in toward earth.

His fingers flew over the keyboard most of the time. Sometimes the energy stream became dormant. Only then could he rest and determine new strategies. During these times he consulted with Janine, querying her about the dynamics of her conversion formula. As he gleaned new information from her he adjusted the energy stream slightly. When the new formula failed to produce the desired results, he reversed his input. When a positive outcome did occur, he made tiny modifications, giving the creators and Champions every edge possible in their battle against the killer portal.

The seeker allowed his thoughts to drift to Conor and Purugama. In his estimation, it had been cruel to send them out against Nemelissi. Of course they had no choice; the Author of All Worlds had to be saved. But surely they could have found another method for his retrieval. He believed Conor and the cougar would find him, they may even send him to a safe place. Nemelissi would destroy them both, however, and eventually find the author, no matter where they tried to hide him.

Nemelissi was a relentless, vicious killer. Nothing had ever stood in its path and survived, and the seeker had no faith that any future outcome might be different. He couldn't focus on that, however. He had duties to fulfill. If it came to pass, he only hoped the corridor would wipe the earth clean before Nemelissi found everyone gathered here. He did not wish to see the carnage that would ensue once the assassin recognized who lay before him in this forest.

TROLOND TAR

CHAPTER THIRTY-SEVEN

It called him by his name!

Conor looked at the hideous creature squatting in front of him. Powerful and menacing, the sight of Nemelissi validated every childhood fear he'd ever had. The pungent odor wafted up from expansive pores opening and closing all over its skin. Sizzling lava bubbled up from within, surfacing momentarily before settling back into an ever-widening hole.

The face of the creature could never be described, hideously ugly and distorted, but at the same time cool and intelligent. Sadism was the only other descriptive element Conor could see in Nemelissi's face. This destroyer was all they had described, a horrible killing machine with a lust for creative devastation.

It called me to battle, using my name!

The creators must have told the truth about his link to the warrior Trolond Tar. Nemelissi had just verified it. Conor stared at the horrible creature, repeating his name silently, over and over again. Trolond Tar, consort to the Lady of the Light. That must be why the creators named him first protector after the battle in the shadow world. It all fit into place now – meeting Purugama, traveling with Maya, the five keys, the cell of shadows and Seefra's chambers. Everything about his journeys with the Champions had led him up to this point. After Nemelissi destroyed Trolond Tar two hundred centuries ago it had changed everything, setting a chain of events in motion that one day far in the future would pit the two warriors against each other again.

Conor felt a peculiar transformation taking place. The power of the equinox became as familiar to him as any other human function. The essence of who he was washed over him, deeply convincing him of his true identity, who he always had been. He blinked his eyes once, transforming into the silver warrior again, the first warrior of the Crossworlds and consort to his Lady. He knew the destroyer squatting in front of him would slaughter her and the rest of her kind without hesitation. It would slice the other Champions to ribbons, leaving nothing but mangled bodies and shattered bones.

Dreams of a good and nurturing system where beings of all kinds could live peacefully, loving everything they encountered, would disappear forever. He did understand. He knew that Trolond Tar fought not only for the creators, but for all beings yearning for the right to be free, to explore and to better themselves. The knowledge lit a fire inside him, stoking the power of the equinox, readying it for battle. Conor raised his right arm, fist clenched, pointing it directly at Nemelissi's forehead. The energy of the sun surged forward from his chest, through his shoulder, firing down his arm like a bolt of lightning. Sighting down his arm, he saw Nemelissi's face twisted into a bizarre smile.

Conor squeezed his fist, giving the power a clean departure point. He looked beyond his fingers one last time, focusing everything on the assassin. He released the energy, using every bit of strength he had to hold his arm in place. A bolt of white-hot power cut into the destroyer at point blank range, blasting right through a spot between its eyes.

The edge of the cliff where Nemelissi sat disintegrated, giving way to the energy cleanly. The bolt traveled to the floor of the cliffs instantly, cutting a huge swath into the ground. Rocks and debris flew everywhere as the fantastic power traced a line in the rocky landscape.

Conor issued a mental command and the energy flow terminated. He felt no ill effects from the transfer of power, but that didn't salve the fear from what he saw at the edge of the cliff. Nemelissi squatted there, still wearing the crooked smile. It sat there, mocking him. But upon closer inspection, Conor realized it really wasn't *there*. He understood now, that it had all been a ruse, fooling him into a false sense of security.

Nemelissi was stalking him from somewhere in the vicinity, and he had no idea where. That's why the attack hadn't come right away, because the assassin had been hiding, watching him, learning. It had placed an image of itself here on the cliff edge, an image that would act and move exactly like the original, but wouldn't be harmed by any magic or cosmic power.

Conor stepped to the edge of the cliff. He peered down, following the water as it fell toward the ground. He looked along the base of the cliff. He couldn't see Nemelissi anywhere. He heard a sound behind him. He jumped, turned and found nothing. Hearing another sound in one of the oases close by, he spun around again. As with the first disturbance, he saw nothing.

He recognized the destroyer's tactic; it wanted to torture him mentally so the battle would be that much easier. Trolond Tar wouldn't allow that kind of tactic to succeed, and that knowledge gave him a fleeting moment of hope. It wanted to break his nerve before showing itself. Perhaps that might be a sign of fear, or at least respect.

It must be supremely intelligent. Along with that, seeing the unstoppable power of the equinox commanded so easily might give even the most feared creature in the Crossworlds pause to reflect.

Conor looked all around the cliff area. His senses blazed with fiery intensity. He looked, listened and smelled everything he could. He had no idea where the assassin would come from, so he allowed his mind to see things in a different way. He didn't try to think logically about Nemelissi's strategy at all. He tried his best to release his mind and let the battle occur as it would.

The stench returned, mildly at first, and then with a vengeance. Conor panicked for a moment before regaining his discipline. He couldn't see Nemelissi anywhere, but he knew the assassin must be close. Closing his eyes, he used his sense of smell to locate it. Moving into of one the larger oases, he placed his back against a tree. He looked everywhere in front of him.

Nothing moved at all. The putrid smell, however, fell around his shoulders like a heavy blanket. His eyes watered. He slapped his hand over his nose, breathing shallowly through his mouth. Closing his eyes again, he listened for any noises out of the ordinary. He recognized a handful of familiar sounds – leaves slapping against each other in the wind, the trickle of the tiny stream, and the small feet of a nocturnal animal skittering across the sandy boulder. He tried as hard as he could to locate Nemelissi, but the assassin had eluded him completely.

As slowly and quietly as it could, the tree Conor had braced himself against came to life behind him. Branches became powerful arms. A few feet above the young Champion's head, a huge burl transformed itself into Nemelissi's head. The assassin's face peered through the wooden mask, the eyes hungrily looking down at its opponent. The thick base of the tree separated into two muscular legs.

Nemelissi emerged from its camouflage, claws flared and teeth extended. The deadly needles of its hair pointed straight down at Conor, bubbling with a fresh dose of poison. If injected into its enemy, the venom would ravage his body for four to five weeks. Nemelissi would enjoy watching him suffer before finishing him for good.

The strategy had been Nemelissi's first mistake. The hair follicles emitted a tiny expulsion of wind as the projectiles shot forward. If it had grabbed Conor with both hands and feet, it might have held him long enough for the needles to find their target.

When Conor heard that tiny whisper, he leapt away from Nemelissi so quickly the destroyer almost became the recipient of his own attack. Conor jumped high into the air and across the oasis, clinging to the upper trunk of a tree like a jaguar in its natural homeland. Nemelissi reacted instinctively, spreading its legs so the needles would miss his feet. At the same time, it looked up at Conor, snarling viciously. Throwing both arms forward simultaneously, it unleashed a set of bizarre electrical explosions toward its enemy. The entire oasis disintegrated – trees vaporized into confetti, bushes vanished and even the large boulders were reduced to random piles of smoking sand.

Conor saw the pulsating light flash toward him with just enough time to react. Throwing a silvery screen in front of him, he placed an impenetrable barrier between his body and the assassin's weapon. Although it protected him, the concussion from the energy blast catapulted his body away from the oasis. His face bloodied by the impact with his shield, he flew nearly a hundred yards. He hit the ground awkwardly, crushing the muscles in his shoulder and pulling the joint apart. He rolled as best he could, finally landing in a defensive crouch. If what they said about Nemelissi held true, the destroyer would follow the initial attack with another immediate assault.

Conor looked at the remains of the oasis, the fires sparkling and burning here and there. He caught sight of Nemelissi just as it pounced toward him. Vaulting all the way from the burning remains of the oasis, it soared straight toward him, screaming hideously. Conor barely had time to stagger back a few steps. He slammed his shoulder back into place, rolled it around once to make sure it worked and pushed off from the ground. His powerful limbs, teeming with the strength of a tiger's hind legs, propelled him directly toward Nemelissi.

The two warriors crashed together in mid-air. Even with Nemelissi's frightening strength, Conor's velocity propelled it backwards toward the oasis. The young Champion drove his opponent into the ground, hoping to inflict as much damage as he could. The destroyer rolled over easily, flicking him from his powerfully-built body like a gnat. Conor bounced up immediately, rushing the creature again. He wanted to attack before Nemelissi had time to call forth a spell against him. Again he slammed the creature to the ground, clawing at its skin, trying desperately to tear one of its limbs from its body.

As his assaults became more violent, Conor felt the power of the Champions burning in his blood. He could feel Therion's strength pouring into his muscles as he tore into Nemelissi's skin and sinew. Even his appearance began to change. Just like when he had fought Fumemos in the dead ocean on the strange world, his hands began morphing into lion's paws. He held onto Nemelissi with a lion's brawny hind legs while tearing into it with his huge, razor-sharp claws. He let the power run freely, gaining the upper edge over a creature never before challenged in battle.

The assassin convulsed, snarling with a rage so powerful even the earth seemed to shrink with fright. Using a blast of kinetic energy, Nemelissi bucked Conor off of its body, standing immediately after tossing his opponent away. It looked at its torn body, enraged at what the first warrior had done to it.

Before Conor could stand or react in any way, Nemelissi spat a small clear vial in his direction. As it approached, the vial expanded. Just before it made contact, Conor tried to remember the name of the substance. He knew what it was. He couldn't believe Nemelissi had control of this magic as well. He wondered if the assassin had any limits at all.

The protection packet engulfed Conor completely. It contracted violently after sealing itself around him, holding his body rigidly in place. He strained against the material, knowing it was useless.

He had used the identical protection against Seefra in his castle many years ago. The packet had withheld the crushing weight of millions of tons of tiles. Conor didn't feel confident he'd be able to free himself, even with the power of the sun at his command. He tried desperately to summon the energy of the equinox, but his limbs simply wouldn't follow his mind. The command kept stalling at the base of his brain.

Conor breathed evenly as he watched the assassin crawl toward him. He attempted to mouth the words of every spell he knew, but the soft plastic of the protection packet prohibited him from speaking the words correctly.

One of his eyes had been sealed shut during his capture. With his good eye he watched as Nemelissi stood in front of him, roughly fifteen feet away. The skin on the creature's body began to swirl, changing its composition completely. The open pores returned, this time they were fewer but quite a bit larger. Instead of acid or noxious gas spilling forth from the openings, to Conor's horror, living creatures spilled out of the assassin's body.

About two dozen cylindrical rodents fell from the gaping holes in Nemelissi's torso. The assassin bent over, picked up one of the strange creatures and held it aloft for a moment. It extended its hand toward Conor, who watched as its skin, muscle and bone dissolved right before his eyes.

Nemelissi shook its hand, flinging the living thing away. It flexed its fingers a few times, restoring the circulation and essential elements to the appendage. Then it looked where it had thrown the strange rodent. It had landed on an area of flat stone, a hard granite surface impervious to all but the strongest substances. The rodent sunk straight down, deep into the stone ledge.

The assassin looked back at Conor, watching him as he stared at the hole in the granite slab. When he looked back at Nemelissi, the assassin smiled while waving its arm toward him. As if controlled by strings attached to its hand, the remaining creatures surged forward.

A choking, gurgling sound reached Conor's ears. Although muffled by the packet, Conor knew Nemelissi was laughing at him.

Mocking him was more like it, due to the ease with which he would dispatch him. Conor struggled against his bonds, straining his right shoulder until he felt it beginning to pop. When he saw the strange creatures closing in on him, he renewed his efforts with a vengeance. It seemed the bizarre things performed two functions very well. They could stick to anything *and* dispense their deadly acids without harming themselves in the least. Conor watched in horror as the first creature came within a foot of his right toe.

He didn't feel the vibrant rush of wind as Purugama soared past his head toward Nemelissi. The great cougar snarled as he fired a series of golden projectiles from his talons. Nemelissi's small servants never had a chance. The magic pellets sought out the strange creatures, exploding on contact and rendering the acid inert. Conor watched the creatures expire and collapse into the gravel. A tiny wisp of smoke sailed up from each dissolving body.

Nemelissi grunted loudly as Purugama grabbed hold of its torso. The big cat pumped its wings courageously, flying toward the heavens with the assassin firmly in his grasp. Tucking his wings and swooping back toward Conor, Purugama uttered a lengthy spell, throwing it at the young Champion. The cougar drifted back and forth in the sky, waiting to see Conor emerge from the protection packet. As soon as he saw him break free, he dove straight for him. Holding Nemelissi tightly with his huge talons, Purugama called down to his apprentice.

"Go Conor," he growled. "You must find the Author of All Worlds. I will keep after Nemelissi."

"No," screamed Conor, "you cannot defeat him!"

"I will not let you perish, Champion," answered Purugama. "Do as I say. Draw forth a corridor and go to him. You must be the next line of defense after me."

Conor opened his mouth to answer, but his words stopped dead in his throat. Still in Purugama's grip, Nemelissi contracted its body and then exploded in a fiery shower of molten lightning.

The enormous blast knocked Purugama unconscious. The great cougar fell to the ground, lifeless, a sack of wet sand smacking hard against the rocks, frightening Conor right down to his bones.

He ran to his friend. He didn't care that Nemelissi had disappeared. If the destroyer was taking aim against him at that very moment, then so be it. He raced over to Purugama, falling onto his shoulder, hugging his huge head fiercely. He couldn't feel any movement at all in the big cat's body, not even a breath or any sign of a heartbeat. In a panic he called to him, the big, beautiful cougar who had come to save him again.

"Purugama!" he called out. "C'mon, buddy, wake up, breathe, do something!" He placed his ear against the fur-covered rib cage, holding his breath in an attempt to sense any movement from his big friend. The cougar lay still, however. No breath of life moved within him. Conor reached out, petting the huge cheek time and again, cooing to Purugama, his closest friend in all the Crossworlds.

The sickening gurgle reached his ears again. Conor turned around. He saw Nemelissi crouched about twenty yards away, its huge arms hanging over its knees. The destroyer's face turned, showing its twisted smile. The laughter continued. It enjoyed the fact that it finished the cougar. Raising its right arm, it examined the claws on its hand meticulously, concerned with nothing more than its next attack.

Conor held his hands against Purugama one last time. Feeling nothing, he stood and faced the assassin, guarding against any further attacks. He took ten or twelve steps toward Nemelissi, stopping suddenly and looking at it from a new perspective.

It had killed his best friend. A truly noble creature had laid down his life for Conor, and this thing squatting in front of him had killed him. Whatever it was – animal, humanoid, neither – Conor didn't care anymore. Purugama was the most astounding creature he had ever met, and this disgusting thing had murdered him.

Conor felt a new power boiling within him, an all too human emotion. He hated Nemelissi with all his heart. The assassin had taken something from him, something he treasured beyond all understanding. He loved Purugama with his entire being; he was a brother, a friend, and yes, even like an uncle to him. He couldn't imagine life without him, and Nemelissi had changed all that. The assassin not only killed Purugama, it took great pleasure in it. Conor looked at the creature with the fire of the equinox burning in his eyes.

"You mutant freak," he said just loud enough for Nemelissi to hear, "your ass is going down!"

In his wrath, Conor unleashed the power of the heavens. There was no plan, no strategy, and no thought process at all. He knew one thing only; he wanted to annihilate Nemelissi more than anything he had ever wanted in his life. The white hot energy of the sun spilled from every one of Conor's limbs. He threw everything he had at the assassin, flinging huge bolts of blazing energy with both hands.

Conor commanded the equinox to explode from his feet, and a battery of glowing spheres with enough power to vaporize small mountains began forming around his toes. He kicked them with all his might, blasting them toward Nemelissi like soccer balls in front of an open net. His attack became brutal, relentless; Conor pummeled the creature repeatedly with enough combined power to destroy the glade of Champions and the realm of the creators a hundred times over.

Every blast from Conor's assault left a smoldering crater fifty feet wide wherever Nemelissi happened to be a split second before. With each strike he became more enraged. He stalked the assassin as it rolled across the rough surface of the cliff trying to avoid the onslaught. Even though he knew Nemelissi would never hear him, Conor called out to it, taunting it, daring it to attack him.

"What are you waiting for?" he yelled, spitting at the ground in its direction. "You're the all-powerful assassin. You slaughtered me during the great equinox war. Why can't you stand against me now? Get up! Hurl your hideous magic at me! Treat me as you treated my friend! I dare you to get up and face me!"

The first warrior had emerged again. He was so furious, tears rolled down his cheeks as he pursued Nemelissi across the rocky surface. He was crying from a sense of loss, but not the loss of his mentor, even though the image of Purugama's lifeless body haunted his mind. The tears came from a loss of innocence. Conor had always fought for his friends, but never with the feeling of passionate hatred which he now experienced. He felt it burning in his soul, and he didn't like it one bit.

He truly *had* become the warrior Trolond Tar – a Champion on the side of good, yes, but a callous killer nonetheless. He pushed the thought aside while sending more energy rocketing toward Nemelissi. The blasts were so powerful he could no longer see the result of the concussion. Still he walked forward, sensing the destroyer more than seeing it. He would not allow it to escape. It had killed Purugama, and now Conor would make certain it did not survive.

When the power of the equinox hit Nemelissi, the destroyer nearly lost consciousness. It had never before encountered such formidable energy. It tried to counter Trolond Tar's movements, but the warrior moved much faster than he remembered from their previous encounter. Three more direct hits blew Nemelissi clear across the surface of the cliffs. Its body slammed against a huge boulder fronting one of the oases, flipping over backwards before ricocheting off a thick stand of trees. Nemelissi barely had time to close the pores on its body before other more powerful bolts of energy blasted his insides to jelly. It could actually feel the bones and muscles of its body beginning to shake apart. It knew it wouldn't be able to stand much more of Trolond Tar's attack. It had to escape, regroup and develop a different strategy before confronting him again.

With fear driving its incredible agility, Nemelissi found the strength to dodge most of the ensuing attacks. Now that it knew what to expect, the assassin managed to elude the driving force of the explosions. If it could avoid taking another direct hit, it might find a way to escape the ancient battlefield of the equinox war. It watched Trolond Tar closely as he prepared to kick one of the strange orbs floating at his feet. Waiting until the last second, it leapt to the right, bounding away as fast it could.

To its horror, it saw the strange glowing ball arcing toward it, as if sensing its movements precisely. With no time to react again, Nemelissi curled into a tight ball, hoping to give the weapon the smallest surface possible to impact. But the efforts proved fruitless. The Champion's shot sailed true, accelerating toward Nemelissi and smacking the assassin dead on.

The flash from the impact nearly blinded it. Its body caromed off two different groups of trees, spinning one way and then another before finally dropping to the ground awkwardly. Three more energy spheres pummeled Nemelissi before the destroyer ever hit the ground. It sensed one of its legs going limp; all feeling had disappeared entirely. Breathing was suddenly quite difficult as well. The assassin held one clawed hand to its chest while supporting itself with the other. It turned its aching head to look at its enemy. Trolond Tar advanced confidently, hands and arms swelling with the invincible power of the sun.

Nemelissi rolled over onto the ground, crumpling into a fetal position. It knew it had to escape immediately. Feeling foolish for allowing the Champion to gain such an advantage, it spat a mouthful of blood in his opponent's direction. It spat again, defying its enemy, mocking him even while facing its own death. Using its swollen tongue as gingerly as possible, it mumbled a hasty spell. It called forth a corridor directly underneath its bloodied, mangled body.

Nemelissi smiled as the portal materialized below. It felt the frigid surface of the membrane solidifying, tickling its stomach as it prepared for transport. It smiled broadly at Conor as it began sinking into the surface of the cliff. The expression was unmistakable. The destroyer congratulated him for winning the first round of their skirmish. It also foretold of more battles to come, perhaps those in which the young Champion might not fare so well. Like a crocodile slowly sinking under the water of a murky lake, Nemelissi melted into the grainy surface of the cliffs, narrowly escaping the fate of the next barrage brought forth from Trolond Tar's hands.

Conor ran to the spot where Nemelissi's corridor shimmered in the dirt. He watched the portal glisten beautifully with a multitude of colors; a stark contrast to its dreary surroundings. Uttering a quick spell and waving his hand over the passageway, Conor used Nemelissi's own magic against it. He secured the corridor to the ground, giving it no chance to vanish until Conor returned to follow the assassin's path.

Assuring himself that his spell would hold, Conor ran back to where Purugama lay on the sandy floor of the cliff. His heart skipped a happy beat when he saw the great cougar's head upright and looking in his direction. Running even faster after seeing this, Conor wanted to jump into Purugama's flank and hug him with all his might. Unsure of the extent of his mentor's injuries, however, he decided against wild abandon, approaching the big cat gingerly instead.

"Purugama," he said, touching one of the golden paws, "you're alive."

"It would take more than a frantic attack to destroy one such as me, my brother," said the great cougar. "I believe the shock of the explosion knocked me unconscious. It may have even induced a temporary coma. But I believe I am well."

The big cat placed his huge clawed feet on the dirt beneath him. He rose, unsteadily at first, flapping his great wings and creating quite a stir around the grounds. He chuffed a few times, shaking his giant head from side to side. After skating with his hind feet for a few moments, he pronounced himself fit for travel.

"What has become of Nemelissi?" he growled.

"Disappeared," answered Conor. "I had it surrounded by the most powerful energy I've ever seen, but it escaped through a corridor. I did manage to trap the portal before it could dissolve."

"An excellent strategy," said Purugama. "The energy you spoke of, tell me more about it. You've never seen any of us using it before?"

Conor brushed his hands against his rough leather pants. A few small puffs of dust shot toward the ground as he tried his best to improve his appearance. He almost resembled a cat preening itself before greeting an audience. "I've never even seen a creator wield this kind of power," he said. "I could have finished Nemelissi right here on these cliffs if it hadn't escaped."

"Interesting," murmured Purugama. "If I had any doubt about

your true identity, Conor, this development erased it for good. There's no question anymore. You are Trolond Tar, first warrior of the Crossworlds."

Conor looked at the ground, kicking a few pebbles away from his feet. He looked back to Purugama, not saying anything right away. He just stared at the cougar, waiting for him to explain his comment.

"Twenty thousand years ago, Conor," continued Purugama, "Trolond Tar alone controlled the source of all power – physical and magical. No one could explain the anomaly, for no other being within the entire system could claim dominion over the forces of the Crossworlds. Even the creators, with all their mysterious abilities, could not convince the sun to bestow upon them the fantastic energy of the equinox. Rather than bemoan their fate, the creators sent an emissary to convince Trolond Tar to join in their cause."

"The Lady of the Light," said Conor.

"Yes," replied Purugama. "Athazia traveled through an infinite collection of corridors, finally reaching a distant world where she found him. To this day she has not revealed its location. I doubt she ever will. She eventually returned with the first warrior, introducing him to the Council of Seven and setting his course for the next millennia. It is said that Trolond Tar was so taken by her beauty and intellect he offered his services before she could request them. Before returning to the realm, she spent a great deal of time educating him about the creators, the Crossworlds and the scope of his duties as first warrior."

"His reign occurred so long ago. I know nothing but what I've been told in stories," continued Purugama. "His power was frightening, legendary. It is said that with a flick of his wrist an entire mountain range would crumble into dust."

Conor felt a small twitch in right arm.

"I have also heard that the power of the equinox could reach across space, even travel to other worlds to exact punishment."

The young Champion felt a powerful surge in the pit of his stomach.

"It has even been said that the energy from the sun could alter time and history, although I've never seen anything to support that statement."

Conor sensed a flood of new information entering his mind. Something seemed to be feeding him new instructions, or providing an entirely new perspective on his powers. He didn't understand it, but he didn't fight it either. He accepted the new aspect of himself, filing the information away for deeper inspection later.

"If Trolond Tar was so all-powerful," asked Conor, "how could Nemelissi defeat him? How could any destroyer overcome someone so invincible?"

"No one can claim perfection, Conor," replied Purugama. "Trolond Tar was certainly not a fool; however, due to his tremendous power, he became careless. You said only moments ago if not for a corridor you might have finished Nemelissi here on these cliffs. Trolond Tar assumed the same thing many centuries ago. Seeing the destroyer bloodied and beaten, he lowered his defenses for a split second. Nemelissi took advantage of that, slaughtering him mercilessly in front of the Lady of the Light.

"I kept myself concealed until I felt certain you needed assistance," the great cougar said. "It almost had you with the protection packet. When I saw Nemelissi spit in your direction, I knew I had to reveal myself.

"You did well, Conor. No one, not even the legendary Trolond Tar, ever laid into Nemelissi the way you did after seeing me fall.

But I warn you, don't ever let up, and never let that creature convince you of its suffering. If you get the chance, destroy it without hesitation, without mercy, Conor. Blast it into a billion pieces; send it through a thousand different corridors to the utmost regions of the Crossworlds. Pulverize it, Conor; make certain it never lives again.

"Trust me," continued Purugama, "it will treat you in the identical fashion should it gain the upper hand. Never forget, Conor, Nemelissi controls a tremendous amount of magic. The protection packet may have caught you by surprise, but I assure you it possesses a huge host of additional weapons. It will use any one of them if it feels it must do so to defeat you. Anticipate everything, ready yourself to go on the offensive, but don't charge blindly ahead. To destroy the ultimate assassin, allow it to exhaust most of its resources. When you are certain its reserves are gone, then go in with everything you have and annihilate it."

"So," said Conor. "I am to face Nemelissi then? You will go to the Author of All Worlds and protect him in case I fall?"

"Yes, I will go. As much as I detest the thought of leaving you here, I haven't the strength to stand against Nemelissi."

Conor watched the great cougar lower his head slightly. He detected a sense of shame in his mentor's soul. He reached out and grabbed a handful of fur at the cougar's cheek. Hugging the golden fur closely, he whispered a few words into Purugama's ear. In return, the cougar spoke his last words of encouragement.

"You must become the warrior again, Conor. Only Trolond Tar can defeat Nemelissi. You are he, I believe it without reservation. The assassin is a ruthless killer. To overcome it, you must become as cold-blooded as Nemelissi."

"I don't see that as a problem," answered Conor, remembering the sensations he felt less an hour ago. He stared at the big cat, nodded his head quickly and called forth a passageway to carry Purugama to his next destination. Assuring himself of the portal's reliability, he ran back toward the assassin's corridor.

Purugama watched him go, uttering a silent plea for his safe return. After doing so, the great cougar tucked his wings into his body and walked through the corridor's blazing silver membrane. His thick tail banged against the perimeter before disappearing from sight.

CHAPTER THIRTY-EIGHT

Despite the seeker's best efforts, the predatory corridor continued moving toward earth. Now only twenty-five thousand miles from the outer atmosphere, the fantastic membrane was dangerously close to affecting the natural ebb and flow of earth's planetary stability. Mr. Hikkins could only imagine what might occur if the killer portal advanced another five thousand miles.

Earthquakes would erupt along every major fissure, affecting tectonic plates on every continent. Some would measure lightly on the Richter scale, causing only marginal damage. Other temblors would no doubt roar past any kind of normalcy, creating chaos in cities around the world. Gigantic glaciers would fracture from the arctic ice flow, raising the sea level and altering weather patterns around the globe. The very ground they stood on would become the bottom of the Pacific Ocean in little time. California might finally "fall" into the sea, as so many had predicted over past decades.

Atmospheric disturbances would wreak havoc the world over as the corridor consumed the exosphere. Rain, hail, lightning without end – truly, the effect would be an introduction to Armageddon. The pandemonium would be so severe, the seeker doubted anyone on earth would even register what occurred when the corridor erased their world from existence. He shook his head, worrying about his ability to halt its advance. He had never before failed a mission given to him by the creators. He did not want this venture to be his first. He looked over at Janine with an expression of deep anxiety.

"We can't stop it, can we?" she asked.

"Never accept defeat until it swallows you whole," answered Mr. Hikkins. "Perhaps Conor will arrive soon. If he adds his energy to the line, it might propel the power beyond the predatory corridor's ability to resist us."

Janine nodded her head, not really believing in their chances. She felt a profound sadness for her world, for all the people she knew and for her inability to perish with Conor in her arms, the only thing that mattered to her now. She wanted to see the end clutched in his embrace. She brushed her hair away from her ears, feeling a strange wind move through the forest. It brought with it a delicious scent, something completely exotic, foreign to her and to her world. Pitching her head back, she breathed in the aroma, inhaling deeply a few times. She wondered if anyone else had noticed the change in their surroundings. She looked back at Mr. Hikkins, who seemed unfazed. She walked her eyes along the line, looking at the creators, the big cats, and finally at the leader of the Crossworlds Champions.

"Mr. Hikkins!" she shouted. "Look at that! Look at Maya!"

The seeker lifted his heavy eyes from the console. When he saw Maya at the beginning of the rear triangle, he suddenly felt re-energized, almost young again. He had felt something peculiar occurring for some time, and knowing Maya quite well, he believed the Lord of the Champions to be the cause of it. Looking at his Lord now, he felt a wave of relief washing over him. Maya had found something, or someone, to assist them. He felt certain of it. Wherever he had traveled, he was now returning with whatever presence accompanied him. For the first time since they arrived at the forests of Redwood County, the seeker smiled, feeling a sincere sense of relief.

Maya retained his transcendental state, eyes closed, perfectly at one with the elements of the Crossworlds. His entire body glowed, awash with a mesmerizing luminescence. His natural coloring had all but disappeared, replaced by a brilliant milky-white radiance. The aura burned strongly, nothing could possibly penetrate it.

While passing the seeker's energy to the other Champions in the line, Maya sat suspended in a deep communion with some presence only he could identify. To casual onlookers, the scene would evoke a powerful sense of spirituality. To others, especially Mr. Hikkins, Maya's transformation simply confirmed his belief in the cat's infinite powers.

Something extraordinary began to occur behind the Lord of the Champions. A magnificent redwood over a thousand years old sparked with a blinding light similar to the one engulfing Maya. The immense trunk of the ancient tree ignited at its base. The pulsating aura raced up the spine of the giant redwood. The coloring matched Maya's perfectly. Two hundred feet of redwood burl, fifty feet around at its base, suddenly came to life like an enormous candle in the forest.

Soon other redwoods mimicked the transformation. Hundreds of massive trees exploded with a similar luminescence, every one of them carrying identical characteristics. All around the gathering of the creators and Champions, giant redwoods began preparing themselves for battle. These were the *fingers of the forest*, the enormous sentinels of earth. Hearing Maya's call, they reacted by providing exactly the type of support he and the others needed. Within minutes, nearly five hundred acres of old-growth redwoods responded to the summons.

"Now, my dear," said Mr. Hikkins, smiling, "watch closely. This will be something you'll remember always."

CHAPTER THIRTY-NINE

"Apache squadron leader," barked the commanding general at Beale Air Force Base, "you should be hovering over the proper coordinates by now. Can you give us a description of the forces deployed on the reservation?"

Major General McKimmey spoke on a headset in his own office. He had direct communications patched into his panel for a specific reason. Accompanying him in his office were the deputy director of the CIA, a defense intelligence agency attaché from Washington, two commanding officers for helicopter attack deployment, his closest peer in rank and authority, General Morosoff, and the Tribal Chairman from the Hoopa Indian reservation. He would never be able to assemble such a gathering in the middle of the base communications control room. The situation called for a delicate hand. He preferred his home court, so he had directed all concerned parties straight to his office.

"Apache leader, do you read?" he asked again. "What's going on out there?"

"Coming over the site now, sir," answered Captain Darren. "Give me a minute to make good visual contact." With a flick of his wrist, he sent a hand signal to his next in command. The officer in the next closest Apache gave orders to follow the lead chopper. The team banked right, staying a safe distance from the stream of energy exploding from the forest below. They made two passes, one quick and high, the second much closer to the tips of the trees, and much slower. Captain Darren took a good, long look before reporting back to base.

"Sir, we see no more than fifteen individuals on the ground. Most of them are swallowed up in what seems to be the energy flow from the beam. They may be the source of the power stream, but I can't see how that could be possible. Two people are off to the side of the energy flow. One appears to be standing at some sort of console. He may be in control of the entire apparatus."

"Destroy the site, General," said the deputy director of the CIA, interrupting the captain's transmission. "Can't you see? They are the source of the wall of plasma. They're drawing it toward us, guiding it into the earth's atmosphere. You must destroy them now."

General McKimmey waved of the CIA man off brusquely. "Continue your report, Captain."

"Sir, you're not going to believe this. The trees surrounding the small group, well, they're on fire but they're not burning."

"Say again, Captain. Say again."

"I'd say close to a thousand trees are glowing very brightly, sir. They almost seem alive, and they all share an identical coloring to the person in the rear of the glowing formation." Captain Darren clicked off his microphone for a brief second before punching the button again. "As a matter of fact, that doesn't look like a person at all."

The CIA man fidgeted. The defense intelligence representatives did likewise. All three pushed forward to address the General, who promptly assured them that if they bothered him again they would find themselves in the outer office.

"Well, Captain Darren," asked the General, "then what is it?"

"It looks like a giant cat, sir."

"*What?*"

"A cat, sir. A common housecat, but very big. I'd say close to twelve hundred pounds, probably twelve feet tall while sitting on its haunches."

The Hoopa Chairman started when he heard the captain's report. Careful not to show any outward sign of emotion, he blinked his eyes once while shifting his gaze to General McKimmey. He waited patiently for his friend to make eye contact. As he knew he would, the general addressed the frantic ramblings of the government men, placating them before turning to look at his long-time friend in the back of the room. The general's eyes reached the Tribal Chairman, who did nothing to acknowledge the contact. The chairman made no move whatsoever, he merely held the general's gaze strongly. The message would get through, of that he felt certain. If the report of a giant cat directing a stream of energy more powerful than anything the earth had ever seen didn't jar his senses, he hoped their silent communication would.

John Woodhaven had lived in the redwood forests of northern California for close to eighty years. Even after his old way of life had been swept aside by the stampede of white development, he had seen things occur in the woods that cemented his belief in the supernatural.

He had been taught during his youth to respect and revere all living things, especially the ancient forests of his homeland. He always carried himself with the utmost dignity when walking amongst the silent giants of the redwood forests.

He held long conversations with the majestic trees, touching the soft burl at the base of their immense trunks. He slept soundly in their bosom, cradled within the gigantic hollowed-out basins at the feet of the oldest trees.

Sometimes he would awaken in the dead of night to the sound of strange creatures walking around his encampment. Having lived for decades in the region, he knew every noise made by the local creatures of his environment. During the strange nights when he heard footsteps close by, he knew without hesitation that the creatures walking around him were not of the earth, or if they were, they rarely left their hovel to venture out for food or water.

Since all life needed nourishment to live, John believed these creatures to be visitors from another place. During those pitch-black nights when one relied on other senses to make their way, John had always been tempted to seek the creatures out, find out who they were, and give himself another reason to believe in the spirits that protected his people. But he had never ventured forth; he never satisfied his curiosity. Part of the reason was fear; one rarely walks boldly into the company of the supernatural.

Reverence prevented him from seeking the creatures out as well. If they *were* here, if they visited earth on a regular basis, he certainly did not wish to frighten them or show disrespect. He believed they came to earth as protectors; he wanted nothing to do with causing their permanent departure.

John Woodhaven believed with all his heart that the cat Captain Darren spoke of had visited his forest many times in the past. He and his companions were here to help the earth, not destroy it as the government men feared. He wanted to convey that message to General McKimmey. He hoped his eyes would tell his story as well as anything.

"Sir," said Captain Darren over his microphone. "I see other cats in the formation as well. There appears to be a tiger, a lion and

I think there is a cheetah sitting in front of the glowing cat. They're all even bigger than the one that looks like a housecat. The power stream seems to be moving through all of them, then directly toward humans in another formation. There is one man standing at the tip of the arrangement. The power beam is passing through him before heading out toward the giant space screen."

The DIA attaché grabbed McKimmey's arm, turning the man around to face him, demanding, "General, on my authority as attaché to the United States Secretary of Defense, I'm ordering you to destroy that site. If you don't act immediately, I'll relieve you and appoint one of your men commanding officer."

Major General Desmond McKimmey looked the attaché in the eye, and then looked at the man's hand on his arm. The DIA attaché took the hint, quickly removing his hand from McKimmey's firm bicep. The two men locked eyes again before the general gave his answer. "With all due respect, sir, go fuck yourself."

The DIA and CIA men moved to protest. General Morosoff snapped his fingers and two imposing staff sergeants moved side by side next to their commanding officer. "Place these men in the brig on my orders," said Morosoff. "No visitors, no communication at all. Is that clear?"

The two men answered as one before marching their charges out of General McKimmey's office.

John Woodhaven smiled within himself. Very imperceptibly, he nodded once to his friend when their eyes met again. Then he sat down on the edge of a side table. If the general had made any other decision, he would have happily given his life to thwart their plans. He felt that strongly about the events presently occurring in the forest.

General McKimmey issued orders to his helicopter squadron.

Interrupting himself periodically, he made Captain Darren repeat his orders at different intervals. The general wanted no interference, especially not from the idiot media circus undoubtedly plunging into Redwood County.

"Are my instructions clear, Captain?"

"Yes sir," returned the flight leader.

"If your squadron encounters any press helicopters, you are to give one verbal caution, fire one warning volley, and if they don't vacate the area immediately, I want you to blow them out of the sky."

"Understood," said Captain Darren.

Major General McKimmey glanced briefly at his counterpart before moving out of the way.

"Captain Carlson," barked General Morosoff.

"SIR!"

"Gather up three companies from the base, the best soldiers you have stationed here."

"Yes SIR!"

"I want the area around the site secured, Sergeant. No one, and I mean no one, gets past your line. If I hear of one person walking within a one hundred yards of that site, I'll have your ass for breakfast tomorrow. Is that clear?"

"Sir, YES SIR!"

"You will barricade, but not interfere. You will at all times respect the sanctity of the lands you occupy. Is that clear, Captain?"

"Perfectly, sir."

General Morosoff knew it would be. Carlson was one of his best men, very dependable and solid. He had recommended him for officer's training, regrettably, of course. He hated losing competent support personnel.

The captain hurried out of the office, peppering commands into his collar radio. By the time he reached his quarters, his line sergeants would have the troops assembled and ready to go. They would finish preparations and he would brief his troops on the way. He felt confident they would reach the site within the hour.

General McKimmey turned to look at the Tribal Chairman. He walked over and leaned up against the table, standing next to his old friend. He loosened his uniform tie, unbuttoning his standard officer's shirt at the neck.

"Well, John," said the general, "do you have any idea what the hell is going on out there?"

John Woodhaven smiled, his entire face beaming. He crossed his arms in front of his body, gripping himself tightly. He quietly answered his friend. "Yes, I do."

CHAPTER FORTY

Giant old-growth redwoods continued coming to life all around Maya and the others in the formation. The coating on the trunks burned so brightly it looked like the middle of the day in the forest. Only Maya, Janine and Mr. Hikkins appeared to notice the bizarre transformations. The others in the line stayed completely focused, using every bit of consciousness to complete their task. The body convulsions continued, but had not increased. Everyone still seemed to be holding their own. Janine looked out into the sky. The predatory corridor filled up the whole world. She felt she could stick out her index finger and touch it. *Whatever you're going to do Maya,* she thought, *do it now, please.*

The old-growth redwoods banded together, harmonizing their ancient brotherhood by creating a seamless unity among their auras. One by one, they joined together, linking the energy stream between them into a matrix of unfathomable power. Slowly at first, and then with greater speed, hundreds of redwood trees turned the sum total of their forces toward their leader, the largest and oldest of their kind. The huge redwood, located directly behind Maya, accepted their combined energy before transferring it to the leader of the Crossworlds.

Janine gasped when the stream overtook Maya. The energy consumed him so completely he disappeared when it reached him. An entirely new composition shot forward through Therion and Surmitang and blasted through Eha like a supernova on its way toward the creators. The Lady of the Light vanished when it swarmed over her, but she stopped shivering as soon as the energy from the redwoods encased her. She must have been channeling five hundred times the power of the original model created by Janine and Mr. Hikkins. The effect, however, was soothing rather than aggravating. Janine watched as each recipient received the awesome power of Mother Nature. Her heart jumped with excitement as the stream swallowed the Lord of All Life before shooting out toward the predatory corridor.

"Amazing," said Mr. Hikkins. "Maya successfully recruited the *fingers of the forest* to assist us. Their power dwarfs anything we could have conjured. I can't wait to see what happens when the increase hits the plasma membrane on the predatory corridor."

The augmented energy stream swept past the Apache squadron, nearly consuming the tiny machines in the immense wave. It traveled at more than Mach five without leaving any sound concussion in its wake. In less than five seconds, the immense power stream impacted the killer portal, slamming against the center with the cosmic force of a thousand stars. *The inner element had to feel the force of the new mixture on the mechanism*, thought Mr. Hikkins, *even in their counsel chamber many light years away.*

The initial impact drove the corridor back ten thousand miles. The endless energy stream continued pressing against the corridor, pushing it farther away from the planet with every passing second. For a moment it appeared earth's troubles were over.

"Proximity increasing at one hundred miles every minute," reported Mr. Hikkins. "Cell reconstruction is commencing as planned. Apparently your formula is working, my dear, just as you believed it would."

Janine acknowledged the seeker's comment with a nod of her head. She felt so excited by the news she could barely contain herself. She jumped into Mr. Hikkins' arms, hugging him tightly. Her world would survive, she had accomplished something sensational, and they hadn't lost anyone in the process.

Not yet, anyway. She thought of Conor, out there somewhere, fighting a psychopathic assassin. Lost in her reverie, forgetting where she was, she squeezed Mr. Hikkins a little tighter. Embarrassed, she released the seeker with a smile, stepping back to straighten her top. She put her hair back behind her ears, a habit of hers when she was working, and glanced at the console screen.

"Are the numbers holding steady?"

Mr. Hikkins was only too happy to focus on his work again. "Perfectly," he said. "It's hard to believe, the power increase per recipient is off the scale, yet not one of them shows any outward signs of stress. An amazing phenomenon, one I would care to study in the future."

Janine stared out into space, watching the predatory corridor shrink in size as the beam continued its assault. "Do you really think its over?" she asked. "Are we finally safe?"

The seeker ran his fingers over the console, adding a little here, steadying the mixture there. "I'll believe we are safe when all of us are resting comfortably back at the realm of the creators. This new development with the forest certainly has given us an edge. Let us rejoice until we are given reason to do otherwise."

"Blast the creators and their imbecile Champions," Shordano

roared. "Am I to believe that one pitiful seeker has halted the advance of a predatory corridor, and has even propelled it back into space, away from earth?"

Jek pinched his mouth at the sound of his superior's cracking voice. Had Shordano listened to his counsel earlier, this would never have happened. The power-mad fool had gone too far, taken too many chances, and now they were paying the price. He watched his Lord pace around the chamber, finally resting his large hands against the back of Jek's chair.

"Well?" asked Shordano, lowering his exasperated face down by his subordinate's ear. "What are our options now?"

"We have no options, as you well know," answered Jek. "When you ordered maximum thrust for the predatory corridor, you released it, leaving it to its own devices. It will fight back against the new opposition, or it will not. If it decides to, I believe it has the reserves to complete its mission. Will it see that as its primary goal, however? That is the real question. It may just decide to obliterate another world altogether. Maybe even our own."

"Pah," said the leader of the inner element. "It would never turn against those who programmed its function. We gave it life, a purpose. At any rate, traveling back to this part of the galaxy would drain most of its resources. It wouldn't be able to do anything but float in space, an ineffective mechanism without purpose."

"Don't be so certain of its inabilities, my Lord," warned Jek. "In its free state, it could easily replace its energy needs by absorbing essential nutrients from a number of natural phenomena in deep space. This is an organic life form, my Lord. It possesses intelligence. It will do whatever it must to complete its mission."

"You give it entirely too much credit, Jek," replied Shordano, now looking out the open window. "It is a machine, a slave; that is all. It will serve us to the best of its ability, and then it will return to its origin or dissolve in space."

Jek lowered his eyes, focusing on the screen in front of him. *The fool has no idea what he's done,* he thought. It's possible the predatory corridor might be able to complete its task on its own, but Jek did not feel altogether certain. If the portal did travel back to its origin, replenishing itself along the way, then they were surely doomed.

He should have consulted Wolbus before any of these developments took place. Perhaps the two of them might have stopped Shordano, locked him in Nemelissi's cell. Perhaps not, though. Their leader was extremely powerful and *utterly insane,* which made him more dangerous than ever.

Jek glanced up at his superior, staring at his back for a moment. He shook his head, wondering what the outcome of all this madness would be. *At least we won't suffer at the hands of Nemelissi,* he thought. *If the predatory corridor turns against us, at least our deaths will be swift and painless.*

The seeker grimaced as he watched the numbers change on his console. He felt reluctant to inform Janine, for she seemed so happy, much more so than at any time since they arrived. As a scientist, however, she would want to know, so Mr. Hikkins made his pronouncement in a clear, strong voice.

"Proximity expansion dropping steadily," he said. He watched the color drain from her face. Without addressing her needs, he continued his report. "Predatory corridor's movement slowing to almost nothing, now moving away from earth at less than five miles per minute."

"Does that mean the extra energy from the trees isn't enough to keep it away from earth?"

"It means the instrument has incredible power reserves," said Mr. Hikkins. "It intends to make a fight of it, and apparently it's doing quite well, at least at this point." The seeker recalibrated the console and ran another series of tests. "I was afraid of that. The portal is moving forward again. Very slowly, but it is progressing in our direction. Worse than that, the cell conversion process has been terminated. Apparently it deciphered our plan and used its own chemical processes to neutralize it."

Janine let her chin drop. She jammed her hands in her pockets, kicking a rock a good distance and bruising her big toe in the process.

"At its current speed, the corridor will intercept the exosphere in eighteen hours. Be happy, my dear. The *fingers of the forest* have bought us a little more time. The killer portal will contact earth; that fact is incontrovertible. I'm afraid it's up to Conor and Purugama, now, and hopefully the Author of All Worlds. Our continued existence proves that they have made contact with the author, and perhaps moved him to a safe place. We are in Trolond Tar's hands, my dear, and we will survive only if he is able to defeat Nemelissi. Let us at least focus our energies on our task here in the forest. The creators and the Champions need us, and we will not fail them."

CHAPTER FORTY-ONE

Conor fell through a hole in the sky, straight toward a putrid pit of bubbling acid. He barely had time to register the contents of the pool below him. He reacted as any warrior would, with fear, panic and a heavy dose of adrenaline. Flaring the fingers of both hands out to the side, he shot ten thin but extremely strong tendrils beyond the boundary of the acid pit. They stuck in the ground like spears, holding Conor above the smelly concoction. No doubt left there by Nemelissi, the acid would have burned him alive had all his senses not been operating in overdrive. Feeling the intense heat of the gurgling mass beneath him, he gingerly pulled one set of tendrils out of the ground. Using the others like a set of poles, he vaulted his body safely away from the pit. He hit the ground running, nursing a pained expression when he realized where he was. Nemelissi had returned to the realm of the creators.

He noticed no one meandering about the lush grounds. Usually the realm would be bustling with creators, and, if not them, their servants would be tending to the many natural wonders present in the gardens. Conor raced through the central courtyard, running past a wing of life-giving water walls. Kicking up to cheetah speed, he sped through a region of steep waterfalls before running through the meditation pools. As he rounded a large cluster of palms by the last pool, he stopped suddenly, throwing a wave of grass and dirt out in front of him.

"Mind of the Creators," he gasped.

Nemelissi sat crouched at the top of a large palm tree, cradling a strange filament in its hand. The line was attached to a large piece of netting. The huge web ran the length of a bubbling pool and was attached to another tree roughly thirty yards away.

The netting seemed alive. Conor couldn't figure it out at first, but then he saw it was filled with a good number of the creators' servants. They squirmed excitedly, especially when the assassin let the line slacken a bit. The servants screamed with terror as one of their company lost an arm or a foot in the acid pit below them. Nemelissi watched with glee, gurgling and laughing every time one its captives lost a limb.

When it saw Conor running toward the pool, the assassin stood straight up in the fronds at the top of the palm. It held the line out in front of it, daring Conor to come forward and force the issue. It saw the young Champion stop suddenly, so it coiled the line around its hand a few times. The tension pulled the servants up away from the boiling acid, causing them to gasp with a frenzied delight. Nemelissi laughed again, letting the line slip almost completely through its fingers. Dozens of beings climbed over each other to get to the top of the heap. The netting levitated for a moment before falling straight down toward the sizzling pool. In a second or two, it would splash into the acid, melting off body parts everywhere. The screams of the servants echoed in Conor's ears, causing him to react with emotion instead of rationally devising a plan.

Reaching into one of the compartments of his trousers, Conor grabbed one of the magical capsules. He held out his other hand toward Nemelissi, motioning for him to spare his prisoners. He talked evenly to the assassin, trying to gather its attention and devise some sort of strategy.

"Don't hurt them anymore," said Conor. "Let them go. Take me instead."

Nemelissi examined Conor's face for any sign of deceit as it held the line loosely in its hand. It wanted more than anything to drop the people into the acid and launch itself at Conor. After thousands of centuries of battle, however, it knew better than to take any opponent lightly. It would draw its enemy in as closely as it could before striking a mortal blow. The horrible face twisted into a blistered smile. Using the last bit of line it held, it pulled the netting high into the air and released it. The web of servants fell toward the bubbling pool, screaming and holding each other as they watched the steaming acid rising up to greet them.

Conor jumped straight toward Nemelissi. In the same motion, he threw the capsule toward the servants in the netting. The tiny projectile hit the surface of the acid pit, changing the molecular structure in a fraction of a second. The caustic pool disappeared entirely, in its place was a rubbery substance with exactly enough flexibility to absorb the impact of the occupants in the netting.

Conor threw his other hand out toward Nemelissi, sending a blast of silver energy toward the destroyer. Had it hit squarely, it would have knocked the creature unconscious.

Nemelissi anticipated the attack, jumping over the wave of energy just as it reached the tree. The destroyer changed directions in mid-air, turning straight for Conor with a freakish back flip. It accelerated toward the young Champion, using nothing but its peculiar magic. Flinging its hands toward Conor, Nemelissi tossed lightning in every direction. No matter how Conor reacted, he was sure to be struck by one of the powerful bolts.

The destroyer wasted no time in summoning another attack. Immediately after sending the magical electricity, Nemelissi reached across its chest, ripping a piece of flesh from its shoulder. Hurling it toward Conor, the destroyer commanded the mangled skin by uttering a strange incantation. The skin reformed itself, morphing into a living spear. It sped straight for Conor's forehead. It would never stop until sinking itself deep into its target. The strange projectile retained the toughest parts of Nemelissi's skin, a bristly scale-like substance harder than most synthetic metals. Even more, for a brief period the spear would enjoy all of its owner's intelligence. No matter what Conor did, no matter how hard he tried to evade the peculiar weapon, the spear would continue to seek him out. Once released by Nemelissi, it floated in the sky for a moment. After recognizing its target, it shot forward like a bullet, speeding through the air so fast it nearly became invisible. Without any defensive reaction by Conor, the spear would find his forehead in less than a second.

The lightning bit into the ground all around Conor, smashing everything into smoking rubble. The strikes seemed to have no end; it was all Conor could do to keep himself from being fried by one of the streaks of metallic energy. He jumped, ducked, spun and ran in all directions, doing his best to avoid a direct hit. A few times the lightning slammed against the ground right beside Conor, charring his trousers and sending a fiery sheet of pain up his leg. This increased his manic gyrations, giving him the energy necessary to avoid most of the remaining strikes.

Even with all the commotion, Conor heard Nemelissi laughing hideously, mocking him. The destroyer enjoyed Conor's panicked attempts at escape. It also rejoiced in the fact that he hadn't yet discovered its second line of attack.

The living spear followed every move Conor made, speeding toward him when it saw a clear path to his forehead, holding its flight like a hummingbird when it couldn't see its target. Finally, when Conor dove out of the way of three consecutive electrical blasts, the spear saw him roll over on his back. It dove for his head, instantly increasing its speed to maximum velocity.

Conor never saw the spear. The projectile hit his headband squarely, disintegrating into a puff of pale green smoke. Conor felt a light dusting from some of the spear's poison burn the skin on his face and his shoulders. He stood quickly, raking his shoulders with both hands and wiping his face frantically. He spat four or five times as well, ejecting any dust that might have reached his tongue. Seeing no more of the lightning, he turned quickly, looking over at Nemelissi. He watched as the destroyer ripped two more patches of skin from its body. Singing its sweet spell, it flung the strange swaths in Conor's direction.

Horrified, the young Champion saw the skin change in mid-air, turning into the same dangerous type of spear that attacked him only seconds before. He did the only thing he could; he turned and ran like the devil. The spears, fully formed now and aware of their target, zipped after Conor with a single-minded purpose.

Even at cheetah speed, the spears closed the distance between themselves and Conor quickly. But the Champion had given himself a few precious seconds to form a defense. He slid around, bracing his body and slowing himself with his right foot. He focused intently on the spears, calculating when they would reach him and which one would strike first. No doubt Nemelissi had altered their point of attack, ignoring the forehead and focusing on a different and more vulnerable area. They sped toward him at an incredible speed, accelerating even more as they closed in for the kill. Conor noted that one of spears came in low, while the other approached at chest height. He waited until the last second before reacting.

Jumping to the right and rolling over on the ground, Conor snatched both spears out of the air simultaneously. The living weapons fought his grip. If he hadn't taken both with all the strength he had, he might have lost one of them. As it was, he merely brought the spears up to his mouth and whispered a spell of his own. Then he opened his hands, releasing the weapons. The two spears levitated for a moment, unsure of their new instructions. Locating Nemelissi roughly five hundred yards away, the two weapons disappeared in a flash. They took off after their new assignment with all the zeal they previously exhibited for Conor.

Nemelissi, confident that his weapons would finish his opponent, hadn't paid much attention to the outcome of his attack. When it heard the high-pitched whine of the spears coming toward it, however, its attitude shifted abruptly. With only enough time to turn its head in the direction of one of the spears, it destroyed the high-flying projectile with a streak of lightning from its right hand.

That motion, however, eliminated any possibility of deflecting the second spear. It found its target, slamming into Nemelissi's right leg. It disappeared into a puff of sickly green smoke, having injected its poison into the destroyer's calf. Nemelissi reared back, howling with intense pain. Its leg bubbled up, contorting into all manner of shapes. With each different configuration, the assassin roared anew, cursing the creators and Champions in a language Conor could not decipher.

Conor followed the spears, running toward Nemelissi in case the assassin managed to deflect the weapons. He heard the ear-splitting scream echoing around the realm. He allowed himself a second of relief, letting the joy of another victory wash over him.

His celebration ended quickly, however, when the earth heaved under his feet, catapulting him high into the air. Spinning uncontrollably, Conor tried to see what had happened on the ground. All he saw were explosions of earth and rock occurring everywhere. He finally caught sight of Nemelissi lying on the ground twisting in agony. With one large, scaly hand gripping its leg, it waved the other about wildly, causing the beauty of the realm to erupt in a freakish display of chaotic destruction. Conor fell toward the ground awkwardly, only to be slapped twice by sections of buckling ground rising up underneath him.

His only purpose now lay in the safety of the creators' servants. In his haste to save himself from the poisonous spears, he had forgotten them completely. Wresting control of his body from the elements, he twisted around in mid-air. The servants, although still tangled in the netting, were not suffering from the massive earthquakes. Nemelissi had been sending its destructive power in only one direction. Conor threw his hands out in front of him, screaming the words of a spell Maya had taught him. He hoped the destroyer wouldn't notice his intent. To his good fortune, Nemelissi, writhing in pain from the poison in its leg, hadn't been able to keep an eye on Conor.

The invisible spell obliterated the netting wrapped around the servants of the realm. After rolling away from each other, most stood and ran from the pandemonium. After a few commands from the senior servants, however, the group collected itself, returning to carry the wounded to safety. A few of the bravest, after delivering their fellows from the battlefield, returned to the site of their brief captivity. They watched their world erupting in front of them, wondering if they might assist the first warrior in some way.

After watching for only a few moments, they turned and ran back to join their group. What was occurring in the realm at this moment was far beyond their capabilities. After giving a plea to the creators for Conor's safety, they began comforting those who suffered from Nemelissi's handiwork.

The injured assassin continued raking its hand back and forth, tearing the environment to shreds. Conor, understanding the insanity of the attack, realized Nemelissi was merely buying time for itself. The spear must have injured it terribly. Conor weighed his options. He could attack here and now, possibly annihilating the realm in the process, or he could force the destroyer to seek another venue to continue their battle.

Summoning the awesome power of the sun, Conor lifted his arm, pointing it toward a garden some distance away. He let loose the energy, watching an enormous streak of white-hot power cut a jagged line into the soil. With the strike, he sliced the realm's garden in two, leaving Nemelissi only one path for escape.

Turning his shoulder to the right, he sent the power out again. The beam ripped into the garden, this time perpendicular to the first cut. He had essentially cut off any physical escape for the assassin, and afterward he crouched down to the ground like a lion hunting in the wild. He stalked Nemelissi with all the silence and cunning Therion would use. He came up behind the creature, commanding his body to breathe slowly. He came within fifty feet, then thirty, and finally within ten feet of his prey.

Quietly pressing his body into a standing position, Conor's foot slipped slightly on a small patch of wet grass. Even in the midst of all the volcanic destruction occurring in the realm, Nemelissi heard the small noise. It turned its hideous head and looked at Conor, wearing an expression of unbearable pain. When it saw him, it snarled in grimacing pain and yet threatening the Champion at the same time. The assassin spat at Conor, spewing a vaporous substance directly at his face. Conor used a defensive shield immediately, an invisible rectangle of impenetrable power. The mist impacted the shield, melting it from side to side and from top to bottom.

Before Nemelissi had another chance to attack, Conor called forth a corridor directly behind the destroyer. It formed instantly, a silvery membrane surrounded by a solid perimeter. Conor extended his palm toward Nemelissi, throwing a blast of nature's energy at the assassin. The impact sent Nemelissi reeling. Conor followed his magic by running directly into his enemy and carrying the disgusting creature into the corridor. The two warriors disappeared into the membrane, leaving behind a stunned group of servants and a mass of earthen flora that used to be the most beautiful garden in all the Crossworlds.

CHAPTER FORTY-TWO

Purugama walked lightly, silently. He came around a forested corner of the Glade of Champions, not entirely startled by what he saw. Sitting quietly in a darkened cove, a place frequented by his long-time friend and brother, Ajur, the Author of All Worlds typed frantically on one of his laptop computers. Purugama watched him for a while without interrupting, curious about the man's impact on everything he knew.

Without the author, no one would exist. The Crossworlds would never have come into being. It was difficult for Purugama to understand. The creators were all he'd ever known. They were the source of all magical energy in the Crossworlds, the answer to all questions, the givers of life and death. Yet, they too bowed before this seemingly irrelevant human.

Without disturbing his concentration, Purugama quietly crouched down a short distance from the author. The great cougar placed his golden head atop his huge paws, which lay crossed over each other in front of the huge cat's body. He kept his breathing quiet, unobtrusive. He watched silently, wondering how one man who looked so common had created everything he knew. He wondered, most of all, whether this man could bring his brother Ajur back to life.

The author wore an exasperated look on his face as he tapped away on his keyboard. Using the second of his laptop computers, the author wrote his story as fast as possible. Good fortune had reminded him to save repeatedly, so when the first laptop shut down, he lost only a tiny fraction of what he had already added to Conor's tale. The computers were a definite concern, but that wasn't what bothered him. He seemed to be fighting against an unseen presence, something that hacked into his hard drive from somewhere far away from the Glade of Champions. The first time it happened he reacted normally, thinking it just another quirk of technology. He reached up to press the backspace button to erase what he imagined were the machine's ghostly thoughts.

At first his solution worked. The strange text disappeared whenever he erased it. After the initial corrections, though, the computer seemed to fight back, running the text forward again as soon as he lifted his finger from the key. After that, the text forced a stalemate against the backspace key. No matter how many times he pressed it, or how hard he leaned on it, the bizarre alien text remained. The author gave up when he realized the backspace key no longer worked at all.

Thereafter, in a frantic attempt to neutralize the invader, the author wrote with abandon. He wrote anything, sometimes the continuation of the story, sometimes gibberish. He found that as long as he typed, the alien author could not interrupt his story.

It became a game of triumph and frustration. The Author of All Worlds would insert a triumph for Conor in his battle against Nemelissi, only to be thwarted by a pause in his thoughts, his alter ego taking over. He would do his best to overwrite whatever elements of the story rose up against him and his Champion. At times he was successful, but at other times his aloofness nearly cost Conor his life. It was only the memory of Conor's headband that saved him from Nemelissi's first attack with the living spear.

In a strange way, the battle became exhilarating. The alien presence repelled any progress the author made in any part of Conor's journey. Whoever wrote in competition with him had turned away every effort to destroy the predatory corridor. He had initially intended for the portal to be vaporized by the energy stream concocted by Mr. Hikkins and Janine. That plan became academic when the killer corridor reenergized, moving forward toward earth again. The insertion of the redwoods as allies against the portal had drained his first laptop, and now the alien writer had even managed to overcome the power of nature. Although the author focused most of his attention on Conor's predicament, he sincerely hoped the earth didn't suffer an identical fate to that which befell Wilzerd.

"Damnit!" he snapped. His musings had cost him the keyboard again. He watched for a moment while individual keys depressed rapidly under his nose. He splayed his fingers out, ready to take control again, when a voice startled him.

"May I be of assistance, author?" said Purugama.

The man jerked his head up. He saw his beautiful creation sitting like a sphinx about twenty-five feet from him. He didn't answer at first; looking at Purugama made him lose all sense of reality.

Purugama rose to his full height. He flared his golden wings, sweeping them up and down. The resulting breeze cooled the author, but also blew a significant amount of debris around. "I repeat my question, sir," said the great cougar. "How may I serve you?"

"You can't," answered the author. "I must be left alone to complete the story. You can stay here by my side, if you like. I'm beginning to realize that anything can happen with this final journey. We might need to make a hasty retreat, depending on who materializes here at the glade. Do you have the ability to create corridors?"

"Have you instilled that skill within my range of magical powers?"

"Oh, I believe so," replied the author. "At any rate, we'll find out soon enough. If I lose control of this keyboard for good everyone might lose their powers – creators and Champions alike."

"Then I will sit quietly while you complete your work."

Purugama crouched again. He began to preen himself but stopped suddenly. He decided to remain still and quiet and let the author work undisturbed. He looked at the man, the simple human seemingly without any powers of his own. *This was the ultimate presence worshipped even by the Lady of the Light?* The great cougar could hardly believe it, and yet, he had seen things far more peculiar during his life in the Crossworlds.

He watched the man battle against his unseen enemy, listened to him curse in the old language of earth. The great cougar chuffed quietly. So, these were the battles of the most revered being in the Crossworlds. The Champions were pitted against hideous and powerful destroyers who time and again pushed them beyond the limits of their abilities. Even the youngest of their ranks had faced overwhelming evil, as Conor did somewhere within the system at this very moment, and this unassuming man, the designer of everything Purugama knew, spent his battles typing furiously into a small box.

It seemed too bizarre for Purugama to comprehend. The big cat rested his chin on his paws again. Almost ready to close his eyes for a nap, Purugama heard the tapping cease for a moment. He opened his eyes to find the Author of All Worlds staring at him. He had closed and locked the little machine. He knelt before it, resting his hand on a strange insignia pasted against the cover.

"I'm very glad you're here, Purugama," said the author, smiling for the first time since he arrived in the Crossworlds.

"As am I," replied the great cougar. "It is an honor to serve and protect you."

"No one could perform that duty better, my friend." The Author of All Worlds walked up to his creation, completely awed by the sight of the Champion. Even at slightly more than six feet tall, the author shrank into insignificance next to the big cat. Purugama towered over him, his golden fur covering hard rows of thick, powerful muscle.

The beast's head could have swallowed the author whole or snapped his body in two with little effort. The author stood in front of Purugama, feeling the massive cat exhale, blowing his hair and clothing back and forth. He reached up and grabbed one of the giant fangs in the great cougar's mouth. It felt rough and coarse near the gum, but clean and smooth down toward the tip of the tooth. Purugama turned his face slightly, trying to break the author's grip. The man held on, fascinated by the reality of his creation. The immense fang looked to be almost twenty inches long. The author's hand seemed childlike as he gripped it. It was almost like holding a baseball bat in his hand; that's how large it seemed.

"Awesome," the author said to no one in particular. "Absolutely incredible."

Purugama turned his head far enough to wrench his tooth free of the man's grip. One of his huge wings pushed against the author, making sure he could no longer hold on. The big cat washed his huge tongue over the tooth a few times, removing the stain of human touch. As he did this, he noticed with some irritation that the author had moved to his side and now stood examining one of his wings. The great cougar ripped the leathery appendage away, but the author simply waited for it to return to the cat's flank. He seemed particularly interested in the base of the wing, near Purugama's body. He began squeezing the muscle, hard enough to make Purugama flinch. The cougar moved away, circling the author, keeping his wing away from the curious man.

"Please," said the author, "I don't mean to offend you. You must understand, Purugama. I created you, and to see you here, alive, right in front of me, well..." The author eyed the leather saddle fastened around Purugama's shoulders. Without asking permission, he walked right up to the cougar's flank, grabbed hold of the side flap and pulled himself up onto Purugama's shoulders.

The great cougar reacted violently. He bucked the author into the air, throwing him to the ground. He turned to face the author, growling a menacing warning. "That seat is reserved for he who earned it, author. Only Trolond Tar occupies that saddle. It is true, you are the Author of All Worlds, and you may have indeed brought me into existence. Never forget, though, that it was the creators who delivered me to the Glade of Champions and gave me my immense size and magical powers. I serve the Lady of the Light, and only the first warrior journeys with me. Try that again and I swear by my brother Ajur I will finish Nemelissi's work before he ever arrives."

The author sat with his head in his hands, rocking back and forth lightly. He was not a young man anymore. The fall had tweaked just about every muscle in his body. "So that's it," he said, grimacing as he tried to rise. Placing a hand on the ground, he pushed himself up gingerly. "You're mad at me for what happened to Ajur."

"He did not have to die," said the great cougar. "Certainly if you hold power over life and death there might have been another way.

Perhaps you could have allowed him to perish somewhere other than the shadow world."

"And if that had happened?" asked the Author of All Worlds.

"Then he would be standing here now, addressing you as I am," answered Purugama. "You had no right to take him from us."

"Tell me something," said the author, now more than a little perturbed at Conor's mentor. "If Ajur had not sacrificed himself for Conor and Janine, do you think they would have survived the battle with Seefra's monster?"

Purugama felt the rage boiling within him. When logic runs headlong into emotion, even the most grounded mind explodes. "There had to be another way!" Purugama roared the answer at the top of his lungs, advancing on the author as he did so. "I was there! I could have flown Ajur to safety! He did not have to suffer such a horrible death! It was your choice! You condemned him to eternal suffering in the bottomless chasm of the shadow world!"

"How wrong you are," replied the Author of All Worlds calmly. "After everything you've taught Conor, how can you react in this way?"

He walked up to Purugama and gazed into one of his golden eyes. "Are you only concerned with your own feelings? Would you rather Conor had perished under the weight of Seefra's monster? Who could battle Nemelissi if that had happened? Don't you see, cat, that the Crossworlds operates in ways that at times may drive you mad? In all the centuries you've served the creators, have there not been other situations that tested your belief in the rightness of things? Has not your faith been taken from you, squashed, re-formed, and then riddled again? Have you not always come back to your senses, accepting the overall meaning of life?"

The logic beat against Purugama's brain, but the great cougar's emotion won out again. "He was my brother!" The big cat snarled viciously at the author, snapping his huge jaws at the man. "I grew up with him! He was closer to me than any other cat I've ever known, and you took him away!

"I had accepted the loss as something that occurs during the course of battle. How do you think I feel knowing you took him from us on a whim! You could just as easily...."

"I could just as easily have spared Gribba's world, and all his people," said the author, completing the cougar's sentence. "Life follows its own course, Purugama, even in the mind of someone like me. You all worship me, even the creators bow before me, but I tell you again that I am just a man. I am nothing special, I hold no outstanding abilities, and I merely tell the tale of the Crossworlds. Some of the story is delightful, but as with life, much of it is filled with struggle and pain. Believe it or not, Purugama, that's what keeps us going. If we didn't have mountains to climb, we would wither away rather quickly."

The big cougar tamped down his emotions, listening to the words the author spoke. He still didn't like them, but what he said made a good deal of sense. He backed up a few paces, giving the author room to breathe again.

"You speak of loss, Purugama," continued the Author of All Worlds. "I feel for you, I sincerely do, and I want you to think about something. I wrote the Crossworlds into existence. I breathed life into the creators, the Champions, Conor, Janine and every being you've helped over the years. You were the first creature that entered my mind many years ago. The first time I thought of you I was only twelve years old, a young boy. Can you imagine?

"Conor emerged from your creation, as did the Lady of the Light and all the other Champions. I gave Ajur his look, his personality, guiding him through his life. I made certain he took Conor under his wing during his journeys with Maya to repair the Corridors. I always gave Ajur a sense of compassion for Conor, even when he first met him as a young Champion."

The author walked up to Purugama, taking a giant ear into his left hand. He rubbed it briskly, and this time the cougar did not pull away.

"I loved Ajur," said the author, looking into Purugama's golden eyes. "Don't you think it broke my heart when he died? I buried my face in my hands at my desk and cried for nearly an hour after he gave his life for Conor. It was a heartbreaking moment for me, don't you see? I love every character in the Crossworlds deeply. You are all as real to me as you are to each other."

The author released Purugama's ear, bopped the great cougar on the forehead with his free hand. "How do you think I felt when you perished after your first journey with Conor?"

Purugama lowered his great head, chuffed at the ground, blasting streams of dust in every direction. "It is difficult," he said, still avoiding eye contact with the author. "The Champions have given of themselves time and time again. Sometimes I feel it wouldn't be too much to ask a small favor in return. But I suppose I understand. Perhaps we expect too much from our deities, forgetting they too have restrictions placed upon them."

Purugama raised his huge head, letting his jaw drop slightly as he looked at the Author of All Worlds. "I apologize for my outburst. Forgive me, author. The rage has boiled inside me for some time."

The Author of All Worlds grabbed Purugama around the neck, holding the big cat tightly. The man inhaled the aroma of the giant cougar, in much the same way he snuffled his own animals at home. "You have nothing to apologize for, cat. If you only knew how much you've meant to me during my life."

"I am happy to serve the Author of All Worlds," said Purugama.

The author released the great cougar, looking into his golden eyes again. "Drop the formalities around me, Purugama. I tell you again, I am just a man, an ordinary human much like Conor."

"Conor might have been ordinary when I first encountered him on that distant mesa many worlds from here," replied Purugama, "but he has, as you well know, matured, and in many different ways. He has rediscovered himself, author, or maybe I should say he has discovered his true self." The great cougar sat and scratched his neck with a giant hind paw. He shook his huge, golden head before addressing the author again. "May I ask you a question?"

"Of course," answered the author.

"How did you know Conor's real identity?"

"Will you believe me if I tell you it came to me merely by chance?"

Purugama stared at the author, mouth open in disbelief. "That cannot be. How can such a metaphysical transformation merely 'occur'? You are the Author of All Worlds, the designer of the Crossworlds. We would all gladly give our lives for you. Without you we would all perish."

"Purugama, listen to me," said the author. "My life is not that different than yours, or Athazia's, Maya's or even Conor's. We all open our eyes every day, complete whatever tasks we deem necessary and then close our eyes at night. We listen to the chaos in our minds, feel tremendous emotional swings, and after all is said and done, we wonder what our lives really mean."

"I have trouble grasping the fact that you struggle with the same troubles a creator or Champion would," said the cougar. "It is difficult when one has lived for thousands of years according to certain principles."

"Perhaps viewing things from a different perspective might introduce new energies into your soul."

"Perhaps," replied Purugama, interested in the author's last comment.

Just as the big cat opened his mouth again, a thunderous crash occurred less than fifty yards away. From out of nowhere, a corridor gleamed in the sunlight on the surface of the lake. With its silver perimeter resting solidly on the water, the glistening membrane ballooned out across the lake's surface. As the portal reformed in an attempt to release its occupants, the filmy interior pulled tightly against the two warriors.

Purugama could clearly see the outline of Conor's body against the silver membrane. He could also distinguish the destroyer's body as well. Nemelissi's huge, muscular form appeared to be wrapped completely around Conor's smaller frame. The great cougar trotted forward a few yards, ready to intercede should his friend require help. He stopped suddenly, gasping at what he saw inside the corridor.

A bolt of blinding, white-hot energy exploded within the membrane. Stretched beyond its limit, the portal imploded when Conor unleashed the power of the sun. Nemelissi appeared first, blown backward more than a thousand yards. The destroyer cleared the water completely, never even dampening a toe as it sailed over the bulk of the lake. Its body slammed against the volcanic rock stacked haphazardly under Maya's resting place.

The entire mountain blew apart under the weight of the explosive impact. Nemelissi disappeared into the sharp rocks, immediately buried under an avalanche of red and brown debris. For a moment it seemed to Purugama as if Conor had finished the assassin.

Conor emerged from the portal, ripping away the remaining pieces of the membrane. He kept his eyes mostly on Nemelissi's progress across the lake, but he also made quick scans around the glade for additional threats. During one of these inspections, he spotted Purugama and the Author of All Worlds. Without saying a word, Conor threw another corridor in their direction. It formed quickly, standing thirty feet across and twenty feet tall. Purugama looked at the glistening membrane, and then back to Conor.

"Away, cat," called Conor. "Go now! Take the author away from this place."

"I will stay in case you need my strength in battle," answered Purugama, not willing just yet to leave his apprentice alone with Nemelissi. "How can you be certain of victory?"

"Follow my orders, cougar!" bellowed Trolond Tar. "I have no time to argue. The Author of All Worlds is all that matters. Take him through the corridor and protect him while he writes. He's the only one who can save us."

Purugama nodded once to Conor, understanding what he didn't care to acknowledge. He was right of course; the author had to be protected at all costs. But the great cougar felt terribly uncomfortable leaving his apprentice alone with Nemelissi.

Something bothered Purugama about their battle. It appeared to be a little too one-sided for Conor up to this point. Just as Drazian had surprised him before, Purugama felt Nemelissi must be holding something back. He felt afraid for Conor, but he obeyed his commands nonetheless. After all, he was Trolond Tar, first warrior of the Crossworlds and the battle was his to win or lose.

Purugama lowered his shoulder for the Author of All Worlds. Seeing the man's hesitation, the great cougar gently encouraged him, promising not to hurt him again. When the author continued to stand apart from the big cat, Purugama exploded.

"Climb into the saddle now, author," he growled, "or I will go myself and leave you here for Nemelissi's pleasure."

The image of the assassin prompted the author to quickly board the giant shoulders. He sat comfortably, one hand grasping the bronze leather strap, the other clutching his laptop laptops. He rocked forward when Purugama stood, but balanced himself again as the cougar prepared for flight. He marveled at the cat's unbelievable strength. They shot through the corridor, disappearing without a trace.

CHAPTER FORTY-THREE

The western edge of the Hoopa Indian reservation resembled an immense spiritual ceremony. Hundreds of giant redwoods, glowing in unison, stood like bristling towers guarding the coastline. A ring of ground troops under the command of Captain Carlson had cordoned off the area, ensuring the security of everyone in and outside the circle of energy.

Thousands of media representatives from around the world pressed against the line of stone-faced soldiers under Carlson's command. Individual questions couldn't even be heard any more. The raging torrent of media competitiveness had finally overwhelmed the beast itself.

"Can you tell us the nature of..."

"Under whose authority...?"

"The people have a right...."

"When do we get to speak to your...?"

Captain Carlson managed the perimeter in a jeep driven by his most trusted line sergeant. He maintained a fifty foot "no media zone" between his men and the growing army of news personnel. Anyone caught with one foot across that line was immediately arrested and shipped back to Fort Beale for detainment.

A few media hacks had tested Carlson's resolve. They spent the rest of their assignment time shackled to a transport plane or inside a temporary holding cell back at Beale. None of the other news representatives challenged Carlson after those first attempts. The world would have to be satisfied with the images they received from far beyond the actual battleground.

If they only knew what was heading their way, what would arrive any second now, they certainly would have prepared themselves.

CHAPTER FORTY-FOUR

Conor slid across the surface of the water. The assassin had suffered injuries, but nothing serious enough to permanently disable it. Nemelissi was far too powerful, too physically imposing to let a mere mountain overcome him. He was in there, under that giant pile of stone, plotting how he would stage his next attack. Conor knew it in the bottom of his soul, and yet he slid forward confidently, challenging the creature to come out and finish the battle.

"Face me, assassin!" he yelled. "Come out from behind your temporary grave and face the unlimited power of the equinox!" He yelled every insult he could think of at the creature, even though he knew Nemelissi wouldn't understand a word he said. The context would serve, though. The assassin would understand his intent well enough.

Conor skated over the shimmering lake, watching the crumbling mountain for any sign of unnatural movement. He came within a hundred yards of the edge of the lake when a concussion blast knocked him flat against the surface of the water. It took every bit of wind from Conor's body. He barely remained conscious, and he couldn't breathe at all. The spell he had used to stay aloft had been obliterated as well; Conor felt his body sinking and struggled to keep his head where the sun could warm it. He looked back at the mountain a split second before it vaporized right before his eyes.

Nemelissi's spell had turned the rock pile into ashes. It stood defiantly at the shattered base, one powerful hand outstretched toward Conor, answering his opponent's challenge. Debris exploded in every direction, a good deal of it raking Conor's clothing and skin as it flew by at hundreds of feet per second.

The assassin stalked toward the lake, once again completely unscathed, dangerous and lethal. The creature seemed to regenerate constantly; Conor's attacks were not slowing it for very long. Now it stood at the edge of the fouled water, one clawed finger pointed at Conor, the other pointed toward the brightly lit sky. It stared straight into the blazing sun and shrieked at the heavens, pulling its other hand up toward the sky as well. Calling out a spell in a language unknown to Conor, the assassin clasped its hands together six times. At the impact of the final embrace, the light in the sky vanished. The sun appeared to blink out, as if controlled by a magical switch, leaving the two warriors in absolute darkness.

Conor waved his hand in front of his face, seeing nothing. He panicked like a child afraid of the darkness after his parents close the door to his bedroom. He gathered himself, helped by the uncomfortable knowledge that Nemelissi no doubt could see perfectly well without light. He had to think and form a strategy against this new threat. He heard a soft swishing sound at the edge of the lake where the assassin had been only seconds before. Then his ears caught a larger splash, obviously a creature diving into the water. Conor looked around, finding nothing to comfort him. It was pitch black. He was treading water in the middle of a deep lake, Nemelissi was coming for him, and there wasn't a thing he could do about it.

CHAPTER FORTY-FIVE

The face-off between the reporters and the men guarding the group inside the perimeter intensified. Every minute it seemed as though another fifty media representatives arrived on scene, accompanied by at least one additional helicopter. Up to this point, Captain Darren and his pilots had performed extremely well. He had the sense to put in a call for another squadron, and between the two groups of military choppers, order had been maintained.

Early on, before he had a chance to arrange his birds, a news chopper had broken through the line. Hoping for an exclusive on the energy beam projecting out toward the bizarre red curtain in space, the crew had flown dangerously close to the power flow. The awesome strength of the energy stream almost inhaled the chopper. If they had actually contacted that much raw power, the news team would have disintegrated instantly along with their chopper. If it weren't for some quick action by Captain Darren's pilots, the news crew might have been lost forever. As it was, their helicopter was now permanently grounded. The media representatives had been escorted to a holding truck not far from the Hoopa reservation. They would spend their remaining time in Redwood County under guard.

Back at the military barrier, things started to get ugly. Over a thousand media representatives, many from other countries and who spoke little English, were focusing their rage at the center of the ring surrounding the glowing redwoods. They had left courtesy and decorum behind long ago. Those who challenged the line were quickly turned away, but more and more of the media hacks began defying the captain's orders. Soon one of the three companies of soldiers had converged at the center of the barrier. They did their best to hold back the growing horde of reporters and their crews.

A few on the outskirts of the main melee tried to crawl through quietly. They were quickly rounded up, but Captain Carlson knew trouble when he saw it. He ordered his driver to pull his jeep up close to the horde of reporters. He would call to the base for more troops, but first he wanted to try and talk some sense into these idiots. He grabbed the remote microphone and flicked the switch.

"Attention," he said in a normal voice. When the crowd didn't react, he cranked the volume all the way up. "ATTENTION! MEMBERS OF THE MEDIA! LISTEN TO ME, PLEASE!"

About half the people clumped together looked over at the jeep. The rest kept wrestling with the soldiers, trying to break through the line. Captain Carlson, angry now, placed the face of the microphone against the metal plating of the jeep. A searing, high-pitched shriek tore through the crowd, forcing everyone, civilian and military alike, to break off and cover their ears. Carlson quickly grabbed the microphone and addressed the crowd.

"Now that I have your attention, I want you all to listen to me. You will not be allowed to penetrate this perimeter. I have full authorization from the government of the United States to use any means at my disposal to stop you. If I order these men to shoot to kill, they will do so without hesitation. The stakes are too high. This area must be protected, and I assure you, it will be."

"We have a right to know what's going on!" demanded one of the media hacks closest to the soldiers.

"The only rights you have here are what we decide to grant you," answered the captain. "The earth is under attack. That is all I can tell you at this point. If you interfere, even in the slightest, it's very possible you could damage our ability to defend the planet. Now, I'm only going to say this once. I want this barrier honored. The next time someone breaks the integrity of that line there will be dire consequences. Is that clear?"

No one answered.

Captain Carlson held the microphone against the steel plating again. When he felt certain everyone had received a good dose, he lifted the microphone again. "I SAID IS THAT CLEAR?"

Almost everyone backed up toward the edge of the barrier. A few of the more brazen reporters, those obviously trying to make a name for themselves or ensure a promotion, stood their ground. They made no move toward the soldiers again, but they also did not return to their side of the safety zone.

Captain Carlson glanced at one of the line sergeants standing near the defiant reporters. The sergeant on the ground ordered his men to arrest them. A minor struggle ensued, but the soldiers quickly subdued the reporters. The media representatives bellowed their objections, twisting in the arms of the sergeant's men. Other crews began gathering at the edge of the perimeter, voicing their displeasure at the treatment of their compatriots.

Carlson stepped out of the jeep to restore order. The scene looked to be disintegrating again and he wouldn't have it. He walked to the edge of the barrier, separating his men from the main bulk of the media horde. He opened his mouth to speak, but no words came forth. His eyes had found something fascinating to look upon. His head turned so he could focus on the event. Over a thousand additional pairs of eyes followed the captain's line of vision. Suddenly the struggle for the people's right to know somehow didn't matter.

A massive corridor flared to life about fifty yards down the makeshift path surrounding the burning redwoods. Purugama jumped through the middle of the membrane, carrying the Author of All Worlds on his shoulders. The cougar, as big as a tank, landed gracefully on his golden forepaws. The huge hind legs followed in perfect unison, highlighting the animal's powerful bearing. The gigantic cat flexed his wings a few times before tucking them back into his flanks. As he walked toward the cluster of shocked media and military personnel, he turned and asked the author if he had fared well during their journey through the corridor.

"I am well enough," replied the Author of All Worlds, "although next time any passageways I design will exist without the temperature extremes."

"If you spend enough time in the corridors, the cold and heat will eventually become unnoticeable," said Purugama.

The author laughed off the remark. "Maybe for someone as huge and powerful as you."

The media horde stood as one, so shocked by the sight of Purugama they had scarcely taken one photo or even shouldered a digital camera. The sight of an ordinary looking human sitting on the giant cat's shoulders only intensified their surprise. When the huge, winged cougar spoke to the man, a few of the weary, beleaguered press corps simply fainted away. They dropped to the ground around their fellows, who did nothing to help them. Those who managed to stay on their feet simply stared at Purugama and his peculiar passenger.

Captain Carlson signaled to his men. They formed an arc in front of the media horde, while half a dozen non-commissioned officers flanked Carlson as he walked forward to meet their strange new visitor. When they closed the gap to twenty feet, the captain held his right hand up for a full second. The men behind him stopped together, as a unit.

"That's far enough," said Carlson to the man riding the giant cat.

"You must let us pass," replied the author. "The fate of the world depends on it."

"That might be precisely why I shouldn't let you through," answered Carlson. "How do I know you're here to help us and not them? With that thing you're riding on at your disposal, you might walk up there and annihilate everyone inside that circle."

Purugama snarled almost imperceptibly. One of Carlson's men raised his M-16, flicking the safety off. Carlson turned to meet his eyes briefly. The soldier nodded, lowering his weapon. Purugama walked forward slowly, not attempting to threaten the captain in any way. The cougar filled the entire trail, muscles bristling with every sturdy step. When he stood face to face with Carlson, he addressed him directly. Cameras and video equipment came to life in the background.

"Look into my eyes, commander," said the great cougar. "Do you see any evil intent? Can you not see that we have come to lend assistance to my brothers and the creators?"

Captain Carlson took a long look at Purugama's stunning golden eyes. He said nothing for quite some time, preferring to let reason take its course. He had learned through his years of military service that rash decisions usually resulted in disaster.

"Commander," continued Purugama calmly, "I will leave the

decision in your capable hands. If it is your will then keep us here, outside the circle. I ask only that you judge my intentions by the events that have already occurred here today."

"Sergeant Aguilar," barked Carlson, still looking into Purugama's eyes.

"SIR!"

"Let them through on my responsibility. Make a hole in your barrier and guide them directly to the beam's origin. Take six men and make sure no one else follows you. Is that clear?"

"Clear, sir!" answered the sergeant. He quickly jogged toward the group of soldiers handling the pack of media representatives. Calling out six names in rapid succession, he guided the men back to the trail. Aguilar turned back to the giant cougar and his passenger. He waved them forward before guiding his men toward the barrier. Giving a few commands to the soldiers standing their posts, the sergeant soon created an opening large enough for Purugama to walk through. He smiled as he watched the giant cat shoulder past his nervous men. The man on the cougar's shoulder nodded to the soldiers individually, according them the respect they deserved. Sergeant Aguilar and his men jogged through the redwoods toward the beam. Every once in a while, Aguilar looked back to make sure his charges followed closely behind them.

CHAPTER FORTY-SIX

Conor did his best to tread water silently. He couldn't see a thing, which only added to his panicked state. He knew Nemelissi had entered the lake. The destroyer would come for him quickly. Conor figured the creature had covered about half the distance between them by now.

He tried his best to file through his options. He could swim for the shore as quickly as he could, but Nemelissi would catch him easily; he felt certain of that. He could use the power of the equinox to relight the sky, but he couldn't be sure of the limitations of Nemelissi's magic. Even the energy bestowed upon him during that magical moment on the cliffs might not be enough to overcome the destroyer's power over nature.

He felt the water move against his legs. Something huge passed beneath him in the murky depths. It could be Nemelissi, or perhaps another creature the destroyer had conjured up underwater. Conor's panic returned, reenergized by the new threat. He reached down with his right arm, passed his hand back and forth in front of his legs. He wanted to fight back, but he couldn't come up with a strategy. Even if he breathed a spell that would allow him to walk on water again, he feared Nemelissi would simply snatch him from the surface before he reached the shore.

Something touched his foot. Conor jerked his leg up, a reaction learned long ago during jaunts into the ocean with his uncle. He did not enjoy things he couldn't see touching him. When it happened he reacted in the only fashion he understood. He knew it would give away his position, but he couldn't do anything else. Nemelissi no doubt had found him by now. These passes were designed to frighten him. It was working quite well. He was scared to death.

He accidentally gulped down a mouthful of lake water, causing him to spit and cough. Conor cursed himself for being so stupid. Struggling to keep his head above water so his lungs could function again, he scraped his hand roughly against his left thigh. He felt the inside of his knuckles brush across three small lumps in the outer stitching of his leather trousers. It didn't register at first, because at the time he touched them, another huge creature of the deep swept alongside him. This one displaced a huge amount of water, carrying Conor ten or fifteen feet from his original position. It bumped up against him, letting the young Champion get a good idea of its true size. Conor inhaled deeply, frightened beyond all sense, as the creature moved by him. As he settled back into the water, his mind recalled the lumps.

The magic pellets! He could change everything about this encounter with just one tablet! He reached down, digging his fingers into one of the small compartments. He touched the tiny pellet with the tip of his index finger. As he felt a sense of relief for the first time since coming to the glade, Nemelissi's clawed hand wrapped itself around his right ankle and shin. He had only enough time to register the sensation before the destroyer pulled him into the murky darkness. Conor hadn't even had time to breathe, and now he flailed away with eyes open, looking for any way to get back to the surface.

His frantic struggle quickly used up what little oxygen he had. As Nemelissi dragged him deeper into the lake, Conor gulped down the last of his reserves. He started to black out. He blinked his eyes once, then twice, horrified by what he saw. One of Nemelissi's creatures swam right by his face. Conor screamed, releasing his remaining oxygen as he dug his finger into the small pocket in his trousers.

CHAPTER FORTY-SEVEN

Purugama walked carefully through the blazing redwoods, carrying the Author of All Worlds on his back. The man no longer held the saddle strap on the great cougar's shoulders. He clutched his remaining laptop in one hand while shading his eyes with the other. The combined energy of the trees' auras burned so brightly he dared not move his hand from his eyes. If he squinted through shaded fingers, he could see in the distance a group of beings shining just as brightly as the trees. *The creators and the other Champions,* he thought, *are fighting the battle against the predatory corridor, a battle I had designed and brought into existence.* He only hoped those of the Light would be successful, because he doubted he would be able to lend them any assistance.

The big cat crested a small rise in the forest. The author looked upon a scene he could barely believe. All he could think of was how grateful he felt that the military had cordoned the area. The media would lose their minds if they saw something of this nature. Half of them would never even get any film, because the other half would trample them on the way to set up their own staging areas. He looked down upon the Champions and creators, standing their positions bravely. He saw an energy stream more powerful than anything he had ever imagined flowing through each of them on its way to the killer corridor.

The author bypassed every other being in his line of vision, letting his eyes move directly to the Lady of the Light. She stood calmly, consumed by enough energy to light a hundred cities. Her glistening silver hair, dancing softly with the electricity sweeping around her body, framed a face and figure that took the author's breath away.

Even under stress, Athazia looked stunning. She held herself gracefully, wearing an expression of composed dignity. The Champions loved her as they did no other and now the author understood why. He had depicted her as well as he could during every journey in the Crossworlds stories. Looking at her for the first time, however, he realized that her beauty had surpassed even his description. He hoped when this was all over he might have a chance to speak with her.

Behind her stood four of the other Champions – Eha, Therion, Surmitang and Maya. He smiled upon seeing Eha, the affable cheetah who always saw the bright side of everything. Surmitang sat behind him, proud, dignified, doing his best to hold a regal bearing while conducting the intense energy flow. The author looked at Therion and gasped. If Purugama was a giant, then Therion was truly monstrous. The author had pegged him at five thousand pounds in previous stories. Looking at him now, he wondered if he hadn't underestimated his girth. While nearly everyone else in the line seemed to struggle with the energy flow from time to time, Therion merely accepted it, added his contribution and pressed it forward. Other than that modest activity, the giant lion looked to be scanning the savannah for an evening meal.

The author shifted his eyes to Maya, the Lord of the Crossworlds Champions. He felt a lump in his throat when he saw him. Except for his great size, he was the same alley cat he knew so many years ago.

Even back then he knew Maya carried a wide variety of special qualities. During the course of his ongoing legend, however, the hooded cat had grown beyond the author's descriptions. He had brought the *fingers of the forest* into this journey completely on his own, and as he sat calmly, fur quivering all over his body, the author couldn't help but wonder how many dimensions existed within Maya's soul. He wondered also whether his old friend would be just as aloof when he approached him again after so many years.

Purugama leaned toward the head of the line, responding to the noise of fern leaves crunching underfoot off to their right. When he turned his head to follow it, he saw Janine running up the rise to greet them. She approached them wearing a wide smile on her face. As she moved up the small hill, her left foot slipped on a damp pile of leaves. Her athleticism saved her. She merely placed one palm on the ground for balance and kept coming forward. After regaining her stride, she looked up again, the smile mixed with a small portion of embarrassment.

Without even acknowledging the man on his shoulders, Janine jumped into Purugama's furry neck. She grabbed two giant handfuls of fur, squeezing herself into that soft spot just above the cougar's massive chest. She breathed him in for a full minute before calling out his name.

"Purugama," she cried, smiling, "thank the creators you're here."

"Keeper," the great cougar answered.

"And Conor?" she asked, smiling. "Has he arrived as well? Is he following you?"

Purugama glanced up at the man on his shoulders. The great cougar seemed to tell him that since this was his story, his invention, it would be his responsibility to deliver any bad news. The author took the cougar's meaning perfectly, although he certainly didn't enjoy the prospect of breaking this young woman's heart.

"I'm afraid Conor is still engaged with Nemelissi," the author said as evenly as he could. He didn't want to sound morose about the prospect. He kept his eyes connected with Janine's, partly because he wanted to give her strength, and partly because he knew how deep her love was for Conor. "We left him at the glade of Champions, my dear. He instructed Purugama to carry me through a corridor of his own construction. Obviously he wanted me to come here, where he felt my safety would be assured."

The eye contact didn't help Janine much. The author didn't sense sadness or fear in those blazing green eyes, he saw nothing but anger. Everyone else belonging to this peculiar group of saviors had offered the utmost in deference to him. Janine had no time for any such pleasantries. Her lover was out there putting his life on the line for all of them.

"He saved your life and you left him there to face that psychotic freak all by himself?" she asked. "Then why are you sitting calmly on Purugama's shoulders? Get down from there, find yourself a place to write and save his life." Janine walked around to the side of the big cat and grabbed the laptop out of the author's hands. She tugged on his pants leg, pulling him over the side of Purugama's muscled flank. "Hurry, start writing the end of this story and make sure Conor comes back alive." Although startled by her disposition, the Author of All Worlds understood and obeyed her without pause.

As he fell off Purugama's back onto the ground, he heard the giant cougar chuckle to himself. Ignoring the cougar's amusement, the author rolled into a crouched position. He brushed away a few fern leaves as he stood, closing his eyes briefly while his hand swept over his face. Squinting one eye open again, he saw Janine's hand extended out to him. He took the delicate fingers in his larger, calloused palm, surprised by her strength. Janine pulled him down the gently sloping hill toward a darkened area off to the side of the power stream.

"This way," she said. "It's the only place within the circle of redwoods where you'll be able to see your screen." She guided him through a thick stand of immense old-growth trees. The author felt quite insignificant next to the impressive giants of nature. He reached out a few times, touching the crusty burl at the base of the trees. Their majesty took his breath away.

Janine guided him to a small opening within the trees. In a cool, dimly lit area no larger than twenty by twenty feet, the author walked up to a level section of a fallen redwood. He could place his laptop on the burl and sit comfortably as he wrote. He walked past Conor's girlfriend and set the spare laptop to the side in its case. He opened the first one, pressed the on button and waited for it to cycle through the startup process.

"You can return to the seeker if you think he needs you," said the author. Janine hadn't stopped staring at him since bringing him to his makeshift office in the woods. "I'll work here until it's over. Then I'll come find you and Mr. Hikkins."

"If you don't mind," asked Janine, "I'd like to stay here with you. I'd like to know when Conor is out of danger."

The author looked at her, trying his best not to let his worried feelings show in his expression. He wouldn't dare tell her about the alien hand competing with him for control of the story. She looked troubled enough already. He knew how intelligent she was, though. If she pushed hard enough, she might figure it out for herself. "Alright, if you think it wise, then

stay here with me. Truth be told, I could use the company."
Janine smiled. She watched the man open the programs on his laptop, saw his eyes focus, his face become increasingly determined.
After a minute or two, she watched him peck away at the keyboard
using only his index fingers. A thumb hit the spacebar every now
and then and maybe one other finger managed the shift key a time
or two. For the most part, though, the author had designed every
journey in the same fashion. She almost giggled watching him, but
tempered elation soon gave way to sincere worry.

Minutes later, the author stopped writing. He held down one
or two keys with his thumbs, willing the command to work by
applying as much pressure as possible. He typed again, trying to
control more aspects of the story. Finally, he gave up completely.
Pulling a thumb disk from his pocket, he inserted it into the side of
the laptop. After copying all of his work to date, he pulled the disk
from its port, capped it and reinserted it into his pocket. Then he
did something that shocked Janine. He closed the laptop, lifted it
high into the air and brought it down with all his might on the bark
of the redwood. The laptop shattered, small components flinging
in every direction. Then he retrieved the backup from its case and
destroyed it as well.

"What have you done?" shouted Janine.

"Maybe I've saved us," answered the author, "maybe I've condemned us, I'm not sure anymore."

"You destroyed your computer!" said Janine. "How can you
write the story without it?"

The author looked at Janine for the first time since he had situated himself on the prone redwood. "I'm not writing the story anymore, Janine. I'm not sure who, but someone, or something, has
invaded my computers."

CHAPTER FORTY-EIGHT

Conor struggled for the small pellet in his trousers. He had no oxygen in his lungs at all. If he took a breath at this depth life would end for him very quickly. He clamped down on his urge to inhale, keeping a mental image of Janine foremost in his mind. If he failed, and Nemelissi escaped, the destroyer might find its way to earth. He would never allow that to happen even if it took a miracle to win the battle.

He shifted his gaze in all directions, looking for the hideous serpent that swam by his nose only moments ago. He couldn't see it, but he felt the lake water responding to its movements. He knew there had to be more than one, either that or the solitary creature moved incredibly fast.

His fear of the mysterious being nearly caused him to forget about Nemelissi. That mistake became academic when the destroyer's hands latched onto Conor's chest and back. After reshaping the appendages into two bizarre, razor-sharp, scaly weapons, Nemelissi slapped them against Conor's torso.

Conor winced with an indescribable agony, feeling another complex potion of poisonous acid seeping into the wounds. He swung his free arm at the destroyer, frustrated by his sluggishness in the thick water. He swore he could hear Nemelissi gurgling, laughing terribly even down here in the black depths of the lake.

Conor felt his strength leaving his body, the poison obviously acting as a paralysis agent. Nemelissi wanted to watch him perish either by drowning or by immobilization. Either way he wouldn't be able to help Janine or anyone else for that matter.

Conor curled his finger around the pellet. It seemed to be the last conscious act he would ever perform. Before blacking out, he recited a spell in the deep recesses of his mind. He remembered the Lady of the Light stressing the need to remember one particular spell. She tested him weekly during their journey to the shadow world. She told him that someday the incantation might very well save his life. She would accept no errors in pronunciation, no mistakes in the timber of the delivery. Conor clearly remembered her telling him that he might have only one shot at getting it right.

At times the young Champion felt put upon by her constant instruction. As he closed his eyes, giving way to his suffocation, he realized she had been right all along.

As Conor finished the spell, forty million gallons of lake water pitched straight up into the air in one massive eruption. Soaring above its former location, the water congealed into a giant oval, leaving every living thing behind in the moist lakebed. The huge serpents called forth by Nemelissi squirmed ineffectively on the hard ground, squealing their displeasure. Thousands of other creatures, natural residents of Maya's lake, flopped or crawled around, looking for their former watery home. The Lady's spell had attacked the molecular structure of the lake itself, sending only the water aloft. How long it would remain suspended in mid-air depended on Conor.

Now revitalized, he opened his lungs wide, drinking in huge volumes of air. Even the inky blackness of the glade failed to dampen his spirit now that he could breathe again. He used the same finger to extract another pellet from a lower pocket in his trousers. Fighting with every ounce of strength he had, he bent his elbow, lifting the pellet to his mouth. Throwing it in, he stuck his index and middle finger into his throat, forcing the tablet down. He tried swallowing; when that didn't work he willed the pellet down into his stomach. He accompanied its journey with another incantation, one much easier to recite but no less important. After finishing his mental narration, he felt a surge of strength returning to his limbs.

CHAPTER FORTY-NINE

"We'd better get back," said the author, looking around the immediate area for any undamaged parts of the laptop. He wanted to make sure nothing left in these woods would function.

Janine stood with her mouth wide open, still unsure of recent events. "Wait a minute," she said. "What do you mean someone else is writing the story?"

"I can't explain it, Janine. I don't really understand it myself. All I know is that as soon as Conor and Purugama entered my world, strange things started to happen. It's almost as if another being came through the corridor with them, a silent, invisible creature with magic powerful enough to compete with me for control of the story."

"That's just great," she replied. "So now you're telling me that Conor is risking his life fighting an assassin you armed with infinite power, and now you can't even help him anymore?"

The Author of All Worlds looked down at the ground. He couldn't face her; he knew the feelings she had for Conor. "I'm afraid not. All we can do is wait and hope the story gives Conor the power he needs to defeat Nemelissi."

"Come on," said Janine, pulling the author along in her wake. "I'm taking you to Mr. Hikkins."

The author had no time to argue. The same delicate, strong

hand grabbed his palm, pulling him down the trail through the redwood forest. The author pulled his free hand up to his eyes, screening the blinding light from the power beams surging through the trees. He trusted his young guide, letting her lead him left and right through small passages between the ferns.

Before long they emerged into the clearing where the energy streams converged. The author lowered his hand; the brightness seemed to bother him less at this location. He saw the seeker maintaining his control platform diligently, working to balance the forces of magic and nature to achieve the greatest effect from the recipients in the line. Mr. Hikkins didn't even look over as Janine towed her strange passenger into his presence.

The author watched the diminutive man work silently at his workstation. He neither looked up nor acknowledged his two visitors. He was used to Janine's soft interruptions; if he sensed another alongside her he gave no sign of admission.

"Mr. Hikkins," said Janine.

The seeker made no comment.

"Mr. Hikkins, please!"

The soft-spoken man looked up at his former student, somewhat chagrined at having to do so. He glanced over at the author, not a pore of his skin changing expression. "So you are the Author of All Worlds?" he asked flatly.

"Yes, although that distinction may soon change."

"Tell him," said Janine. "Tell him what you told me."

The seeker touched a few commands on his screen. Without looking again at the man standing to his left, he commented on their situation. "You have lost control of the journey?"

"How did you know?" said the author and Janine simultaneously.

"An educated guess," answered Mr. Hikkins. "One must always prepare for such contingencies. An unfortunate turn of events, one we have no power to bend to our advantage. Let us hope our young Champion saved a few tricks for his opponent."

"What?" gasped Janine. "That's all you two can say?" Conor's girlfriend scanned the area around the energy flow. She saw the great cougar lying on his haunches near Maya, protecting his Lord. She admired his loyalty for one second before calling out to him.

"Purugama, we're leaving!"

"You can't be serious," said the author.

"I won't allow it," added the seeker.

"Then strike me down," Janine said defiantly. "You two can stay here and hope all you want. I'm going to help Conor."

"I'm sorry, Janine," injected Purugama, walking up to join the conversation. "I cannot allow you to put yourself in jeopardy. If the Lady of the Light doesn't blast me into oblivion for letting you put yourself in harm's way, then Trolond Tar surely will."

Janine stood there, fists clenched so tightly she could feel warm blood seeping from her palms. "Purugama," she said. "I am the Keeper of the Keys, and I order you to take me back to the glade. We are going to help Conor fight Nemelissi, even if it costs us our lives. Is that understood?"

Purugama shifted his golden eyes to the seeker. Mr. Hikkins did not return his gaze. He wanted no part of the decision. The author took in the great cougar's gaze, answering with reason and not emotion.

"She's got a point. She is the Keeper. It gives her the right."

"Very well, then," said Purugama. He turned to Mr. Hikkins. "A corridor back to the glade, if you please, seeker."

Mr. Hikkins looked at the Lady of the Light, who stood quietly, completely involved with guiding the energy stream to her fellow creators. He rotated his gaze to the left, looking toward the leader of the Champions. Maya, still suspended in his private communication with the *fingers of the forest*, had already called forth the corridor for Purugama and his passenger. Standing a few feet to his left, a shimmering golden doorway patiently waited for the travelers to access the membrane.

Janine pulled herself up into Purugama's saddle, locking her feet into the stirrups as well as she could. She took hold of the strap, ordered Purugama forward and held on with everything she had. This wouldn't be her first time aboard the giant cat, but she had never flown by herself. As the big cat rumbled through the forest toward the corridor, she did her best to roll with the massive body underneath her. When Purugama jumped into the membrane, Janine crouched low in the saddle, one hand on the strap, the other firmly entrenched in the golden fur.

The seeker watched the two of them disappear into the portal. He returned his attention to the board, meticulously monitoring every development. Every few seconds he made minor adjustments, sometimes increasing the energy flow, at other times pulling it back or balancing it a little. It looked like a successful operation, but the author noticed the consternation in the seeker's face. He decided Mr. Hikkins had become closer to Conor and Janine than he cared to admit. *Strange*, he thought, *how characters in a story grow beyond their basic descriptions.*

"Don't worry about them," counseled the author. "Even with everything that's happened I'm sure we'll see them again very soon."

"I agree," replied the seeker. "You gave Conor an alarming sense of resourcefulness, although they are not my primary concern at this moment."

"Why?" asked the author. "What's happening with the beams?"

"The energy stream is performing beyond our expectations," said Mr. Hikkins. "However, the predatory corridor is most determined. I place its distance from earth at less than twenty-two thousand miles."

"Isn't that a little close?"

Mr. Hikkins shot the author a perturbed glance. "It's more than a little close, sir. When the portal crosses the twenty thousand mile barrier, the earth's exosphere will be sucked into the membrane. When that happens, atmospheric chaos will follow."

"How long until the barrier is breached?"

"Sixty minutes. Ninety if we're lucky," answered the seeker. "So you see, author, whether or not Purugama returns with his two passengers, we still may not be able to save earth."

CHAPTER FIFTY

Conor called out to the heavens, commanding them to obey the voice of Trolond Tar. The horizon flashed once, then twice, but darkness remained. Nemelissi's magic continued to cast a deep shadow over the Glade of Champions.

Conor broke Nemelissi's grip, rolled away from the destroyer and stood facing the stench and the warmth he felt from its body. He tore the headband from its perch and wiped back the soaked hair from his eyes. Replacing the headband, he taunted Nemelissi.

"The ultimate assassin fails again," spat Conor. "I am here, alive in front of you, Nemelissi. Is there no spell powerful enough to subdue me? You killed me before, but you can't get the job done this time, can you?"

Nemelissi slammed its palm down on the damp lakebed. The entire glade shook under the weight of the destroyer's frustration. It turned, sniffing around for its servants – the giant, gruesome sea monsters whose purpose had been thwarted by Conor's magic.

He heard three of them languishing near the center of the lakebed. The assassin pulled three strands of hair from its head, dropped them to the ground and ordered them forward. As they inched away from their master, Nemelissi opened a few pores on its forearm. A green, steaming liquid squirted from the skin, covering the strands of hair with the boiling essence. The bizarre follicles came to life immediately, shooting across the damp ground toward the struggling serpents. The moment they made contact, the physical construction of the creatures changed completely. No longer dependent on hydrogen in the water for their lives, the serpents stood on strong, newly-emerging legs.

Shaking the scaly gills from their necks, they inhaled deeply. The skulls of the creatures changed as they swallowed the breath of life. Sharp fangs emerged from expanding jaws, deep-set eyes spread to both sides of the skull, and elongated ears stretched down the sloping necks, detecting everything around them.

One of the creatures howled with pleasure after the transformation. The others quickly answered. All three sniffed for the scent of Nemelissi's enemy. They listened for the heartbeat of their master's prey. In no time at all, they had pinpointed Conor's location. Nemelissi gurgled as he watched his monsters heading toward Trolond Tar.

Conor didn't need light to understand what had occurred. The three lumbering giants made such a racket he could almost sense their exact location. He knew they were coming for him now, but he also knew he enjoyed a small advantage. He had spent many days here at the Glade of Champions. He knew the size of the lake, the distance to the forest, and at precisely what distance into the forest the trees became dense. He knew the creatures could see in the dark, but not as well as in daylight. If he could lead them into the trees, he might have a chance. With a little time, he might be able to devise a way to defeat them.

A glowing doorway appeared high in the sky. Conor looked up hungrily, hoping it might be a delayed reaction to his spell. Just as quickly as it appeared, however, the light blinked out, leaving the young Champion in darkness again. Conor ran toward what he felt was the wall of bushes fronting the forest. He had no idea if he ran in the right direction, but he knew the size of the lake. If he traveled very far without breaking through the bushes, he would know to shift direction and run the other way. He heard the creatures turning to follow him. Conor stopped for a moment, listening intently for the sound of Nemelissi's clawed feet scraping across the soft dirt of the lakebed. He heard nothing but the transformed serpents pounding their way toward him. The assassin had disappeared.

Encased in an inky darkness only a spell from the shadow world could provide, Purugama soared high above the Glade of Champions. Janine hugged the cougar's shoulders tightly, crouched low against his fur for protection. The ghostly darkness covering the glade unnerved her; she called out to Conor two or three times out of a sense of panicked frustration. Purugama soothed her before strongly suggesting she keep her voice down. The darkness, although frightening, served them as well as Nemelissi.

The big cat realized that Conor might be helpless in the shadows. He weighed the options for only a few seconds before calling for the sun to reveal itself. Having never used a spell given to him by Athazia before, he wondered if it would overcome Nemelissi's powers. When the shining blue sky returned to the glade, he thanked the Lady of the Light silently. Dipping his left wing, he instructed Janine to begin searching for Conor.

"There!" she shouted. As soon as they completed the turn she saw him running full bore toward the forest.

"Mind of the creators," Purugama gasped. "Look at the lake." The cougar lost his ability to speak as he soared under the suspended lake water toward Conor. Both he and Janine craned their necks, looking at the bottom of the lake floating above them.

Looking down toward the glade again, they watched as three gigantic creatures rumbled across the lakebed, running full tilt after Conor. Purugama tucked his wings into his body, sloping down directly toward his apprentice. The big cat veered slightly to his left, taking a course toward the slowest of the creatures. He told Janine to hold onto his fur tightly and to be ready for any sudden movement.

Conor never broke stride when the sun appeared in the sky again. He looked around once to get a bearing on the creatures chasing him. After that he summoned Eha's cheetah speed, hoping to reach the forest well before them.

At fifty yards from the forest's edge, he heard one of the creatures squeal in agony, tumble over and fall dead on the lakebed. He continued running, not exactly sure what had happened. As the first few branches of the bushes guarding the forest slapped against his cheeks, he heard another attack.

This time he turned. He grabbed the first tree trunk he passed, holding it for ballast as he swung around to examine the ruckus on the lakebed. He saw golden flashes raining down on the creatures from high in the air. Purugama's cosmic bullets blew apart the hide of the second monster, who took a few more instinctive steps before crashing down in a pile of muscles and meat.

Conor saw the last creature coming for him, but he stood fast, now that only one of his enemies remained. He jumped out in front of the tree, calling forth the power of the equinox. The slow-witted creature never had a chance, nor did it realize what kind of power it was bracing itself against. It obeyed its master's commands – loyalty to Nemelissi was all that mattered.

Conor released the power, bracing his back against the tree for support. He opened a larger channel this time, allowing a greater amount of energy to blast through his arms. It hit the huge creature square in the face. The white-hot beam split the creature in two lengthwise. Fortunately for the animal, death was immediate and painless. The two halves flopped over, hitting the lakebed with dull thuds occurring almost on top of each other.

Stunned by of the sun's power, Conor forgot to call it back while he watched the creature die on the lakebed. The massive energy stream continued forward, streaking across the glade like a laser beam, finally slamming against the base of a mountain. As it did with the creature, the beam sliced through the dense rock without slowing. It would have continued indefinitely had Conor not regained his senses and commanded the power to return to him. With the sun's energy neutralized, Conor grabbed a large branch, holding himself up while gathering his strength again.

"Quite impressive, Trolond Tar," said Purugama. The great cougar emerged from the trees with Janine casually sitting on his shoulders. "The legend holds true."

Conor spun around quickly, ready to respond if the voice he knew so well was another of Nemelissi's tricks. When he saw Purugama, he knew instantly who had come to rescue him. The big cat had brightened the sky, eliminated two of the assassin's creatures and landed so softly in the forest Conor hadn't even heard him coming.

"Conor!" cried Janine as she jumped from the leather saddle. She ran to him, jumped into his arms and kissed every part of his face. Janine squeezed her boyfriend with all her strength. Conor couldn't hold back his joy at seeing her, no matter how dangerous it was for her to be here. He returned her embraces, kissing her nose, ears and lips. He wondered if their love would always feel so fresh and full of passion.

Purugama turned his eyes from the reunion. He couldn't understand emotional human interaction. He would allow them a few moments together before delivering what he felt would be terrible news. After annihilating the two creatures and watching Conor dispatch the third, Purugama had landed in the forest for a reason.

While Conor regained his strength, Purugama had listened to the trees, leaves and debris surrounding them. He crooked his ears, listening to the entire glade, his home for more than a dozen centuries. He knew every sound, every nuance, anything native to the glade.

In the same sense, he knew every sound the glade could *not* naturally produce. The great cougar had listened intently, closing his eyes to allow for maximum concentration. Nemelissi no longer resided in the Glade of Champions. It had sent the creatures after Conor as a distraction. While Purugama and his brother fought the serpents, it had cleverly disappeared. It used the creatures to mask the sound of an emerging corridor. It didn't take a genius to determine where Nemelissi had gone.

"Conor, Janine," said Purugama, interrupting their reunion. "We must leave immediately."

Conor looked over at his big friend. "What is it? What's happened?"

"Nemelissi is no longer here," replied the cougar. "The assassin has left the Glade of Champions."

Conor understood immediately. He left Janine standing alone as he ran to climb aboard Purugama. He mounted the saddle in one athletic leap. Janine, refusing to believe that their momentary reprieve had vanished, stood in the place where she and her boy-friend last held each other. She turned her head and looked at Conor. Finally understanding, she ran to Purugama's side. Conor lowered an arm, lifting her bodily into the saddle behind him.

"Where did it go?" she asked as she wrapped her arms around Conor's waist.

"Back to earth," answered Conor, snapping the leather strap in frustration. "This whole battle has been nothing but a decep-tion. Nemelissi wanted to wait until the author was completely helpless. When you arrived here with Purugama it knew the time had come. It sent the creatures after me, knowing you would come after them. It left the glade as soon as Purugama fired the first vol-ley."

"Mind of the creators," gasped Janine, "how long do you think it's been there?"

"I wonder how many of the soldiers Nemelissi has already dis-patched," said Purugama. "Their weapons will be largely ineffec-tive against it."

"The Author of All Worlds," gasped Conor, "we must save him." He slapped Purugama's shoulder as he called forth a corridor. "Go, cougar. Fly!"

CHAPTER FIFTY-ONE

Nemelissi crept silently through the shaded trunks of the redwood forest. The destroyer inhaled deeply, swallowing the wonderful aroma of damp redwood burl. Sneaking through the ferns, it allowed numerous furry leaves to lightly scratch its muscular arms and torso. The grotesque assassin contemplated returning here after its mission. Spending the remainder of its life in such a place did not seem unappealing at all.

Turning toward the light inside the reservation, Nemelissi walked another hundred yards before scampering up the base of one of the smaller trees. Finding a sturdy branch fifty feet above the ground, the destroyer gazed patiently at the scene below. A small city of people, not unlike those it encountered on its journey to find its target, stood in a loose assembly around a central field of bright lights. Hundreds of trees, very similar to the one he occupied, displayed a brilliant light which connected all of them in the immediate area together.

Nemelissi scanned its objective. A small, organized band of people held a much larger group at bay. The smaller group was all dressed alike, and they carried weapons. Nemelissi filed that information away for when the time came to make use of it. The larger group, those kept outside the lighted circle, didn't seem to be much of a threat. They acted in discord with one another, jostling for position while carrying bizarre instruments on their backs and shoulders. The destroyer knew instinctively they were not weapons. It also knew that an attack through their ranks would provide the greatest amount of chaos, just the diversion it would need. Raising its head, Nemelissi looked beyond the perimeter of lights, beyond the flaming trees to the central gathering area. It vaguely spied the configuration of creators and Champions, spotting Therion more easily than the others. The giant lion stood out from a thousand yards away. *He could pose a problem,* thought the destroyer. Eha and Surmitang were easily dispatched, but Therion's bulk gave him an advantage even Nemelissi couldn't match.

The creature's head twitched when it caught sight of the Author of All Worlds. He stood next to a similar but smaller individual who seemed to be monitoring something in front of them. Squinting, the assassin looked as closely as it could at the author.

Nemelissi did not enjoy great aptitude with reason. Still, it could not understand its jailer's orders. *How could an assassin of its caliber be sent after so a meager a target? No matter,* it thought. *The assignment would be completed.* Whether it returned to annihilate its jailers remained to be seen.

Before attacking, Nemelissi scanned the entire area, looking for the best angle of attack. The large group of bustling humans would provide an escape from the organized forces holding them at bay. The assassin had tussled with beings of this sort before. It recognized the technology each of the men carried. It would find a way to neutralize their advantage before turning them all to ash.

Nemelissi looked up again, focusing on the Author of All Worlds. The destroyer emitted a low, lengthy growl, preparing itself for battle. Grasping the branch in one huge hand, it dropped to the ground quietly. Using the tallest of the trees ahead of him as a guide, Nemelissi jogged lightly toward the outermost circle of media vans.

Conor, Janine and Purugama broke through a corridor high above the Hoopa reservation. Sailing back and forth on an invisible grid, they looked for any disturbance occurring in the forest below. They spotted the author immediately, keeping their arc of flight always within easy striking distance of his position. If anything started to happen, they wanted to be on the ground as quickly as possible.

"We should leave the Keeper down below, on the ground," suggested Purugama. "If a battle ensues, it would be better if she were not aboard."

"No, Purugama," said Conor. "Whatever happens from here on in, I want her with me; just as I would always want you by my side."

Conor felt Janine's arms slide around his waist. She hugged him tightly, burying her cheek in his shoulders.

"Very well," replied Purugama. "I suppose six eyes are better than four. I only wished to secure your safety, Keeper."

"I know that, Purugama," said Janine, "although I feel safest when aloft with you."

"Keep your eyes sharp, then," said Purugama. "If Nemelissi truly is here, there's no telling what might happen first."

CHAPTER FIFTY-TWO

"You men!" barked Captain Carlson. "Brace the gap in that line, and don't let one of those idiots through!"

Carlson shook his head. Things were beyond his control. The supplemental troops hadn't arrived yet, although they should have reported for duty over thirty minutes ago. The media horde had tripled in the last hour, and more were arriving every minute. *They would have their story after all,* thought Carlson, *though it might not be the one they came here to get.*

"No, no, not there. Over *there!*" Gesturing wildly, Carlson ran up the hill to gather his thin line of troops into a semblance of a blockade. Halfway up the hill he turned his gaze toward a chorus of screams coming from the rear of the media mob. There were so many people milling about, Carlson couldn't see what caused the trouble at first. Suddenly, his mouthed dropped as he witnessed a bizarre and frightening scene.

Media vans flew in every direction, bouncing off giant redwoods like toys thrown about during a child's tantrum. The vans and support vehicles slammed into each other, careening off boulders and trees before crashing to the ground again. Any media personnel caught in the chaos had no time to try and duck for cover. The dark magic caused the vehicles to move with an unnatural speed. A van would be stationed normally one second, the next it would fall on its side, slide across the fern-covered soil and take to the air as if some invisible hand had grabbed hold of it.

Some news people were simply crushed underneath tons of falling automobiles. Others were knocked askew, most of the bones in their bodies shattered. They lay in the ferns, crying weakly. The vehicles seemed to sense those who remained alive, however, returning to finish them off in a violent crash of metal and rubber.

"Hold your line!" roared Captain Carlson. Even as he issued the command, he knew it would never happen. At least three thousand media representatives ran straight for the soldiers on the small hill. They came forward with the adrenaline of terror in their blood. They had seen something supernatural within their ranks and they wanted nothing more than to get away from it.

Carlson's men could have opened fire at point blank range, but it wouldn't have slowed them one bit. They were going to over-take the barrier, and once they were beyond it they would keep running. Who knew what would happen when they reached the interior of the circle of light.

Carlson let a twisted thought snap through his mind before dismissing it. He assumed that when the media saw what was oc-curring over the hill, their first thought would be to turn back and retrieve their cameras so their crew could be first with the story.

"What is going on out there, captain?" bellowed Major General McKimmey into his desk microphone. "I told you to hold that line no matter what! Now you tighten ranks and turn those idiot reporters...."

"With all due respect, sir, that's impossible. If the additional troops had arrived on time we might have had a chance. Some-thing happened out here, general. I'm not sure what. I don't think

I can explain it. There's a force of some kind, a power I've never seen before."

"Those troops should be no more than half a mile from your location, captain," said McKimmey. "I want you to reform your line with the other companies, drive those media fools back where they belong, and...."

"General!" interrupted Carlson, speaking rapidly, "those troops are driving into an ambush. Pull them back, turn them around. Don't let them come any closer!"

"Captain Carlson," said the general, "I'm not reading you. Say again, sergeant."

Carlson looked out to the road beyond the wreckage of media vehicles. He saw the bright headlights of the Beale Air Force Base personnel carriers rounding the last turn around the highway into the immediate area. They began rumbling off the main road, disbursing into an arc while the soldiers disembarked under orders of their superiors.

"Forget it, sir," said Carlson into his field microphone. "You can't help them now."

"Look at that," said Conor, pointing toward the chaos occurring below them in the forest.

"Nemelissi's work, no doubt," added Purugama. "A simple distraction, that's all."

"What do you mean, simple?" replied Conor. "People are dying down there. We should go down and...."

"And what?" interrupted the cougar. "Give the destroyer exactly what it wants? If you focus on its diversions, it will surely complete its task. One second after we land in the midst of that terrible scene, Nemelissi will surely find the Author of All Worlds. It would slice the seeker to ribbons before bathing the author in a pool of corrosive acid."

Conor sat quietly on the big cat's shoulders. "Yes," he said while scratching the cougar's ear. "You're right of course, but there must be something we can do for them."

"They are responding in the best way they know," replied Purugama, as he watched the terrified mass of people charging through the trees toward the line of soldiers.

Janine leaned over and spoke into Purugama's ear. "How will we know when Nemelissi is ready to strike?"

"With Nemelissi, one can never know," answered the cougar, making a lengthy turn out over the tips of the redwoods. "We will do our best to watch for a pattern of attack that leads in the direction of the assembly. It will not approach from the rear, for Nemelissi fears Therion's size and strength. Most likely the assassin will hope to draw attention away from the Champion's position, giving it a free path to the author."

"You mean something like that?" said Conor, pointing down to the mad rush of the media horde. Purugama swooped down fifty or sixty feet so they could get a better look at the rushing mass of screaming people. The great cougar scanned the crowd, looking for any individual whose gait appeared slightly different from the others. He didn't think Nemelissi had hid itself among them, and he saw nothing indicating such a possibility. Purugama pumped his leathery wings, lifting himself and his passengers away from the mad scramble. He would let the soldiers deal with the news people. His quarry was still hidden somewhere within the giant redwoods.

Nemelissi camouflaged its body against the rich brown trunk of a massive tree. Standing completely still, the assassin became invisible to the soldiers. Dealing with armed opposition hadn't been in Nemelissi's original strategy, but the creature didn't mind a little exercise before the final battle.

It took a deep breath, grasping the gigantic trunk with both hands. Without making a sound, it lifted itself from the forest floor. Pulling with hands and feet, the assassin climbed to a height of almost two hundred feet. Settling itself, it watched the two companies of soldiers disperse, preparing for their advance.

Nemelissi shook its head, wondering at the stupidity of most warrior groups. No doubt staying in a tight pack would make its job very easy, but their present formation would allow it to eliminate small segments of their forces undetected. *If only there were time,* Nemelissi thought. *It would be quite amusing to send the soldiers into frenzy.* As it was, Nemelissi would force them to fire on each other. It would watch from the trees as the small assembly of soldiers devastated their own ranks.

"Form up and prepare to advance," shouted Sergeant Wolfe. Keep the line staggered but steady. You're under my orders until we join with Captain Carlson's unit."

Wolfe's two companies fanned out among the redwoods. In squads of twenty soldiers each, they marched steadily toward the rear of the media staging area. Some of the soldiers came upon pieces of twisted metal, bumpers or doors that used to be attached to satellite vans. They said little to each other while picking their way through the debris. When they encountered the first of the mangled bodies, they still maintained their silence. Eyes began flicking to other soldiers in the line, however. Each member of the squadron could smell fear in their fellows.

"Steady," said Sergeant Wolfe into his shoulder microphone. "Keep your focus on the mission, not what's around you right now."

A small stream of liquid fire appeared from deep within the forest. It shot forward into the line of soldiers, striking Sergeant Wolfe's bulletproof vest. Sizzling like a piece of bacon on a hot plate, it sliced through the vest and into Wolfe's chest. The sergeant dropped like a bag of cement, never even able to give a final command to his troops. Wolfe flopped down on the soft, padded trail, his face buried in the fragrant fern leaves.

"Sarge is dead!" screamed a private standing six feet from Wolfe's body.

"Keep moving forward," sounded a voice in a distant microphone. "This is Corporal Jennings, assuming command. Hold your formation and move steadily toward...."

Another silent spark of green flame appeared in the giant trees. It focused for half a second before zooming toward the corporal. The stream of acidic fire went straight for her helmet. It slapped the corporal's headgear so hard it nearly knocked her over. The green flame splattered against her helmet, the fire forming into a spike. It drilled through the helmet easily. Corporal Jennings slapped her right hand against her head, knocking the helmet off in an attempt to thwart the attack. She never had a chance. By the time her brain sent the command to her arm, the smoking fire had already passed through her helmet. She died before her legs buckled. She hit the ground in much the same way Sergeant Wolfe did – completely lifeless.

Five seconds later, all hell broke loose. With no one in command

and dozens of voices flying through the headsets, the supplemental troops became easy prey for Nemelissi's ploy.

From two dozen locations surrounding the remaining troops, blazing emerald fire rocketed from the forest toward the soldiers. At precise intervals, members of the twenty-second infantry began dropping to the ground, various parts of their anatomy burned to cinders. Nemelissi knew exactly how to move the soldiers from a state of intense trepidation to one of complete horror. It watched from its high perch as all remaining order on the ground departed.

The soldiers, fearful they would be the next target for the strange phenomenon, began firing in all directions. The rounds sprayed everywhere, cutting into men, women, trees and anything else within a hundred feet of any soldier with an M-16. A few of those who remained calm shouted for the rest of the soldiers to cease fire. Their calls fell on deaf ears, however, as the hail of bullets snapped through the redwoods, echoing far into the night.

Nemelissi smiled. Its strategy had worked perfectly. Only fifteen or twenty of the soldiers remained standing. They would be easy enough to dispatch. In their dazed condition, it had only to rush through their ranks and dismember them before moving on to the Author of All Worlds.

"Yes, I see it happening," said Purugama, answering Conor's plea as the soldiers cut each other to ribbons. "We cannot intervene, young Champion. By doing so, you would open the door of opportunity for Nemelissi."

Conor watched the smoke rise up from the one-sided battle in the forest below them. The remaining soldiers cried out for their superiors, or for anyone they knew within their ranks. Conor could sense severe shock rampaging through those still living. If Nemelissi came for them, they wouldn't have a chance of defending themselves. He felt Janine's strong hand pinching his rib cage. She wanted him to help those troops, and she was letting know in no uncertain terms.

Conor grabbed her hand, pushing it away from his side. "I'll meet you back at the seeker's monitoring station. Purugama, watch over my girlfriend."

"Conor, no!"

Ignoring the cougar's attempt to stop him, Conor swung a leg over Purugama's neck and jumped. Falling more than three hundred feet through the towering redwoods, he used the thick branches and leaves to slow his descent. He dropped the last forty to fifty feet, free falling to the soft fern-lined forest floor.

He rose to his full height, standing toe to toe with a very nervous looking private. The M-16 in his hands found its way toward Conor's chest.

"I'm not your enemy," the young Champion said quickly. "I've come to help you. We have to move fast if you want to escape your attacker."

The private looked right through Conor. He examined the strange young man wearing the leather outfit capped with the elaborate headband. He held his rifle aloft, preparing to fire at the first sign of threat. A single drop of perspiration ran from underneath his helmet, down his forehead, by his right nostril and down his cheek. This seemed to bring him back to his senses.

"What do we do?" asked the private.

"Follow me," said Conor, jogging in the direction of the other soldiers. He wanted to collect them quickly, lead them to the interior where the seeker might find refuge for them. The others fell in behind Conor and his first recruit. They passed the remaining wreckage on their way toward another thick stand of trees.

Conor turned, encouraging the troops running behind him. When he looked ahead again, he barely had time to reach out and snare another of the screaming projectiles. This one had been aimed directly at the private's stomach, but Conor managed to intercept it before it hit its mark. He slapped his hands together, suffocating the flame within his palms. Ordering the soldiers to halt and quiet down, Conor listened for a sound he knew quite well by now.

He could sense Nemelissi's breathing, even its heartbeat if the assassin were close enough. After a moment or two, he gave the soldiers a hand signal. He wanted them to take a wide circle around the trees. This would lead them directly to the rear of the line, right past Therion. If he played his cards right, he could cut Nemelissi off before the assassin could intercept the soldiers. He nodded his head once, telling the private to lead the others toward the interior.

Conor watched the soldiers walk briskly through the blinding lights of the huge redwoods. Out of the corner of his eye, he saw a large shadow mirroring their movements.

CHAPTER FIFTY-THREE

"Proximity to earth measured at twenty-thousand, three hundred forty-four miles," reported Mr. Hikkins. The seeker ignored the madness occurring all around him. Media representatives had stormed the perimeter of the circle. They stood toe to toe with Captain Carlson's troops, staring at the incredible scene in front of them. To Carlson's credit, he managed to corral the media at the outer edge of the gathering. He made it very clear that the fun was over; anyone passing through his line of soldiers would be immediately shot. The media horde saw the expression on his face. No one challenged his authority.

"Exospheric balance beginning to unravel," continued Mr. Hikkins. "Weather patterns in this hemisphere should reach cataclysmic proportions by sunrise."

The Author of All Worlds looked around him. The giant redwoods gleamed with ethereal power. The creators and Champions, weary from hours of punishing energy transference, stood or sat proudly, trying their best to save Conor's world from a final desperate act by the Circle of Evil. The author looked beyond the energy line, up around the perimeter of the circle. Hundreds of media people and soldiers jostled for position. Some of the camera operators had indeed gone back to the vans for their equipment. A few had already shouldered their cameras, the red lights indicating a live feed.

The author looked back at Mr. Hikkins. Staring at the seeker, the man felt light-headed thinking about everything that was happening. "I created all of this," he said blankly to himself. He felt a throbbing pain lance through his heart. He wanted terribly to help the creators fight for earth's survival. Without control of the story, however, there was nothing he could do. He had no special powers, nor could he join the line and transfer energy toward the predatory corridor. He felt so inept, so completely helpless. He would be swept into oblivion along with everyone else on earth. He cared little for his own life. He only wished there was something he could do to help others.

The author looked out toward the sky. The blood-red membrane of the killer portal filled his whole world, and yet he could tell that night was fading. The earth's rotation would soon bring the dawn and with it the final breath of life for earth.

SACRIFICE

CHAPTER FIFTY-FOUR

Conor ran swiftly through the redwoods. He held the advantage here in this forest of old-growth giants. Having spent a great deal of time in this part of California, he knew how to make good time under these conditions. Keeping Nemelissi's shadow in sight, Conor flanked the line of soldiers, making sure he could jump in to defend them at a moment's notice.

The troops still held their weapons close to their bodies, for security's sake no doubt. Certainly they realized that anything less than a rocket-propelled grenade wouldn't slow their pursuer for a second.

The shadow dipped down into the ferns. It disappeared behind one of the larger trees. Conor noticed it and jumped the distance between where he stood and the lead private. He stood to the side of their line, slapping each on the shoulder as they passed by him. As the last five brushed past, he saw the shadow emerge from the ferns beneath a charred trunk of burl. The camouflage spell began to fade, and Conor stepped into the trail. He faced Nemelissi as the assassin walked confidently toward him.

"Now, private!" he yelled. "Head for the line of soldiers on the next hill, and make sure you don't leave anyone behind."

The troops didn't hesitate. They saw three more companies from Beale less than a hundred yards away. They ran for the safety of greater numbers. Perhaps they could return to help their benefactor after collecting themselves. Right now, though, they wanted nothing more than to leave the strange, haunted forest behind.

"Stop," ordered Conor, standing fast on the trail between Nemelissi and the soldiers. "Your fight is with me, not them."

The shadow wavered, and then disappeared. In its place stood the assassin, flexing its muscles while altering the composition of its skin. The sickly pores opened and closed, releasing smoke, a yellowish-green liquid, even a peculiar creature or two. Opening its mouth wide, the destroyer showed Conor row after row of needle-sharp teeth. It gurgled a few times, closing its mouth and smiling, seemingly for Conor's amusement. Then it looked toward the interior of the energy stream. It smiled again, this time more broadly. The gurgle returned, but instead of attacking, the destroyer sat down on the trail, staring at Conor as if it wanted to play cards with him.

The interior of the blazing circle erupted in screams or horror. Conor looked around, and then back at Nemelissi. The assassin smiled again, evaporating into nothing right before Conor's eyes.

"Mind of the creators, not again!" Nemelissi had used its image to lull Conor into a tragic mistake. While he stood guarding the trail against a phantom monster, Nemelissi had ambushed the Author of All Worlds.

The young Champion crouched, calling forth the strength of Therion's powerful hind legs. In one fantastic leap, Conor sailed through the air all the way to the seeker's workstation. He landed directly in front of Mr. Hikkins, who had safely positioned the author behind him. Conor looked back the other way, seeing a snarling three thousand pound winged cougar standing between him and Nemelissi. Purugama challenged the destroyer, swiping a huge, golden paw every time Nemelissi took a step in his direction. The assassin confronted Purugama many times, but the sight of the cougar's giant claws convinced it to back off.

Conor took in the entire scene, making up his mind instantly. Although he didn't see Janine anywhere, he trusted his mentor had delivered her to safety. The young Champion threw an immobilization spell at Nemelissi, hoping to momentarily delay any further action on its part. Happily, the spell hit the real thing, not another of its wraithlike imitations. Nemelissi struggled mightily, but the sparkling envelope held fast. Purugama advanced, smacking the assassin in the head a few times for good measure. This fueled Nemelissi's anger, allowing it to break free of the first few layers of the magical cage.

Conor grabbed the author by the shoulders, dragging him over to the edge of the bluff. Trusting in Purugama's flying skills, Conor took one last look at the author's eyes before hurling him into the abyss. "Don't worry," he told the Author of All Worlds. "I know what I'm doing." With that final comment, Conor pushed the author over the edge of the cliff. Strangely, the man didn't utter a sound. He merely fell silently toward the roaring ocean three hundred feet below.

Conor turned, shouting a command to his mentor. "Purugama! The author! Fly!" When the great cougar turned, Conor locked eyes with him. Purugama knew instantly what he was expected to do. He left the ground without looking back at Nemelissi. The huge, leathery wings propelled him toward the edge of Conor's world. The cougar sailed over the precipice, soaring straight down toward the falling man. With the author's rapid descent, he would smash into the rocky surf in seconds. Purugama flapped his giant wings, reaching out with his forepaws toward the author's upper torso.

Knowing Conor's plan, Nemelissi shed the last of the immobilization spell and ran past the seeker toward the bluff. It never sensed Conor coming toward it through the trees. With no time to react, Nemelissi instinctively held a strong hand out to its side, claws bared in the hopes of deflecting the attack.

Conor brushed the arm aside, running headlong into the destroyer, pouring all his weight into his right shoulder. The destroyer crashed to the ground, pummeled by the physical strength of all the Champions combined. It tried to rise and attack, but with blinding speed, Conor called forth the power of the equinox. The energy blasts knocked Nemelissi backward toward the magical beam holding back the killer corridor. Time and again Conor channeled the energy through his limbs, hammering the creature relentlessly. He drove Nemelissi closer to the power stream, hoping to trap it within the limitless energy of the creators, Champions and the *fingers of the forest*. Perhaps if he could force Nemelissi into the stream, the creature might be swept away, maybe even gobbled up by the membrane. Conor had no idea what might happen then, but at this point he really didn't care. He wanted Nemelissi out of the way so he could help defeat the killer corridor.

Six feet from the edge of the power beam, Conor could barely advance another step. The emanation from the stream repelled anything coming close to it. Conor dug his heels in, blasting Nemelissi dead center with a barrage of strikes that would have carved a mountain to shreds. The destroyer stepped back, its skin merely rippling from the force of the energy behind it. Conor watched as one arm and then another flew backward, locked in place by the powerful energy stream. Nemelissi's back arched, its pain-streaked face fighting with everything it had against Conor's onslaught. At the last moment, the creature's hair, a living weapon, streaked forward, wrapping itself around Conor's body.

The Champion couldn't save himself. He was going to be drawn into the power beam alongside Nemelissi. He fought the hair follicles, trying to free his limbs with the last few seconds he had. No spell emerged from his lips, no strength found its way through Nemelissi's powerful magic. Nothing could save him. Conor felt his feet lift off the ground as he and his enemy flew into the heart of the beam.

Purugama tucked his giant wings against his body, letting his weight carry him down toward the author. At the last second, no more than eight feet above the sharp rocks of the northern California coastline, the great cougar flared his wings and snatched the Author of All Worlds back from oblivion. The man groaned from the pain of Purugama's crushing grip. The force of the ascent pulled against the great cougar's muscles and tendons as well, forcing him to release an anguished cry to the heavens.

Purugama flew up and over the edge of the cliff. Before setting the author down near the seeker's workstation, he noticed the battle between Conor and Nemelissi raging dangerously close to the energy stream. He gently placed the author on the ground.

A second later the big cat was in the air again, flying toward his young apprentice. Before he had time to figure out how to help Conor, however, Nemelissi had turned the battle in its favor again. The destroyer was dragging Conor into the beam, and Purugama would never close the distance in time to help him. When he saw

Conor disappear into the blazing energy stream, he howled in frustration. He knew he couldn't do anything to help him now. Purugama turned toward the interior of the circle, heading back to the only person he could aid in any way.

"Nemelissi dragged Conor into the beam," said Purugama after landing next to the seeker.

"Yes," said Mr. Hikkins, busily tapping away at his makeshift keyboard. The seeker wore a peculiar smile on his face.

Purugama growled. "I see nothing funny about the fact that our Champion will be burned to a cinder long before he reaches the membrane of the killer corridor."

"Stay your anger, cat," said the gentle, diminutive man. "Conor and the assassin are alive and well inside the energy stream, although I couldn't tell you why. The temperature inside that beam is immeasurable, Purugama, but something has intervened and is keeping them alive."

"What will happen when they reach the membrane?" asked the cougar.

"No one can answer that," said the seeker, "and seeing as how there is little we can do to alter their course, I suggest we await the outcome of their battle."

Purugama stared at the seeker. He saw the strange smile return to his cheeks again. The man knew something, of that he felt sure. He either didn't want to spoil the surprise, or he truly didn't know what the outcome would be and didn't want to cause a severe letdown should the wrong result occur.

"What is it, seeker?" asked Purugama. "Your look is one of happy anticipation, a rare expression for one such as you."

"Prepare yourself, cougar," said the seeker. "I believe we've reached the end of this particular journey."

"Why do you make that claim?" replied Purugama. "You've just refused to recommend an outcome for Conor's battle with Nemelissi."

"That is true," said the seeker.

"Well, then," growled the great cougar, stepping uncomfortably close to the seeker.

"One way or another," responded Mr. Hikkins, "we will soon see an end to this altercation. The predatory corridor has broken the twenty thousand mile barrier. As we speak, the exosphere of this planet is being drawn toward the membrane. When that occurs, it will not matter whether the killer portal finishes what it has begun. The atmospheric convulsions caused by the elimination of the exosphere will exterminate every living thing on earth. By absorbing the planet, the corridor will only be consuming what natural life remains on a dead world."

"Then why are you smiling, if I may be so bold?" said Purugama.

"Because," said the seeker, "Conor is still alive. He is headed straight for the membrane. Has he not saved us before? Does he not possess qualities too complex for either of us to understand?"

Purugama stamped at the ground a few times. He couldn't share in the seeker's enthusiasm, not just yet.

"Did you not select Conor Jameson as your apprentice many years ago?" asked Mr. Hikkins.

Yes, thought Purugama, *I had.* And with that thought, he smiled, too.

CHAPTER FIFTY-FIVE

Conor fought the assassin with every magical spell he could summon. Nemelissi did the same, throwing the most hideous creatures it could conjure in Conor's direction. Their combined energies neutralized every attack thrust upon one another. Frustrated with the lack of progress, the two combatants charged each other within the white-hot mists of the energy beam. They struggled mightily, brawn against brawn, until at last the destroyer overcame the Champion, wrapping him in a column of powerful arms and legs. The four hands connected to Nemelissi's limbs raked Conor's skin, pulling bloody chunks of sinew and bone from his torso. After distracting the young Champion with a deep scrape across his chest, Nemelissi called forth one of its most powerful spells. It hit Conor squarely between the eyes, blinding him and freezing every muscle in his body.

The two warriors sped toward the predatory corridor's membrane at over eight thousand miles an hour. Nemelissi, seeing a chance for a small measure of rest, reared back while examining its prisoner. It breathed heavily, nourishing itself while its strength returned. It had Trolond Tar exactly where it wanted him, it would not allow him to escape again. As it played out twenty thousand years ago, the outcome of their battle would repeat itself today.

Conor's eyes were glued shut. As hard as he tried, he could not budge. He wanted to reach up and rub the outer skin around his eye sockets, but he found his arms unresponsive. He hadn't lost his sense of motion; however, he knew he and the assassin were zooming straight toward the membrane. He had no way of knowing how close they were, or how much time remained before they splashed into its center, disappearing forever.

As bad at the situation seemed, Conor found his mind floating in an oddly calm environment. He had lost his eyesight, so the other senses had pooled their resources to quiet his soul. He allowed his mind to float away, pursue any direction it pleased and bring back any memory it desired.

Conor began replaying every journey he had taken with his brother Champions. He relived everything, the initial confusing journeys with the great cougar, his dangerous adventures with the beguiling Lord of the Champions, even the desperate mission with Janine to retrieve the five keys of the creators.

Conor realized in his semi-comatose state that their incarceration and torture had been a small component of a much larger and greater journey, one he had been destined to undertake from a time long before the human race had come into being. The battle in the shadow world had been proof of that. He fought bravely alongside the most courageous beasts he had ever met. Even the loss of Ajur somehow complemented the entire voyage, for they had soundly defeated the Circle of Evil.

Now he sensed the end of his journey approaching. Conor coasted along in the power beam, secure in the knowledge that whatever he needed to defeat Nemelissi would be shown to him at the correct time. It became a moment of clarity. Even though blinded by Nemelissi's magic, he could suddenly see perfectly through his mind's eye. He saw a brilliant light. Within that light stood Athazia, creator of the Crossworlds. She held something out to him, a golden band roughly a foot in diameter. She placed it on his forehead, but before doing so, she showed him the insignia branded in the center of the ring. The letter "C" stood out in Conor's mind, and within his soul he heard the Lady of the Light repeat the phrase she spoke that day.

"Before your journey is complete, you will understand the meaning of the letter."

The crest burned a symbolic image into Conor's mind. The three definitions he wanted to offer the Lady before departing for the shadow world had indeed been wrong. He understood her meaning now. He thanked the creators for their wisdom. He felt an extreme sense of calm overtake his entire body.

The destroyer's spell fell away like an overcoat falling to the ground from a man's shoulders. Opening his eyes, he saw Nemelissi clearly through the blazing fire of the energy stream. Conor reached up, removing the headband as he covered the insignia with his palm. Holding it to his lips, he stared at Nemelissi while uttering a single word.

"*Capture,*" whispered the first warrior.

Nemelissi's eyes went wide as the headband leapt from Conor's fingers, springing forward toward the assassin. It threw its arms out wildly, trying unsuccessfully to deflect the golden crown. With a last desperate attempt at escape, the destroyer turned toward the approaching membrane, trying to swim into its mists to escape the all-powerful instrument of the creators.

It never had a chance. The greatest and most powerful cell the keepers had ever constructed took shape right before Conor's eyes. A hideous contraption, the cell was never designed to be an exterior set of tiles or bars of any sort. This time the keepers had outdone themselves. This cell worked from within its intended target. The organism it detained became a partner in the cell's molecular structure. Retaining its rigid organic composition, it held its victim firmly in place. Its method of capture, however, was sickening to witness, and horrible if one were the intended prey.

The headband expanded rapidly while collapsing around Nemelissi's muscular form. Golden spines shot forward in every direction, piercing the destroyer's skin, driving into its organs, muscles and bones. The creature who had annihilated Trolond Tar twenty thousand years prior to this day shrieked in horror as the golden cage swept through every molecule in its body. The beautiful crown worn by the creators' warrior had become their decisive weapon against the ultimate assassin. Nemelissi could do nothing to stop it from finishing its task.

The assassin's body involuntarily wrenched forward to a sitting position, placing Nemelissi's face directly in front of Conor's. The Champion grimaced, gasping loudly as he watched the cage flood through the creature's body, spilling out of every orifice, no matter how small. Golden spikes no larger than threads poured out from Nemelissi's eyes, nose, mouth and ears. Other filaments of a similar size forced their way through the tiny openings of its fingernails, nipples and genitals. Even the assassin's hair, a formidable weapon in its own right, gave way to a series of tiny golden follicles. The hair that flowed freely within the swirling energy of the creators' and Champions' power beam now shot straight out from Nemelissi's skull, frozen in a golden halo of magical adhesive.

Conor watched the cage solidify within the assassin's body. The only movement came from deep within the eyes. Nemelissi's soul spoke through the hateful gaze. Conor understood perfectly; he saw the willingness to destroy him even while Nemelissi's power had been neutralized. All it wanted to do was break the spell, attack and kill Conor and return to the redwood forest to annihilate everyone else.

Conor listened as the bones in Nemelissi's body started to snap. The cage had completed its injections, now it would finish its work. He watched its eyes as the cage pulverized the assassin. The hatred never left Nemelissi's soul, to the last breath it would despise its enemy. If it could not claim victory in their battle, it would never allow Trolond Tar to see an ounce of regret for the life it led.

The cage compressed, crushing the life from Nemelissi. Conor watched the volcanic eyes blink for the last time. His own lashes closed once, and then afterward he forgot about his opponent. He looked ahead at the approaching membrane. He knew he had only a few minutes left before impacting the predatory corridor. He had no idea what would happen then. He could be sent to some forbidden portal a billion miles from earth. He thought of Janine, finally safe back home. At least he had accomplished that goal.

The more he thought, however, the more he realized that as long as the predatory corridor remained, no one would be entirely safe. In that one moment of understanding he finally came to terms with his true identity. Up to that point he had lived his life as Conor Jameson – student, soccer player, boyfriend, son and brother. It was as if his childhood had been a hiding place, somewhere to keep him safe until the appropriate moment. At that time he would meet a giant winged cougar in the Crossworlds system. It all made perfect sense to him now. He knew why he had been born, what he was meant to do and what would happen if he failed.

Conor turned toward the corridor's membrane. The energy stream poured over his shoulders like a psychotic jet stream. The blazing white color of the power beam nearly blinded him. Ahead, all he could see was the bright crimson color of the gigantic portal. He fought to keep control of his senses, but nevertheless, he kept his eyes pointed straight toward the membrane.

Clasping his hands together with arms fully extended, he fell to his knees in front of the predatory corridor. He called forth the power of the sun, the unparalleled energy of the twice yearly equinox. He closed his eyes, bowed his head and summoned the primal force.

"*I AM TROLOND TAR!*" he yelled, releasing the power in one devastating spasm. The concussion inside the energy stream knocked him backwards at twice the speed he had been approaching the screen. Conor's limp body zoomed back toward earth, his head slumped over in a shock-induced coma.

CHAPTER FIFTY-SIX

"Look!" screamed Janine, pointing toward the predatory corridor. The author followed her line of sight, exclaiming wildly when he saw what caused her excitement. The crowd packed around the circle's interior roared its appreciation, pointing and gesturing toward the sky directly in front of them. Mr. Hikkins flicked a glance in the direction of the portal. After gleaning the information he needed, he returned his gaze to his instruments, for he knew that whatever occurred in the sky held no sway against empirical evidence. The seeker stared at his screen, waiting for confirmation of what everyone saw with their own eyes.

The initial blast from the energy in Conor's fists knocked the predatory corridor completely off its axis of attack. The monstrous wall of power, stunned into near submission, tried its best to absorb the immeasurable energy sent against it. The color of the membrane, so deep a shade of blood, began fading as the equinox unleashed even more bolts of unfathomable power. Red dissolved into pink, which soon gave way to white, the color of the sun's intensity at the exact moment of the equinox. The predatory corridor rocked uncontrollably in the sky, its mammoth image shrinking by the second.

The sun's power seemed to be driving it back toward its launch point. Then, in one gigantic surge, the energy of the equinox flattened itself over the entire corridor. A second later, a brilliant flash exploded in the sky above the earth. When the blinding light faded, leaving the stars shining against the moonlit sky, the predatory corridor had been obliterated. Not one shred of its former existence blotted the western skies. It looked as if it had never even entered lunar space.

"Destruction confirmed," reported the seeker. "Former bioreadings exist nowhere within the scanning capacity of these instruments."

"Are you saying earth is no longer in danger?" asked the author.

"The exosphere appears to have survived the initial magnetic influence," said Mr. Hikkins. "Whether there are any lasting effects remains to be seen. I will only confirm that the predatory corridor is no longer any concern of ours."

Janine jumped into Mr. Hikkins' arms, nearly knocking the man down with her exuberance. "He did it!" she yelled. "Conor did it! He saved us!"

Her comment caused the Author of All Worlds to quickly glance past Janine. He looked at the sky, now nearing the break of dawn, searching for any sign of Conor or Nemelissi. The two warriors seemed to have disappeared as soon as the fireworks started. The only indication of their existence lay in the shrinking energy stream.

While still connected to the creators, the Champions and the giant old-growth redwoods, the power beam retracted toward earth with alarming velocity. The author looked over at Mr. Hikkins, who must have noted the phenomenon well before he did. The seeker once again tapped away at the console below his fingers, trying to construct any information he could regarding the energy stream. The author looked back at the power beam. Its pace had quickened, its speed must have been well over Mach ten. He wondered what would happen if it impacted against earth with that much velocity.

He looked over at the formation of Champions and creators previously guiding the energy forward from the massive redwoods. Nothing unpleasant seemed to be occurring within their ranks, so the energy couldn't be backtracking toward earth. If it were, there would be a terrible repercussion against every single recipient. *No,* thought the author, *something strange is occurring.* But for some reason he didn't feel it would end badly for them.

CHAPTER FIFTY-SEVEN

"Captain," said a tired and cross Major General McKimmey, *"I want our party on site in no less than thirty minutes."*

"Yes sir," replied Captain Darren, firing up the MH-53E Sea Dragon helicopter. He pulled the big bird into the sky in a matter of minutes, leaning it into the wind toward their destination. After handing the controls off to his co-pilot, Darren turned around to face the general and his party. One of the passengers struck him as quite odd, but Darren didn't flinch after making eye contact with him.

"Sir," he said into his communications link. "I recommend we land just beyond the immediate staging area. There's a clearing fifty meters from the end of Carlson's line. If you can forward your orders to him during our flight, he may be able to position his troops so we'll have direct access to the site."

"Excellent, Captain," answered McKimmey. "Make it so. I'll handle the logistics."

Captain Darren saluted his superior officer. Turning back into the cockpit, he held a quick conversation with the co-pilot before taking back control of the chopper.

"ETA twelve minutes, sir," he said into the link.

"Right on schedule," said McKimmey. "Carlson's men are moving into position as we speak."

Captain Darren floated the Sea Dragon in a wide circle around the perimeter. The giant redwoods, the tallest and heaviest trees in the world, still glowed brightly with their magical contribution to the line of Champions and creators. On the ground, the peculiar man at the console had been joined by two others; another man and a younger woman, college-age at best. The others formed their ranks perfectly, still standing strongly in defense of earth.

Major General McKimmey peered out one of the side windows of the Sea Dragon. He looked at the bizarre line-up of individuals consumed by the immense energy stream. The robed humans he could almost swallow, although anyone from earth standing in the way of that much power wouldn't be around very long to tell about it. *They had to have come from somewhere else, but where, and what type of phenomenal powers did they possess?* The general shook his head. Every minute he involved himself in this fiasco meant another day trying to explain it to the brass. He felt certain he would be dragged over a bed of hot coals for the orders he already ignored. *They'd no doubt take their sweet time with it, too,* he thought.

If the robed humans weren't bad enough, the gigantic wild cats at the end of the line would surely stretch an already difficult description. He stared at Therion, thinking the lion must weigh at least ten thousand pounds. *Christ,* McKimmey thought, *if it went up against an Abrams or a Bradley tank, I'd give odds on the lion and probably win.* The other cats looked imposing as well. McKimmey scratched his cheek, wondering how he would ever explain things.

"Don't worry," said John Woodhaven to his boyhood friend. He clapped McKimmey on the shoulder. "It will all work out to everyone's advantage. Be happy you are alive to witness such an event. It isn't every day one of the mysteries of life unfolds before your eyes."

CHAPTER FIFTY-EIGHT

Mr. Hikkins watched the energy stream draw back toward the bluffs of the Redwood County forest. As it neared the shoreline, its pace slowed considerably. The seeker stared at the far boundary of the beam as it approached. The infinite power no longer bristled uncontrollably at the tip. Mr. Hikkins knew who lay within that refuge. He did not know, however, whether their Champion still lived.

After making landfall, the beam pulled through the line of creators and Champions. One by one, the recipients dropped to the ground after being released from their task. None of the creators moved a muscle after collapsing. Their strength depleted, they lay on the ground as lifeless as mannequins.

Even proud Surmitang submitted to the total loss of bodily strength. The huge tiger tried his best to maintain posture. After faltering a few times and resurrecting himself, he finally slumped over on his right side. He did his best to land without wrinkling his fur, so his stripes would be pleasing to look upon. When his tongue flopped out of his mouth, he used his last bit of strength to emit a chuff of disgust. Therion and Eha had given in immediately. They were cats, after all, and no feline would ever refuse a good nap under any circumstances.

After the power beam passed away from Maya, the leader of

the Champions remained in his upright sitting position. He didn't seem the least bit fatigued by the exercise. Mr. Hikkins wondered after this, until he saw great numbers of redwood trees flicking off their energy streams. Maya stood at attention until every tree had returned to its normal living state. A split second after the last redwood dismissed its magical beam, the Lord of the Crossworlds Champions crumpled to the ground. Mr. Hikkins ran over to examine the cat for injuries. After he saw Maya's tail flick back and firth a few times, however, he relaxed and returned to his workstation.

"Do you think he's alive?" asked the Author of All Worlds, looking up at the bizarre cell floating above their camp.

"I can't believe he's come this far only to perish now," replied the seeker.

The huge, golden sanctuary hovering above the gathering slowly began to descend. As it drifted within eye level, the seeker, the author and Janine peered through the translucent window. Conor, asleep or lost forever, lay peacefully within the confines of the cell. Upon touching the ground, the cell blinked lightly seven times before disappearing altogether. A soft cushion holding Conor was the only part that remained.

Janine dashed down the small hill, crying Conor's name repeatedly. She fell to the ground by his side, gripping his lifeless hand, cooing to him. She gazed at his face, so peaceful in repose. She wondered if she would ever hear him speak again. Thinking about all the plans they had talked about, she began to cry softly, squeezing his hand again and again. She couldn't shake the feeling that this final journey had taken him from her for good.

"Oh, Conor," she wept, "I love you. I love you so much."

Janine felt a delicate but strong hand fold over her left shoulder.

She turned to find the Lady of the Light kneeling beside her. The woman looked haggard, but awake and willing to assist Janine with her attempts to revive her boyfriend.

"Please, let me," said the Lady, gingerly moving into position.

Janine wanted to push her away. She wanted every one of the creators to return to their realm and never bother them again. They had taken everything from Conor. He had never denied any of their requests, answering their calls selflessly. Now they had taken the only thing that ever mattered to her. She wanted to scream at the Lady of the Light, but in the end, she simply moved aside. If anyone could help him, she could. She was his only hope.

The Lady of the Light examined Conor carefully. She wouldn't dare tell Janine, but she wasn't encouraged by what she found, or failed to find. Conor possessed no life essence at all. The force of the equinox must have blasted his spirit into a billion different dimensions. The Lady uttered dozens of incantations. They fell on a lifeless body, for Conor did not stir in the slightest. She opened her soul to him, delivering a pure source of light and power directly into his body. The silver aura resembled an umbilicus, ethereally connecting the Lady of the Light to her Champion. She fed the power to him, hoping for a flicker of life to appear. At long last, she pulled her energy back into her soul. She wanted to bow her head and weep, but she would not draw Janine into her misery. She looked around slowly, meeting the eyes of the supreme councilor.

"Athazia," said the Lord of All Life. "Let me."

"If you mean to use the golden wings," she said, extending an arm and looking her Lord in the eye, "you must not. You know the consequence."

"I more than anyone, my Lady," he replied. He looked down at the young man's face, the warrior who had returned to them after so many centuries. "Has he not earned the right? Has your Champion not proven his worth? Have I not earned the privilege of joining my mate at the far reaches of the system?"

"We need you," said the Lady. "The Crossworlds needs you."

"The Crossworlds will survive," said the Lord of All Life. "As will you and the rest of the council. You will take my seat as supreme councilor, Athazia. It is as your father decreed. All that was meant to be is finally coming to pass. I am pleased to have played a small part in the transition."

"You played more than a small part, my Lord," said Athazia, taking the creator's cheek in her hand. "Your stewardship has created the Crossworlds we all enjoy."

The Lord of All Life smiled. He asked Athazia to guide Conor's companion to a safe distance. Then, holding his hands aloft, he clapped them together repeatedly.

Immediately thereafter, he held them stiffly out to his sides. A golden energy, more robust than anything Janine encountered thus far in all her journeys through the Crossworlds, shot straight up from the supreme councilor into the sky. As it fell back toward him, it altered its form and color. The energy grew paler by the second, finally coalescing into a bright white cone that swallowed him completely. Throbbing quietly, the energy slowly began dissolving. When it finally evaporated, the Lord of All Life had vanished.

In his place there stood a stunning bird of prey. Everyone gathered around the perimeter gasped with wonder at the sight of it.

"A white winged kite," whispered Janine. The Lady of the Light squeezed the girl's hand. They exchanged an understanding glance.

The kite called out to the sky, in much the same way it had done at the bottom of the deep crevasse near Conor and Janine's high school. The bird of prey snapped its head around, looking for the great winged cougar somewhere in the crowd. When it spotted Purugama, it locked eyes with Conor's mentor. The bird's snowy white head bobbed up and down a few times, a strange signal to the big cat. Purugama simply returned the gaze. He bowed his head once toward the bird, an acknowledgement of kindred spirits. Whatever communication passed between the two, no one would ever know, but after they looked away from each other, the white kite stepped gingerly toward Conor. Crouching in a comfortable position, the huge bird of prey unfolded its golden tipped wings. Extending them out to their maximum arc, the bird locked its feathers together at the tips. It looked straight down at Conor's face, chirping a soft but piercing cry over and over. It seemed to be singing to the unmoving Champion.

A golden luminescence appeared at the tip of the kite's wings. Slowly, the syrupy coating moved down the wings toward the bird's torso. It merged them together to form a perfectly symmetric golden ceiling over the first warrior.

The kite chirped again. A shower of golden flakes fell from the wings down onto Conor's body. When the first flake touched his leg, Conor's foot involuntarily twitched. Janine grabbed the Lady's arm. Athazia wrapped her in a loving embrace. Conor would live; they would will it to be so together.

The shower increased. The rain of golden life-giving particles danced all over his body. His entire form emitted a mild glow even as he lay there motionless.

As dawn pulled night away from the heavens, additional grains of life began falling from the sky toward the white winged kite. Thousands, and then millions, of tiny motes zoomed down from all directions. They slipped silently into the golden wings, joining the Lord of All Life in his bid to revive Trolond Tar, first warrior of the Crossworlds.

No one in the immediate vicinity uttered a sound. They were witnessing the reanimation of life by some deity they could never fathom. Everyone in the area held a collective breath as they watched the young man lying underneath the towering bird of prey.

Conor stirred. He expelled a small cough from his lungs, and then another. Rolling on his side, he raised his left arm in an attempt to shade his eyes. He looked out at the crowd and saw Purugama standing close by him.

The great cougar held his right forepaw out in front of him, pads held straight up, a gesture to his brother Champion. Conor understood at once. He rolled back to the ground, looking up at the amazing bird of prey, so like the one that helped him and Janine escape Seefra's chasm. He blinked his eyes, allowing the sparkling golden rain to wash his body clear of injury and pain. Then he stared into the eye of the kite, into its unblinking eye that held within it all the wisdom of the Crossworlds. He grinned, and in that all-knowing eye he swore he saw the kite smiling back at him.

The shower of endless particles falling from the sky finally began to wane. The fiery wings, burning so brightly they resembled the glistening arms of a golden statue, cooled while slowly separating. The beautiful bird of prey, weakened but determined to complete its task, folded its wings against its feathered, white body. Stepping away from Conor, the white winged kite called out to the sky again. Apparently thanking the Crossworlds for their involvement in his resurgence, the kite sang to the sky for a few minutes before quieting itself. Then it turned to look at Conor.

The kite extended a wing, calling on the young Champion to rise. Conor did as it requested, and when Janine saw him standing under his own power she couldn't restrain herself. As she broke away from the Lady of the Light's embrace and ran to her boyfriend, the huge throng of troops and reporters cheered at the scene.

Janine leapt into his arms. Showering him with kisses, she squeezed her body against his as strongly as she could. After a minute or two, feeling no return excitement or any emotional sensation of love from him, she held his shoulders apart from hers. She looked deeply into his eyes. She saw her boyfriend standing before her, but she glimpsed someone else at the same time. Conor stood there, without humor, without the old mischievous glint in his eye. He looked much more like a warrior returned from a titanic battle.

The first warrior gently removed Janine's hands from his arms, excused himself politely, and walked softly over to the Lady of the Light. Athazia stood regally, tired and soiled though she was, accepting her Champion's advance.

"Trolond Tar," she said, locking eyes with him.

"My Lady," he answered, gracefully bending a knee while lowering his head.

Janine stumbled after the love of her life, silently begging for an explanation. She reached out to him, tears dropping lightly on her flawless cheekbones. She tried to grab him from behind. She wanted to fall upon his back and never let go of him again.

Purugama moved forward to halt her advance. Even Eha had recovered enough to understand the danger. The cheetah lunged forward, reaching out with a striped forepaw. In the end it was the seeker who caught her first. Mr. Hikkins had seen the dilemma long before the others. He grabbed Janine with a surprisingly strong grip.

"Not now, my dear," he whispered into her ear. "You must not disturb them. They have waited two hundred centuries to be reunited."

The area had gone quiet once again. No one made a sound as the strange young man knelt before the glorious creator. Major General McKimmey and his entourage had arrived at the scene only moments before. They too watched with mute fascination. McKimmey's entourage looked upon the event with mouths agape. Only John Woodhaven took in the occurrence with a placid, knowing expression. The old Hoopa tribal chairman smiled wryly as he watched his lifelong friend try to assimilate the event.

The Lady of the Light waved a delicate hand over her head. Instantly, a shower of shimmering, silver sparkles consumed her from head to toe. When the sprinkling ceased, she stood completely transformed. The disheveled, battle-weary creator had disappeared. In her place stood Athazia, Lady of the Light and supreme councilor of the creators emeritus. Her beauty was unsurpassed; she positively glowed as she looked down upon her consort.

"You have performed brilliantly, my Champion," she cooed, smothering Trolond Tar with her luxurious, velvet voice.

"All for the glory of your greatness, my Lady," returned the kneeling youth.

"I have missed our time together, Trolond Tar," she said. "It has been far too long since you held me in your strong, capable arms."

"Command me, my Lady, and I shall do so again."

"Rise, Champion," said Athazia, lifting his chin with the fingers of her right hand. "Come to me, now."

The first warrior allowed her to assist him. He lifted his eyes to the stunning creator. As he rose to stand before her, his gaze remained locked on her silver-flecked, multicolored eyes. Stepping forward, he took hold of the nape of her neck in his left hand. He passed his right arm around her waist, gripping her oblique muscle softly but firmly. He pulled her to him and they stood, body to body, forehead to forehead, losing themselves in each other's eyes.

The Lady of the Light allowed her consort to physically command her. She fell into his powerful grip, sliding her arms along his shapely, muscular back. She felt his ribbed stomach and dense pectorals pressing against her body.

Her eyes never left his, but more than once she felt passionately faint. She had counted the days for so long, waited a thousand lifetimes to feel his embrace again. She broke from his gaze, letting her head fall onto his shoulder. She whispered her love for him. As she did, another shower of silver flecks formed above her. It began as a halo, widening slowly until it hovered over both of them.

The silver shower began anew, a thick sprinkle falling around the Lady and her Champion. Increasing in density, soon the rain masked every movement the two of them made. The last thing anyone saw before the pair disappeared within the silver cone was Trolond Tar lifting Athazia's face to his. As he joined her in their first kiss in over twenty thousand years, the wall of silver became opaque, closing them off completely.

CHAPTER FIFTY-NINE

"Captain Carlson," barked *Major General McKimmey.*

"Sir!"

"You are to be commended on your command. I selected you for your ability to operate under exactly this type of pressure."

Carlson stood at rigid attention listening to the general's praise.

"Now I want you and your troops to back these media folks away from here and I mean pronto. See to it personally that they board their rigs and leave the area. Anyone found inside the Hoopa Indian Reservation in one hour will be arrested for trespassing. Is that clear, Captain?"

"Perfectly, sir," answered the captain. "Are we heading back to base?"

"That's affirmative," said McKimmey. "Captain Darren and his crew will remain behind with us. Now get moving."

Captain Carlson jumped to his orders immediately. A few protests rose up from the media horde, but within minutes all of them had turned back toward their vehicles. Carlson's troops formed an arc behind them, hurrying them along and scooping up any stragglers.

McKimmey turned toward his friend. John Woodhaven nodded his head, thanking the general for giving him a peaceful stage.

The Hoopa tribal chairman looked across the clearing at the immense hooded cat. The black and white tabby had awakened and was busy cleaning its fur. It seemed oblivious to everything around it. Indeed, as he crushed the crisp fern leaves littering the ground while walking over to address Maya, the big cat never once looked up. John Woodhaven came to stand directly in front of his lifelong mystery. When Maya continued with his tasks, the tribal chairman spoke to him.

"You are the strange visitor in the forests of my youth," he said.

Maya stopped licking his rear leg momentarily, but did not look up. "Yes," he replied.

"I have dreamed of meeting you all my life," said Woodhaven. "You are my strongest spirit guide. You've given me great power over my lifetime."

Maya twisted his body into a more comfortable position. He stopped preening, looked at the man in front of him. "Why did you not reveal yourself, John Woodhaven? You had so many chances, and yet you refused to come out from your place of hiding to meet me."

"I feared for my life," said Woodhaven, shocked that the giant cat knew him by name. "What if I was wrong, and Haphap or Ququ had tricked me?"

"Conquering fear brings the greatest of all rewards. Don't you believe that?"

"Yes, of course," said Woodhaven. "But I haven't been completely honest. I felt frightened at the prospect of meeting you. You possess great powers, and I am merely one man, a lowly being briefly inhabiting Mother Earth."

"You have powers I cannot even touch, John Woodhaven," answered Maya. "You have looked within yourself your entire life.

That is good, for the energy of life exists within all of us. The living world holds many secrets, however. Spend the remainder of your time here communing with all that surrounds you. Draw the magic of the natural world into your soul. You will find strength you never imagined."

"Will you come again to the forests of my youth?" the tribal chairman asked.

"I will."

"Will you give me a sign that it is you walking among the trees?"

"I will call out to you. We have much to discuss, John Woodhaven."

Maya turned his gaze slightly to his left. He saw another man walking up the rise to greet him. The Lord of the Champions didn't immediately recognize him, but something about his manner flicked a memory deep in his mind. He knew this man to be the Author of All Worlds, but something more attracted his attention. The way he walked, his smile, something about him tugged at his heartstrings. The man approached and recognition suddenly flooded the big cat's memory.

Before the author even reached the small hill where Maya and John Woodhaven sat together, the big cat rose, standing on all fours nimbly. A sound came from deep within his soul, a bizarre call, one neither the Champions nor the Lady had ever heard. A cry of some sort, somewhat sad, but mostly a call of recollection poured out from Maya's lungs. The Lord of the Champions walked briskly toward the author, anticipating the man's steps perfectly. He reached the author's side, waiting for a moment to see if he might reach out to him. The author stood still, cooing to the big cat in a way he reserved especially for him.

"Maya," he said quietly, firmly. He repeated himself, never touching the big cat or moving toward him at all. "Maya!"

The big black and white tabby left all decorum aside. He yowled happily, rubbing vigorously against the author. Back and forth the big cat moved, nearly knocking the man down more than once. All the while, the author called out quietly to the leader of the Champions, enjoying every moment of their reunion.

"Maya, you big tom cat, you," said the author. "I've missed you, boy."

Maya continued talking to the man, his confidante of long ago during the ancient times. The man had befriended him, spent more than a little time with him every night after returning from his day's toil. Maya breathed in the man's scent, looked into his eyes and raked his feet with his claws as he passed by him again and again.

The author reached out, dragging his fingers through Maya's glistening fur. He grasped the strong shoulders, rubbing his old friend the way he used to outside both of their homes. Touching him brought back all the old memories.

Maya suddenly flared. His tone changed abruptly. The Lord of the Champions lashed out at the author, swiping a forepaw with claws fully extended. He caught the man's hand, the one that had touched him, drawing blood and more than a little pain from the author. He crouched, ears back, sending him a low, guttural warning.

The author reared back, exploding in laughter. He threw his hand out a few times, teasing Maya for a minute. The big cat fired his paw out viciously, trying to inflict more damage. The author was ready for him this time; however, he never touched him again.

"Still the same old Maya, eh boy?" As he had done so many

times long ago, the author turned and walked away from his old friend. Perhaps he would meet him again somewhere, in a place where they could spar. That's what he loved about Maya. You didn't pet him, he petted you. Any attempt at altering that set of rules met with swift reprisal. He turned back one last time and sent a high-pitched whine through his pursed lips. He watched Maya's ears prick as he listened to the sound they had shared long ago on earth.

CHAPTER SIXTY

The creators assembled in a circle around the white winged kite. Understanding what their leader had sacrificed in order to save the first warrior, and after reviving themselves they fell into place around their longtime leader. Their equidistant alignment left one place unoccupied. They waited quietly for the Lady of the Light to return and sanctify the departure of the supreme councilor.

The silver cone shimmered softly. The multitude of flecks blinked out one by one, first slowly and then with greater speed. Athazia and Trolond Tar stood as they had before disappearing, embracing tightly while gazing into each other's eyes. When the halo rose above their heads again, finally vanishing altogether, the Lady of the Light gently removed herself from Trolond Tar's strong grasp. Stepping down from the soft dais, she immediately moved to her place within the circle of creators emeritus. The others looked at her, acknowledging her as supreme councilor. Even the first councilor, long believed to be next in the line of succession, bowed his head to Athazia. She smiled broadly at him. She would need his assistance during the years to come. She felt especially glad for his acceptance.

The white winged kite, depleted from using the golden wings, called out to the Crossworlds in a series of hollow, piercing cries. The ghost-like bird of prey repeated its calls, patiently summoning his mate. The circle of seven formed an acoustic ring around the kite, amplifying the pleas as they rose to the outer reaches of the Crossworlds.

After what seemed like an endless sequence of rhythmic projections, an answer came from somewhere far above the cliffs. High in the sky, so tiny it appeared as another fading star, another kite flew down toward its companion. Almost identical to the white kite on the ground, the supreme councilor's mate circled above the gathering, calling out repeatedly to the creator she had known since the beginning of time. He answered, summoning new reserves of strength now that she had descended from the heavens to join him. The visiting kite held a strong fascination for Janine, for she recognized the bird of prey immediately. This was the one who had come to rescue Conor and her from the chasm. *Was she creator, Champion, or something else entirely?* Janine watched the interplay between the two birds with wondrous appreciation.

The kite perched within the circle of creators unfolded its wings. He flapped them slowly at first, and then with a few quick beats he launched his white feathered body into the air. The other kite, unsure of her mate's ability to sustain flight, dove under and around the bigger bird, hoping to catch him if he should falter. Together, the two stunning birds of prey swept higher and higher into the sky. They called out to each other, happy in the freedom they sought for so long. They dove at each other playfully, beginning the mating ritual that would result in a child of their own. The ring of creators watched until the two kites had disappeared completely. They heard one final set of calls, and then nothing. The transfer had been accomplished. The position of supreme councilor now fell to Athazia.

The seeker watched his student gaze longingly at what used to be Conor Jameson. Reasoning that his time with the workstation had come to an end, he walked silently over to her side.

"Janine," said Mr. Hikkins softly. "Please, sit down. Let me speak with you."

Janine loved Conor with all her heart. She had stood there alongside the Lady of the Light, waiting for his return. She had lost her ability to breathe upon seeing his lifeless body lying in the middle of the gathering. Now her mind swam in a pool of a thousand emotions.

"Please, my dear," repeated the seeker. "Sit."

She eyed her old high school math teacher. She hadn't looked at anyone other than Conor since his return from the energy stream. She saw the patient demeanor, the caring attitude. Finally she sat on a smooth rock coated with a fine sheet of micro-ferns. She stared into his eyes, letting him know that drivel would not be tolerated.

"The man you saw with the Lady of the Light is no longer Conor Jameson," said the seeker, well aware of her need for directness. "Conor may have left this world while battling Nemelissi, but it is Trolond Tar who returned."

"It *is* Conor!" Janine demanded. "He's the same man I've known since high school." She bit the words off sharply, hoping to convince the seeker with her conviction.

"No," said Mr. Hikkins. "I assure you, he is not."

Janine would not be put off. "No one changes that much, or that quickly. It must be a result of the power beam, or the interaction with the predatory corridor."

"My dear," said the seeker, patiently resting a hand on Janine's arm, "Conor made his choice long ago. During the initial stages of his battle with Nemelissi, he agreed to accept the power of the sun in a cosmic transference. It occurred at the precise moment the equinox formed over the ancient battlefield. Once the power entered his soul, he was destined to evolve into the warrior you see before you now. He is Trolond Tar, first warrior and consort to the Lady of the Light. All that was Conor Jameson has been transferred to a safe destination within the Crossworlds. His spirit will be safely guarded into eternity, I assure you."

She interrupted the seeker. "*I love him!* What gives them the right to take him from me?"

"They did no such thing, Janine. He made the choice. Never forget that. He saw the imminent conclusion of our struggle here in this forest. He knew earth would be destroyed. He knew countless other worlds would suffer the same fate. He forfeited your future together, yes, but in the same decision he saved you and everyone you love."

Janine sat still, quietly absorbing everything the seeker told her. Tears streamed from her emerald eyes, flooding her cheeks and dropping silently to the ground. She wiped them away vigorously, not caring whether she damaged the delicate skin around her cheeks. She fought for the right not to accept the seeker's version of events. In the end, though, her disciplined mind was forced to accede.

"May I talk to him one more time?" she asked. "Is there any of Conor left in him?"

"Unfortunately, no," replied Mr. Hikkins.

Acting on her own impulse, Janine jumped up and ran down the small rise toward Trolond Tar. She would take her chance while the Lady of the Light was engaged with the other creators. She boldly walked up to her boyfriend, demanding acknowledgement. Her body language allowed no other response from the first warrior.

"Thank you," she said, staring into his eyes. "You saved us, all of us. You saved our world. Thank you."

Trolond Tar returned her gaze serenely, standing tall and strong in front of the young woman. "It is my honor to serve you. I serve all creatures of the Crossworlds, as my Lady commands."

Janine stepped closer and placed a hand on the warrior's chest. "Conor, don't you recognize me? It's Janine. We've been together for years. Look into my eyes, tell me you don't know who I am."

Trolond Tar gently removed the young woman's hand from his leather tunic. "I apologize. You must have me confused with someone else. Please, if you will excuse me."

"No!" said Janine. She wrenched her hand away, grabbing the leather neckline of the warrior's outfit. "You are Conor Jameson. You attend Redwood State University and play on the varsity soccer team. Coach Rumsey. Do you remember that name? Oh, Conor, don't you remember anything?"

"He will never recall any part of his former life, my dear," said the Lady of the Light. Trolond Tar immediately stepped away from Janine, addressing his Lady formally. She acknowledged his service before turning back to Janine. "I am sorry, Janine. I'm afraid Conor no longer inhabits this human form. Only the first warrior, Trolond Tar, exists now. I assure you, though; Conor is safe wherever he presently exists."

Janine exploded, hurling insults at Athazia. "You wanted him for yourself! All this time you've been planning to take him from me! How dare you stand here trying to pacify me!"

The Lady of the Light felt nothing but love for the brave young woman. "Is that truly what you believe? For if that is true I must profess my guilt. I did want him for myself. I've longed to feel his touch for so many years I cannot count them. But it is Trolond

Tar I awaited, not Conor Jameson. Conor belonged to you heart and soul, my dear. He loved you. You know that. He loved you so deeply he made the ultimate sacrifice for you. He gave his identity over to the true warrior he had always been."

The Lady brushed a tear from Janine's cheek. The Keeper of the Keys did not flinch, nor did she continue her bitter verbal assault.

"From the very moment Purugama laid eyes on that little boy sitting on the mesa so many years ago, we knew our search had ended. Even then, Conor displayed many qualities of his warrior lineage. As he grew and experienced the challenges posed by the Circle of Evil, we became more convinced of our choice. After thousands of years, the first warrior had returned to us, reincarnated in the form of a small boy.

"I wish to make something very clear, Janine," the Lady continued. "Conor always had the option of retaining his own identity. No one forced him to call forth the equinox, or to accept the responsibility of that much power. It is a choice he made freely, of his own will." Athazia let the words sink in before continuing. "Do you believe that Conor made that choice without once thinking of you, of the life he could share with you, of your feelings for each other? We are all selfish beings to some extent, I assure you, my dear. The choice did not come easily for him. In the end, he picked the only course that would ensure your survival. That was always his paramount concern. He wanted you to live even if it meant losing you forever. He loved you, Janine. With all his heart he loved you."

The Lady of the Light took the crying girl into her arms. Janine fell against her shoulder, sobbing uncontrollably. The painful convulsions nearly masked the touch of a strong hand against her shoulder. She turned to see Trolond Tar offering a moment's consolation. The first warrior smiled, nodding his head lightly, giving his ardent approval to the one who had sacrificed so much for the woman he loved. Trolond Tar understood, for he would give his life under any circumstance to protect his creator.

The warrior's sympathy propelled Janine into a new round of passionate weeping. She had seen a small morsel of Conor's personality flash toward her the instant she met Trolond Tar's gaze. The recognition crushed her. From a space deep within her soul, her heart broke anew. The streaks of pain battered her so strongly she could barely keep her feet. She clutched Athazia's shoulders, gripping the Lady of the Light with all of her strength. The beautiful creator cradled Janine in her arms, speaking softly to her while letting the warmth of her aura pour over the young woman. At long last, Janine's convulsive tears ended. She rested her head on Athazia's shoulder, breathing evenly, staring at nothing.

"I will escort her back to her home, my Lady," said the unassuming voice of the seeker. Mr. Hikkins had quietly moved behind Janine, waiting for the opportunity to assist her. He had grown quite fond of her over the last five years. Her beauty held men spellbound, that was certain, but so much more about her appealed to him.

Janine possessed a magnificent mind. He saw limitless potential in her academic pursuits. She would become an important physicist or chemist someday, perhaps even advising world leaders and scientific symposiums along the way. More than that, Mr. Hikkins saw in Janine an emissary for a better world. *Perhaps,* he thought, *she might guide earth toward the light once again.* The seeker had always imagined a world of altruism instead of selfishness. He wondered if Janine Cochran would become the leader they had all waited so long to serve.

"If you will call forth a corridor, I will see that she returns safely to earth."

"Thank you, seeker," said the Lady. "I presume you will stay with her, to ensure her transition back to her old life."

"I would be honored," replied Mr. Hikkins.

Athazia grabbed Janine's strong arms, gently pushing her away. She looked into her stunning green eyes, seeing strength in her she saw in few others. "You must return home, Janine. The seeker will guide you. He will also stay behind as an instructor at your place of study. He will provide anything you need over the course of the next year. If you cannot bear the pain, and there will be pain for a while, my dear, seek out his counsel. Besides being brilliant with numbers, he is wise beyond all understanding."

Janine stood in shock. The realization of her great loss hurt her physically. The Lady of the Light took Janine's chin in two fingers, elevating it slowly. "You will overcome this loss, I promise you. If you ever need me, or any of the Champions, call and we will attend you."

"Do you swear?" asked Janine, her face lighting up for the first time since the Lady addressed her. "If I call for you, or any of them, do you swear you will come to me?"

"I will not swear," said Athazia. "I will affirm my promise to you, Keeper. You served the Crossworlds valiantly while imprisoned for almost two years. We will come to your aid should you require anything at all."

Janine smiled weakly. She squeezed the Lady's hands warmly before turning to address the seeker. "I'm ready." She took Mr. Hikkins' hand in her own, walked down the hill toward a clear place away from the giant redwood trunks. They passed the general and his party, exchanging glances briefly before continuing on. When they arrived at the clearing, the seeker turned and nodded in Athazia's direction.

A dazzling silver fire flew from the Lady of the Light's fingertips. Arcing over everyone standing in the interior, it found its target directly behind Janine and Mr. Hikkins. As if tipping a bucket of paint above a blank floor, the silver fire splashed against an invisible wall, forming a strong, rectangular corridor behind the two travelers. The perimeter of the portal solidified quickly, the membrane following equally as fast. Janine turned her head one last time and looked at the face of the man she loved so deeply. The warrior stood passively, staring at her with eyes she did not recognize. He nodded his head once, signaling his farewell. She smiled, but the pain inside her brought tears to her eyes again. With great sadness, she turned at long last, grasped the seeker's hand more firmly, and walked through the corridor that would escort her back to earth and a life without Conor.

CHAPTER SIXTY-ONE

The Lady of the Light dabbed her eye lightly, brushing away a solitary tear caught on one of her eyelashes. She glanced at Trolond Tar, standing at ease beside her, always ready to protect. Her eyes found another man, standing at a respectful distance but with a visible desire to speak to her. She brushed her gown with both hands, presenting a regal presence to the Author of All Worlds.

"My Lady, if I may speak with you."

Athazia knelt before him, head bowed. Trolond Tar followed suit, almost in the same motion. Maya and his four Champions encircled the small group, taking up their usual protective positions around their creator. Before kneeling, Athazia noted an element of curiosity in the Champions' eyes.

"We are yours to command, author," she said with a mixture of regal authority and submissive posturing. "You may speak as long as you wish, for it was you who brought all of us into existence."

The author fumbled for something to say. Indeed, he *had* designed every creature and being in front of him, but one does not encounter royalty and unimaginable power without pausing to reflect. He had so many questions for her, but in reality, he merely wanted to sit in her presence and talk with her a while.

"Please, rise, all of you," he said. When they hesitated, he asked again. Finally, the Lady of the Light, the first warrior and the Champions lifted their eyes to the man. He looked at each of them in turn, returning his eyes to Athazia after each creature had been acknowledged. She radiated before him, the silver aura bristling with anticipation. Her mouth quivered with many questions. She held herself in check, however, waiting for the mysterious yet common man to address her.

"What will become of Conor, now that Trolond Tar has returned?"

The Lady of the Light sparkled, and then composed herself. Her eyes gave away her surprise, even as she answered the author's question.

"Surely you know the answer to that," she said. "You are the Author of All Worlds. If the answer hasn't appeared yet, you will deliver it to us shortly." She smiled at the man, her expression one of comfortable assurance.

The author looked into her eyes, into the eyes of everyone gathered before him. *Should I tell them what I told Janine only hours ago? How would they receive the news? What would become of the Crossworlds?* After much internal discussion, he decided to be honest with them. After all, freedom is something one best enjoys with complete understanding.

"My Lady," he began. "I have no knowledge of Conor's whereabouts. I had no idea Trolond Tar would emerge at the end of this journey. I was afraid Nemelissi might defeat Conor, giving the predatory corridor the freedom to consume earth. The truth is I haven't been writing this story for quite some time."

Surmitang burped. The huge Sumatran tiger had been in midbreath when the author delivered his statements. The shock of it forced the air from his lungs quite abruptly. The proud tiger did his best to act as though he had not been the perpetrator. His body language gave him away, however.

"How can this be?" asked the Lady. "You are the Author of All Worlds. Without your guidance, nothing can take place within the Crossworlds."

"I don't fully understand it myself," replied the man. "A presence slowly took control of my writings. It seemed as though a being, or a group of beings, was supporting Nemelissi's efforts in its battle with Conor."

"The Inner Element," whispered Athazia. The Champions stirred. Trolond Tar remained silent, unmoving.

"Perhaps," said the author. "Or perhaps it was someone or something else entirely. I honestly don't know. The conversion happened so mysteriously I couldn't come to any conclusions."

The author stepped closer to the Lady of the Light. "What I do know is that my association with the Crossworlds has come to an end. I am no longer the Author of All Worlds, or of any world. The story falls to you now, Athazia. You must initiate the journeys now. All of you must contribute – the creators, Champions, every being on every world within the system. You are no longer controlled by the whims of one mind. The Crossworlds belongs to you. You can make of it what you will."

Athazia and her Champions stood in a state of collective shock. At first they couldn't comprehend what the author had communicated to them. Eha broke the silence by bounding up to the author and licking the man's face from chin to forehead. The cheetah laughed a few times, causing the author to chuckle as well. The man looked at the massive, spotted cat in front of him. Throwing decorum to the dogs, he stepped toward Eha, wrapped his arms around the coarse fur and hugged him tightly. Of all Purugama's friends, he loved Eha the most. The cheetah could bring a smile to the face of almost anyone. He broke away from hugging

Eha and lost his balance, nearly toppling over to one side. He felt a something huge nudging his backside. He turned, looking at a large face surrounded by stunning, striped fur. He grabbed one of Surmitang's ears, the extra eye for a Sumatran tiger. The huge tiger lifted his head, staring straight into the author's eyes. The man felt overwhelmed. The tiger's head was easily nine feet from ear to ear. He reached out, grabbed a handful of the gorgeous fur and pulled his face into Surmitang's jowls.

The huge tiger obeyed its instincts at first. He began pulling away from the author but then caught himself. Forgetting his vanity, he threw his infamous pride aside and embraced the author roughly. Pulling the man off his feet, he crushed him in an embrace of striped fur and slobbery jowls. A resounding purr shot forward from Surmitang's chest, tickling every pore of the author's body. The sound resonated around the small group, causing Eha to laugh anew while watching Surmitang's unnatural display of affection. At length, the huge tiger released the author. The man stumbled backwards, almost falling into the immense arms of the largest Champion of all.

Therion caught him by placing a vast paw against his back. The giant lion eased the author up into a standing position, leaving his paw in place until certain he had regained his balance. The man turned to thank his unknown benefactor, nearly falling down once again at the sight of Therion. The lion was so immense it nearly blocked out the sun's light.

"Are you well?" asked Therion.

"Yes, I-I think so," answered a clearly unnerved author.

"May I express my infinite gratitude to you?"

The man's expression changed. He looked at Therion, extremely curious. *How could a beast as large and imposing as him thank anyone for anything?* "Whatever for, Therion?"

"For allowing me to return from the forbidden corridors, to join the Champions once again in their struggle for what is right and good."

The author remembered – the journey to repair the corridors. Therion had turned traitor and tried to destroy Conor. He remembered the ending as well, when the creators had dragged Therion down from the light into a forbidden portal. It had nearly broken his heart to write an ending like that for such a noble beast.

"I'd always intended for you to return to the glade, Therion," said the author. "The battle for the Crossworlds could not have been won without your strength and valor. Even more than that, I understood your anguished memories of your home and pride. I knew you to be of good heart, good soul. Even as the creators sentenced you to a life of solitary reflection, I began thinking of how to resurrect you in another journey. I am pleased to know my judgment of your integrity was correct."

The giant lion sat staring at the author. Unblinking, Therion gazed at the man with burnished golden eyes, quietly taking his measure. Then he let his great mane fall about his face while bowing low to the man standing before him. He did not offer a paw, nor did he approach the author with any intent to exchange pleasantries with him. He merely acknowledged the man, silently offering thanks for generously watching over him.

The author nodded his head once to Therion, understanding his nature and ways, not willing to disturb the big cat's sentiments. He would take whatever the Champions would give and ask for nothing more.

He turned to see Trolond Tar standing close to the Lady of the Light. Not knowing exactly what to say, he walked up to the stoic Champion, placed his left hand on the warrior's right shoulder and smiled to him. "You have returned, Trolond Tar. The Crossworlds will forever celebrate your victory over Nemelissi and the predatory corridor. Guard your Lady well, obey Maya and see to it that the Champions remain ready to defend the helpless at all times."

The warrior nodded. The author returned the gesture, giving the young man one final instruction. "The one who sacrificed himself so you could return enjoyed a wonderful sense of humor, Trolond Tar. I urge you to seek that part of him within yourself. If you look hard enough, you may find it. I assure you it will serve you well during the next two hundred centuries."

Trolond Tar nodded again, this time with an accompanying smile, small though it was. The author turned back to Athazia, addressing her respectfully.

"I must return to my home. It is long past time for me to try and rescue what little is left of my life. I have a family who will be wondering after me, a wife and four cats actually."

Eha smiled at this announcement. Surmitang did the same. Even mighty Therion chuckled lightly at the revelation.

"Purugama will escort you back to the corridor that brought you here," said the Lady. Without asking, she approached the author and gave his cheek a delicate kiss. Withdrawing, she gave the man a dazzling smile. "Thank you. From the bottom of my heart, I thank you. You will remain the Author of All Worlds in the minds of every Crossworlds inhabitant. We may indeed be free now, but it was you who designed our worlds, who gave us life. Promise me you will return at some point in the future, if only to gauge our progress in the stewardship of our new destiny."

"I will, my Lady," said the Author of All Worlds. "I promise you I will return."

CHAPTER SIXTY-TWO

"Your instruments are flawed, Jek!" bellowed Shordano. *"Either* that or you are the cause of the error. No force in the Crossworlds could obliterate a predatory corridor the size of a living planet."

"I tell you I speak the truth!" shouted the third arc of the inner element. His aura flared as Jek moved aside, leaving the panel exposed for Shordano. "See for yourself!"

The absolute ruler kicked the levitating chair to the side, disgusted with his subordinate for even thinking he might be interested in such menial functions. "Perhaps I should call Wolbus to the chamber. With someone intelligent operating our sensors we might be able to ascertain the corridor's whereabouts."

Jek had had enough. He had faithfully served Shordano for centuries. Up until a few months ago he would have given his life to save his Lord. In that period of time his assessment had changed, however. Shordano had lost his mind. His insane lust for power and revenge had taken him to the edge and beyond. Now his maniacal dreams would kill them all. He spat at the feet of his Lord. Jek had never confronted him before; he cared little for any punishment that might come his way. He looked at the shocked expression on Shordano's face, the glint of fear in Shordano's eyes. It turned to utter horror when Jek spoke again.

"You don't need Wolbus. I know the predatory corridor's current course."

Shordano recovered quickly. "Then call it forward. Press it back into service. Destroy the world of Conor Jameson!" The absolute ruler looked upon his servant's stillness. It sent him into a frantic rage. "At once!"

Jek slowly guided the chair back to the workstation. He did not sit, however. He merely watched Shordano twitch and shake with an impotent desire to have his orders followed. Jek actually smiled at his Lord. He would never understand. Even if he told Shordano the truth, he would refuse to accept it until their planet was consumed by the very instrument they created.

"Enjoy your tempest, *my Lord.*" Jek bit off the last two words, mocking the being he had worshipped for so long. "Your tenure as absolute ruler will end soon enough. The predatory corridor we set against earth will destroy this planet within minutes. It has returned, as I knew it would when you increased its power to maximum. We lost control of it at that second, and Trolond Tar has sent it back to annihilate us."

"Preposterous! Even the first warrior of the Crossworlds cannot summon that much power."

"Trolond Tar commands the equinox! The oracle spoke truly, for the first warrior has returned. He has defeated Nemelissi, and now he sends our destruction racing through the stars toward us. You have killed us, you fool. Your insane drive for vengeance has sealed our fate."

Shordano stood placidly, his hands elevated to chest level. It appeared that Jek's musings were finally breaking through the iron discipline of the absolute ruler. That discipline had carried the Circle of Evil from victory to victory for millennia. In the end, however, his twisted defiance would destroy them all. Shordano jerked his body around, keeping his feet planted on the ground.

He looked out the window, the one porthole left for them to view their world. He picked the star out of the sky. He sensed it more than anything else, and as he continued to stare he noticed the odd fluctuations in the light pattern. *The predatory corridor,* he thought.

It had found them, or rather Trolond Tar had found them and sent it reeling through space toward their planet. Shordano chuckled briefly, a sick look overtaking his face. He held his position, watching his death approach. He didn't even notice Wolbus entering the chamber behind him. He stared, chuckled and fell to the floor in a crumpled pile of quivering nerves.

The killer portal vacillated through space like a drunken gyroscope. The impact of the sun's energy had rendered most of its functions inert. The elements that remained instructed the corridor to proceed directly to its launch point. The portal immediately obeyed, flying through space at an incalculable speed. The immense organic monstrosity pulverized stars and debris on the way to its final mission. When it reached the outer edge of the galaxy containing the Circle of Evil's home world, the predatory corridor slowed and began taking what readings it could.

148,611 kilometers diameter

1.122×8^{19} kilograms mass

Approximately 3 grams/centimeter^3 density

Planetary composition: 22.6% Iron, 31.5% Oxygen, 11.2% Silicon, 6.7% Magnesium, 2% Nickel, 3.9% Sulfur, and 3% Titanium.

Indigenous life forms: few

Population: scattered. Two or three hundred sentient beings planet-wide

Approximately four billion years old with seventy two billion kilometers^2 total area.

A series of distorted blinks, not nearly as precise as before, informed the corridor the device could now commence operations.

The giant corridor steadied itself. The perimeter of the portal expanded rapidly but irregularly. The membrane formed as well as it could. No longer perfectly flat, its surface had become concave, no doubt from the severe impact with Trolond Tar's sunburst. It moved into position, flanking the planet as it rotated on its axis. It began moving forward. The crimson membrane swirled with a sickening mixture of distorted colors. The predatory corridor would complete its mission even in its damaged state. It took pride in its abilities. Trolond Tar had commanded it. It would perish before failing its new master.

After ascertaining Shordano's condition, Wolbus stood and approached the lookout window in the chamber of the inner element. He gazed out across the expansive terrain, once more wondering what might have been. He lifted his eyes to the sky. The hideous membrane looked to be no bigger than a red window drifting aimlessly through the stars, but its rapid growth dispelled that myth. It approached their world at a frantic pace, hoping to complete its mission before it expired from its injuries.

Wolbus felt another presence close by. He turned and saw Jek standing on the other side of Shordano's sunken form.

"Shall we stand him up so he can witness the end with his own eyes?" asked Wolbus.

"If it were any other day I'd say yes," responded Jek. "Today, however, I think it best if we leave him be."

The two arcs of the inner element turned toward the window again. Broken and discolored, the predatory corridor already filled half the sky. Wolbus wondered what might have been under different circumstances. Jek marveled at the tenacity of the organic machine. Minutes before his death, his final thoughts revolved around the brilliant combination of corporeal life and technology.

"Let us strive to find each other again, Jek," said Wolbus. "I enjoy working with intelligent beings."

"Perhaps our rejuvenated souls will cross paths in another dimension," replied Jek. "Perhaps not. In any case, we have accomplished much during our time in the Crossworlds."

"Have we?" asked Wolbus.

The immense predatory corridor crashed into Shordano's world like a top running out of steam. The section of the globe encountering the membrane disappeared without a trace. The unfortunate remainder exploded violently as the perimeter collided with the outer rim of the planet's surface. The boundary of the portal cut across the exterior of the planet, slicing into mountains, oceans and deserts like a dull scalpel. The portal became confused by the multiple sensations it encountered. It tried desperately to alter its course. It wanted to please its new master by sweeping the world cleanly away from the system.

In its effort to correct its functions, the corridor lost more control than it gained. Larger sections of the planet escaped the membrane, only to be cut to pieces by the perimeter as it followed the portal's every move.

Soon the operation became schizophrenic. The device swept back and forth in a frantic attempt to dissolve what remained of the inner element's world.

At length, the borders of the portal began to fracture. They could not sustain themselves under the manic pressure the membrane continued to deliver. The right edge cracked at the midpoint of its line. Two of the other borders immediately broke apart from the added strain. The top and left borders disintegrated completely, leaving the bottom edge alone trying to maintain membrane integrity. In its final desperate attempt to complete its mission, the predatory corridor struggled mightily to keep its passageway intact. The end became a foregone conclusion, however, as the final border broke apart. The membrane quickly dispersed, spreading itself into the galaxy among the frayed remains of Shordano's world.

The portal would never know how perfectly it had executed Trolond Tar's commands. The world of the inner element had been obliterated, and in completing its mission the predatory corridor had destroyed itself. The danger from both had been eliminated. The Circle of Evil and its creation had been utterly destroyed by its own precise design.

CHAPTER SIXTY-THREE

Before departing for the realm, the creators and Champions did their best to leave no footprint in the redwood forest. John Woodhaven, General McKimmey and his men assisted the strange beings any way they could, conversing lightly when they felt it might be appropriate. Captain Darren formed a strong friendship with Eha as the cleanup commenced. The pilot used his human hands to pick the forest clean while Eha followed behind, using his huge, striped tail to smooth out the grounds. Therion and Surmitang accompanied the creators, summoning spells and potions that remade the forest into its original state.

The Lady of the Light left to examine the wrecked hulks of the media vehicles. The reporters had abandoned anything that no longer functioned. They left their dead under orders from General McKimmey, who promised to process the remains for shipment to the families. They would rest at Beale Air Force Base until relatives came forward.

Athazia gazed upon the carnage Nemelissi had brought forth against the innocent onlookers. She would not allow the assassin's cruelty to negatively influence so many lives. She raised her fingers to her lips, delivering an ancient spell into the palm of her hand. She had not called on her father's spirit since the day of his passing. For this situation, however, she would use every means at her disposal. The incantation lasted more than five minutes. When she believed she had spoken the words correctly, she focused her mind on the scene before her. Cementing the images of the broken bodies and twisted vehicles in her mind, she threw her hand out in front of her. Pulling it from left to right, she covered every inch of the damaged landscape.

When she completed her restoration of the forest, only the indigenous residents remained. Every truck, van, and discarded scrap of any vehicle strewn about the landscape had been swept away from the Hoopa reservation. The remains of the soldiers and news people vanished as well, no doubt restored to their former selves by Athazia's father. The Lady of the Light hoped the troops at the nearby base would accommodate their new guests physically and psychologically. They would have interesting stories to tell, of that she felt certain. She turned back to the interior, watching the small group of creators, Champions and earthlings preparing the area for their departure.

"Captain Darren," said the general. "I believe our time has come. Make preparations for departure."

"Yes sir, general," replied the captain. The stocky man punched Eha in the shoulder. He received a vicious swipe across his forehead from the cheetah's long, bristly tail. Captain Darren jumped at Eha, locking his right arm around the big cat's neck. Eha shook him off easily. They said their goodbyes, with heartfelt promises to look each other up someday. Darren jogged off toward the chopper, barking commands into his shoulder microphone. His co-pilot would soon begin firing the large rotor and prepare the helicopter for travel.

John Woodhaven stood next to his lifelong friend. They watched the peculiar group of creators as they gathered themselves together. The Hoopa tribal chief put a hand on the general's shoulder.

"Thank you, Des," he said. "You could have handled this a dozen different ways and made things much easier for yourself. I know you've put your hand in the fire this time. I assure you the world appreciates it."

Desmond McKimmey nodded once, pursing his lips together in acknowledgement of Woodhaven's comments. He would be demoted for his actions, but after witnessing the day's events, he didn't care one bit. He had been prepared to walk away from his career anyway, and now was as good a time as any to retire. He would never forget what had happened here. As a matter of fact, he planned to visit this place with his good friend from time to time.

The general watched the mystical lady in the glowing silver robes walk by him. As she rejoined the others resplendent in their regal garments, the stalwart warrior took up his position beside her. He wanted desperately to speak to the strange young man. He felt he knew him from somewhere. That couldn't be possible, though, for he was certainly not of this world. McKimmey heard the blades of the chopper behind him, at full speed delivering a precise cadence. He motioned to Woodhaven and his attendants. Together, they walked out of the redwood forest toward their ride home. After securing themselves in the helicopter, McKimmey watched as John Woodhaven stared back at the interior. The tribal chairman had locked eyes with the giant leader of the Champions. He refused to look away. He had found his spirit guide. He would imprint the image of Maya in his mind so he would never forget him.

The first councilor called forth an expansive corridor. The

creators, followed by Trolond Tar and the Champions, walked through the shimmering membrane, leaving no sign of their temporary occupancy. The corridor washed over itself, checking for any further duties. Sensing no more travelers, it shot a pulse of organic energy to each corner of the perimeter simultaneously. The rim of the corridor blinked once, signaling its intent to reduce its dimensions. The blazing portal shrank to the size of a pinhead before vanishing altogether. To the casual hiker, it would seem as though the forest remained as it always had, a natural environment full of mystery and intrigue.

DECLARATION

CHAPTER SIXTY-FOUR

Janine sat alone in the stands of the Redwood State University football field. Even while sitting on the highest bench, she still had to lean back as far as she could in order to see the top of the shortest redwood tree. She enjoyed sitting up in the stands by herself. The wind climbed the steep roads from the bay, passed through the school grounds and brought the salty aroma of the shore straight to her. The giant redwoods completely circled the sports complex, except for a small area next to the gymnasium. This was her special hiding place; she spent time up here mostly by herself. If others occupied the stands when she arrived, she wandered back and forth until they left. She wanted no one to share in her private moments. No one except, of course, her boyfriend.

Sitting alone, she thought longingly of Conor. She recalled how she had shared her secret site with Conor. They would stare into the forest and imagine what might be waiting for them within the trees. They had designed their own brand of hide and seek here, with the amazing sounds of the Champions thrown in for a dash of excitement. They would wait until the last possible moment before running down the steps, across the field and into the deep green forest, he at the north end and she at the south. They would hide and hunt at the same time, looking for each other while protecting their positions. At first, Conor would always win, finding Janine in a matter of minutes. As the games went on, though, Janine became quite adept at following her boyfriend's every move. She beat Conor nearly every time after those first few months, causing him to remark about her excellent tracking abilities. Even with his exceptional gifts, she had bested him time and again. Had Conor not been so competitive, he might have called it off after losing so many consecutive challenges. He hadn't done so; however, because he felt the new trait she displayed was something worth nurturing. They played their game every weekend, sometimes after classes during the week as well.

Janine raised her eyes to the sky, gray and cloudy as always this time of year. She recalled the happy times with a forlorn, expressionless face. She had been back at school nearly a month now. The pain of being without Conor hadn't lessened in the slightest. She drifted around campus with a hole in her heart she thought she'd never fill, smiling bleakly at passersby, completing assignments robotically. Even her experiments with Mr. Hikkins had taken on a morose, lifeless aspect. The third time they met in the lab, the seeker had expressed his extreme concern for her wellbeing.

"Miss Cochran," he had begun, always using the surname when dealing with students. "I cannot instruct you in matters of love. I will not order or urge you to put aside the memories you have of Mr. Jameson."

For the first time in his life, the seeker touched one of his protégés. He cradled his right hand around Janine's left cheek, lifting her eyes to meet his. "Please, my dear," he said softly, "you must find something, some way to fill your life with happiness. I know you'll never replace the void left by Conor's absence, but you cannot continue down this path. I don't want this for you; neither would the creators you served so brilliantly. Conor, most of all, would want you to be happy. He gave his life for you, Miss Cochran. He would want you to make the most of it."

"He's not dead!" she said, exploding in Mr. Hikkins' face. She threw her notes onto the floor, angry at the seeker for even mentioning it. "You said so, the Lady of the Light said so, and even the warrior confirmed it. He is somewhere, at least his soul is, or whatever it is that makes him human. I'll find him, I swear I will."

"You cannot," claimed the diminutive seeker. "His essence was absorbed by the sun's power at the moment of the equinox. Even the creators have no idea where he might be."

"I'm taking a leave of absence from school."

"Miss Cochran, *please.*"

"I'll be leaving this Sunday after the state championships."

"You cannot retrieve him. Even if you do, what will be left of him, a thought, a whim, maybe a moment's breath of feeling?"

"I'll be leaving this Sunday. Please make the necessary arrangements with the attendance office."

Mr. Hikkins began picking her papers off the floor. He set her notes on the lab desk in a tidy pile. "Miss Cochran, your work, the science award, you're sure to win first prize this year. Don't throw that away on a meaningless quest."

"Meaningless to whom?" she had asked before storming out of the lab.

She sat in the stands watching the sun kiss the horizon. Redwood State had put up a strong showing, but without Conor they couldn't successfully face the powerful Baker College soccer team. Redwood State had lost the state title by one goal, a very respectable achievement without their star player.

Janine issued a silent plea to the creators for assistance with her quest. As she slowly negotiated each step in the stands of the football stadium, she looked into the lush redwood forest. She inhaled the evergreen aroma of the giant trees. When she reached the edge of the forest, she crouched for a moment, gathering a handful of fern leaves. She felt the soft, grainy texture while kneeling at the base of a tree that lived long before her most distant relative had been born. She stood, dropping the leaves to the ground, brushing her fingers against her blue jeans. As the sun dipped into the bay a few miles west of where she stood, the Keeper of the Keys disappeared into the canopied twilight of the Redwood National Forest.

CHAPTER SIXTY-FIVE

Deep in the Glade of Champions a young man stood next to a golden winged cougar. The wind buffeted his warrior's leathers, rippling the fabric against his muscular chest. The first warrior of the Crossworlds stared out into the abyss, seeing nothing and everything with eyes as sharp as a hawk's.

"Your thoughts, Tar," said Purugama. "They trouble you."

The young warrior said nothing in return. He looked over at his brother and friend. No emotions adorned his face. No body language gave away his innermost feelings. He stared at the cougar with expressionless eyes.

"You cannot share your troubles with me?" asked Purugama. "I mentored you through the course of your reincarnation, and yet you stand silent in the face of my concern?"

"Ajur," said Trolond Tar quietly.

Purugama understood completely. He missed the jaguar every day of his life. Ever since their final battle together when the brave cat gave his life for Conor and Janine, he held out hope that he might see his brother again.

"I had hoped to meet him. The glade cannot be the same without his presence," said the warrior. "Don't misunderstand me; it is good to be here with you, Purugama. Seeing the others lifts my spirits as well. Yet there is a terrible void without Ajur among you."

The great cougar chuffed quietly. He wanted to discourage the warrior from thinking such thoughts, but he thought better of it. Instead, he offered a small kernel of the Lady's teachings.

"Let us keep a warm place in our hearts for Ajur. Perhaps the memories will aid us in our journeys for the creators."

"Perhaps," said Trolond Tar while sitting down, holding onto Purugama's fur for support. He kicked one of his feet out in front of him, scuffing up a mild spray of dust with his sandal. He looked out over the glade below them and saw Ajur's forest, Maya's crumbled mountain, Therion's lake and the tracks left in the ground by Eha's endless sprinting. The sky beamed with pure sunlight, clear, blue, infinite. The winds died down somewhat, creating a beautiful scene that failed to invite any tragedy whatsoever. The Glade of Champions served its inhabitants perfectly. The cats and the warrior would always return here after every journey, eager to rest and engage in recreation with one another.

Trolond Tar, first warrior of the Crossworlds, sat on the high bluff with his most trusted friend and brother. He reached up behind his head, grasping a handful of Purugama's chin whiskers. He massaged them lightly, listening to the great cougar purr softly. Pulling his legs toward him, the warrior balanced his taut forearms on his knees. Letting his head fall back against the furry chest, he spoke softly to Purugama.

"Tell me, cat," he said, looking straight out into the sky. "Tell me again the story of Conor and the Crossworlds, and how Ajur saved us all."

A note from Kevin Gerard...

The most fulfilling reward during the journey to write and publish Conor's story has to be the fact that I actually completed the task. I've made a contribution to humanity; no one could ask for a greater legacy than that. I'm thankful for whomever or whatever shaped me into the person I am, one who ignores ominous warnings and dares to stride down paths that would make others cower.

I've said this to many people: I don't think I so much decided to write Conor and the Crossworlds, I believe Conor's story was seeking an author and I somehow was chosen for the honor. The fact that the mighty Champion, Purugama, came to me when I was a boy strengthens that belief. I'm truly grateful for that destiny.

Now that the five books have been published, the obvious question is, where do we go from here? The story ends with some intriguing surprises and a few disturbing riddles, the most glaring of these having to do with our two human protagonists, Conor and Janine.

Much to Mr. Hikkins' dismay, Janine has left college to find the man she loves. She does not accept Conor's transformation. She refuses to believe that he and Trolond Tar are one being. She packs what she needs and steps boldly into the Redwood Forest at sunset. Who knows what awaits her within the mystical pillars of the ancient, burly giants? What we've learned about her so far gives us hope. Janine is a very bright, very logical young woman, and *very* resourceful. I believe if Conor is out there somewhere, she will find him and bring him home.

And Conor? What truly happened? Was Conor really Trolond Tar all this time, even as a frightened ten-year-old boy listening to

Purugama shoulder his way through the jungle? Or did Mr. Hikkins and the Lady speak truly, and Conor's spirit departed the instant he collided with the face of the immense corridor. Perhaps at the moment of reincarnation he embarked on a journey to find Ajur. It's possible he'll wander through the forbidden corridors for some time, seeking worlds we are presently unaware of, or maybe he'll travel on the astral plane with Maya, learning the deep secrets of the Crossworlds. I honestly don't know the answer, and I believe that's the true magic of writing fantasy novels.

Other questions arise as well. How will Trolond Tar's reincarnation affect the spiritual balance of the Crossworlds? Prior disturbances, as when Purugama failed to prepare Conor for their initial journey, or when Conor broke his promise and told Janine about the Crossworlds, produced disastrous consequences. Will Trolond Tar's command of the equinox powers introduce new challenges for the creators and Champions? Might he become an instrumental actor in Janine's quest to find Conor? Does he have an evil twin, similar to the Lady of the Light's twin sister, the Lady of the Shadows?

What is to become of the Champions of the Crossworlds? Now that we believe the Circle of Evil has been utterly destroyed, shouldn't the Champions be given passage back to earth, to live out their lives after giving service to the creators? Can we say goodbye to the most attractive characters in the Conor and the Crossworlds story? I would certainly not want to read another series of books if they didn't contain the wonderful antics of Purugama, Surmitang, Therion, Eha, and of course, Maya. Yes, there is a new Champion, a timber wolf named Wolbiter, and he will figure prominently in Janine's quest in the sixth book. Will he be the leader of a new company of Champions? Will the great cats join him and his brothers somewhere within book seven, eight, or nine? It's hard to say, but wonderful to consider.

I've traveled the country speaking about Conor and the Crossworlds to students everywhere. They've asked many questions, but the two I heard most often were, "Are there going to be any more books in this series?" and "Are you going to make movies out of these books?" To the first question I'll say this; I've never stopped thinking about Conor's story, and I'm always entertaining ideas for books six through ten. Whether or not they become published novels is another matter. I've sacrificed a great deal, financially, emotionally, even physically, to make Conor's story available to enchanted children everywhere, even beyond American borders. Young readers in Canada, the United Kingdom and Australia are reading Conor's adventures. Perhaps by the time this novel reaches the shelves, children in other countries will also have the chance to enjoy them.

To the second question I've always made my point very clear. I say to the students, "Everyone here has the power to make these books into movies. If you scream loudly enough, Hollywood will hear you and grant your wishes." I hope your lungs are strong, my readers, my Champions, because I want this story to continue as much as you do, and I already know the movies will be amazing!

May all of you achieve every dream you can imagine.

Onward!

Kevin Gerard